DARK SHAMAN

THE LOST TREASURE

THE CHILDREN OF THE GODS
BOOK NINETY-EIGHT

I. T. LUCAS

Published by Evening Star Press, LLC.

EveningStarPress.com

ISBN: 978-1-962067-86-7

CONTENTS

ELUHEED

July 2, 1840

Rain clouds hovered over Mount Ararat's steep slopes as Eluheed made his way up the familiar path, hoping it wouldn't start raining before he reached the cave. At these elevations, sudden thunderstorms and heavy precipitation could create dangerous conditions even for an experienced climber like him.

He wasn't worried about hypothermia, but icy conditions could mean slipping and falling, and there was a limit to what his body could repair.

It was too late to go back, though. Besides, he'd already missed the summer solstice by nearly two weeks because of the weather, and he could delay no longer.

This was the time when the veil between worlds was

supposed to grow thin, and there were certain rituals he was obligated to perform.

After all, he was a shaman even if he was temporarily displaced.

Eluheed chuckled bitterly.

What had been supposed to be a temporary displacement, a way to save and hide the most precious of treasures, had turned into a very long exile, and he'd lost hope of ever going back.

For better or for worse, this was his home now.

A hawk circled overhead, its cry echoing off the mountain's face, and Eluheed paused, watching its flight pattern with the practiced eye of one who knew how to read nature's signs. Except for the worsening weather, nothing seemed amiss.

Just a hunter seeking prey among the rocks.

He continued the ascent, his boots finding purchase on rocks he'd climbed countless times before, each step bringing him closer to his hidden treasure. The cave entrance lay another hour's climb ahead, concealed behind a wall of rocks, the narrow opening visible only to someone who knew exactly where to look.

Suddenly, the ground beneath his feet trembled, and Eluheed froze. The tremor lasted only a heartbeat, so slight that he was tempted to dismiss it as his imagination, but he knew better. These mountains had been his home for hundreds of years, and he knew them well. Tremors were common, but the question was whether they would intensify or die out.

Fifty-seven years prior, the mountain had erupted, as it also had four centuries before that. He'd survived on both occasions, but only by sheer luck. Many hadn't.

His charges were in no danger, though, even if it got much worse. This mountain was as close to their natural habitat as it got, and they were built to withstand whatever it could unleash. Nevertheless, Eluheed quickened his pace.

Another tremor, stronger this time.

He climbed faster, his legs carrying him up the slope that would challenge a mountain goat. His leather satchel bounced against his side as he leaped from boulder to boulder, no longer caring if there were any other climbers on the mountain to witness his unnatural agility.

The cave was close now, perhaps two hundred meters above. He could see the distinctive rock formation that marked its location. He'd built it himself, making sure it was unmistakable, so he could always find it.

Then the world around him exploded into chaos.

The earthquake struck with a force that threw Eluheed to his knees. The mountain groaned, a sound that seemed to come from the very heart of the earth below. Rocks the size of houses broke free from the slopes above, tumbling past him in a deadly cascade.

Eluheed pressed himself against an outcropping, shielding his head as debris rained down. Through the thunder of falling stone, he heard something that made his blood freeze —a deep, resonant crack from somewhere far below, as if the mountain itself was splitting apart.

"No," he breathed, though the word was lost in the cacophony.

The shaking intensified. It wasn't merely an earthquake now.

The mountain was awakening.

Eluheed had lived long enough to recognize the signs. Volcanic gases began rising from the new fissures, sulfurous and choking. The temperature climbed, and he could feel the heat through his palms where they pressed against the rock face.

He had to reach the cave.

Fighting against the bucking earth, Eluheed struggled upward. A boulder crashed down where he'd been standing moments before, pulverizing into dust. He leaped over a widening crack, barely catching the opposite edge as the gap yawned wider behind him. His fingers dug into crevices as he hauled himself up.

The cave entrance was just ahead, still sealed, still intact. Relief flooded through him. If he could just—

The explosion knocked him backward, a blast of super-heated gas and ash erupting from the mountain's peak. Eluheed's vision went white as the shockwave hit, his body tumbling through the air like a leaf on a gust of wind. He slammed into a rock face, the impact cracking ribs that immediately began to heal.

When his vision cleared, the world had transformed into a nightmare.

The sky had turned black as night, choked with volcanic ash that fell like hellish snow. Lightning crackled through the ash clouds, illuminating the mountain in terrible flashes. And below, far below where the villages nestled in the valleys, the screaming began.

Eluheed looked up toward the cave's entrance, or where it had been. The entire face of the mountain was gone, sheared away in a massive landslide that was even now racing down toward the inhabited areas below. Millions of tons of rock and earth, moving with the speed of an avalanche.

"No!" This time he screamed the word, his anguish lost in the mountain's roar.

His charges, his sacred duty, were buried beneath half a mountain, lost perhaps forever. The weight of his failure crushed him more thoroughly than any falling rock could have.

But the distant screams cut through his despair.

There were thousands of people below, toward whom death was racing at an impossible speed.

Eluheed turned his back on the obliterated cave and on his charges that would continue to slumber under the rocks without him and bolted toward the village below. The landscape blurred past as he descended at incredible speed, leaping over chasms that hadn't existed minutes before. The landslide thundered behind him, a wall of death that grew with every meter it traveled, collecting rocks and earth into its hungry mass.

The first village appeared through the ash fall—Akhuri, home to nearly two thousand souls. The small houses clustered around an ancient church, their inhabitants confused by the darkness and the shaking earth.

"Run!" Eluheed roared as he burst into the village square. "Run for your lives!"

An elderly woman stood in her doorway, frozen in terror. "The world is ending," she wailed. "God has forsaken us!"

"God wants you to run." Eluheed grabbed her arm, practically lifting her from her feet. "Now!"

But it was already too late. He could feel the landslide's approach through the ground, a vibration that grew to a roar that drowned out all other sound. Some of the villagers ran screaming, while others stood frozen, staring up at the mountain they'd lived beneath all their lives, unable to comprehend that it was about to kill them all.

Eluheed dropped the old woman and sprinted toward the church, where children were running out, their teacher trying to herd them away from the incoming disaster.

The landslide crested the ridge above the village like a tsunami of earth and stone. Eluheed had seconds at best.

He grabbed a boy, then a girl who couldn't have been more than five. He could only save so many.

The teacher pushed more children toward him. "Take them. Save who you can."

He grabbed two more when the houses started to explode into splinters. The church, which had stood for five hundred years, vanished in an instant. The screaming suddenly stopped, replaced by the grinding roar of millions of tons of debris flowing.

Eluheed ran, four children clutched against his chest, his legs pumping with desperate strength. The ground beneath him was disappearing, consumed by the advancing wall of destruction. He leaped over a stone fence just as it was swallowed up, the children screaming in terror.

Ahead, the ground rose slightly—not enough to stop the landslide, but perhaps enough to slow it. Eluheed pushed harder, his muscles burning. He could feel the heat of the debris flow now, the friction of so much moving earth raising the temperature to lethal levels.

They crested the rise just as the landslide caught up to them.

Eluheed threw himself forward, curling his body around the children as they tumbled. Rocks battered him, tearing flesh that immediately tried to heal. A tree branch punched through his shoulder. He screamed but didn't let go of the children.

They tumbled in the chaos for what felt like hours but was probably only seconds. Then, miraculously, they were thrown clear, ejected from the edge of the flow onto solid ground.

Eluheed uncurled, checking each child. Bruised, terrified, covered in dust and blood—but alive. All four of them.

Behind them, the landslide continued its destructive path, heading for more villages below. Eluheed could already see the dust cloud rising from where Akhuri had been. Two thousand people gone in less than a minute.

"Stay here," he told the children, setting them in a cluster by a large rock. "Don't move. I'll come back for you."

The oldest boy grabbed Eluheed's torn sleeve. "Don't leave us!"

"I have to try to save others," Eluheed said, prying the small fingers loose. "Be brave. Watch the little ones."

He didn't wait for a response. The landslide was heading for the monastery of St. Jacob, where dozens of monks lived. Perhaps he could still save them.

But as he ran, Eluheed knew it was hopeless. The scale of the disaster was beyond his abilities. He was just one immortal, and he couldn't stop a mountain from falling.

The monastery bells were ringing when he arrived, the monks standing in the courtyard, some praying, others trying to gather precious manuscripts.

"Leave everything!" Eluheed shouted. "Run! Now!"

An elderly monk, presumably the abbot, responded with an eerie calm. "If God wills us to die today, we die."

"God gave you legs to run," Eluheed grabbed the man's arm. "Use them!"

But the monk pulled free, smiling sadly. "You run, my son. Save who you can. We will meet our fate here."

Eluheed wanted to scream at the foolishness, but there was no time. Younger monks were already fleeing, and he helped herd them toward relative safety. Behind them the ancient monastery, repository of centuries of knowledge and faith, vanished beneath the unstoppable flow.

The rest of the day blurred into a nightmare of desperate rescues and terrible failures.

At the Russian military barracks, he found the soldiers mobilizing.

The Sevjur River, dammed by the massive debris flow, began to flood upstream villages. Eluheed and the soldiers spent hours pulling people from the rising waters, diving again and again into the muddy torrent.

By nightfall, the immediate danger had passed. The mountain was still rumbling ominously, occasional pyroclastic flows glowing like rivers of hell on its flanks, but the great landslide had spent its fury.

Eluheed stood on a hillside overlooking the devastation, his clothes in tatters, his body covered in cuts and bruises that had healed a dozen times over. Below, the landscape had undergone a transformation. Where villages had stood, there was only raw earth. The monastery, the town, and entire communities had been erased as if they had never existed.

9

In the distance, survivors huddled around fires, their wails of grief carried on the ash-laden wind. He had saved many throughout the terrible day, but thousands had perished.

Somewhere beneath those millions of tons of rock and earth lay his sacred charges. The treasures he had sworn to protect were lost. How would he ever find them? The entire face of the mountain had collapsed. It could take centuries to search through all that debris.

Eluheed then remembered the children he'd left behind. He needed to retrieve them and deliver them to someone who would find them help.

Relieved to find the children where he had left them, he carried them to the soldiers, who were in better shape than most.

"You saved many today," their commander said. "Thank you."

"I didn't save enough."

The commander nodded. "There is nothing left for us here. We will help organize the people as best we can and then go back to Russia."

"Can I come with you?"

There was nothing left for him here except grief and a crushing sense of failure.

"Of course," the commander said. "After we are done here."

Eluheed nodded. He would go to Russia, learn what he

needed to learn, acquire the necessary skills, and someday, somehow, he would return and reclaim what was lost.

The mountain rumbled again. Ash continued to fall like grey snow, covering the devastation in a shroud of volcanic dust. Tomorrow, the full scope of the disaster would become clear. The dead would be counted, and then the long work of rebuilding would commence.

2

ELUHEED

Eighteen months ago.

Lord Navuh's ridiculously lavish receiving room reeked of expensive cigars, fear, and greed. The cigars belonged to the lord, the fear to Eluheed, and the greed to the Pakhan.

"What do I need a shaman for?" the lord of this godforsaken island asked. "I do not need to speak to the dead. In fact, I prefer not to. And I do not need a witch doctor either."

Navuh was as impressive as he was terrifying—tall, broad-shouldered, with the bearing of an emperor and the cold eyes of an executioner. He was also into theatrics, wearing an intricately embroidered caftan over an equally luxurious gown. All that was missing was a turban and a neatly trimmed beard, but he was clean shaven, and his sleek black hair was styled in the latest fashion.

The man was too handsome and too young for a cruel warlord who ruled over this entire mystery island. He seemed to be in his early or mid-thirties, but his eyes looked ancient and cold. If Eluheed hadn't known better, he would have thought the guy was an immortal. But to the best of his knowledge, Eluheed was the only immortal on Earth, and there were no others or, at least, there weren't supposed to be.

He resolved to say as little as possible. He was just a simple human with some small shamanic ability, which Gorchenco hoped to barter to the lord.

Too valuable to kill but not interesting enough to investigate.

The Pakhan crossed his legs and smiled, the expression never reaching his cold blue eyes. "Elias is not a regular shaman, Lord Navuh. Instead of functioning as a bridge to the world of the spirits, he can sometimes predict the future."

Eluheed kept his gaze fixed on the elaborate Persian rug beneath his feet, counting the threads to keep his mind occupied. One hundred and seventy-two years had passed since Mount Ararat buried his charges, and in all that time, he'd managed to avoid situations like this one. He'd been careful, moving every decade or so, changing identities, and using his abilities sparingly to earn a living, never revealing their full extent.

Until a month ago, when he'd made the catastrophic mistake of giving Dimitri Gorchenco a true reading. He should have lied.

Navuh's dark eyes sparkled with interest. "What kind of future?"

The sound of the distant waves breaking against the shore rose to roar in Eluheed's ears, a mockery of the paradise this island pretended to be. This was no tropical haven but a fortress.

Gorchenco spread his arms as if in apology. "Elias's abilities are modest but useful. He can predict events such as pregnancies, marriages, and deaths. But most importantly, he can predict betrayals, which I know is extremely valuable to you."

Eluheed cursed himself for the thousandth time. He hadn't known who the man was when he'd entered his shop in Leningrad. Gorchenco had seemed like just another wealthy client seeking mystical guidance. The reading had started as theater, the kind of vague predictions that could mean anything. But then his real gift had stirred, and he'd seen the betrayal coming—Gorchenco's right-hand man plotting with his main rival to stage an assassination so he could take over as his natural successor.

The words had spilled from his mouth before he could stop them.

A week or so later, after the prediction proved true and saved Gorchenco's life, four goons appeared in his shop. They'd bound and blindfolded him, and several hours later, he'd found himself in the Pakhan's estate, serving as the oligarch's seer.

Eluheed had thought that was as bad as it got. He'd been wrong.

After a failed escape attempt, he'd been loaded onto a private plane and flown to this island in the middle of nowhere. Now he was sitting before someone who made Gorchenco look like a choirboy.

Navuh's smile was pure malevolence. "How much do you want for him?"

The words hit Eluheed like a kick to the gut. Was he being sold like a slave?

"I don't want money." Gorchenco leaned back in his chair with the confidence of a man holding good cards. "I want a guarantee that I will remain your sole arms supplier for the next decade."

A decade. Eluheed's heart sank. Whatever business these men were conducting, it was substantial enough that exclusive rights were worth dragging him to this island and offering him like a bargaining chip.

Navuh nodded slowly, considering. "First, let's see if he's worth anything. If he predicts something useful, you've got a deal. If not, I'll kill him."

The casual way he said it made Eluheed's blood run cold. Had he survived volcanic eruptions, earthquakes, and centuries of wandering only to die at the hands of an arms dealer on a private island?

He couldn't die.

Not here, and not before he fulfilled his duty, no matter how impossible it was or how unlikely it seemed that he would ever succeed in delivering the treasure to where it belonged.

He'd better come up with something useful or die at the hands of this sociopath.

"Well, seer?" Navuh's voice cut through his thoughts. "Who is going to betray me?"

The question hung in the air like a guillotine. Eluheed could feel both men watching him, Gorchenco with nervous anticipation, Navuh with predatory interest. He had seconds to decide how to play this. With too little information, he'd be deemed useless. Too much, and he would be deemed a danger.

"I will need to touch you, Lord Navuh." He kept his voice steady despite his racing heart. "That's the only way I can predict things that are connected to you."

Navuh's expression darkened, and for a moment, Eluheed thought he'd made a fatal error. Physical contact was not something this man permitted lightly.

"If you don't need skin-to-skin contact," Navuh said, "I'd prefer that you touch me over my sleeve."

"It needs to be skin to skin," Eluheed insisted, though every instinct screamed at him to back down. "I need to hold your hand."

The lord looked at him as if he were a piece of gum he'd scraped off his shoe. The disgust in those dark eyes was palpable, mixed with a curiosity that might be the only thing keeping Eluheed alive.

"Very well." Navuh extended his hand across the space between their chairs. "You may touch my hand."

Eluheed reached out, his movements careful and deliberate, giving Navuh's security no reason to be alarmed. The moment his fingers made contact with Navuh's palm, the vision slammed into him with the force of a sledgehammer.

Power.

Ancient power that had nothing to do with money or weapons. For a moment, Eluheed was confused by the sheer weight of years he sensed, but then understanding came—this man was old, far older than he appeared, with centuries of violence trailing behind him like a blood-soaked cloak.

He was an immortal, a very old one, even older than Eluheed, but the how of it was irrelevant at the moment, and Eluheed pushed the disturbing revelation aside to focus on the question Navuh wanted an answer to.

Family connections radiated from Navuh like a spider's web. Sons, many sons, some by blood but most adopted, each with a different thread of loyalty and ambition. And there, like a wound in the web, was the betrayal Navuh feared.

A son. Not just any son, but one that Navuh cared about. The vision sharpened. The man had Navuh's dark hair and dark eyes, but he lacked his father's cruelty.

The son was good, trapped in an evil empire and trying to minimize the damage it caused. The son walked a tightrope between his father's expectations and his own moral compass.

He couldn't give Navuh that information. But he had to give him something.

"A son," Eluheed said, his voice hoarse. "A son will betray you."

Navuh's hand tightened around his, the grip becoming painful. "Which son? I have many."

"I can't see clearly," Eluheed said, and it wasn't a lie. His gift never gave clear visions. "He is far away from here."

That seemed to narrow the options because Navuh's crushing grip on his hand eased a fraction. "When?" The word came out sharp as a blade.

"I don't know." This part was also true. "The future is fluid. It could be soon, or it could be years. It's not something that puts your life in danger. He's not after your head."

"What form does this betrayal take?" Navuh leaned forward, his dark eyes boring into Eluheed's. "Does he steal from me? Sell information to my enemies?"

Eluheed felt pressure inside his mind and realized that the lord was trying to enter his thoughts or maybe compel him to say things he did not want to.

Sweat beaded on his forehead despite the air-conditioning, which was practically freezing the room. He had to shield his mind but not appear as if he was doing so. He had to give enough to be valuable but not enough to sign the son's death warrant.

"The vision is unclear," he said. "I see conflict. Your son doesn't wish you harm—that much is certain. The betrayal comes from conscience, not ambition. He's a good man trying to do what he believes is right."

"That narrows it to one name only." There was contempt in his voice that could have curdled milk. "I thought I taught him better. I thought that I raised him strong. I am very disappointed."

"Perhaps that's the entire betrayal," Eluheed ventured, then immediately regretted it as Navuh's eyes narrowed dangerously.

"Explain."

Eluheed swallowed hard. "He might not be doing anything to undermine you, but he is disappointing you, and that feels like a betrayal. It shouldn't, though. You should be proud of him."

The silence that followed was deafening. Navuh hadn't moved, hadn't even blinked, but Eluheed could feel the violence coiled within him, ready to strike.

He'd made a grave mistake.

Eluheed wasn't in a position to tell the lord what he should or shouldn't do or feel. One wrong word and he'd be dead before his next heartbeat.

The problem was that he'd already misspoken, and he was counting the heartbeats until his execution.

"I should be proud?" Navuh spat.

He had to save the situation somehow. Perhaps flattery would soften the blow that was sure to come.

"It takes tremendous strength to go against someone as powerful as you, Lord Navuh," Eluheed whispered. "Your son has backbone. Perhaps you can work things out with him."

When Navuh released his hand, Eluheed had to stop himself from cradling it against his chest. The immortal lord leaned back in his chair, studying him with those terrible, dark eyes.

"Tell me more," he commanded.

This was dangerous territory. The son had always had a conscience. He'd played the part expected of him while secretly working to minimize his father's damage. But telling Navuh that would mean revealing how long the deception had been going on.

"I see... a woman," Eluheed said, grasping for glimpses of the vision that might be half-truth. "She doesn't turn him against you, but his love for her shows him that there are other paths."

"A woman." Navuh's laugh was like breaking glass. "I should have known. It's always a woman. The weakness that eventually brings down all great men."

Navuh stood abruptly, and Eluheed tensed, ready for the killing blow. But the lord walked up to his own portrait, hands clasped behind his back as he gazed at it.

"Did you see anything else? Other betrayals? Other threats?"

Eluheed hesitated. He'd seen glimpses of plots and schemes, but they were too fleeting to make sense of. He reminded himself that he should appear valuable but not dangerous.

"There are always threats," he said. "And opportunities. I didn't see much beyond what you asked of me, but I got a glimpse of something in Iran. You should establish a greater presence there."

With careful manipulation, perhaps he would convince the lord to take him back to Ararat.

Navuh returned to his chair and leveled his gaze at Gorchenco, who had remained silent throughout the reading.

"Your shaman has some skill," he said. "The question is whether that skill is worth a decade of exclusive arms deals."

Gorchenco straightened, sensing opportunity. "The betrayal he warned me about saved my life."

"And now he warns me of betrayal, too." Navuh's fingers drummed on the armrest. "Tell me, seer—can your visions be changed? If I know a betrayal is coming, can I prevent it?"

This was the question Eluheed had been dreading. The truth was complex—some futures were fluid, others seemed carved in stone. And sometimes, knowing the future was what caused it to come true.

"The future is like a river. You can dam it, divert it, but water always finds a way to flow. You might prevent the specific betrayal I saw, but your son's conscience is harder to change. The best advice I can give you is to work with him and not against him."

Navuh's smile was ice. "You are right. It might not come true, which is why I need to keep you around for when danger draws near. You will be my personal seer, available to me at all times."

The good news was that Navuh wasn't going to kill him right away. The bad news was that he was to become a prisoner on this island with no way to escape unless he could somehow convince the lord to send him to Iran.

Navuh turned to Gorchenco. "Your shaman has earned you a decade of exclusive dealings." He offered the Russian his hand. "Congratulations."

The mobster smiled broadly. "Thank you, Lord Navuh. I'm sure Elias will serve you well."

"He'd better." The threat in those two words was unmistakable. Navuh turned back to Eluheed. "This island is your forever home now, and the sooner you accept your fate, the more comfortable your life will be." He smiled, and the expression was scarier than when he didn't. "If you give me valuable information, you will be rewarded. You'll have access to plenty of beautiful women, if that's what you fancy. If you prefer men, that can be arranged as well."

How progressive of him.

Eluheed chose not to respond.

His charges were buried beneath a mountain, and now he was buried too, in a different kind of tomb.

"Where are you going to keep him?" Gorchenco asked.

The lord thought for a moment. "The harem. It's the safest place on the island because none of my sons or warriors can access him there. I won't have them trying to extract predictions or using him against me." Another cruel smile played at his lips. "No one gets in without my explicit permission."

The harem.

A gilded cage within the larger prison of this isolated island, but it was better than a dingy cell in a dungeon.

3

KIAN

Present Day

The aroma of Chinese takeout filled Kian's penthouse at the keep, the familiar scents of sesame oil and soy sauce wafting through the modern space. He checked his watch, then glanced at Esag, who sat on the leather couch embodying that peculiar immortal paradox of an impossible age and a permanently youthful face.

At two thousand and one years old, Kian had long held the distinction of being one of the clan's oldest, but that title had become almost meaningless lately. First Wonder had arrived, older than even his mother, though the millennia spent in stasis made that a technicality at best. Then Toven had appeared, crushing all records with his seven thousand years of actual lived experience. The Kra-ell refugees had added their own complexity to the age hierarchy—

some had spent seven thousand years in stasis pods, making them more like Wonder than Toven in terms of real-life experience. The same held true for Ell-rom and Morelle.

And now there were Esag, Davuh, and Roven—each having marked over five thousand years of living the day-to-day, the entirety of it spent awake and aware, believing themselves the last of their kind. The weight of those millennia showed not in Esag's unmarred face, but in the depth and wonder of his gaze, as if he was still amazed to find himself among his own people once more.

"They should be here soon," Kian said, reaching for another spring roll. "Andrew is punctual to a fault, but Tim is never on time. It's almost like a point of pride with him."

Esag speared a piece of beef with his fork and smiled. "I'm not in a rush. This is excellent. I'm glad that Tim insisted on takeout from the Golden Dragon."

Across the table, Anandur snorted. "Tim always makes insane demands in addition to the exorbitant prices he charges. He could try the patience of a saint."

"He's the best forensic artist in the country," Kian said. "Probably the world. Which is why we put up with him."

"And also why we are willing to pay him ridiculous amounts of money," Anandur added. "Don't forget that part."

Kian leaned back in his chair, studying Esag. The ancient immortal had been in the village for just over two weeks now, but this was his first venture outside its protective boundaries. "Tim doesn't know about immortals. As far as he's concerned, we're just a private organization with deep pockets and unusual requests."

Anandur chuckled. "As long as the checks clear and we keep him supplied with food from his favorite restaurants, he's happy to draw whatever we describe. Though he does complain a lot and he's rude, so be ready for that."

Esag nodded. "I have a lot of experience deflecting questions, and if someone is stubborn, there is always thralling, right?"

"True," Anandur said. "Tim's talent is so extraordinary that we suspect he might be a Dormant, but he's such a pain in the ass that we are hesitant about bringing him into the fold."

"That seems rather harsh," Esag said between bites of beef and broccoli.

"You'll understand when you meet him," Kian said.

Esag put his fork down. "How do you find Dormants? In five thousand years, Davuh, Roven, and I never encountered a single immortal or Dormant. We thought we were the only survivors."

Kian felt a pang of sympathy for the guys who'd spent millennia believing their entire race had been wiped out.

"We were in the same situation," Kian admitted. "We knew they were out there, but we didn't know how to identify them. Then one day, Amanda decided to study neuroscience. She became a professor and started researching people with paranormal abilities. Her theory was that

Dormants might manifest stronger psychic abilities than what can be found in the general human population, and she was right. The first Dormant she found through her research was Syssi, my wife."

"Lucky you," Esag said.

"Indeed, but I was so jaded by that point, so tired of the endless revolving door, that I didn't even want to meet her despite Amanda's urging. The Fates conspired to put me in a position where I had to visit Amanda's lab, and the moment I saw Syssi, it was as if I had been struck by lightning. I knew immediately that she was the one."

"You're fortunate," Esag said. "To find your truelove mate is a priceless gift. I'm jealous."

"You'll find yours too. You've certainly earned it."

"Perhaps your sister could help?" Esag sounded hopeful. "Does she still conduct the research?"

Kian chuckled. "I'm afraid Amanda's track record isn't as impressive as that story might suggest. She found two Dormants through her research—Syssi and Michael. Every other Dormant who's joined the clan has been brought to us by the Fates, not scientific method."

"The Fates," Esag repeated. "They only reward those who have suffered greatly or who have sacrificed much for others. I do not deserve their boon."

"On the contrary," Kian said. "You should be at the top of their list. You've certainly suffered enough, spending five thousand years believing all of your people were gone except for your two companions. You also sacrificed by leaving everything behind to search for Gulan. It saved your life, but you couldn't have known that at the time. The Fates conspired to save you."

Esag shook his head. "That wasn't a sacrifice because it wasn't my choice. Khiann commanded me to find her, and I was following orders."

"Would you have said no?" Anandur asked. "If he gave you the choice?"

"Of course not." Esag looked a little flustered to be asked that question by Wonder's mate. "I was the reason she ran. I felt responsible for her drastic reaction."

"Then that was your choice." Anandur reached for one of the take-out boxes and emptied its contents onto his plate. "You sacrificed the cushy life your fiancée represented to go looking for the girl whose feelings you hurt."

When the doorbell chimed and Anandur walked to the front door to answer it, Kian looked at his watch. "Finally. Twenty minutes late. If he complains about the food being cold, I'm going to empty the noodles over his head."

As Andrew and Tim entered, the difference between them was striking, and not just because Andrew was handsome and Tim wasn't. His brother-in-law was dressed in a well-fitting suit, while Tim looked like he'd gotten dressed in the dark after a three-day bender. The little hair he had was sticking up at odd angles, and the t-shirt he wore under his unbuttoned dress shirt proclaimed, 'I'm Not Antisocial, I'm

Selectively Social.' He also carried an oversized art case that seemed to weigh him down on one side.

His nose twitched like a bloodhound's as he eyed the Chinese food.

"Is that moo shu pork?" he asked by way of greeting, not bothering with hello. "And spring rolls? And..." He pushed past Andrew, following his nose. "General Tso's chicken! You beautiful bastard, you actually got everything on my list!"

"Hello to you, too, Tim," Kian said dryly.

Tim was already at the table, carefully setting his art case down next to his chair and grabbing a plate. "Yeah, yeah, pleasantries, whatever. Do you have any idea how long it's been since I had decent Chinese? The place near my apartment closed, and everything else tastes like cardboard soaked in soy sauce."

"Maybe if you cooked—" Andrew began.

"Cook?" Tim looked genuinely offended. "Why would I waste my time on cooking when other people can do it for me? That's like asking Michelangelo to mix his own paint. A waste of genius."

Anandur caught Kian's eye and mouthed, "Michelangelo?"

"Tim, I'd like you to meet Esag," Kian said in what he hoped was a patient tone. "He's the one you'll be working with today."

Tim glanced up from loading his plate, giving Esag a quick

once-over. "You look a lot like that one." He waved his chop-sticks at Anandur. "Brothers? Cousins?"

"Soul brothers," Esag said.

"Oh, you're British. How exciting." Tim went back to piling food on his plate. "Who do you need drawn?"

"An old friend," Esag said. "Someone I have not seen in a long time."

"How long ago is a long time? Because memories fade and details get fuzzy. Last year? Five years? Don't tell me this is some childhood sweetheart thing from thirty years ago."

Esag opened his mouth, possibly to say five thousand years, so Kian quickly intervened. "The time frame isn't important. Esag has an excellent memory for details. He's an artist himself, but he works in a different medium."

That got Tim's full attention, and he actually looked at Esag. "What's your passion?"

"Carving," Esag said. "I carve figurines."

"Requires patience I don't have. When you see me work, you'll get what I mean. I'm usually done in under an hour." Tim turned his attention back to the food, still loading his plate, which by now held enough to feed three people. "Did you order crab Rangoon?"

"Over there." Anandur pointed at a closed box. "Not a single one of us is a fan of that dish."

Tim's face lit up like a child's on Christmas morning. "More for me. Do you have beer?"

"In the fridge in the kitchen," Anandur said. "If you want it, you'll have to get it yourself. We are not your servants."

"Fine." Tim pushed away from the table. "No one touches my crab Rangoon."

"I think it's time," Kian said when Tim was out of earshot, searching the refrigerator for treasures.

"Time for what?" Andrew asked.

"To tell Tim about his potential heritage and give him the choice. I feel guilty about putting it off for so long."

"We don't have a compeller with us," Andrew said. "If Tim rejects the idea, or if he's not ready to come with us to the village right away, we'll have to thrall him to forget what we tell him, and that doesn't make sense. We can do it some other time. Perhaps when Kalugal wants a portrait of his father drawn."

"Tim will want to come." Kian scooped some fried rice onto his plate.

"Based on what?" Anandur snorted. "The guy's about as cooperative as a rabid wolverine."

"Not when he has something to gain," Kian said. "And this is a bigger gain than any he has extorted from us over the years."

"So, what's the deal?" Tim returned with two bottles of beer and an opener. "We're doing this tonight or what? Because I've got a Netflix marathon planned for tonight, and—" He stopped mid-sentence, finally seeming to notice the tension in the room. His eyes narrowed, darting between the faces watching him. "Okay, what's with the weird vibe? Did someone die? Because I don't do memorial portraits."

"No one died," Kian assured him. "Finish eating, then you and Esag can get started. You can use my office."

Tim studied him suspiciously. "You're being weird. Weirder than usual, I mean. What's really going on?"

"Nothing you need to worry about right now," Kian said. "Just do what you do best."

"Fleece rich dudes with too much money to spend while eating their food?"

Kian offered him a chilled smile. "I wanted to say that you draw impossible things from descriptions, but fleecing me and eating my food works too."

Tim shrugged and turned to Esag. "Give me five minutes to finish what's on my plate, and then you and I get to work. Once I start, I don't like interruptions. Bathroom breaks ruin my flow."

Kian stifled an eye roll. Apparently, food breaks didn't interfere with Tim's flow because he'd taken them during every portrait he'd drawn for the clan.

"No problem," Esag said. "I'm ready when you are."

In more or less five minutes, Tim gobbled down everything on his plate, wiped his mouth with a napkin, and got up. "Let's do this." He grabbed his art case and headed out of the dining room without waiting for Esag to follow.

"Charming," Esag murmured as he got up and exited behind Tim.

Once they heard the office door open and close, Andrew moved to sit next to Kian. "Do you really want to do this?"

Kian chuckled. "No, but my conscience demands it, so it's going to be done."

"Anyone want more moo shu?" Anandur gestured at the containers.

As time crawled by, Kian busied himself with going over emails and responding to Shai's questions. The Chinese food containers slowly emptied as the guys kept digging in, and at some point, Tim emerged to fill up a plate and take it with him to the office without asking Kian if it was okay to do so.

Oh, well.

If he made a mess, Okidu would clean it up.

Finally, after what felt like hours, the office door opened. Tim emerged first, looking surprisingly subdued.

"I don't know who your guy is," Tim said, jerking his thumb back at Esag, "but he's got the best visual memory I've ever encountered. Like, scary good. Every detail, every proportion—it was like he was looking at a photograph in his mind."

Esag followed, carrying a large portrait. He gestured at the table. "May I?"

"Please," Kian said.

They had just finished clearing the boxes, and Anandur wiped the table clean, so it was safe.

Esag set the portrait down, and Kian felt his breath catch. He'd seen the previous sketch Tim had done of Khiann from Annani's memory, but this was a different Khiann, or rather, a different facet of him. There was mischief in his eyes instead of the loving expression that Annani remembered, and he looked younger, probably as Esag remembered him from their early years together.

The face that looked back from Tim's drawing was noble but approachable, with dark hair and intelligent eyes that seemed to hold both wisdom and humor. There was strength in the jaw, kindness in the slight curve of the lips, and something indefinable that spoke of respect earned rather than demanded. He looked like someone Kian would have liked to know.

"This is Khiann exactly as I remember him." Esag kept staring at the portrait, his eyes filled with awe. "Tim is incredible."

"It's perfect," Kian said.

"Of course, it is." Tim preened. "I don't do imperfect. Though I gotta say, this guy must have had excellent genes. That facial symmetry is unreal."

If only he knew.

"Speaking of genes," Andrew said, "Tim, there's something we need to discuss with you."

"If this is about my fee, it's non-negotiable," Tim said immediately. "Talent like mine doesn't come cheap."

"It's not about money," Kian said. "It's about you. About what you can do."

Tim's expression grew greedy. "Do you have another assignment for me?"

"Not at the moment." Kian leaned back in his chair and crossed his arms over his chest. "But I'm sure I will have many more in the future. That wasn't what I meant, though. Your talent isn't normal," Kian said bluntly. "You know that, right? The way you can capture perfect likenesses from verbal descriptions alone and produce photo-realistic depictions that can trigger facial recognition, that's a talent so unique and so unparalleled that there is no way an ordinary human can do that."

"Of course not. I'm one of a kind—" Tim stopped and frowned. "Ordinary human? Did you mean ordinary guy?"

Evidently, Tim possessed not only a sharp eye for detail but also a sharp mind that didn't miss much.

Kian just looked at him, letting him absorb the implications.

"What the hell is that supposed to mean?" Tim asked.

"It means that you might be more than human." Kian smiled. "It means that you might have godly genes. I'm sure the thought has crossed your mind from time to time. You seem like the type to have a little bit of a god complex, only in your case, it's justified."

"Naturally." Tim stared at him for a long moment. Then he laughed, but it was a nervous laugh. "Okay, you got me. Is this some hazing thing? Or a reality show? Where are the cameras?"

"No cameras," Andrew said. "No joke. We're completely serious. You might be a dormant carrier of special genes, and we have a way to test that hypothesis."

Tim snorted. "What if I do? Does it make me royalty or something?"

"Not royalty, just someone with the potential to become immortal."

Tim's face went through a series of expressions—disbelief, fear, and finally, something that looked almost like hope.

"Immortal," he said flatly. "Like, live-forever immortal?"

"Yes," Kian confirmed. "I know you've wondered about Andrew's transformation and how he became taller and younger looking. The story about the rejuvenation spa and spinal realignment was obviously fabricated. He was a Dormant, and we activated him." Kian waved a hand over everyone present. "All of us here are immortal."

"This is insane," Tim said, but he didn't sound like he disbelieved them. Instead, he sounded like someone whose world had just shifted on its axis. "You're telling me that you are all immortal, and that I might be one of you?"

"Potentially," Kian said. "The only way to know for sure is to test it."

"How?"

"You'd need to fight one of us," Anandur said. "Get our aggression up enough to produce venom, then get bitten. If you're a Dormant, you'll go through the transition."

"And what if I don't?" Tim asked.

"If not, nothing happens," Kian said. "You remain human, and we can make you forget this conversation ever happened."

"Make me forget?" Tim's eyes narrowed. "How? And did you say get bitten? And venom?"

"We can make you forget by thralling you," Andrew explained. "Which is a form of mental influence. It's not dangerous if done right, and we can tell you more about the getting bitten and venom parts after you confirm that you are on board with the testing."

Tim was quiet for a long moment, processing. "Why tell me now?" He asked the question Kian had been expecting. "You've known me for years."

"We weren't sure, but the more of your creations we see, the more evident it becomes that your talent is supernatural, which is often an indicator of the presence of godly genes. You are not getting any younger, and the transition takes a toll on the body. The older you are, the more difficult it gets. It can even be deadly, but we haven't lost a transitioning Dormant yet. I just need to tell you that so you can make an informed decision."

Tim narrowed his eyes at Kian. "What's the catch? There's always a catch."

"No catch. After you transition, you will move into our secret village. You can continue working for the government just like Andrew does, or you can quit your job and devote yourself to art. All living expenses are covered, and you'll even get a small allowance. What you earn from your art is yours to keep."

A grin spread over Tim's face. "Where do I sign?"

4

ELUHEED

.

Present Day

T he morning sun beat down on Eluheed's back as he knelt in his herb garden, the small patch of cultivated herbs that he had turned into his personal sanctuary within the gilded prison of Navuh's harem.

A wide-brimmed hat protected his head and the back of his neck from direct sunlight, but it didn't do much good in shielding him from the heat and humidity. It was sweltering outside the underground structure that contained the elaborate labyrinth of the harem, and the only thing that made the garden bearable was the breeze coming off the ocean. Still, the neat rows of feverfew and chamomile that he had planted emitted pleasant medicinal scents, mixing with the salt air that drifted over the cliff face, so as imprisonment went, this wasn't half bad.

His freedom was restricted, and there were certain rules he had to follow, but other than that, it wasn't much worse than other places he'd lived in, and in some respects, it was better.

That didn't mean that he could stay, though.

He had to find a way to escape this godforsaken island before Navuh realized that his shaman was not aging and therefore wasn't human. He also needed to return to Mount Ararat and find a way to dig out his treasure.

Eighteen months had passed since Gorchenco had sold him to the warlord, and in that time, Eluheed had used every opportunity to search for gaps in the harem's security so he could one day escape. So far, he hadn't found any, but he'd managed to carve out this small corner of purpose to keep himself from going insane in his otherwise purposeless existence.

Almost two centuries had passed since that fateful day when his sacred treasure had been buried beneath millions of tons of rock, and in all that time, he hadn't amassed the means or even the knowledge of how to dig his cache out.

Living with that failure was a heavy weight he carried in his heart, a burden far worse than the tropical heat or his enslavement to the ruthless warlord who ruled over this island and was the master of this harem.

"Elias!" Sonia called from the servants' entrance. "Mika's fever hasn't broken. Do you have anything more that you can give him?"

The harem's clinic was stocked with every modern medicine anyone could think of, but since the ancient doctor who had been dispensing it had passed away, the staff had been relying on Eluheed's natural remedies.

He'd been treating the boy with willow bark tea and cooling compresses, but since his condition wasn't improving, he should be given proper medicine. The problem was that his mother was stubborn and didn't trust medications that came in capsules and pills.

"I'll prepare something stronger," he said, brushing dirt from his knees as he stood. "But you should put in a request for proper pills from the island's main clinic. Most of what we have here is expired. Besides, I'm not a physician, only a natural healer, and I'm not qualified to dispense antibiotics."

She shook her head. "You are the closest we have to a doctor right now, and I trust you to take care of my Mika."

When she disappeared back inside, Eluheed let out a breath. This was what his existence had been reduced to—playing physician to the trapped souls who, like him, would probably never leave this place alive. At least his herbs gave him a reason to rise each morning that didn't involve staring at the rocks at the bottom of the cliff and contemplating that only available exit point.

The drop was nearly three hundred feet onto jagged rocks and churning waves. His body would shatter on impact, and the ocean would claim whatever remained. Even his remarkable healing abilities had limits. The question that haunted him wasn't whether he'd survive, he knew he wouldn't, but whether he had the right to abandon his duty through this ultimate exit strategy.

Of course, he had no right.

He was the only one who knew where the sacred treasure was buried and, as long as he drew breath, there remained the possibility, however remote, of escape and redemption.

Gathering fresh feverfew leaves and willow bark, Eluheed added them to his leather pouch alongside dried elder-flower and ginger root. The garden had been his one successful negotiation with the powers that governed the harem, which were surprisingly reasonable in that regard. The whole place was like an oasis of normalcy, an island within the larger island that was its direct opposite.

Out there, he'd learned, it was all about war and debauchery.

A strange combination, but he had to admit that it made a certain morbid, practical sense. The warlord needed to keep his army satisfied, and he also needed to finance it. Women and drugs were the answer, and the added bonus of the illicit enterprise was the secrets learned and extortion material collected.

Eluheed was about to head toward the servants' quarters when the sound of feminine laughter froze him in place. The musical quality of it, like silver bells in a gentle breeze, could only mean one thing—the warlord's concubines were taking their morning stroll, and he needed to disappear.

The rules were explicit and unforgiving. Servants like him, those who were not granted leave to interact with the ladies in any shape or form, were supposed to make themselves invisible when Navuh's prized possessions ventured out of the building. The penalty for breaking this rule was solitary confinement in a room the size of a coffin, and that was just for the first transgression of any kind. A second transgression meant being taken out and handed over to the guards, and no one knew what happened to them afterward.

Eluheed didn't want to find out.

The problem was that he had nowhere to go. The ladies were approaching from the direction of the main exit of the aboveground pavilion, and they were following their usual path that would take them directly past his garden. The servants' entrance lay on the other side of the pavilion, and the only other escape route led to the cliff's edge.

His only other option was to drop to his knees, press his forehead to the ground, and stay in that position until they passed.

Their voices grew clearer, and despite every instinct screaming at him to cover his head with his hands and block his ears with his arms, he couldn't help but listen.

"I told her that mixing copper oxide with lead would give her the turquoise she wanted, but the proportions were completely wrong." This voice held the casual arrogance of someone who'd never been contradicted. "Now she has a kiln full of muddy green disaster."

"Rolenna is too impatient," another replied. "Like when she tried to create dichroic glass without understanding the metal oxide layers?"

More laughter, and then a third voice. "At least she is trying to learn a new skill and create something beautiful. I wish I had a talent for something other than learning obscure languages. I am so sick of doing the same thing day in and day out for eternity. Immortality is a curse, not a blessing."

Eluheed's breath hitched.

He'd suspected Lord Navuh was immortal, but evidently, he wasn't the only one. The ladies were immortal as well, and the members of the house staff who had known them for years had kept it a secret from him.

Why hadn't they told him?

It wasn't as if he was ever leaving this damn place, so who would he tell?

So far, the one piece of juicy gossip he'd heard was that the warlord's black heart belonged entirely to the first lady, and that the other concubines were merely decorative additions to maintain his image. The other part of that gossip was that they were allowed to pick lovers from the male servants of the harem as long as these males resembled the lord in appearance, so he could claim their sons as his own.

Whether that was true or not, Eluheed had no proof one way or another. The men didn't talk, which they for sure would have if they'd gotten to sample from the lord's exquisite candy box.

"Oh, Tamira," the first voice said with fond exasperation. "You have as much talent as Rolenna, and she would be delighted if you joined her efforts to produce glasswork. It doesn't matter whether or not you succeed right away because you have endless time to get it right."

"Liliat is correct," someone else said. "I tried metalworking last year and nearly burned down the workshop until I got the flow right. We all need something to occupy our time with, even if we're terrible at it."

The footsteps drew closer, and Eluheed hunched lower, his forehead pressing so hard against the dirt that he was sure it would bear the marks of all the small pebbles.

The scent of expensive perfume wafted over him, something exotic he couldn't identify.

Driven by suicidal curiosity, he lifted his head a centimeter off the ground, just enough to view what was in front of him from under lowered lashes. He caught a glimpse of silk-slippered feet passing mere yards from his position.

One pair paused, and his heart nearly stopped.

"What a lovely herb garden." The voice belonged to the one named Tamira. "I heard we have a gardener who knows his way around medicinal herbs."

"Keep walking," Liliat chided. "We shouldn't stay out in the sun for too long. I want to get to the gazebo and sit in the shade."

The feet moved on, but not before Eluheed had caught a flash of azure silk and a fall of long, dark hair that gleamed like polished obsidian in the morning sun. He didn't dare lift his head further, but that brief glimpse was seared into his memory.

The ladies continued their conversation, discussing a new shipment of books for the library and speculation about when the next supply run would bring the new swimming suit collection from the mainland.

Only when their voices faded completely did Eluheed allow himself to raise his head and breathe properly again.

Tamira.

The name echoed in his mind with uncomfortable resonance. He'd lived for centuries, had known countless women, but something about that voice and that brief glimpse had penetrated deeper and affected him more strongly than it should have.

"The forbidden fruit," he muttered, pushing himself to his feet. "That's the allure."

The lovely concubines belonged to the warlord even if he didn't visit their beds and was devoted solely to his first lady. And if the rumors were true and the lord had no problem with his concubines dallying with members of the staff, it was only with those who looked like him.

Eluheed didn't look enough like Navuh to be considered, and until today, that hadn't bothered him. There had been enough lovely female staff members who'd happily shared his bed during the months he'd spent in the harem.

In a place like this, monotony and boredom were the enemies, and every newcomer was welcomed with open arms. Especially one who looked young, was decently attractive, and knew his way around medicinal herbs.

The warlord had been true to his promise, and Eluheed had been given a private room in the servants' quarters that had its own exclusive bathroom. It was modest in size and furnishings, but it had everything Eluheed needed, and it was luxurious compared to the places he had lived in before.

He'd entertained quite a number of maids and cooks in there since his arrival, and not just to provide spiritual guidance and herbal remedies.

As the service elevator descended to the servants' quarters, Eluheed remembered how impressed he'd been, when he had first arrived, by the architectural genius that had gone into building the harem's seven underground levels. Now the pyramid felt like a tomb. Everything here existed in artificial illumination that could never replace the real thing.

Sonia was waiting outside her room, her face drawn with worry. "He's wheezing so badly."

The boy most likely needed antibiotics, and it was easy enough to get them. The island had a large clinic that served its population and the resort guests. The doctors and nurses working there were not allowed to enter the harem, and those working in the harem were not permitted to leave it, but it was possible to submit a request for medications to be delivered.

He followed her inside to where Mika lay on a narrow bed, his eight-year-old frame shivering beneath the blankets. The boy's forehead burned with fever, and his breathing came in labored wheezes that spoke of fluid in the lungs.

"How long has he been like this?" Eluheed started mixing herbs in a ceramic bowl he'd brought with him.

"Since dawn. I've been sponging him with cool water like you showed me, but he's still getting worse."

"You need to ask for antibiotics to be brought from the clinic. There is a limit to what I can do with herbs from my garden."

She nodded. "I know. I already did. Someone is supposed to deliver them this afternoon."

He let out a relieved breath. "Good. The antibiotics will do the heavy lifting while I'll provide relief in other ways. Can you get me some hot water and honey?"

While Sonia fetched what he needed, Eluheed examined the boy more closely. The fever was high, but what worried him more was the rattling in Mika's chest.

When Sonia returned with the requested items, he set about preparing a concentrated tea of elderflower, willow bark, and thyme. He added honey to make it palatable and helped prop Mika up enough to spoon the mixture between his cracked lips.

"Small sips," he instructed Sonia. "Every twenty minutes, if you can manage it. I'll prepare a chest compress with euca- lyptus and peppermint oils to help his breathing."

Eluheed finished preparing the compress and showed her how to apply it. The eucalyptus scent filled the small room, and Mika's breathing already seemed marginally easier.

"I'll check on him again this afternoon," he promised. "Send word if his condition changes. Hopefully, the antibiotics will get here soon."

He left mother and son, returning to his own quarters to wash the herb residue from his hands and change out of his dirt-stained clothes. The small mirror above his washbasin reflected a face that hadn't aged in centuries—lean features, brown eyes that turned hazel in direct light, hair that was mostly medium brown but was streaked with lighter strands, bleached by the sun. Eluheed was handsome in an unremarkable way—nothing like Navuh's commanding presence, striking features, and much darker coloring.

He would never be allowed near the lord's concubines, and even if he were, they would probably not find him attractive enough to deserve a second look. Not that he wanted to get entangled with any of them and father children for the warlord to claim.

And yet, as he changed into clean clothes, Eluheed's thoughts drifted to azure silk and dark hair, to a silky voice that had evoked an unexpected reaction.

Tamira.

Even her name seemed to carry a musical quality.

When a knock sounded on his door, he opened it to see Arnav standing out in the corridor.

"Lord Navuh wants to see you in his office," the guy said.

Eluheed's stomach clenched. Navuh's summonses were never predictable in their timing, but very predictable in their nature. The warlord was paranoid and always wanted to know about people conspiring against him.

That was Eluheed's main value to Navuh—to warn him about betrayals.

He followed Arnav through the winding passages to the elevator that led to the uppermost level, where the lord's private quarters in the harem were located.

They emerged into opulence, a stark contrast to the servants' quarters below. Here, marble floors gleamed beneath crystal chandeliers, and priceless artwork adorned the walls.

Navuh's office in the harem was even more opulent than the one Eluheed had been brought to originally by Gorchenco. The lord of the island sat behind a massive ebony desk, his attention on documents that probably detailed some new terrible and senseless war in the making.

"Leave us," he commanded Arnav without looking up.

The servant bowed and retreated, closing the heavy door with a soft click that sounded like a trap springing shut.

Navuh raised his dark eyes to study Eluheed.

"Shaman," he said as a form of greeting.

"My lord." Eluheed bowed.

"Sit down." Navuh waved at the chair in front of his desk.

That was good. If he wanted Eluheed to sit, he wasn't going to execute him for daring to look at the feet of his concubine or for feeding him misinformation.

"Thank you, my lord." Eluheed lowered himself to the edge of the chair.

"My son evaded capture," Navuh said, sounding almost pleased. "Your visions about his escape routes were far from accurate."

He had done his best to provide information that would almost get the son caught, so it would be deemed reliable, but still allow the guy to escape, so Eluheed wouldn't have his death on his conscience.

"My apologies, my lord." He dipped his head. "My visions leave a lot to be desired. I was surprised that they were even remotely accurate."

"Indeed." Navuh leaned back in his throne-like chair. "I have to admit that they are still quite impressive."

Eluheed wasn't used to getting compliments from Navuh. Something was afoot, and he wondered what game the guy was playing with him and why.

"Thank you, my lord." He dipped his head again.

"Tell me, shaman. Where is my wayward son now?"

"I would need to touch—"

"Yes, yes." Navuh extended his hand with the air of someone making a great sacrifice. "Let's get this over with."

Eluheed looked inward, into the radiant place that provided him with glimpses of the future, and as soon as he took the lord's hand, the vision flowed through their connection with surprising clarity.

At first, he saw the son with his lovely female companion surrounded by well-wishers who were welcoming them into their community, but then the visions changed, turning apocalyptic.

The island was ablaze as figures moved through the smoke and chaos. The double fence around the harem melted like wax. And through it all, he had a sense of ending, of empires crumbling and prisons opening.

Eluheed gasped, jerking his hand back instinctively.

Navuh's eyes narrowed.

"What did you see?"

Think. He had to think. The truth was too dire and dangerous to reveal. Messengers of doom were often executed. But lying to Navuh carried its own risks.

"Change," he said carefully. "Something is coming, though the specifics remain clouded."

Usually, he could only sense connections, so the vision he'd seen was the first of its kind, and he wasn't sure how to interpret it. Fire and smoke didn't necessarily mean exploding bombs. They could be symbolic.

"Is my son leading the change?"

Eluheed shook his head. "I didn't see that."

"What kind of change did you see?" Navuh asked.

"I saw upheaval, but whether it threatens you directly, the island, or simply represents shifts in the wider world, I cannot say."

Navuh leaned back, fingers steepled beneath his chin. "You're being deliberately vague."

"My gift is finicky, my lord, and I can only report what I see. The interpretation is yours to make."

"What you saw disturbed you. I could see it on your face."

Eluheed chose his words like a man navigating a minefield. "Change is always disturbing, especially change of the magnitude I witnessed. But whether it will come tomorrow or decades ahead, whether it brings opportunity or threat—these things remain hidden from me."

For a long moment, Navuh stared at him, those ancient eyes seeming to peel back layers of deception. Then, unexpectedly, he smiled.

"You know what I think, Elias? I think you saw something that you don't want to share with me." He stood, moving around the desk with predatory grace. "But resisting me is futile. Do you know why?"

Eluheed remained silent, knowing that anything he said would be twisted to serve the warlord's agenda.

"Because I can force you to tell me about the true nature of your vision." He looked into Eluheed's eyes. "Tell me everything you saw."

It wasn't the first time the lord had tried that trick with him, and as usual, Eluheed pretended that he was forced to say things he hadn't intended to say while repeating what he had said before in so many words.

When Navuh's strange power slid off him without finding purchase, Eluheed wondered how well it worked on others.

It must be effective, or Navuh wouldn't be trying to use it on him.

After listening to Eluheed's answer and realizing that he had nothing more to add, the warlord dismissed him with a wave of his hand and returned to his seat behind the desk.

Outside, Arnav was waiting to escort Eluheed back to the servants' quarters and ensure he didn't wander around the upper levels, peeking where he wasn't supposed to.

Destruction was coming to this place, but Eluheed hadn't lied when he said that he didn't know the when or how or even why.

5

TAMIRA

A s Tamira and her companions made their way back from the gazebo, the air was already thick with humidity, promising another sweltering day in their tropical prison, but at least it hadn't rained today. The monsoon season was the worst time on the island. She still remembered the days they had lived in what was now northern Lebanon. It had been so much cooler there and not as restrictive.

The concubines had always resided in a harem, but back then, the security guards had been posted to keep them safe from unwanted intruders and not to keep them imprisoned within. She still remembered going shopping at the market, providing small charities to the local humans, and having a life that was much more well-rounded under Mortdh's rule than what it had turned into under his son's.

When she'd belonged to Mortdh, her duty had been to plea-sure the god and, if the Fates willed it so, bear a child, and it hadn't been a terrible burden at all. Mortdh had been generous with his affections.

After Mortdh's demise, Navuh had taken over, installing Areana as the queen of the harem shortly thereafter. Naively, Tamira had thought that things would get better since he wasn't interested in any of his father's concubines and had given them freedom to choose human lovers as long as they resembled him so he could claim their children as his.

That illusion had been quickly shattered when they'd discovered that any sons born in the harem would be taken from their mothers and raised elsewhere in the compound. Even Areana had been subjected to the same fate. Her mate had taken the two sons she'd given him away from her and had them raised by the Dormants in the breeders' enclosure. The boys grew up with vague memories of their birth mothers, if any, and became warriors and commanders in Navuh's army.

The one exception was Kalugal, who had somehow remembered Areana and had managed to sneak into the harem on occasion as a little boy. He had inherited his father's compulsion ability, which was how he was able to make the guards let him through, but Areana had feared for his life and told him not to do that.

How could she love a male whom she considered a threat to her children?

Navuh didn't care what happened to his own sons, and he cared even less about what happened to the daughters of his so-called concubines.

Only two girls had been born to the harem ladies and taken away to the breeders' enclosure. After that, Areana had negotiated with Navuh to let the girls remain in the harem and grow up with their mothers. Still, they were not allowed to transition, and they had lived and died as humans.

Both fates were cruel, and Tamira had a hard time hiding her deep resentment of Navuh from Areana, who loved him despite being subjected to the same cruelty.

Love was apparently not only blind but also completely misguided and misplaced.

If Tamira hadn't known better, she would have been prompted to believe that Navuh had Areana under a thrall, but that wasn't the case. The Fates must have hated Areana when they'd burdened her with a truelove mate like Navuh.

Then again, Areana was the only one on the planet who was capable of reining in Navuh's cruelty and insatiable appetite for power. If not for her, the world would have been in an even worse place than it was now.

The harem didn't have a connection to the outside world, but that didn't mean that Tamira had no idea what was going on. What she knew came from books that were lagging a few years behind current events, but at least she had that narrow window into the world, and as long as she kept her head down and pretended to be contented with her lot, she could continue to order books from the catalog approved by Navuh and get them delivered to the harem's ever-growing library.

It was a delicate balance, one she'd perfected over thousands of years.

As they passed the herb garden, she scanned it for the gardener she'd seen there at the start of their morning stroll, but he was no longer there, and she was surprised to realize that she was disappointed.

She'd caught only a brief glimpse of him earlier when he'd dropped to his knees and pressed his forehead to the ground, his wide-brimmed hat sliding forward to hide his face but revealing his sun-streaked, light brown hair. The posture of abject submission should have been pathetic, but something about the tension in his shoulders and the way his hands had splayed against the earth as if grounding himself had caught her attention.

Or maybe it was his bottom that had been sticking up in the air. It was a nice, masculine bottom, and after living for as long as she had in captivity and seclusion, even that was a source of excitement.

"Did you find anything interesting among those herbs?" Liliat asked.

Tamira realized that she'd slowed her pace and had been staring too long at the neat rows of plants. "I'm just appreciating the garden. Someone has been growing medicinal herbs for what seems like a while, and I only noticed it now because of the strong smell."

Raviki laughed from ahead of them. "Are we really reduced to admiring plant life for entertainment? What's next, placing bets on which wave will reach the highest on the cliff?"

"Don't mock," Liliat said. "Remember the time we spent cataloguing cloud formations? Or when Beulah convinced us to learn seventeen different forms of calligraphy?"

They reached the entrance to their underground palace, the temperature dropping blessedly as they descended into the climate-controlled interior. The transition never failed to remind Tamira of descending into a tomb—fitting, perhaps, since they were all buried here.

She could barely remember her life outside the harem, before she had been delivered to Mortdh as an offering by her father, but she remembered a house full of windows, with a front and back yard, and children playing outside.

There had been joy there that was lacking inside the various compounds Navuh had built for his people over the millennia.

Why had the Fates cursed her with beauty?

If she hadn't been so strikingly beautiful, she wouldn't have been offered like a sacrifice to the god, and she could have mated an immortal of equal station and built a home and a family with him.

Then again, if what Navuh had told them was true, the world she'd left behind was gone and the gods were dead and with them all the immortals and humans who had lived in Sumer.

Before entering the dining room, the three of them stopped at the jade-inlaid basins to wash their hands, a ritual unchanged over the millennia.

The scents of fresh bread and coffee greeted them, along with the quiet murmur of voices.

Areana sat at the head of the table, her ethereal beauty undiminished by age or captivity. Beside her, Tula was gesturing animatedly about something, her latest man-toy seated at her side like a trained pet. Beulah and Sarah occupied the chairs across from them.

"Good morning, ladies," Areana greeted them, her voice soft and melodic. "I apologize for missing the walk. Since Lord Navuh informed me last night that he expected a busy day and was leaving at sundown, I thought I would be able to join you today, but something urgent came up that I needed to attend to."

When Areana had first arrived, Tamira had been sure that her gentleness was feigned. No female got to be the head of a harem without being a ruthless cutthroat. But it was impossible to fake a character for thousands of years, and in the end, she had to concede that Areana was indeed a gentle soul.

That didn't make her weak, though. Or timid. She managed the harem efficiently, maintaining the elaborate fiction that this was a functional household rather than an expensive prison and mostly succeeding. Thanks to her, the human staff enjoyed an almost normal life in the harem.

"You missed nothing of note," Liliat said, taking her usual seat, third chair on the left. "Unless you count our fascinating discussion of Rolenna's latest artistic disaster."

Rolenna cast Liliat a glare that should have killed her on the spot. "My artistic disaster, as you called it, was part of my training. No one gets to be a master artisan on their first try." She smiled cruelly. "I still remember your astronomy phase."

"That was different," Liliat protested. "I successfully mapped the visible constellations from this latitude."

"After two hundred years of trying," Raviki pointed out.

Tamira settled into her chair and reached for the coffee pot. The familiarity of routine was a balm for some, an ever-present thorn for her. How many thousands of mornings had played out exactly like this? The same faces, the same seats, the same elegant place settings?

"Actually, there was something different today," she said. "I saw a new gardener in the herb garden."

Sarah looked up from her book, while Beulah set down her teacup. Even Tula paused in whatever she'd been talking about with Tony.

"A new gardener?" Areana's perfectly shaped eyebrows rose slightly. "We haven't gotten anyone new in months."

"New to me, then. I haven't noticed him before. He was tending the medicinal herbs, and when we approached, he prostrated himself, trying to follow protocol."

"Smart man," Raviki said. "You remember what happened to the last one who dared look at us without Lord Navuh's permission."

"That was seventy-five years ago," Beulah said, her voice tinged with its usual bitter edge. "And he also dared to speak."

"Hardly a capital offense," Sarah added dryly.

Five thousand years had worn away most of their capacity for outrage, leaving only a weary acceptance of the rules that governed their cage.

Tony shifted uncomfortably beside Tula, and Tamira felt the familiar pang of sympathy for the newest addition to their prison. He was still new enough to be horrified by casual mentions of callous executions.

Unlike the simple laborers Navuh provided to the harem, Tony had been someone before his kidnapping. He was on his way to becoming a professor of bioinformatics or something like that. He'd explained once that it was about working with computers and genetics. But in addition to his technical expertise that none of them could properly grasp, he could actually string together complete sentences and discuss a variety of topics.

He was like a breath of fresh air, but it was almost cruel to give them someone intelligent to talk to who wasn't going to last. It reminded them of what was out there in the world that they would never have access to. Companionship with an equal, intellectual discourse, and perhaps the possibility of connection beyond the hollow relationships they maintained with their rotating cast of human lovers.

In a few decades, though, Tony would be dead, and they'd still be here, having the same breakfast, the same conversations, the same empty eternity stretching before them.

"You must have seen Elias," Tony said. "And he's not a gardener. He just grows medicinal herbs to provide cures to the human staff."

"Oh, Elias." Areana nodded. "I've seen his name on the roster, but his occupation wasn't specified, so I assumed he was part of the general staff."

"Well, he is," Tony said. "But some say that he's a shaman or used to be before being captured and brought here."

"A shaman?" Sarah leaned forward. "Like a witch doctor?"

Tony shrugged. "I'm not sure. Shamans are supposed to be spiritual guides. They communicate with spirits, perform rituals, and heal using plants and prayers. But Elias seems more like an herbalist. He makes teas and poultices and other natural remedies for the servants."

"How long has he been here?" Tamira asked.

"I think it has been about eighteen months. He's a quiet guy, but I hear that he's very popular among the single ladies."

An unexpected surge of jealousy surged through Tamira. "Is he good-looking? I didn't get a good look since his face was planted in the dirt and his ass was in the air."

Tony shrugged. "He's okay, I guess. I didn't pay attention. He's doing amazing things with those herbs he's growing, though, so maybe the ladies are grateful and repay his kindness with favors."

It sounded to Tamira as if Tony was envious of Elias's success with the ladies, even though he shouldn't be because Tula had claimed him as hers.

Areana sighed, the sound carrying five thousand years of resignation. "I've been meaning to remind Navuh that we need a proper physician in the harem. Dr. Petro's passing left the human staff vulnerable. And even we might need a physician's services if any of us needs help delivering a baby."

An uncomfortable silence fell over the table. None of them wanted to become pregnant, but Navuh forbade them the use of contraceptives because he wanted more sons. The only way to prevent pregnancy was complete abstinence or other methods that always left them unsatisfied.

Not that Tamira had ever been truly satisfied with any of her numerous human lovers. She still hadn't forgotten the immense pleasure of a venom bite and the euphoria that followed. She hadn't enjoyed one since Mortdh's death five thousand years ago, and she still missed it and yearned for it.

"I hate the idea of dooming another soul to life imprisonment, but the humans need care," Areana said. "I doubt a shaman can replace a proper physician."

"We are all doomed here," Tula said. "Dead people walking."

"Don't be morbid," Areana chided, though her tone lacked conviction.

They'd all contemplated a final escape at some point over the millennia. The cliff called to them, promising an end to the endless days. But hope and uncertainty held them back. What if a miracle happened and they were freed? What if the gods were not dead and they were looking for their people?

Then there was the possibility that the drop wouldn't kill them, and they would suffer unimaginable pain, only to go back to jail or worse. Navuh was a vindictive bastard, and he would find creative ways to punish anyone who dared to disobey him by seeking death on their own terms.

"Elias sounds interesting," Tamira said, to steer the conversation and her own thoughts back to safer ground. "It would be nice to have someone new to talk to."

"He seems like a nice guy," Tony said. "A bit strange though." He chuckled. "Given where I am and who you are, saying that Elias is strange sounds like a joke."

"How is he strange?" Tamira asked, not caring that she was showing too much interest in someone she shouldn't.

"I can't put my finger on it." Tony lifted his coffee cup and took a sip. "He treated a cut on my hand and gave me something for headaches. He doesn't know that you are all immortals, and the rest of the staff has been instructed to tell him as little as possible. I don't know why. All I know is that Navuh requests that he be escorted to his office in the harem almost every day. No one knows why, though, and the staff is speculating that the lord must have headaches or some other affliction that Elias is taking care of."

Tamira was beyond intrigued.

She couldn't care less about Navuh's dealings with Elias, but she was extremely curious about what he could do for Navuh.

Then it registered that Tony had seen Elias up close, so he must know what he looked like with no guessing involved.

"Can you describe Elias to us?" The question slipped out before she could stop it.

"Not like the usual type Lord Navuh brings in," Tony said. "The coloring is similar but lighter, and the features are more European. Maybe Eastern European? Russian? I'm really not an expert on ethnicities."

Definitely not Navuh's type. Which explained the segregation. Five thousand years of carefully maintaining the fiction that all children born in the harem were Navuh's required strict control over which males had access to his concubines.

"That must be why he's kept apart." Sarah voiced Tamira's thoughts. "Can't have children who don't fit the mold."

"As if any of us are eager to bear any children," Liliat said, then caught herself. "We have our duty, of course. But we are not eager."

Another uncomfortable silence. They'd all borne children over the millennia, and all of them other than two girls who had died as old humans in the harem had been taken away.

It was a wound that never healed, no matter how much time passed.

"Shall we discuss the week's activities?" Areana asked, gracefully changing the subject as she'd done ten thousand times before, and turned to Rolenna. "I filled out the form to request additional supplies for your glass workshop."

"Thank you." Rolenna dipped her head. "At the rate I'm going, I will need a lot before I produce anything adequate."

The conversation shifted to safer ground, the seven of them taking part in the eternal dance of making their captivity bearable. But Tamira's mind wandered to the herb garden and to the man who cultivated it.

"Tamira!" Tula said. "You're not listening."

"Sorry. What?"

"I asked if you wanted to join us for cards this afternoon. Tony's teaching us Texas Hold'em."

"Poker?" Tamira laughed a little more loudly than was appropriate. "What's next, cigars and brandy?"

"That's a great idea." Tony grinned. "We can do that while playing poker."

"I'll pass." Tamira waved a dismissive hand. "I think I'll work on my translations this afternoon."

"Those Sanskrit texts?" Raviki wrinkled her nose. "You've been working on them for over three hundred years."

"It's a lifetime project," Tamira defended. "And it's not as if I'm short on time."

That earned her rueful laughs. Time was the one resource they had in abundance—endless, crawling, suffocating time that stretched before them like the vast ocean surrounding the island.

Later, as they left the dining room, each heading to her quarters, Areana fell in step with Tamira. "You seem intrigued by Elias, and I don't remember the last time you were interested in a man. I'm going to speak with Navuh today about him. I will tell my mate that he should remove the restrictions from the shaman because it's medically necessary." She smiled. "After all, keeping the mind sharp and engaged is as important as keeping the body satisfied."

"Indeed." Tamira nodded, trying to look amused rather than eager.

Areana studied her with those kind eyes of hers. "Be careful with your heart, my dear. You cannot give it to a human."

"I know," Tamira said quickly. "I'm just bored and in desperate need of having someone new to talk to."

Areana's cautious smile turned bright. "Absolutely. I'm sure that my mate will not begrudge you such a small boon."

6

TIM

"*Mi casa, su casa*." Thomas led Tim down the hallway to his spare bedroom. "My previous temporary roommate moved out only a week ago, and when Ingrid asked me if I was willing to host another newcomer for a couple of weeks, I said why not? I got used to having company, and now the house feels empty."

Tim had a feeling that Thomas would soon regret his hospitality.

In his experience, people could tolerate him in small doses but quickly got tired of him when exposed to his particular brand of humor for longer than a few minutes. He didn't blame them. He gave them plenty of reasons to dislike him, but hey, it was better to be hated for being nastily funny than for no reason at all.

"What happened to your other roommate? Was he also a dormant carrier of those super genes who transitioned to better things?"

"No, Din was already an immortal." Thomas opened the door to the bedroom. "He was visiting from Scotland and decided to stay. He and his mate, Fenella is her name, they got their own house."

Tim wasn't really listening. Instead, he was admiring the room.

It was nice. Like a magazine picture, nice. The room was spacious, featuring a king-sized bed, a small seating area facing the sliding doors that overlooked the backyard, and a large screen mounted on the wall. Everything looked new and clean. Compared to this, his apartment in Santa Monica looked like a hovel.

An expensive hovel.

He was shelling out nearly three grand a month on a one-bedroom in a building that was at least seventy years old with appliances that hadn't been updated in the last thirty years, just because it was within walking distance from the beach, like twenty minutes of walking and no view, but who was counting, right?

"Thank you," he remembered to tell Thomas before dropping his duffle bag on the floor. "I appreciate you opening your home to me."

His late mother would have been proud of him, remembering how to be polite.

Frankly, it was difficult to drop the snark after decades of perfecting it, but he was a guest, so he at least had to try.

"You are most welcome." Thomas offered him a bright smile that transformed him from enviably good-looking to jaw-droppingly handsome.

This village of perfect immortals was not the heaven Tim had imagined. It was his personal hell—a troll in the land of Barbie and Ken dolls.

"Would you like to join me for a drink?" Thomas asked.

"That's the best offer I got today."

Thomas chuckled. "I would think that the prospect of immortality would be a better offer than a drink."

"A drink isn't going to kill me, and it's going to calm my nerves. Can't say that about the transition Andrew told me about."

"True that," Thomas agreed.

Andrew had been telling Tim bits and pieces about immortals and gods throughout the drive to Tim's place and then to this hidden village. He'd told him how some other immortals called Doomers wanted the immortals Andrew was with dead, but after a while, it had all become one big salad in Tim's mind. All he could think about was the upcoming induction ceremony that sounded like something from a horror movie.

"So, on a scale of one to ten, how likely am I to die during my transition?" Tim asked.

"We've never lost a Dormant during transition, so I would say very low."

"That's what Kian said." Tim shuffled after the guy into the living room. "But you all have that look. You know, the one people get when they're trying not to mention that your fly is open or you have spinach in your teeth."

"I assure you, your fly is closed, and your teeth are clean."

Tim snorted. "Smartass. You know what I mean."

Thomas leaned against the kitchen counter, arms crossed. The guy was massive—not just tall but built like someone who bench-pressed cars for fun. Tim tried not to feel like a hobbit in comparison. A pudgy, balding hobbit who hated to walk, let alone bench press anything.

"The transition can be difficult," Thomas said. "Some Dormants lose consciousness for days or even weeks, and the older you are while undergoing it, the tougher it gets. But you'll have the best care possible. Our doctors have plenty of experience with transitions by now, and they will take good care of you." He flashed that beautiful smile again. "Instead of focusing on how difficult it will be, focus on all the benefits you will reap. You'll improve in every way you can imagine."

Andrew had improved, that was true, but he'd been a good-looking guy before his transition. Tim still couldn't believe he'd fallen for Andrew's explanation that a Swiss spa was responsible for all the changes he'd undergone, including growing taller by what looked like two inches. Spinal realignment, he'd said, and Tim had believed him.

What a fool he'd been.

Still, he had no illusions about becoming a model after his transition. Remodeling a shack wasn't going to turn it into a mansion, no matter how much was invested into fixing it. The only way to make it look good was to demolish it and start over from scratch, but they were not talking about rebirth and reincarnation. They were discussing ways to improve on what was already there.

"Unless this transition comes with a complete body reconstruction, I'm still going to look like the 'before' picture in a fitness ad."

Thomas laughed. "Chances are that you will look like the after picture, but it won't come without putting in the work."

"Yeah, well," Tim muttered. "I'm starting from a deficit, and I'm not good at setting goals and sticking to them. My idea of exercise is walking from the couch to the fridge."

Thomas laughed, and he didn't try to counter the self-deprecating statement, which Tim appreciated in a twisted way. At least the guy was honest.

Tomorrow was the big day, his induction ceremony, and after hearing what was involved, Tim had hoped that Andrew would volunteer to be his inducer, but he hadn't exactly jumped at the opportunity, claiming that it required a precision he hadn't mastered yet. Translation—he didn't want to put his mouth on Tim's neck, and he couldn't even blame him.

Tim wouldn't have wanted to bite his wobbly neck either.

Andrew didn't like him, but that was fine. He preferred to be feared rather than pitied. Anyone talking shit about him found lovely caricatures of themselves tacked to every surface in the building. His personal favorite was Jenkins from accounting, whom he drew as a weasel in a suit, counting pennies while the building burned around him.

Thomas pushed away from the counter and walked over to the bar. "What's your pleasure?" He opened the glass doors to reveal quite a collection of fine whiskeys.

"Holy shit," Tim breathed. "Is that a Macallan?"

"Aged thirty years." Thomas pulled out the bottle and poured two generous measures.

Tim accepted the glass reverently. "This stuff costs more than my car."

Thomas lifted an eyebrow. "I was under the impression that you are being paid well by the government and doubling that with all the private commissions you are accepting."

"Yeah, but I don't like spending my money. I'm a hoarder. My car is a twenty-year-old Honda Civic."

"That's another benefit of becoming immortal." Thomas lifted his glass. "You'll get a special car equipped with self-driving and windows that turn opaque. I'm sure you noticed that when Andrew brought you here."

"Yes, I did." Tim took a small sip from the superb whiskey, determined to savor it. "Your hidden vampire lair. That's essentially what you are, right? Vampires? The whole biting and venom thing is like something from a horror movie."

"We're not vampires," Thomas said. "We don't drink blood, we don't burn in sunlight, and we don't turn into bats."

"Shame about the bat thing. That would have been useful." Tim studied Thomas. "Hey, since we're going to be roomies and all, do you want to tell me your story, starting with how old you are?"

"I'm not much of a storyteller."

Right, so he was the silent type. Although that wasn't the impression Tim had gotten so far.

"Come on, give me something. I'm nervous as hell about tomorrow and could use the distraction."

"What would you like to know?" Thomas asked.

Bingo! When snark failed, it was pity to the rescue.

"The biting thing. How does it work? And don't give me the sanitized version. I want to know what I'm in for. Does it hurt? Can it kill me?"

"It hurts, but only for a moment. As soon as the venom hits your system, you'll go on the best psychedelic trip of your life. We've never had a guy die from being injected with too much during the induction ceremony, but theoretically, it's possible."

"Great." Tim took another sip. "You look like a competent fellow. Can you be my inducer?"

It was a long shot, but there was no harm in asking.

Thomas shook his head. "I'm not the right person for that."

"Why?"

"I lack the required finesse. The bite needs to deliver exactly the right amount of venom. Too little and the transition fails. Too much and it can be fatal."

Tim's hand tightened on his glass. "But you've just said that no Dormant ever died from too much venom."

"That's because we're very careful about who performs inductions. Only those with excellent control are permitted."

"And you don't have excellent control?"

Thomas's jaw tightened. "I'm out of practice. I haven't induced anyone in centuries."

That sounded like an excuse. The guy just didn't want to do it.

Tim held out his glass. "I'm going to need more whiskey."

Thomas obliged, pouring another generous measure.

"You know..." Tim studied the amber liquid, "I've been thinking about this whole thing. What if it doesn't work? What if I'm not a Dormant? That would be such a tragic waste of my two-week annual vacation time."

Thomas shrugged. "I'd say it's worth sacrificing to find out whether you can turn immortal or not. If you try and fail, you'll just go back to your life, and we'll make you forget that this ever happened. We can even implant fake memories of a wonderful vacation in your head."

"You make it sound so appealing."

"It is. Just tell whoever is going to do the thralling your preference. Paris? Tokyo?"

"Can I ask for a hot babe to accompany me on my imaginary vacation?"

Thomas's expression turned doubtful. "That depends on how good that person's thralling is. It's easier to implant visual memories of locations than the emotional complexity of a relationship."

"Right." Tim emptied the second shot down his throat.

It was such a waste to drink fine whiskey that way, but it was an even bigger shame that he couldn't get a hot babe even in his imaginary holiday.

Who would want to hook up with a guy who looked like him and had the social skills of a Rottweiler?

Hot babes weren't exactly lining up to spend time with him.

"Have you ever heard about Perfect Match?" Thomas asked.

Tim snorted. "Who hasn't? They run commercials on late-night TV when lonely schmucks like me are awake and seriously contemplating shelling out three grand for a three-hour mind hook-up with some random chick that could be a guy pretending to be a babe."

"We have them in the village and they are free for our use. The wait-list is long, but if you put your name down now, you might be able to enjoy it before your two weeks are up. At least you won't be wasting your vacation time."

"You know what? I'll do that."

Thomas smiled and poured more whiskey into Tim's glass. "Let's drink to the wonders of modern technology and the relief it provides lonely souls like us."

Tim nearly choked on the whiskey. "You? Lonely?"

"It's not that easy for immortals. It's not like we can have human girlfriends, and the immortal females in the village are either our relatives or already mated."

It was shocking that an Adonis like Thomas was lonely as well and also comforting in a very selfish way.

Tim felt some of the tension ease from his shoulders. Maybe it was the whiskey, or maybe it was the fact that he had that in common with a stud like Thomas.

"So, any advice for tomorrow?" he asked after a moment. "I mean besides 'don't die'?"

"You'll need to put up a fight," Thomas said. "But you don't have to last long, and you don't need to be afraid. Just trust your inducer and let it happen."

"Let it happen. Right."

"You will be overpowered, and it's better to surrender willingly than to feel helpless."

7

AMANDA

Amanda shifted Evie on her hip as she followed Syssi up the path to Annani's house. Her daughter's chubby fingers were tugging on her short hair with the determination of a one-year-old who had decided to change her mommy's hairstyle from short to bald.

"Gentle, sweetie," Amanda said, carefully extracting the strands from Evie's grip. "Mommy needs that hair attached to her head."

Beside them, Allegra toddled ahead, refusing to sit in the stroller or be carried. "Nana!"

Syssi hovered behind her, letting the girl walk on her own but ready to catch her if needed. "Yes, sweetie, we are going to Nana's house."

Amanda smiled at the exchange. Allegra had a strong personality—confident, precocious, and absolutely certain the world revolved around her. Which, in their little corner of it, wasn't far from the truth.

She adjusted Evie again, this time to prevent her from grabbing the necklace that hung temptingly within reach. "I'm dying of curiosity. Mother says that this version of Khiann is so spectacular that she can't take her eyes off it."

"Two different versions of Khiann." Syssi's voice carried a wistful note. "It must be surreal for her to see him through someone else's memories."

They reached the door, where Allegra was kicking it with enthusiasm. Once, twice, three times before Syssi scooped her into her arms. "We don't kick doors, sweetheart. It's impolite."

Allegra glared at Syssi. "I want Nana!"

It was funny how the little girl remembered to speak in full sentences when she was angry.

The door opened to reveal Ogidu, his broad face creasing into a smile that was still a little mannequin-like but seemed almost human. "Mistress Amanda, Mistress Syssi. And the young mistresses. The Clan Mother is expecting you."

"Nana!" Allegra twisted in Syssi's arms until she put her down and then darted past the Odu before anyone could stop her, her little feet pattering across the marble floor.

"I'll get her," Syssi said with a sigh and rushed after her daughter.

Amanda smiled at Ogidu. "How are you doing today?"

She'd gotten into the habit of asking the Odus about their day, like she would have done if they were people, because that was what they were becoming.

"Very good, mistress." He inclined his head. "Thank you for asking."

"And how is my mother doing?" She didn't really expect a response because that would require the Odu to understand her mother's mood, which was probably beyond his capabilities at this stage.

"The portraits have stirred memories." The Odu surprised her with his answer. "The Clan Mother has been observing them throughout the day."

Amanda's heart ached for her mother, who'd spent five thousand years mourning a love she'd believed lost forever. And now, with hope so close she could almost taste it, the waiting must be excruciating.

They found Annani in her living room, already being climbed on by an enthusiastic Allegra. The goddess sat on her couch, looking impossibly small and delicate as she helped the little girl onto her lap.

"My darling girl," Annani said, her melodic voice filled with warmth. "Give your Nana a kiss."

Allegra complied eagerly, never shy about showing her affection. "I made a picture."

"You did? What did you draw?"

"A dragon."

For some reason, the answer seemed to startle Annani. "What happened to drawing pictures of Princess Sparkle?"

Allegra shrugged. "I like dragons."

"That's her latest obsession." Syssi sat on the couch next to Annani. "Since she's started watching this new animated series about dragons, she's been drawing nothing else."

When Amanda sat on Annani's other side, Evie demanded to be transferred to her grandmother.

Amanda passed Evie over, watching as her mother settled her little girl on her other knee, balancing both grand-daughters with a big smile on her face. Evie reached for Annani's face, patting her cheek with a drool-covered hand. "Nani," Evie said seriously, as if imparting great wisdom.

"Yes, darling." Annani was unbothered by the baby drool now decorating her cheek.

"Can we see the portraits?" Syssi asked. "I'm dying to see them one next to the other."

"They are hanging in my bedroom, but Ogidu can bring them here."

The Odu bowed. "Right away, Clan Mother."

He returned a moment later carrying two large canvases. "Where should I put them, Clan Mother?"

"Against the fireplace," Annani said. "That way we can look at them from here."

The Odu cast a worried look at Allegra, probably thinking of all the ways she could destroy the portrait. He didn't know that Evie was already walking as well, and no less destructive than her slightly older cousin.

Amanda got off the couch and walked over to where the Odu was standing with the two portraits in his arms. "Perhaps you can put two chairs with their backs to the fireplace and prop the portraits on the chairs. I'll hold them for you."

Grateful for the advice, Ogidu handed her the canvases, and she finally could get a look at Tim's newest creation, or rather a copy of it.

The original was with Esag, serving as an inspiration for his carving.

"They are two facets of the same beautiful man," she said.

Annani nodded, her eyes glistening with tears she would never let fall.

Once the portraits were properly situated on top of the chairs, Amanda returned to the couch and sat next to her mother. "Are you okay?"

Annani nodded. "Of course."

Amanda leaned forward, studying the two images. The first she'd seen before, the one Tim had drawn from Annani's description. It showed Khiann as powerful and commanding, but with eyes full of love and tenderness. In the second portrait, Khiann was younger. His face held mischief, his smile crooked and challenging. There was an energy to him, a sense of barely contained vitality that practically leaped off the page.

"He was quite the charmer, wasn't he?" Syssi asked.

"Not if you asked him," Annani said. "He claimed that he was always proper, a dutiful son whom I had to seduce into courting me. But looking at him through Esag's eyes reveals a facet of him that he kept hidden from me."

"I'm sure he hid nothing from you," Amanda said with a grin. "I remember you telling me that the two of you got into a lot of mischief during your courtship."

Annani smirked. "It was all my doing. I had to tempt Khiann into breaking the rules."

Amanda had a feeling that Khiann had cooperated with Annani's shenanigans because it was fun, and he'd only pretended to be pulled into them against his will.

"My Khiann was playful, passionate, and on occasion irreverent. He made me laugh until my sides ached."

Allegra, who'd been unusually quiet, pointed at the younger portrait. "He's pretty."

"Yes," Annani agreed. "I find it curious that Cyra, Yasmin's little girl, called Khiann a pretty man too. Or a doll man."

Her mother had told Amanda about Cyra's prophetic dreams, and that the girl had seen four others buried in the sand with him.

Amanda studied the details of the portrait that Esag had inspired more closely. "Has Esag started working on a new figurine?"

"He has been carving for days," Annani said. "He has carved many versions already, but none satisfy him. Hopefully, now that he has the portrait to inspire him, he will manage to make one with the spark that will trigger a vision."

"Speaking of visions," Syssi said, "I could try—"

"No." Annani put a hand on her arm. "Not yet, my dear. The universe is not generous with visions, as you well know. Let us give Esag more time. If he fails, then I will ask you to take another look."

Syssi nodded. "That's wise."

Annani laughed. "Khiann would never have accused me of wisdom. He called me cunning and sharp, but he was unhappy with my reluctance to study commerce. It was so boring." She sighed. "Those were the good times, though. I miss them so much. If I knew then what I know now."

"And what's that?" Syssi asked.

"That family is the most important thing. I should have been kinder and more understanding toward my mother. I should have spent more time with my father when I had the chance."

Amanda took her daughter from her mother and pressed a kiss to her cheek. "Who is going to have a big party this Sunday?"

"Evie!" Her daughter pointed at herself. "Evie, princess."

"That's right, sweetheart. Every girl is a princess on her birthday."

"One already," Annani marveled, reaching for Evie's tiny hand. "It seems like yesterday you were born, little one."

"It's going to be a party to remember," Amanda said. "I'm planning something unique."

"How unique?" Syssi asked, looking suspicious.

"I'm not telling. It's a surprise."

"Amanda—"

"Nope. My lips are sealed. You'll just have to trust me."

Syssi burst out laughing. "When you say the words unique and party in the same sentence, I get scared. Really scared."

Annani smiled. "Whatever you are planning, Amanda, I'm sure it will be wonderful."

"How much damage can one alpaca cause?" Amanda muttered.

"Paca!" Evie exclaimed, clapping her hands. "Paca!"

"No alpacas," Syssi said firmly. "Amanda, I mean it."

"Do you really think I would bring alpacas to a one-year-old's birthday party?" Amanda asked innocently.

"Yes," Annani and Syssi said in unison.

"Your faith in me is touching," Amanda said, lifting Evie and turning her around to face her. "Don't listen to them, baby girl. Mommy's going to throw you the best first birthday party ever."

Allegra tugged on Annani's sleeve. "Nana, can I play in your room?"

"Of course, darling." Annani helped her slide off her lap.

"You really shouldn't let her play with your jewelry or your slippers," Syssi said.

Annani's feet were so tiny that Allegra could play dress up with her shoes. The girl had a thing for shoes almost as bad as her aunt.

"She's getting so big," Syssi said, watching them go. "Sometimes I can't believe she's just a little over one year old. She talks like she's much older."

"She's a smart little girl, and she's surrounded by adults." Amanda leaned back against the couch cushions.

"Do you think Allegra might have transitioned already?" Syssi asked. "She's been spending a lot of time with your mother lately."

"It's possible." Amanda lifted the teacup Ogidu had served. "I wish my Evie had transitioned already, so I could stop worrying so much about her."

The doorbell ringing was followed a moment later by the sound of familiar footsteps, and as Kian strode into the room, his face brightened when he saw Syssi.

He walked over to the couch, taking the spot their mother had vacated only moments ago. "How are my girls doing?" He kissed Syssi's cheek and then leaned to kiss Amanda's.

"I'm so touched." Amanda put a hand over her chest. "You haven't called me your girl since I turned seventeen."

He chuckled. "That was about the time that sweet Amanda was replaced by hellion Amanda."

"Daddy!" Allegra's voice carried from their mother's bedroom. "I'm wearing Nana's shoes!" She waddled into the living room in a pair of Annani's silk slippers.

Kian stood and met her halfway. "Come to Daddy, Princess." He swooped her into his arms and spun her around.

"Kian, no," Syssi said. "Put her down."

"You're no fun," Kian said, but he was smiling.

Amanda watched the scene with contentment. These moments—family gathered together, children playing, laughter filling her mother's often too-quiet house—these were what mattered most.

Evie had reached the coffee table and was pulling herself up to standing, eyeing the portraits with interest.

Kian studied the images. "It's fascinating what a difference perspective makes."

His mother nodded. "Khiann looks so happy in the one drawn from Esag's memory. He lost some of that joy when he moved into the palace. He felt stifled there."

"But he had you," Amanda said. "He loved you with every fiber of his being."

"He did." Annani walked over to the portraits and smiled. "But as important as love is, it is not everything. That is why I let him go on that caravan expedition. I should not have done that. I should have been firm and demanded that he stay by my side, even if it caused a rift between us. If I had done that, the entire history of gods and humans would have been different."

Annani lived with so much guilt that it must be crushing.

"You don't know that," Syssi said. "In fact, you know that it is not true because it probably wasn't Mortdh who dropped the bomb on the assembly. It was most likely the Eternal King's doing."

Annani shook her head as she sat on the couch next to Syssi. "Even so, they needed the right circumstances and a scape-goat to cover their tracks, and we played right into their hands."

"Some futures are set," Syssi said quietly. "And no matter what we do, they are going to play out the same way. This was a major fork in the history of Earth, and it was inevitable. The Fates knew what was coming, and they did their best to mitigate it. They saved you, and they saved Khiann."

Annani let out a breath. "You are right, and I owe the Fates a huge debt of gratitude. I just wish they had made it a little easier for us to find him."

8

AREANA

Areana watched Navuh slice into his perfectly prepared lamb, noting the relaxed set of his shoulders and the absence of the perpetual furrow between his brows. Such moments of peace were rare enough to be treasured, even if they were as fleeting as morning dew in the desert.

"The wine is excellent," she said, lifting her glass to admire the deep burgundy color. "From the new shipment?"

"A 1947 Château d'Yquem." Navuh's lips curved in satisfaction. "Sahid outbid three collectors for the entire lot, with my approval, of course." He leaned toward her and took her hand. "Nothing but the best for you, my love." He kissed the back of her hand.

"You spoil me." She smiled.

"It is my pleasure to do so."

It was, but only on his terms.

Areana took a sip, letting the complex flavors bloom on her tongue. After five thousand years, few pleasures remained that could truly surprise her palate, but Navuh's dedication to acquiring the finest of everything for her occasionally yielded gems like this.

"Speaking of acquisitions," she said, setting down her glass, "I wanted to discuss something with you."

His hand paused halfway to his wine glass. "Oh?"

The single syllable carried a weight of suspicion that would have silenced most people, but Areana had not survived five millennia as Navuh's mate by being easily cowed. She had mastered the art of navigating his moods, like a caravan leader deciphering wind patterns. She knew when to adjust her course, when to capitalize on the prevailing winds, and when to patiently endure the storm until it subsided.

"There is a new resident in the harem." She cut a delicate piece of asparagus. "Well, not really new since he has been there for the past eighteen months, but he is relatively new. His name is Elias."

Navuh's shoulders tensed, the moment of peace evaporating like smoke. "What about him?"

"You should permit him to interact with the ladies." She kept her tone light, conversational.

"No." The word came out sharp and final. "He does not look enough like me to be allowed to father their children. How do you even know of him? His instructions were to stay away from you and my concubines, like all others who do not bear any resemblance to me. "

Areana smiled, the expression both gentle and knowing. "My darling, you should know by now that nothing happens in the harem without my knowledge. I know everything that goes on within these walls."

"Apparently." His dark eyes narrowed. "But as you mentioned, he has been in the harem for eighteen months already, and he has only now come to your attention. How did that happen?"

"Elias has been treating the human staff with his herbal remedies, so of course, the rumors about him spread. He's quite skilled, from what I understand. The servants call him their shaman." She paused to take another sip of wine. "Which brings me to another related matter—we desperately need a proper physician for the clinic. Sonja and Mariam are expecting, and we don't even have a midwife. I can probably manage, but I would prefer to have a qualified medical professional on hand for when their time comes."

She knew she was sealing some poor physician's fate by asking, but there was really no way around it.

"I'll arrange for someone to be brought in," Navuh said. "But that doesn't explain how you became interested in Elias and why you want him mingling with the concubines."

"Tony mentioned him," Areana said. "The ladies were intrigued by someone whom the staff refer to as a shaman. They crave someone new and exciting who can actually engage them in conversation and alleviate their boredom. No offense, but the males you bring for them to play with are not intellectually compatible with ladies who have lived for over five thousand years and used that time to acquire the knowledge of several scholars. Good-looking lovers are just not enough to satisfy them."

"They have Tony for conversation," Navuh pointed out.

Areana laughed. "Tula has claimed Tony entirely for herself, and she's not sharing him."

"Then I'll bring in more men." Navuh's jaw set stubbornly. "Men who resemble me and can carry on an intelligent conversation."

"Right." Areana put down her wine. "That is going to be extremely difficult, my love, since you are one of a kind and no other flesh and blood male can resemble you both in looks and brains."

That got him to smile. "I agree. So, what is the solution?"

"Perhaps it is time we reconsidered that particular require-ment. Especially nowadays, when genetic testing can prove and disprove paternity with ease, having sons who look like you is much less relevant."

His expression darkened dangerously. "On the contrary. It makes it even more important. The children born in this harem must be believable as mine, or such tests will be brought up. We can't have that."

"My love," she said gently, "you could always say the boys take after their mothers. You've done it before when the resemblance was marginal."

"Elias looks too European even though he's not," Navuh said. "I believe he's Armenian."

Areana sighed. "You have been complaining about the ladies not conceiving lately. When was the last child born to any of them? Fifteen years ago?"

He nodded. "Eighteen. I'm suspecting that they are using contraceptives against my explicit wishes."

"The Fates decide who conceives and when, my darling. But perhaps in order to conceive, the ladies require genuine passion, real excitement, something to stir hearts that have grown weary with five thousand years of sameness." She looked into his eyes. "Immortal conception is different from that of humans. Ovulation happens on demand when the female's body recognizes a compatible male. Maybe all these handsome simpletons are simply not enough?"

"Are you saying the men I provide are inadequate?"

She heard the dangerous edge in his voice but pressed on. "I'm saying that variety is the spice of life, especially for females who have lived as long as we have. You are gorgeous, my darling, and any male who resembles you is blessed with good fortune. But even the finest wine grows tiresome if it's all one ever drinks."

His eyes blazed as he reached for her hand. "Are you getting bored with me?"

She gasped. "Never! We are truelove mates. You are the only one I will ever want."

Navuh deflated and pushed his plate away, his appetite apparently gone. "Elias is not particularly handsome, and I don't find him particularly knowledgeable either. He has good instincts, which is why I keep him."

That was something she wanted to find out more about, but now was not the time to annoy Navuh with questions.

Areana leaned back in her chair, taking her wine glass with her. "They might discover that Elias is no more interesting than the other males you made available for their use, but sometimes just the excitement of something new and different might have a positive impact."

He narrowed his eyes at her. "You seem to have given this considerable thought."

The suspicion in his voice made her tread carefully. "I think of little else but the well-being of those under my care. The ladies grow listless, going through the motions of their daily routines without true engagement, and they grow reckless in an effort to find stimulation. Take Rolenna's glassmaking experiments for example. I fear for her safety."

"Why do you think one unremarkable male who calls himself a shaman will change that?"

"I do not expect him to perform miracles. But if even one of the ladies finds renewed passion with him and conceives a son, it is worth the small concession."

Navuh was quiet for a long moment, his fingers drumming against the table. She waited, having learned that patience was often her strongest weapon in these negotiations.

"Fine," he said at last. "I'll speak with Elias."

"Thank you." She kept her triumph from showing on her face.

"Don't look so pleased with yourself," he said, but there was a hint of amusement in his voice now. "I know you too well, my dear. This isn't just about providing variety for the concubines."

"Oh?" She affected innocence. "What else could it be about?"

"You're bored as well, and you are looking for excitement even if it is to witness one of the ladies flourish with a new male."

She couldn't deny it, so she didn't try. "Perhaps we all need something new to get our blood pumping. Even you seem to find Elias interesting enough to keep him on hand."

His expression shuttered immediately. "That's different."

"Is it?" She topped off both their wine glasses. "What does a shaman do for the great Lord Navuh? Brew headache remedies? Create soothing teas for stress? You have no need for any of that."

"He's useful in other ways," Navuh said. "That's all you need to know."

"Come now," she coaxed. "We've been together five millennia. Surely you can tell me why you keep him around."

Navuh was silent for so long that she thought he wouldn't answer. Finally, he said, "He is intelligent, and he has a good strategic mind. What I find the most useful, though, is that he is completely removed from the Brotherhood's operations. Sometimes, an outside perspective is valuable. Elias doesn't know the various participants and he doesn't have any direct involvement in any of our activities. I can present scenarios to him hypothetically, and he provides insights unclouded by politics or personal interest."

It was plausible, but Areana knew her mate too well to believe it was the complete truth. There was something else, something he was deliberately keeping from her. But she knew better than to push him to reveal more.

"That is very wise," she said instead. "He is a neutral sounding board, and that can be valuable."

One of the fundamental truths of their relationship was that they did not share everything with one another. They were bound by love and fate, but their goals were not the same. She worked to minimize the damage his ambitions caused, while he worked to expand his power regardless of the cost. It was a dance they'd perfected over the millennia, neither able to change the other, but willing to coexist because they had love and devotion despite it all.

"When will you speak with Elias?"

"Tomorrow," he said.

"Wonderful." She raised her glass. "To new possibilities and at least one more son."

He moved around the table to her, one hand coming up to cup her cheek. For a moment, his thumb traced the line of her cheekbone with surprising gentleness. "You know I can deny you nothing."

"I know you tell yourself that," she said softly. "Even as you deny me the things that matter most."

His hand dropped away. "Areana—"

"Navuh."

He kissed her forehead, a gesture both tender and dismissive, and left without another word. She stood alone in the candlelight, surrounded by the remains of another meal that had ended too soon.

Five thousand years, and still they danced around each other, never quite meeting in the middle.

He kept his secrets, and she kept hers.

9

LOKAN

L okan was lured to the kitchen by the intoxicating aromas of rosemary and garlic. He knew that Carol loved to cook. After all, that was how they had initially met, when he was captured by the Guardians and brought to the dungeon. She had seen a portrait of him drawn by Dalhu and talked Kian into allowing her to prepare and serve his meals. Things progressed quickly and happily from there. However, she'd never really done any cooking while they'd lived in Beijing.

They'd embraced the cosmopolitan life, eating out for all of their meals, and she'd seemed happy, but seeing her now, wearing leggings and an oversized t-shirt that slipped off one shoulder, humming as she worked, Lokan realized that his mate assumed personalities with the same ease she changed outfits.

The female who'd always worn designer clothing and high heels had been replaced by a homebody.

Her hair was back to blonde, which was a sign of things getting back to normal, but not really.

Lokan missed the hustle and bustle of Beijing and the intensity of the fashion world. There had always been some fire he'd needed to put out, people to charm, supply problems to solve. Now he had nothing to do other than doomscroll social media and look for the Brotherhood's fingerprints all over world affairs.

A bombing in Syria, political upheaval in three African nations, and economic instability in South America that coincidentally benefited certain arms dealers. Follow the chaos, find the Brotherhood. Follow the slaughter, find his father.

The thought of ending Navuh once and for all flickered through his mind as it had done countless times before, but he could never actually complete the thought, let alone make concrete plans.

It wasn't love. He'd never loved his father. How could anyone love a monster?

It was something else. Fear, perhaps, but not of Navuh. Fear of what would happen after. Who would control the Brotherhood?

Some of Lokan's so-called brothers made Navuh look reasonable by comparison. If any of them took over, the chaos would just grow, but what was most likely to happen was a battle for power that would create a vacuum and destabilize half the world.

"Lokan?"

He looked up to find Carol watching him with concern. "What?"

"Can you watch the oven while I get ready? The timer should go off in just a few minutes, and I need you to take the roast out right away or it will get dry."

"No problem. Consider it done."

She tilted her head. "Are you sure? You seem distant. Is something bothering you?"

He forced a smile. "I'm just browsing the news."

"That's a mistake." She took his phone and set it aside. "No doomscrolling allowed at dinner parties."

He pulled her onto his lap, wrapping his arms around her waist. "It didn't start yet. Besides, I wouldn't call it a party."

"What else would you call having two couples over for a home-cooked meal?"

"An interrogation disguised as social niceties?" He nuzzled her neck, breathing in the scent of her hair. "My brother and Kian are going to spend the entire evening trying to figure out what to do with us."

She laughed. "I will welcome their input. It's not like we know what to do with ourselves now that we no longer run a fashion business or pretend to. We need to figure out how to live a normal life."

"We're not normal people."

"Perhaps we are not," she agreed, "but we can pretend."

He studied her face, noting the tension around her eyes. She was worried about him.

"I love you," he said.

Her expression softened. "I love you too, and I worry about you. You are restless, and I can't blame you, but I don't know what to do about that."

"I'm adjusting," he admitted.

"To not having someone trying to kill us?"

"To irrelevance." The words came out harsher than he'd intended. "I need to be more than a refugee from my father's insanity."

Carol cupped his face in her hands. "It's been ten days. Give yourself time. You'll figure it out."

"You're feeling it too. The boredom. The sense that we should be doing something more than playing house."

"I like playing house."

The oven timer beeped, breaking the moment.

"Go get ready." He helped her stand. "I'll take out the roast." The vegan dish she'd prepared earlier was in the warming drawer. Something Thai that smelled delicious, even though it was made with tofu.

She kissed him, quick but thorough. "Cover it in foil so it doesn't dry out."

"Yes, ma'am."

As she disappeared down the hallway, he turned his attention to the oven. The roast looked perfect, golden brown and crackling. Carol had always loved to cook, and since returning to the village, she'd thrown herself into domesticity. He loved every meal, every moment spent with her in this idyllic, safe community, but they both needed more.

The doorbell rang just as he was done covering the roast as per Carol's instructions, and he added a dish towel on top for good measure before answering the door. He found Kalugal and Jacki standing on the front porch.

"Lokan." Kalugal pulled him into a brotherly hug that felt good and awkward at the same time.

They hadn't been close while Kalugal was still in the brotherhood. In fact, Lokan had been annoyed by how quickly Kalugal had risen in the ranks despite his youth and inexperience. He hadn't known the truth about their parentage, and that out of all his numerous brothers, Kalugal was the only one he was actually related to.

"Jacki." He kissed his sister-in-law's cheek. "You look lovely as always."

"Thank you." She gifted him with a smile.

"Come in." He stepped aside. "Carol's getting ready. As usual, she has prepared enough to feed an army."

"I heard that she's a great cook."

"She is. If I don't get busy soon, I'll get fat from eating too much." He patted his flat belly.

Carol walked into the living room, transformed from a domestic goddess to the polished beauty he was accustomed to seeing. Her curly hair was perfectly styled to frame her cherubic face, her makeup was flawless, and the dark pink dress she wore hugged her curves, making her legs look endless in the matching heels.

"You look absolutely stunning." Jacki pulled Carol into her arms.

"So do you," Carol said.

Jacki waved a dismissive hand. "You'll have to impart the fashion knowledge you gained to me because I'm clueless. I always wear the same types of outfits because I can't figure out what else will look good on me."

The doorbell rang again before Carol could respond. This time it was Syssi and Kian, and another round of greetings ensued.

"Let's adjourn to the dining table," Carol said once all the embraces and compliments had been exchanged.

Lokan helped Carol serve, falling into a rhythm as if they had done this a thousand times before. Was it a couple thing? Were they so attuned to each other that they could perform any task in perfect synchrony?

The thought sent a wave of comforting warmth through him. Each of them was capable and formidable in their own right, but together, they were a force of nature. They would figure this out.

Hey, perhaps they could start a new fashion business from scratch?

The clan would provide them with all the fake documentation they needed, and he had plenty of money stashed away from all the side hustles he'd run behind his father's back for nearly a thousand years.

"This is delicious," Syssi said after her first bite of the Mung bean and tofu stir-fry.

"I want the recipe." She chuckled. "Not that Okidu would let me sneak into the kitchen and cook anything, but I can give him the recipe."

"It's easy," Carol said. "The secret is plenty of freshly grated ginger."

"Write it down for me, will you? Okidu needs exact instructions. He's very literal."

"I will," Carol promised.

"How are you both adjusting?" Jacki asked. "It must be quite a change from Beijing."

Carol and Lokan exchanged glances.

"It's been nice," Carol said. "Peaceful. Wonderfully, blissfully peaceful. For about three days."

"And then?" Kian prompted.

"And then the boredom set in," Lokan said bluntly. "We're used to operating with our tanks filled with adrenaline. This feels like retirement, and I'm not ready for that lifestyle yet."

"You're not retired," Kalugal said. "You're regrouping."

"For what?" Lokan set down his fork. "What's the next move? Because watching our father's organization tear the world apart via news feeds isn't productive."

Kian leaned back in his chair, studying them both. "The Brotherhood's influence is growing, and we need to counter it. I've been toying with an idea of creating a task force that will undermine their influence."

"Their network is too vast, too entrenched," Lokan said. "If you cut off one head, three more appear."

"I'm talking about political influence." Kian took a sip of wine. "Something that can be achieved with a small force of skilled operatives."

Carol perked up. "Go on."

"The Brotherhood has been placing their people or compromising existing officials in governments worldwide. We need to do the same, but instead of using blackmail and bribery, we'd use the one secret weapon the Brotherhood doesn't have. Beautiful, charming, immortal females."

"A honey trap operation." Carol grinned. "I love it."

"What I have in mind is more sophisticated than that." Kian refilled his and Syssi's wine glasses. "I'm talking about long-term influence, not just information gathering. We can guide policy decisions, counter Brotherhood initiatives, and in doing so, save countless lives."

Carol sighed. "I would have loved a job like that. It's right in my wheelhouse. But I'm happily mated, and my seduction days are behind me."

Lokan didn't like to be reminded of Carol's days as a courtesan. The thing was that she hadn't done that just for the money. She'd loved the power she'd wielded over men and the attention and gifts they'd showered her with. He didn't have the right to be jealous because he hadn't been celibate until he'd met her either, but it was healthier not to think about the sheer number of men she'd been with.

"You could train others," Syssi suggested.

"Train them in what?" Jacki laughed. "The art of manipulation? Men are so easy that no training is needed. All a beautiful woman needs is the intent. Smile, show some skin, pretend to be fascinated by their boring stories, and their minds will be like putty to their thralling."

"You'd be surprised," Carol said. "There's a difference between getting a man's attention and maintaining influence over time. It requires finesse, intelligence, and the ability to become whatever they need you to be while keeping your own agenda hidden."

Lokan watched his mate warm to the topic, her eyes brightening with interest. This was the Carol he'd fallen in love with—sharp, cunning, incredibly brave.

"Have you started assembling your team?" Carol asked Kian.

He grimaced. "I don't know who to approach with that. Mey and Jin, who are perfect for that kind of operation, can't do it because they are mated and running a business. Eva could be great as a consultant, but she can't do field work for the same reason."

"What about the paranormals from Safe Haven?" Syssi asked. "I know that they can't thrall, but some of them might have talents that can be useful in other ways."

"Eleanor and I have discussed bringing them to the keep for testing," Kian said. "We've decided to do it in stages rather than relocating everyone at once."

"That might be problematic," Syssi said. "They've formed such a tight-knit community."

All eyes turned to Jacki, who had been part of the government's paranormal program before running away along with Jin.

"Actually, it might be good for them," she said. "That kind of insular community can become limiting. Some distance could help them grow as individuals."

"Who would oversee the testing?" Carol asked.

"Julian," Kian said. "He will arrange the inductions for the men without the ceremonies we usually do for Dormants. We are still not sure what to do about the women. Since they are all in committed relationships, they might want to wait for their partners to transition and induce them once their fangs and venom are ready for that."

"I could help explain things," Jacki offered. "They know me."

"And I can do the recruiting in the village," Carol offered. "I know which females might be interested in something like that."

Kian nodded. "That would be tremendously helpful. Thank you, both."

Lokan felt something ease in his chest. Carol with a purpose was Carol at her best.

Kalugal shook his head. "You have enough on your plate, my love. Perhaps you can just give pointers to Carol, and if anyone needs more convincing, you can do it over a video call."

Jacki let out a breath. "That's true. I always overestimate what I can accomplish in a day."

Kalugal took her hand and kissed the back of it. "You accomplish more in a day than most people do in a month."

"What about you?" Kian turned to Lokan. "Do you want to assist your mate? You have insight into the Brotherhood's operations that none of us have."

"You want me to help my mate train women to seduce politicians?" Lokan raised an eyebrow. "That's progressive."

"It could help them understand what they will be working against," Kian said. "You know how they think and how they operate."

Lokan nodded. "I can do that. I think. I'm not sure what's going on with those enhanced soldiers and how we are supposed to deal with them. We encountered them in Mongolia. My father's way of saying hello. They were stronger, faster, and nearly impossible to put down. I couldn't get into their minds."

Kalugal regarded him with curiosity in his eyes. "How is your ability progressing?"

Lokan shrugged, uncomfortable with the scrutiny. "It's still not strong enough to affect most immortals. It only works on the weak-minded, but it saved us nonetheless."

Kalugal put his wine glass down. "I find it interesting that the ability to manipulate immortals only started to manifest recently. We share the same genetics, and I've been able to do it since I was a boy."

"I have a theory," Syssi said, turning to Lokan. "You are over a thousand years old. Your abilities should have manifested a long time ago. I think fear held you back—fear of your father. When you met Carol, when you had something worth fighting for, you stopped holding back. Does that make sense to you?"

Lokan nodded. "I thought it was just being around someone as wonderful as Carol rubbing off on me, but perhaps more than one factor influenced the development of my abilities."

"Fear can be a powerful inhibitor," Syssi said. "And love is an equally powerful motivator."

"Speaking of fear," Kalugal said, "these enhanced soldiers worry me. If Navuh can create an army of them, we don't have an answer for that. Not yet anyway." He looked at Kian. "Any estimates on those robots William and Kaia are designing?"

Kian shook his head. "Won't be ready quickly enough to prevent a hell of a lot of bloodshed."

Lokan frowned. "Are you talking about creating a robot army?"

Kian shrugged, and Kalugal nodded.

"That's the future, Lokan. Our father's goons will not win this war for the control of humanity. Robots equipped with artificial intelligence and guns will, which would be Annani's ultimate revenge. Without her, that knowledge wouldn't have been developed for another thousand years or more, and by that time, it would have been too late."

Kian refilled his glass again and took a sip. "You are an optimist, Kalugal. So many things can go wrong between now and when the robot army is ready to defend the world. Hell, for all we know, that army could turn against us. The Eternal King had all the Odus on Anumati destroyed for a reason."

"Yeah, his own quest for power," Kalugal said. "That's why I think they will benefit us. My father is like the Eternal King. He would do anything and everything to achieve his goal of world domination. The Eternal King believed that the Odus would stand in his way, so I say let's put their inferior cousins in front of my father's army."

10

ESAG

The small closet that served as Esag's workshop held the lingering scent of cedar shavings and the faint sweetness of the oils he used to finish his carvings. The final product would be made with stone, but wood was easier to work with, and he could create many more figurines until he was satisfied with the result.

Only then would he switch to stone and create the masterpiece that would induce a prophetic dream.

In theory.

There were no guarantees of that happening even if he got the figurine just right.

Sitting hunched over his workbench, he was looking at Khiann's portrait as the figurine was taking shape beneath his hands. The mischievous eyes of his childhood friend seemed to taunt him, egging him on like he used to when they were both young lads.

"You'd find this funny, wouldn't you?" Esag murmured to the portrait. "Watching me sweat to produce an image of you in wood. I can just hear your stupid jokes."

Esag sighed, the knife moving with the muscle memory of five thousand years. He didn't need to look down anymore —his fingers knew the wood's grain, could feel where to coax out the curve of a cheekbone or the angle of a jaw.

A shadow fell over him, but he didn't lift his head.

"Roven and I are heading to the Hobbit Bar," Davuh said from the doorway. "It's time to call it a day and have some fun. Put the wood aside and come with us."

Esag didn't look up from his work. "I can't. I need to finish this one."

Roven joined Davuh in the doorway, both of them crowding the narrow space. "You haven't left this damn closet for anything other than food and sleep."

"I also left it to take showers and attend dinners." He kept working even though his friends had a point.

"The clan ladies, Esag," Davuh said with a grin. "They've been asking about you. This village is like a free candy store for immortals, and you are behaving like a monk."

Esag's knife paused for just a moment before resuming its steady rhythm. "I can't think of anything else until I fulfill my duty to the princess."

Roven laughed. "In all the years I've known you, you could never resist female companionship. But when you could finally find a proper mate among your own kind, you're spending all of your time in a closet like a hermit."

The words stung. Esag set down his knife and finally looked up at his friends—brothers, really, after all they'd been through together.

"Go," he said, forcing a smile. "Have fun. Drink some of that excellent whiskey Atzil keeps behind the bar and look for your truelove mates. Maybe you'll get lucky tonight."

Davuh shook his head. "Don't you want that too?"

"What I want is to finish this figurine so we can find Khiann. Nothing is more important than that."

The two knew better than to argue with him when he got into one of his moods. They'd learned over the millennia when to let him be.

"Well, good luck," Roven said. "I hope you finally get what you are after tonight."

"Thank you." He got the knife going again.

Esag heard their footsteps fade down the hallway, heard the front door close, and then he was alone again with his thoughts and the half-formed face of a god who'd been gone for five thousand years, but possibly not dead.

That was the whole point of this exercise, wasn't it? To create something that might trigger a vision, that might lead them to where Khiann was sleeping beneath the sand.

The portrait showed Khiann young and laughing, full of life and mischief. It was nothing like the formal painting

114

Annani had, where he looked regal, the epitome of the romantic hero.

This was Khiann as Esag had known him—friend, brother, and co-conspirator in countless adventures.

Khiann was the better male, though, and not just because he was a god and Esag was only an immortal, his servant.

His mind drifted, as it often did during these long hours of carving, back to those days in Sumer when the world had been younger and full of possibility, when he'd been engaged to Ashegan and desperate for a way out.

When Gulan had been in love with him.

He squeezed his eyes shut, trying to push away the memory, but it came anyway. Gulan in the garden, tall and strong and beautiful in her own unique manner. The way she'd blushed when he'd complimented her. The way she'd thrown him over her shoulder with such ease. The way she'd kissed him back with innocent passion before running away.

And then his spectacular failure. His insulting offer. The hurt in her eyes when he'd suggested she become his concubine.

"Stupid," he muttered, not sure if he was talking to his younger self or the wooden figure taking shape in his hands. "Stupid and selfish."

He'd thought he was being practical. Ashegan had the connections his family needed. Gulan had his heart. Why not have both? It had seemed so simple, so reasonable. Many immortals had similar arrangements.

But Gulan wasn't like other immortals. She was honest to her core and incapable of duplicity or compromise when it came to matters of the heart. She'd loved him, and he'd thrown that love back in her face as if it were worthless.

The knife bit too deep, and Esag cursed as he nearly ruined the curve he'd been working on. He set down the blade and rubbed his tired eyes.

Wonder had never brought it up. Not once since he had arrived in the village had she mentioned the pain he'd caused her. She was gracious and kind in a way that made his guilt worse. He'd rather she turn her back on him or demand an apology, something. But she simply treated him as an old friend, as if those painful memories belonged to different people.

Maybe they did.

Thousands of years changed a person. The young male who'd been too weak to stand up to social pressures and his family's demands was long gone. The girl who'd run away rather than watch him marry another had become a confident woman who'd survived for millennia and found her truelove mate.

The Fates had a sense of humor about these things.

Esag picked up a piece of sandpaper and began smoothing the rough edges of the carving. This was his favorite part— when the raw wood began to transform into something refined, something that captured not just the physical appearance but the essence of the subject.

He thought about what Roven had said. The clan ladies were asking about him. The possibility of finding a mate among his own kind. It should have excited him. After five thousand years of loneliness, the chance of companionship, maybe even love, should have had him racing to that bar.

But every time he thought about it, he saw Gulan's face. Not Wonder's—Gulan's. The girl who'd loved him with so much passion and whom he'd failed so spectacularly.

Some mistakes couldn't be undone, though, and some hurts couldn't be healed. He'd had his chance at love and had thrown it away for family obligations that, in the end, hadn't mattered at all. The cataclysm had come, and Ashegan, his parents, and his sisters were all gone in an instant.

He'd sacrificed Gulan's love for nothing.

Khiann's eyes emerged from the wood, that knowing look that suggested he saw more than he let on. He'd warned him not to lead Gulan on. Had he known about his feelings for her? Probably. He'd ordered Esag to find her and not to return without her because he had known that Esag was the reason she'd escaped, and that any harm that overtook her would be Esag's fault.

He'd searched for her, and once he'd realized the scope of the destruction that had befallen their lands, once he'd understood that the world they'd known was gone forever, he'd searched some more. But Gulan had vanished without a trace.

For centuries, he'd wondered. Had she made it to Kemet? Had she found happiness there? Had she thought of him at all, or had she forgotten the stupid squire who'd broken her heart?

Finding out she'd survived, that she'd been asleep in stasis all this time, that she'd woken to find love with Anandur, was a tremendous relief. She was happy. She'd found someone who valued her properly, who saw her worth and cherished it.

Everything Esag should have done but hadn't.

The figurine was nearly complete now. Just a few more details—the slight upturn of the lips that suggested Khiann was about to say something clever, the way his hair fell across his forehead. These were the things that would make it real, that might spark the vision Esag needed.

He held the carving up to the light, comparing it to the portrait. It was good work, maybe some of his best. But was it good enough? Would it capture whatever essence was needed to trigger a vision, even though it was made from wood and not stone?

"Only one way to find out," he murmured.

He set the figurine down and reached for his finishing oils. This was the final step, the one that would bring out the wood's natural beauty and preserve the carving for years to come. As he worked the oil into the grain, he thought about permanence, about the things that lasted and the things that didn't.

Even now, after all this time, he could close his eyes and see Gulan in that garden, sunlight catching the lighter tones in her dark hair, her green eyes wide with wonder as he'd told her she was beautiful.

She'd been so surprised by the compliment as if no one had ever told her that before. As if she didn't know that her strength was magnificent, her loyalty precious, her heart pure gold.

"I should have broken that engagement and married you properly, given you the life you deserved."

But the truth was that he hadn't been her truelove mate. He'd been merely an infatuation, an object of desire for a young girl who was growing into a woman.

What she had with Anandur was the real thing, and that was what the Fates had planned for her all along. Esag hadn't been meant to be hers, and apparently, he hadn't been meant to be Ashegan's either.

Was his truelove mate waiting for him somewhere out there? Had he earned the right to such a boon?

He'd suffered, but he hadn't sacrificed. Not when a sacrifice had been required of him.

11

KIAN

"Magnus has volunteered to be Tim's inducer," Kian told Syssi as he put on his jacket. "Or rather, Vivian volunteered him after hearing that no one else wanted to do it."

"That was kind of them," she said. "Magnus is perfect for this."

"Let's hope so. Tim is in no shape to provide a physical challenge, but in his case, he doesn't even need to memorize offensive poetry to irritate Magnus. He does that naturally. I just hope he's not stupid enough to insult Vivian or Ella. Even Magnus has his limits, and he might beat Tim into a pulp if he says something about his mate or daughter."

Syssi lifted a brow. "They are both coming to the ceremony?"

Kian winced. "There will be no ceremony. Just Tim and Magnus in the ring, but yeah. Vivian mobilized the entire family to support Tim because he had no one else."

She frowned. "That's not right, Kian. Tim deserves a ceremony like anyone else." She pulled out her phone. "I'm calling Andrew and telling him that he needs to show up. He's been working with Tim for the past six years. They might not be friends, but they are coworkers, and he should show his support."

"Andrew? It's Syssi. Tim's induction is tonight...Yes, I know...That's not the point. He's your colleague, and you should be there...Thank you."

She ended the call and turned to Kian. "Maybe if we shower Tim with love and support, it will encourage him to be nicer."

Kian pulled her close, pressing a kiss to her forehead. "You're sweet, but Tim is probably irredeemable. He's made being ornery into an art form."

"No one is irredeemable."

"Well, he's not a criminal," Kian conceded. "Having no social skills and being proud of it isn't illegal, and that's why we are offering him this opportunity, and who knows? Perhaps it will make things more interesting to have a resident grouch in the village. Every community needs one, right?"

"That's a terrible attitude." But Syssi was smiling as she said it.

They paused at the door to the nursery, where Allegra was sleeping peacefully, one small fist curled against her cheek. The sight never failed to make Kian's heart expand with protective love.

"Okidu," Syssi called softly.

The Odu emerged from his room. "Yes, mistress?"

"We're going to the gym to attend an induction. Please keep an eye on Allegra. If she wakes up and asks for Mommy or Daddy, call me?"

"Of course, mistress."

Allegra rarely woke up at night, so Kian wasn't worried, and even if she did, she would probably just demand that Okidu turn on the television for her. She was a cunning little thing, and she knew who she could manipulate and who she couldn't.

The walk to the gym was pleasant, and the village was quiet and peaceful at night. When they got there, it was already busy, and Kian was surprised to see many more people than he'd expected to be there.

It seemed like Vivian had called around and organized a bigger showing for Tim, who might not appreciate such a turnout for what he considered to be public humiliation.

He was already in the ring with Magnus, the Guardian was saying something to him, and Tim was actually listening and nodding.

The guy wore a tracksuit that seemed brand new and hung loosely on his soft frame, making him look even more out of place in the gym.

"He looks nervous." There was pity in Syssi's voice.

"He should be. He's about to fight a Guardian."

They entered to find Vivian seated on a mat next to the ring, wearing a yoga outfit and displaying an elegant posture. Ella sat beside her, looking more casual than her mother but similarly excited. Parker and Lisa sat on Vivian's other side, and several Guardians were standing in a group around Julian, listening to something he was telling them while gesticulating with his hands. Roni and Sylvia were present as well.

As Kian walked over to the group, Vivian waved Syssi over. "I didn't know you were coming."

"I figured I'd add my support," Syssi said, sitting down next to Ella. "Thank you for roping Magnus into this," she said quietly. "Tim's reputation precedes him, and people didn't want to be tied to him with bonds of friendship forever."

Vivian smiled. "My Magnus can be friends with anyone. He will be a good influence."

In the ring, Magnus was demonstrating a hold, moving slowly so Tim could see exactly what would happen. Tim nodded along, but his face had taken on a grayish cast that suggested he was anxious despite his attempts at bravado.

"How is your newest patient?" Kian asked Julian.

"Out of shape but otherwise surprisingly healthy for a guy who thinks exercise is walking from the couch to the refrigerator and back."

Andrew arrived looking like he'd rather be anywhere else. "I can't believe I'm here at this hour. People with little kids should be exempt from attending these midnight ceremonies."

"I'm here." Syssi wrapped her arm around her brother's middle. "You'll live."

"You guilted me into it." His expression softened as he glanced at Tim. "He does look like someone who needs all the support he can get."

Kian had planned to keep things simple, but Syssi was right —Tim deserved a proper ceremony. He hadn't brought the ceremonial wine, but the ritual could be done without it.

He walked up to the ring. "Are you two ready?"

Up close, Tim looked even more nervous, sweat already beading on his forehead despite the cool temperature in the gym, but he nodded.

"Ready as I will ever be," he said.

Kian turned to the small crowd and lifted his hand to draw everyone's attention. "We are gathered here to witness Tim's attempt at transformation. He comes to us vouched for by his ability and sponsored by..." He paused, realizing they'd never formally assigned Tim a sponsor.

"By me," Andrew said. "I vouch for him."

"I second that," Magnus added. "In the short time I've known Tim, I've seen his commitment to this process. He asks good questions and listens to the answers."

Magnus was always generous with his praise.

Kian nodded, adapting the formal words in his head. "Tim comes before us, vouched for by Andrew and seconded by

Magnus. Who volunteers to take on the burden of initiating Tim into immortality?"

"I do." Magnus stepped forward, his tall frame dwarfing Tim.

"Tim, do you accept Magnus as your initiator? To respect his guidance and honor the gift he offers?"

Tim swallowed hard, his usual sarcasm nowhere to be found. "I do."

"Does anyone have any objections to this pairing?"

Silence greeted the question, though Kian caught a few surprised looks. Usually, this part of the ceremony was a formality. Tonight, the silence carried weight.

"Then let us proceed," Kian said. "Magnus, Tim, you may begin."

Tim shed the top of his tracksuit, revealing a t-shirt that proclaimed 'I'm Not Anti-Social, I'm Anti-Stupid.' Evidently, he couldn't resist making a statement, or maybe he just didn't have any plain t-shirts.

"Remember what we practiced," Magnus said.

"I do," Tim said.

"You've got this," Magnus encouraged. "Ready?"

Tim nodded, raising his hands in an approximation of a fighting stance that would have made any Guardian in training wince. Magnus circled him slowly, giving him time to adjust.

"Any time now," Tim said, nervous energy making him bold. "Unless you're waiting for me to die of old age first."

Magnus smiled. "There's the Tim I was expecting. Come on then. Attack me."

Tim lunged forward with all the grace of a tranquilized bear. Magnus caught him easily, using his momentum to spin him around. For a moment, Tim actually managed to stay on his feet.

"That was good," Magnus said. "Again."

Kian didn't know whether Magnus was dragging this out because he hadn't managed to produce venom yet or to give Tim the illusion of actually putting up a fight.

They repeated the process several times, with Magnus gradually increasing the speed and force. Tim was sweating profusely now, his breathing labored, but he kept coming.

"He's got guts," one of the watching Guardians murmured.

The next exchange was faster. Tim threw a genuinely decent punch that Magnus deflected before sweeping Tim's legs. Tim hit the mat face first, or rather stomach first, but immediately started fighting against Magnus's hold, bucking and twisting, his face red with effort.

Magnus's fangs descended, his body somehow responding to the pitiful struggle.

"You weigh as much as a damn car!" Tim hissed.

Magnus shifted his hold, applying more pressure. Tim's struggles became more desperate, less calculated. The scent of aggression filled the air—sweat and adrenaline and the primal response to combat.

"Almost there," Vivian said, but Kian didn't know who she was trying to encourage, Tim or Magnus.

Magnus's eyes were glowing now, his fangs fully extended. He lowered his head toward Tim's neck, and Tim actually whimpered.

"It's okay," Magnus said, his voice rough with the effort of control.

The bite, when it came, was precise. Magnus's fangs pierced the skin cleanly, delivering venom for exactly thirty seconds before he pulled back. Tim's entire body went rigid, then limp.

"Is he okay?" Andrew asked.

"He will be," Julian said.

Tim's eyes had rolled back, showing only whites, and Magnus carefully turned him onto his back. "I hope I gave him enough."

That was why the induction was tricky. Too much could kill, and too little didn't do the job.

"He's fine," Julian announced after checking Tim's pulse.

"I'll take him to the clinic." Magnus lifted Tim's unconscious form.

"I'll come with you," Vivian offered.

Usually, the Dormant would go home and be cared for by his mother, if he was still a teenager, or by his partner, if he was older. However, since Tim had neither, it was decided to take him to the clinic and monitor him there. It wasn't fair to ask Thomas or even Andrew to do that.

"I hope he'll change after his transition," Andrew said as Magnus left the gym with Tim, Vivian, Julian, and Ella.

"Body-wise, he will probably improve. But personality-wise?" Kian shrugged. "Not likely, unless he meets a guiding angel while he's out."

Andrew chuckled. "Perhaps the physical improvement will make him less of an ass."

Sometimes the physical changes brought confidence, and immortality brought peace. Sometimes joining a supportive community brought out the best in people, and sometimes, it just gave them new ways to be difficult.

Time would tell which way Tim would go.

ELUHEED

The familiar path to Navuh's office on the first level felt different this time. Eluheed's escort seemed more relaxed, and he wondered why he seemed less like someone leading a prisoner and more like a guide.

"The lord is in a good mood today," Arnav offered as they approached the heavy doors.

That was unusual. The guy rarely spoke beyond what was necessary, and Navuh's moods were typically variations on paranoid and calculating, not good.

"Thank you for the heads up," Eluheed said, though he wasn't sure if a good mood was better or worse than the usual.

Arnav knocked, waited for the command to enter, then opened the door for Eluheed before retreating to his post outside.

Navuh sat behind his massive desk. "Sit," he commanded, gesturing to the chair across from him.

Eluheed sat, keeping his expression neutral while trying to assess his jailer's mood. Arnav was right. Something was different about the lord today.

"Tell me about your healing knowledge," Navuh commanded.

The question caught Eluheed off guard. "What would you like to know, my lord?"

"The herbs in your garden and the remedies you make from them. How extensive is your knowledge?"

"I can treat simple ailments." Eluheed held his hands in his lap. "Fevers, headaches, minor wounds, digestive issues. But the harem needs a proper physician, my lord. There are limits to what plant medicine can accomplish."

"Such as?"

"Such as someone who can dispense antibiotics. We have a boy with pneumonia right now, and until he got antibiotics, he wasn't getting better with what I could do for him. I could ease his symptoms, help with the fever, but I couldn't cure the infection."

Navuh's lips curved in a mocking smile. "What kind of shaman can't cure common maladies like pneumonia? I thought you people channeled divine healing."

The insult stung, but Eluheed had endured far worse in his centuries of wandering. He lowered his head in apparent shame. "I'm not a very good shaman, my lord. My abilities are limited."

"Limited." Navuh leaned back in his throne-like chair, studying him with those ancient, calculating eyes. "And what about your spiritual guidance? Can you at least manage that, or are you equally incompetent in matters of gods and mortals?"

This was some kind of a test, but Eluheed wasn't sure what Navuh was testing him for. In the long months he'd been stuck in this godforsaken place, no one had asked him for spiritual guidance. Advice, yes, but even that was rare. Mostly, people sought him out for his herbal remedies.

This could be to test his general knowledge. Or maybe to verify that he wasn't calling himself a shaman for nothing?

Eluheed had to give Navuh something that sounded profound, but without revealing the foundation of his own beliefs and the practices he'd followed when he was a real shaman. He drew upon centuries of observing human faiths and weaving together threads from various traditions.

"Spiritual guidance is not a skill one learns. It comes from within. It's about understanding the fundamental truths that unite all seeking souls."

Navuh's eyebrow arched. "Enlighten me."

Eluheed took a breath. "All spiritual traditions speak of balance between light and darkness, action and stillness, the material and the divine. In the East, it is known as yin and yang. In the West, they speak of virtue and sin. But beneath these dualities lies a deeper truth."

He paused, watching Navuh's face for any sign of recognition or displeasure. The warlord's expression remained neutral, attentive.

"The ancient Egyptians understood this better than most," Eluheed continued. "They spoke of Ma'at—truth, justice, harmony, balance, not as abstract concepts but as the fundamental order of existence. When we align ourselves with truth, we find peace. When we deceive others or ourselves, we create chaos."

"Truth," Navuh repeated, something flickering in his dark eyes. "It's an interesting choice. Why truth and not benevolence or kindness?" He said those words with obvious contempt as if they were sins and not virtues.

"Truth has many faces, my lord. The truth we show the world, the truth we tell ourselves, the truth that exists regardless of our perception of it. A shaman's role is to help others navigate these different truths and find their authentic path."

"What is your authentic path, shaman?"

The question was a trap, but Eluheed had navigated such snares before. "To serve where I am needed, to heal what I can, and to accept what I cannot change. The ancient texts speak of dharma—duty aligned with cosmic order. My dharma led me here."

Navuh snorted. "Your dharma? Or your bad luck?"

"Perhaps they are the same, my lord. What seems like misfortune may be the universe placing us exactly where we need to be. The Sufi mystics say that the poison and the cure often come in the same cup."

"Sufis." Navuh's tone dripped with contempt. "Whirling madmen lost in ecstatic delusions."

"Yet they understood something profound," Eluheed pressed on, warming to his theme. "The divine speaks through beauty, through poetry, through the intoxication of the soul. They knew that rigid orthodoxy kills the spirit, while divine madness can set it free."

"Are you calling me rigid?"

"I would never presume, my lord. I speak only of spiritual principles. The Taoists say that the rigid tree breaks in the storm, while the flexible reed survives. Strength can take many forms."

Navuh was quiet for a long moment, and Eluheed wondered if he'd gone too far. Then the warlord smiled—not his usual cruel smirk, but something almost genuine.

"I can see how all this nonsense might appeal to the ladies," he said.

Eluheed frowned. "My lord?"

"My ladies are bored. They require entertainment." Navuh drummed his fingers on the desk. "I am devoted to my first wife, the Lady Areana. I'm not involved with any of the females. They satisfy their needs with selected male servants."

Eluheed let his eyes widen in apparent shock, even though he'd heard the rumors.

"Normally," Navuh continued, "I prefer these males to

resemble me. For obvious reasons. But I'm making an exception in your case."

Eluheed's heartbeat accelerated, and he started sweating. "I'm honored, my lord," he managed.

"There are rules." Navuh's voice took on that strange quality that Eluheed had felt before, the push of compulsion that slid off his mind like oil on water. "You will not speak to anyone about your prophetic abilities. You will not discuss anything that passes between us in these meetings. You will not use your position to gather information about my operations. Is that clear?"

"Yes, my lord," Eluheed said, letting his voice go flat as if the compulsion had taken hold. "I understand completely."

"Good." Navuh's voice returned to its usual smoothness. "From now on, you may look upon the ladies when you encounter them. You may engage them in conversation if they initiate it. If they invite you to share meals or other activities, you will comply."

The implications hung heavy in the air. Eluheed struggled to find words.

"Furthermore," Navuh continued, "you will treat them with absolute respect. You will attend to their needs with diligence and skill. They are my treasures, and I expect you to treat them as such. Is that clear?"

"Crystal clear, my lord," Eluheed said.

Navuh leaned forward, his dark eyes boring into Eluheed's. "Do you know why I put you in the harem?"

Because it was the best-guarded prison on the island, but Eluheed pretended not to realize that.

"You said that it was the safest place for me and also convenient for you, my lord."

"Correct. The harem is the most secure location on this island. I allow select people in, but no one ever gets out unless it is in a casket. My power-hungry sons cannot reach you here, and my commanders cannot bribe or threaten you." Navuh smiled one of his creepy smiles. "You see, Elias, you are a unique treasure, and I keep my treasures safe, protected, and exclusively mine to do with as I please."

Navuh was telling him that he was like the harem ladies.

"I'm protecting my assets," Navuh continued. "You should count yourself fortunate."

"Thank you, my lord," Eluheed said, pouring genuine feeling into the words. "Your wisdom in keeping me safe is matched only by your generosity in allowing me to bask in the presence of your ladies."

Navuh's eyes narrowed. "I don't appreciate false platitudes or flowery speeches. Save those for the concubines—they might like them."

"Yes, my lord."

"You're dismissed. The head housekeeper is waiting outside. She'll show you to your new quarters."

Another surprise.

Eluheed rose, bowed deeply, and made his way to the door. His mind was reeling. Free access to the ladies. New quarters. The golden cage was becoming more elaborate, intriguing, and its bars were now glinting with diamonds, but it was still a cage.

Outside, he found Shalini, the head housekeeper. Her expression was neutral, but he caught a glimmer of curiosity in her eyes.

"Follow me," she said briskly. "Lord Navuh has instructed me to find you appropriate quarters on the second level."

The second level was one level below where the lord and his first wife resided, and where Navuh's office was located.

Eluheed followed Shalini to the elevator. "Who else lives on the second level?"

She cast him an amused glance. "All the ladies except the first wife, who occupies the entire first level with Lord Navuh. The doctor had a room there when he was still alive, and you are getting his. Tony also has a room there."

He remembered Tony, the American who'd cut his hand and also needed headache remedies.

The second level was a big upgrade from the servants' quarters on the seventh level, which was the bottom and largest one. The carpets were thick beneath his feet, the air scented with subtle perfumes, the lighting soft.

"Tony's room is there," Shalini indicated a door halfway down the corridor. "Yours is here." She opened a door to reveal a suite that made his previous quarters look like a closet.

The bedroom was spacious, with a large bed covered in luxurious bedding. There was a seating area, a desk, and even a small balcony that overlooked an interior courtyard. The bathroom had a full tub, not just a shower.

"This is more than I expected," Eluheed said.

"The ladies' companions are well cared for," Shalini said. "Speaking of which, has one of them already claimed you?"

Eluheed's breath caught. "Claimed me?"

"Lady Tula has exclusive rights to Tony. The other ladies may speak and dine with him, but he shares intimacies only with her."

"I see." His mouth felt dry. "And the other ladies?"

"They share the available men, those who are allowed, of course. But none have taken a permanent companion." She studied him with shrewd eyes. "Until now, perhaps. So, has one of them claimed you?"

Was this an elaborate trap? The lord's way of finding out that Eluheed had broken the rules?

"No," Eluheed said, his voice suddenly hoarse. "No. I haven't even looked at them, and they haven't looked at me. It was forbidden."

Shalini moved to the door. "Your belongings will be brought up within the hour. The ladies typically take their main meal at sunset in the common dining room that's located at the end of this corridor. You are expected to join them."

"Will they know about Lord Navuh's decision to allow me here?"

"Lady Areana will have informed them by now." She smiled knowingly. "Did Lord Navuh tell you what is expected of you?"

"I am to provide entertainment to bored ladies."

She snorted. "Well, yes. That's how it will start. Lord Navuh is interested in sons, but none of the ladies have conceived in many years. He hopes that variety and spice will lead to conception."

Eluheed swallowed. "I see." He was expected to function as a new breeding bull.

She left him standing in his new quarters, staring at the opulent space that was a vast improvement over the room he'd been occupying for the past eighteen months.

This one might hold possibilities, being closer to the surface, and perhaps even uncovering the hidden tunnel that the lord used to come and go. Eluheed had never seen him arriving through the gates in the double fence surrounding the harem, so the only logical conclusion was that there was a tunnel. Either that or Navuh was a demon who dematerialized in one place and materialized in another.

But that wasn't what Eluheed really wanted to think about

right now. His mind conjured an image of azure silk and dark hair, a musical voice that had asked about his herbs.

Tamira.

Would she be at dinner? Would she claim him for herself?

Did it matter? He needed to find a way out of the harem and not get involved with a lady who was someone else's treasure. Eluheed had his own treasure to take care of, and he couldn't allow himself to get sidetracked.

He moved to the balcony, looking out at the artificial paradise of the courtyard. Fountains played in the eternal twilight of the underground complex. Exotic plants bloomed in carefully tended beds. It was beautiful, in its way. A perfect illusion of life.

Across and to the sides were the balconies of the ladies' quarters, and above, across the entire span of the top level, the first lady and the lord's, and scaling the walls to get there didn't look difficult. The access to the tunnel the lord used must be in his rooms, and it was possible to reach them from this illusion of a garden.

Perhaps that's all any of them had here—illusions. The ladies were pretending this was a home rather than a prison. The servants pretended they had chosen this life. Navuh was pretending his paranoia was wisdom, his cruelty strength.

And now Eluheed was pretending to be a human shaman while hiding centuries of secrets and a sacred duty he could never abandon.

13

RUVON

R uvon checked his appearance in the mirror one more time, straightening his shoulders and pulling them back. Three gym sessions in a week weren't enough to create dramatic changes, but his trainer had been right—posture made all the difference. When he stood properly, he looked less like a man apologizing for existing and more like someone who belonged.

"Shoulders back, chest out, chin up," he muttered, repeating his trainer's mantra. "Confidence is ninety percent presentation."

That meant not walking around hunched over like—what had Gareth called it? The Hunchback of Notre Dame.

Ruvon had to look that up, and then he spent an evening watching the animated movie because the live-action version looked too depressing. It had been illuminating. And mortifying. But also strangely hopeful, because even the hunchback had found love with the beautiful Esmeralda.

Although in the Disney version, she'd chosen the handsome captain instead.

But the resemblance between the animated Esmeralda and Arezoo had been striking enough to make him pause the movie several times. Same lustrous dark hair, same golden skin, same graceful way of moving. Arezoo's eyes were brown instead of green, but everything else...

He would never tell her about that comparison, though.

Ruvon grabbed his wallet and headed out, his heart already racing at the thought of seeing her again. Over a week had passed since their first date. They still spent time together at the end of her shifts in the café, but not wanting to overwhelm her, he'd waited to ask her out on another date.

They'd shared conversations over coffee, poetry readings, smiles across the table, and brief touches of hands, but no kisses. Not since that perfect moment at the lookout point when she'd taken control and shown him exactly what she wanted. The memory still made his chest constrict with something between joy and terror.

He was in love.

The realization had hit him a while ago, sometime between their third post-shift coffee and the fourth time he'd caught himself staring at her instead of his computer screen.

Ruvon had never been in love before. He'd experienced attraction, even affection, but nothing like this consuming need to be near Arezoo, to make her smile, to make her happy, to prove himself worthy of her.

It was terrifying.

As he approached her house, Arezoo emerged before he could knock, just as she had on their first date.

The sight of her stopped him in his tracks.

She wore a white sundress printed with bold black and yellow flowers that made her golden skin glow. A tiny black cardigan that looked more decorative than functional was draped over her shoulders. Her hair fell loose around her face, and she'd done something with cosmetics that made her eyes look even larger and more expressive.

"You look beautiful," he said, the words inadequate for what he wanted to express.

She did a little twirl, the dress flaring around her legs. "Do you like it? It's new. I bought it with my first paycheck from the café." There was pride in her voice. "My first purchase with my own money."

A cool evening breeze rustled through the trees, and he frowned when he noticed her slight shiver. "It might get cold later. This pretty sweater doesn't look warm."

"I'll be fine," she said, linking her arm through his with an ease that expressed growing comfort. "Besides, the pub will be warm."

He swallowed his rebuttal that it would be cold on the way back home. She was so happy about her new outfit, so proud of buying it herself. He would never wish to dim her joy.

"You'll be the most beautiful woman there," he said instead.

She squeezed his arm. "I bet you say that to all the girls."

"I've never said it to anyone before."

The words came out sounding more serious than he'd intended, and she looked up at him with those big, brown eyes of hers. For a moment, he thought she might kiss him again, right there in front of her house where her mother and her many aunts could see. But she just smiled and tugged him forward.

"Come on. I don't want to miss Fenella's readings. I brought something for her to read." She lifted her arm, showing him the delicate bracelet she wore on her wrist.

Warning bells went off in his head. "Are you sure that's wise? Fenella makes up most of what she says, and her aim is to entertain, which means that she says potentially embarrassing things."

"Then we'll laugh about it." She bumped her shoulder against his arm. "Don't be such a worrier, Ruvon. Fenella is family, remember? She won't say anything cruel."

Family. The word sat uneasily with him. Arezoo's father was family too, and he'd been willing to trade her to the highest bidder. Ruvon had gotten so angry when she'd told him about it that for several days he'd contemplated going to Iran, finding the bastard, and beating him up.

But he kept those thoughts to himself. Arezoo chose to trust Fenella, embracing this new family despite everything she'd been through. He wouldn't dare poison that noble resilience, his own anger issues notwithstanding.

When they reached the pub, night had fully settled. No light spilled from the shuttered windows, but the sounds of laughter and conversation grew louder as they approached, and the music drifted out on the evening air.

The moment they entered, Fenella spotted them from behind the bar. She waved them over enthusiastically, then turned to shoo away two males who'd been sitting directly in front of her.

"Off with you two," she said cheerfully. "You've already had your readings tonight. Make room for the young couple."

One of the males grumbled as he stood, "The girl might be young, but Ruvon isn't."

Fenella laughed. "Ruvon's a youngling compared to these gentlemen." She gestured to two males sitting at the other end of the bar. "Ruvon, Arezoo, meet Roven and Davuh. Roven and Davuh, meet Ruvon and Arezoo."

Everyone in the village had heard about the three ancient immortals who had been found in Egypt, and he'd seen them during their welcoming party, but the truth was that he remembered only the tall redhead who looked like Anandur, Wonder's mate.

After the four of them exchanged greetings, Fenella shook her head. "Ruvon and Roven. You're going to confuse me. One of you needs to change your name."

"I was named first," Roven said with a grin. "So, it will have to be you, Ruvon. Perhaps you'd be Novur? It's your name spelled backward, and it has a nice ring to it. Like new and voyeur."

"No, thank you," Ruvon said. "I'm kind of fond of my name, and it will be too difficult to get used to a new one, especially one that rhymes with voyeur."

Arezoo was looking at him as if she were just discovering that he had a sense of humor. He liked the appreciation in her gaze. It made him want to square his shoulders and sit up straight.

"So, darlings." Fenella regarded them with mischief in her eyes. "Did you bring me anything to read?"

Arezoo slid the bracelet off her wrist and handed it to her. "It was my grandmother's. She gave it to me when I turned twelve."

Fenella took the bracelet, making a show of examining it from all angles. She closed her eyes, pressed it between her palms, and hummed dramatically. The nearby patrons quietened, leaning in to catch whatever pronouncement she'd make.

"Oh my," Fenella said, her eyes popping open. "This bracelet has seen some things."

Arezoo leaned forward eagerly. "What kind of things?"

"Love," Fenella intoned. "Deep, passionate love. Your grandmother was very happy when she wore this." She paused dramatically. "I see...more. Kisses. Many, many kisses."

Arezoo's cheeks flushed pink, but she was smiling. "Whose kisses?"

Fenella pretended to concentrate harder. "Someone close. Someone who looks at you like you hung the moon and stars."

Ruvon felt heat crawl up his neck. How did she know about the kiss? Did she actually read it from the bracelet? Arezoo hadn't worn it the night they'd kissed.

"Also," Fenella continued, her eyes twinkling, "I see dancing. Maybe a wedding? No, wait—that's further off. First come many more kisses." She waggled her eyebrows suggestively.

"Fenella!" Arezoo protested, but she was laughing.

"Your turn," Fenella said, handing the bracelet back and turning to Ruvon. "What have you got for me?"

Ruvon reluctantly unclasped his watch, an expensive piece that Kalugal had gifted him years ago. It was one of the few possessions he truly valued—not for its monetary value but for what it represented. Kalugal had presented it to him after he'd successfully upgraded their entire security system.

Fenella whistled appreciatively. "Now this is a timepiece. Swiss?"

"German, actually."

"Even better." She cradled the watch as if it were made of spun glass. "Let's see what stories you tell, shall we?"

The performance this time was even more elaborate. Fenella stood up, holding the watch to her ear as if listening to whispered secrets. The pub had gone nearly silent, everyone waiting for the revelation.

"This watch has counted many hours," she began. "Lonely hours. Working hours. Hours spent proving worth through service and skill." Her expression grew more serious. "But its owner's time of loneliness is ending. I see...transformation. A transformation of the heart."

Ruvon shifted uncomfortably. This was hitting closer to home than he'd expected.

"There will be challenges," Fenella continued. "Old fears to overcome. Trust to be rebuilt. But the reward..." She opened her eyes and looked directly at him. "The reward will be worth it."

She handed the watch back with a softer smile than her usual theatrical grin. "Also, kisses. Lots and lots of kisses. You two are going to be absolutely nauseating to be around. Off with you." She waved a hand. "Find a table and make room for new readings."

They found a small table in the corner, and Ruvon helped Arezoo with her chair, earning himself a smile that melted his heart.

"She means well," Arezoo said once they were settled. "But you were right. It was a little embarrassing."

"It wasn't that bad." He twisted his watch around.

"Can I do a reading for you?" Arezoo extended her hand.

He arched a brow. "Are you developing new talents I should be aware of?"

She smiled. "I might be. Now, can you hand me that nice watch?"

He took it off and handed it over.

Arezoo closed her eyes, pretending to concentrate. "This watch has seen a lot. It has witnessed its owner being lonely for a very long time because he was scared of letting anyone in. His soul ached from the things he'd been forced to do, things he did to survive, but he never let it make him cruel."

Ruvon's throat felt tight. "That's...very insightful."

"I recognize the signs," she said softly. "I see them in the mirror every day."

Before he could respond, the lights dimmed, and Din took the stage with his guitar. The pub erupted in applause.

"Have you heard him play before?" Arezoo asked.

"No. I didn't even know he played."

Din started with a haunting ballad, his voice rich and warm. The pub quieted, everyone drawn into the melody.

"It's beautiful," Arezoo whispered. "What's it about?"

"Lost love," Fenella said, placing a plate of appetizers on their table that they hadn't ordered. "On the house."

She pulled up a chair without invitation. "Atzil is covering for me so I can watch my man perform."

"It's about a warrior who comes home to find his village destroyed and his love dead," Fenella explained quietly. "He spends the rest of his life wandering, looking for a way to join her in the afterlife, but cursed to keep living."

"That's heartbreaking," Arezoo said.

"That's Scottish music for you. We're a cheerful people, really. We just express it through tragic ballads and heavy drinking."

Din finished the song to thunderous applause, then immediately launched into something more upbeat that had people clapping along.

"That's more like it," Fenella said. "This one is about whiskey."

"Also a Scottish specialty," Ruvon observed.

"We're a people of many talents." She stood. "Enjoy your evening, you two. And remember what I said about kisses. My visions are never wrong." She winked before walking away.

"She's not subtle," Arezoo said.

"No, she's not." Ruvon gathered his courage. "But she might have a point."

"About what?"

"The kisses."

Arezoo's cheeks pinked, but she held his gaze. "What about them?"

"I've been thinking about our kiss nonstop and wanting to do it again."

"Then why haven't you?"

"I didn't want to pressure you."

"Ruvon." She leaned forward. "I kissed you first, remember?"

"I do, and I cherish every moment of that kiss."

14

ELUHEED

The knock on Eluheed's door came just as he'd finished arranging his few possessions in the closet of his new quarters. When he opened it, he found the American standing in the hallway, a broad smile lighting up his face.

"Hi," Tony said. "Welcome to the palace."

"Thank you." Eluheed stepped aside, gesturing for him to enter. "Though I'm not sure 'palace' is the word I'd use."

Tony laughed as he walked in. "It's all about perspective, my friend. Compared to the servants' quarters below, this is definitely palatial. May I sit down?"

"Yes, of course. Forgive my manners." Eluheed gestured at the armchairs that were facing the balcony that was over-looking the interior garden.

It almost felt like being topside. Almost.

"Thank you." Tony settled into an armchair and leaned back. "Nice view."

"Is yours different?" Eluheed took the opposite chair.

"No, it's the same." Tony crossed his legs. "I like the view of the courtyard. It makes the rooms feel less stifling."

"You mean less like a prison."

"Well, yes." Tony smiled as if they were discussing the weather. "I'm so glad to have another male's company up here finally. Someone intelligent to talk to. Since the old doctor kicked the bucket, I've only had the ladies to talk to, and as lovely as they are, it's not the same."

"In what way?" Eluheed prompted.

"You know." Tony waved a hand. "Let's just say that after so many years of living in isolation with no interaction with the outside world, their conversations get repetitive."

Eluheed found it interesting that Tony hadn't mentioned Tula, who was supposed to be his partner.

Perhaps Tony didn't care for Lady Tula?

"If you don't mind me asking..." Eluheed spread his legs and leaned forward, resting his elbows on his knees and inter-lacing his fingers. "Why are you in the harem? How did you end up here?"

Tony's smile turned rueful. "Probably for the same reason you're here, my friend. Quality breeders to provide Navuh with intelligent sons." He laughed, but there was no humor in it. "He got tired of having gardeners and maintenance workers father his adopted sons, and now he seeks quality."

The casual way Tony discussed being used for breeding made Eluheed's skin crawl. But he kept his expression neutral, maintaining the façade of mild curiosity. "Why doesn't the lord do it himself? The ladies belong to him, so he can do as he pleases with them. What better way to ensure quality offspring than to father them himself?"

Tony snorted. "Lord Navuh's only redeeming quality is his love for Lady Areana. He's devoted to her and her alone. He's not attracted to the others, although I don't understand why. They are all beautiful, and let me tell you, they are horny. I've never encountered females with such an appetite for sex."

Eluheed was starting to dislike Tony, even though he hadn't said anything particularly offensive about the ladies. A healthy sex drive was nothing to be ashamed of, especially in a place like this.

Still, even though he'd heard about Navuh's devotion to his wife, hearing it confirmed by Tony painted a complex picture of the ruler of this island—a terrifying, paranoid warlord on one hand and a loving husband on the other. It was an unusual combination.

"There are other ways to impregnate females that don't require unfaithfulness to his wife," he said casually. "Artificial insemination is a viable option."

Tony shrugged, a gesture that seemed to be his default response to the absurdities of their environment. "Who knows what goes through his mind? The lord might find masturbation distasteful. After all, he's as old as dirt, and back in the day that might have been considered immoral or unbecoming or something that only peasants did."

The comment about Navuh being older than dirt hung in the air between them, but Eluheed chose to ignore it. How much did Tony know? How much was safe to discuss in this room?

"What do you know about the lord?" Eluheed asked, keeping his tone low.

Tony's eyes sharpened. "What do you know about him?" He turned the question back on Eluheed.

Eluheed weighed his options. How much could he trust Tony? In a place built on secrets and surveillance, paranoia was a survival skill.

"He's a warlord, and he's the ultimate authority on this island. That's all I know."

Tony nodded. "That's true, but on a scale you probably can't imagine. Lord Navuh is plotting to take over the world."

As Eluheed's eyes darted around the room, searching for the telltale signs of listening devices, the movement wasn't lost on Tony, who understood his concern immediately.

"That's not a secret," Tony said with another of his casual waves. "Everyone in the harem knows it. The ladies discuss it openly. Well, as openly as one discusses anything around here."

Eluheed doubted that Navuh's plans for world domination were openly discussed in the harem. They might be known but not discussed. Then again, who were they going to tell?

He'd been told more than once that no one ever left the harem unless it was in a casket.

Tony shifted in his chair, his expression growing more animated. "I've been meaning to ask you about your herb garden. That's the real reason I am here. I'm fascinated by your knowledge of natural remedies. It's such an important skill to have, and I learned it the hard way when I needed something for my headaches and there was no doctor in the clinic to help me."

The sudden change of topic was jarring, but Eluheed recognized it for what it was. Tony was either eager to redirect the conversation to safer topics, or he was trying to hint at something.

"I'm happy to share what I know," Eluheed said. "I'm waiting for more seeds to arrive, so we will have a greater variety. Especially now, when the harem doesn't have a doctor, it is important to cultivate as many medicinal plants as possible in this climate and share my knowledge with the staff so they can use them in case something happens to me."

Tony frowned. "Are you expecting something to happen to you?"

Eluheed spread his arms out. "We are all human and susceptible to illnesses and other misfortunes, like the good old doctor who passed before his time. It is important to share what we know with others." He smiled benevolently. "That's how we get to be immortal."

It was bait, and Eluheed hoped Tony would bite and tell him that Navuh was immortal.

"That's true." Tony rose to his feet without taking the bait. "Would you mind showing me your garden? My knowledge of plants is embarrassingly lacking. I'm a bioinformatician, and I'm supposed to know those things, but I have a horrible memory."

"Of course." Eluheed immediately understood the subtext. "Would you like to go right now?"

"Why not?" Tony's face lit up. "Let me just grab a notebook and pencil from my room. I want to write everything down." He motioned for Eluheed to follow him.

The door to Tony's room was two down from Eluheed's, and when he opened it, the first thing that struck him was the books. They were everywhere—stacked on shelves, piled on the desk, even forming small towers on the floor.

"Where did you get all these books from?" he asked.

"The harem has an extensive library," Tony said, retrieving a notebook and several pencils from his desk. "Since you were prohibited from interacting with the ladies, you weren't allowed there. But now that the restriction has been lifted, you can use the library, the pool, and all the other wonderful amenities our underground paradise offers."

The sarcasm in Tony's voice when he said 'paradise' was

subtle but unmistakable. He definitely saw their gilded cage for what it was.

They took the elevator to the surface level, and the moment they stepped outside the climate-controlled environment, the heat and humidity of the tropical island hit them. Eluheed had grown somewhat accustomed to it during his months of tending the garden, but Tony seemed bothered by it, and he wiped sweat from his forehead with the back of his hand.

"How do you stand it?" Tony asked, looking wilted after less than a minute of enduring the outdoors.

"You get accustomed to it." Eluheed led the way to his herb garden. "The breeze helps."

When they reached the garden, Tony surprised him by getting down and sitting cross-legged on the ground. He opened his notebook and pulled one of the pencils out of his pocket. "I'm going to sketch the plants and make notes next to the sketches so I remember what instructions go with which plant."

As Eluheed crouched beside him, ostensibly to point out different herbs, Tony kept his head bent over his notebook, pencil moving in quick, sure strokes.

"You're really good at this," Eluheed said. "The sketching."

"Thank you," Tony said with a bright smile before bending over the notebook again. "There are cameras out here as well," he murmured, his voice barely audible. "Keep your head down when you talk so they can't read your lips."

Eluheed tensed. This whole thing stank of a setup. The sudden lifting of restrictions, the move to better quarters, and Tony's exuberant offer of friendship all could have been staged by the paranoid lord of this island to get Eluheed to disclose his secrets.

He bent over a patch of feverfew, pretending to examine the leaves. "What do you hope I can tell you?"

Tony's pencil kept dancing over the page. "Do you know that the lord, his ladies, and most of the soldiers on this island are all immortal?"

Eluheed forced his hands to remain steady as he pointed to another plant. The direct question required a careful response. He chose to feign ignorance, letting surprise color his voice. "What are you talking about? Is this your idea of a joke?"

"I'm serious." Tony kept his head down. "Think about it. Have any of the ladies come to you for remedies in the eighteen months you've been here?"

"No, but that's because I wasn't supposed to interact with them."

"Fair point." Tony flipped to a new page, starting a sketch of the chamomile. "But who took care of them after the old doctor died? Who treated their ailments, their aches and pains?"

Eluheed pretended to consider this. "Perhaps they didn't need care. They're all young and healthy."

Tony's chuckle was low and knowing. "Young? My friend, they're as old as human civilization itself. But that's not exactly a secret in the harem. Everyone knows." He paused. "Everyone except you, apparently. I'm surprised a clever fellow like yourself hasn't figured it out yet."

"I don't understand." Eluheed maintained his façade of confusion. "How should I have been supposed to guess that? And if everyone knows, why did no one tell me?"

"Good question." Tony's pencil scratched across the paper. "Most people figure it out eventually. The staff are afraid to talk openly, but the ladies can basically do as they please because they have Lady Areana's protection. They speak freely among themselves and with their companions." He glanced up briefly, his eyes meeting Eluheed's. "Naturally, they're careful not to say anything offensive about Navuh himself when in range of the many listening devices. Even Lady Areana's protection has limits."

Eluheed pointed to another section of the garden, and they shifted positions, maintaining the pretense of a botany lesson. The sun beat down mercilessly, and he could see sweat dripping onto Tony's notebook, smudging some of his sketches.

"How did you find yourself on this island?" Eluheed asked. "And how did you end up in Navuh's harem? You said he was interested in quality breeding stock, but that implies looking for the right males, and I know no one was looking for me. I was brought over by one of his associates." And sold like livestock, but he chose not to mention that.

Tony's expression darkened. "I was lured here under false pretenses. A job offer too good to refuse, working on cutting-edge genetic research." His laugh was bitter. "I wasn't meant to serve in the harem, though. Navuh lured many highly educated men to the island for his larger breeding project, but because I look enough like him—dark hair, olive skin, the right build—I was sent here instead. The other guys get to go home after they are done providing their services, but no one leaves the harem, so I'm stuck here until the day I die."

Chills ran down Eluheed's back despite the oppressive heat. "What larger breeding project?"

"Trust me, you don't want to know." Tony turned to a fresh page. "My job here is simple—to get Tula pregnant and provide Navuh with an intelligent son he can claim as his own. The problem is that Tula doesn't want to have a child, and I can't blame her." Tony's voice dropped even lower. "Do you know what happens to the children born here?"

Eluheed shook his head.

"The boys are taken away as babies. Removed from their mothers as soon as they're weaned, sometimes sooner. They're raised in the Dormant enclosure and told that Navuh is their father. When they are old enough, they are moved to the war camp, turned immortal, and trained to be warriors." Tony's pencil pressed harder against the paper. "They never know who their real mothers are. Navuh's excuse is so none feels superior to the others and all are judged on merit alone."

"What happens to the girls?" Eluheed asked.

"The girls born to the ladies fare a little better, I suppose. They're allowed to stay in the harem, raised by their mothers. But they're not allowed to become immortal. They live and die as humans." Tony looked up, his eyes holding a mixture of anger and sadness. "It's a particular kind of cruelty to let a mother watch her daughter age and die while she remains young forever, but it's a better fate than what awaits girls who are born to dormant mothers in the breeding enclosure or are sent there. They are not allowed to transition either and grow up to become breeders like their mothers." Tony sighed. "Even the harem ladies are breeders, just of higher caliber."

Something about what Tony had said bothered Eluheed. If becoming immortal was a choice and not a birthright, how did the dormant children transition into immortality?

"You said that the girls are not allowed to become immortal. That implies it's a choice, something that can be granted or withheld."

Tony studied him for a long moment. "You really don't know, do you?"

"I'm beginning to realize there's a great deal I don't know," Eluheed admitted, which was true enough.

Tony bent back over his notebook, sketching with renewed focus. "The immortal males have fangs and venom. When they bite someone who carries the dormant godly genes, it activates them. The person goes through a transition and becomes immortal, but only the boys are induced."

Eluheed's mind reeled. Fangs and venom? His own path to immortality had been completely different. These immortals were an entirely different species.

"The sons born to immortal or dormant females and human males can be activated when they reach puberty," Tony said. "They get induced by older immortals and become warriors in Lord Navuh's army of immortal soldiers."

"Why not induce the daughters as well?" Eluheed asked.

"Navuh wants them to remain dormant because their fertility is as high as human females when they're dormant. Once they transition to immortality, their fertility drops dramatically. He wants breeders, not more immortal females. That's why the boys are removed from the Dormants' enclosure as soon as they reach puberty and moved to the training camp. The Dormants are kept away from immortal males so they don't get activated by mistake or purposely."

"That's monstrous," Eluheed spat, forgetting to maintain his pretense of casual interest.

"Welcome to Navuh's world," Tony said dryly. "Where women are breeding stock and men are cannon fodder."

Eluheed felt sick. He'd known Navuh was evil, but the industrialized approach to breeding an army was on another level.

"The girls born in the Dormant enclosure are doomed to the same fate as their mothers," Tony added quietly. "Generation after generation, trapped in a cycle of breeding more soldiers for Navuh's insane quest for world domination."

Eluheed's mind raced as he tried to process everything Tony had told him. Immortals with fangs and venom. Dormant genes that could be activated. Breeding programs designed to create armies.

What kind of crazy world had he stumbled into?

15

TAMIRA

The inner garden was Tamira's favorite place in the harem, and as she sat at her favorite bench by the fountain with a book in her hands, she positioned herself so she had a clear view of the balconies.

Elias had been moved to the second level earlier that day, and the news had spread through the harem's invisible network with typical efficiency, whispered between servants and confirmed by Areana's announcement at breakfast.

Tamira couldn't contain her curiosity about the man who was supposedly a shaman, but she couldn't simply knock on his door. That wasn't how a lady operated, although she could see Tula doing just that.

Well, she wasn't Tula, and she valued the art of subtlety, of letting things unfold naturally or at least to appear to. So, she waited, turning the pages of her book and occasionally lifting her eyes to check the balconies.

The book in her lap wasn't a prop, though. She'd gotten it in the latest delivery a few days ago and had been reading it ever since. *The Power of Intention: Manifesting Your Heart's Desires* was an interesting read.

The fountain's steady cascade provided a modicum of privacy, its white noise potentially masking conversation from listening devices. She knew better than to trust it completely, of course.

In the harem, privacy was an illusion.

Even with the fountain obscuring sounds, cameras could capture lip movements, and anyone who'd lived long enough could read lips, provided they knew the language being spoken. She didn't know where the cameras were hidden, but she assumed the tropical foliage camouflaged them. Her room and the rooms of the other ladies were free of such devices, allowing them some privacy, but the public areas were a different story. Tula claimed that Tony's room was also bugged, so Tamira assumed that Elias's room was bugged as well, but that wasn't something she was worried about at this point.

She wondered what languages Elias spoke. Over the endless years of her captivity, she'd collected languages like other women collected pearls. Each new tongue mastered was another small victory against the monotony, another way to fill the centuries. Her accents might not be accurate because she'd learned most of them from books and hadn't heard them spoken, but her vocabulary in many of them was extensive.

These days, learning was easier than ever with books on tablets that could translate words with the press of a finger. When she'd been a girl in Sumer, only the gods had possessed such miraculous devices. Now, everyone used them, but the harem's tablets were regrettably connected only to an internal server. Lord Navuh didn't allow the harem to be connected to the internet, which she'd read about and seen in movies.

Their window to the outside world was narrow and carefully monitored—a vast library of approved books and films —but it was what it was, and she did her best with what was available to her.

The book grew warm in her lap as the afternoon progressed. Tamira had not chosen this title because she wanted to impress the newcomer with her reading material, but she hoped that a shaman would have opinions on manifestation and spiritual desire.

She closed her eyes and tried to practice what the book preached. *Come out*, she willed, picturing Elias appearing on his balcony. *Be curious. Come down to the garden.* The author claimed that focused intention could reshape reality, that believing strongly enough in an outcome could make it manifest. It sounded like New Age nonsense, the kind of philosophy that flourishes among humans who have decades to fill with meaning, not millennia. But what harm could it do to try?

As the garden door's hinges squeaked, Tamira knew it was Elias, some instinct deeper than logic confirming what her intention had supposedly manifested. A smile bloomed on her face before she could stop it, an expression of delight that she immediately tried to temper.

She opened her eyes and saw him standing just outside the door, scanning the garden. When his gaze found her, she saw a flicker of recognition, but she knew it wasn't of her specifically, but of what she represented. One of the ladies. One of the untouchables who had suddenly become touchable.

A flutter of excitement started low in her belly, something she hadn't felt in a long time, but it wasn't only because she found Elias pleasant to the eye, although he was.

He was tall but not overly so, and his build spoke of natural strength rather than cultivated bulk. Broad shoulders tapered to a trim waist; his chestnut-brown hair was streaked with natural highlights that looked sun-kissed, even in their artificially illuminated environment, and his face was handsome in an understated way, with strong features softened by an expressive mouth.

Those lips, perfectly shaped and lifting now in a gentle smile, commanded her attention. This wasn't the smile of a boastful male who expected females to fall at his feet. Neither was it the timid expression of someone overwhelmed by his surroundings. He walked toward her with measured steps, maintaining eye contact without staring, his gait relaxed but purposeful.

As he drew closer, she caught his scent—soap and shampoo, the particular combination the harem provided that managed to smell both expensive and institutional. He'd showered recently, probably in preparation for dinner with the ladies.

He stopped at a proper distance and bowed, the gesture formal but not obsequious. "Good afternoon, my lady," he said in accented but fluent English. "Allow me to introduce myself. My name is Elias."

The language choice pleased her. He must have noticed that her book was written in English and made the correct assumption that she spoke the language.

She dipped her head in return, deliberately signaling that she regarded him as an equal. "My name is Tamira. Would you like to join me?" She placed her hand on the bench beside her, the gesture both an invitation and a boundary. Here, but no closer.

Not yet.

"I'd be delighted." He settled onto the bench at a respectable distance, close enough for conversation but far enough to maintain propriety. His eyes flicked to the book in her lap. "That's an interesting choice of reading material."

She smiled, letting a hint of mischief color her expression. "A coincidence, I assure you. I didn't expect to meet a shaman today who might have opinions about the topic."

It was only partially a lie. She'd intended to meet Elias, had orchestrated this *chance* encounter with careful deliberation. However, the book's subject matter was truly unrelated, a happy accident that provided an easy opening for conversation.

"So, you know who I am." His tone held amusement rather than concern.

She nodded, seeing no point in pretense. "We don't get many newcomers in the harem, so it wasn't difficult to guess your identity. I'm surprised that you speak English so well, though. Tony didn't mention that you spoke to him in his native tongue when he sought relief from you for his headaches."

His smile transformed his face from merely handsome to something that made those butterflies in her stomach take flight. The expression reached his eyes, crinkling them at the corners in a way that suggested he smiled often. "Tony didn't leave me much choice since he speaks no other language with any fluency, but I could ask you the same question. I would never have guessed you were an English speaker if not for the book in your hands."

"I speak many languages," she said, running her fingers along the book's spine. "When you live as long as I have, you need to fill the years with something. I chose to learn languages."

"That's admirable." He shifted slightly, angling his body toward her. "How many languages do you speak?"

"Twenty-three fluently, perhaps a dozen more conversationally." She watched his eyes widen slightly. "Though I suspect some of my pronunciation is not accurate. Books can teach vocabulary and grammar, but they're poor substitutes for living conversation."

"Still, twenty-three languages." He shook his head in wonder. "That's several lifetimes' worth of study."

"Yes," she said softly. "It is."

The gravity of those lifetimes was almost physical for both of them. For a moment, she saw him processing the implications, adding up the years it would take to master so many tongues. His expression shifted, surprise giving way to something more complex—sympathy, perhaps, or understanding.

"I assume that Tony has told you about us," she said. It wasn't a question.

He nodded. "Earlier today. I had no idea. I'm still trying to process this. It's hard to believe."

"What's hard to believe? That we're immortal, or that we've been here so long?"

"Both," he admitted. "But mostly the time. Five thousand years is..." He trailed off, apparently unable to find words adequate to encompass such a span.

"It's just a number," Tamira said, surprised by the bitterness that crept into her voice. "Like twenty-three languages or seven underground levels or one lovely fountain. After a while, the numbers cease to have meaning. They're just markers we use to pretend time is passing, that things are changing."

She hadn't meant to say so much, to reveal the hardship of her captivity so plainly, but something about him invited confidence, perhaps the same quality that made people seek him out for healing.

"It's still extraordinary," he said quietly. "I understand how the long years could become a burden, especially in an enclosed space like this, but it is still a marvel."

She nodded. "To me, this is just the way it is, but I realize how shocking it must seem to you."

The fountain continued its endless cascade beside them, throwing tiny droplets that sparkled in the artificial light. Tamira was absurdly grateful for its presence and the white noise that might grant them a small measure of privacy for their first conversation.

"Your English is quite good," she said, steering them to safer ground. "Where did you learn it?"

"Here and there," he said with a slight shrug. "I've traveled extensively, and English has become the common tongue of commerce and education. It seemed practical to master it."

"Practical," she repeated, smiling. "You're a practical man, then?"

"I try to be." He glanced at her book again. "Though I suppose a shaman can't call himself practical without sounding like a hypocrite."

"Why not? The gift of healing seems very practical to me."

"Some would say that mixing herbs and offering spiritual guidance is the opposite of practical. They'd prefer their medicine in pill form and their spirits firmly ignored."

"These people haven't lived long enough to see the patterns," Tamira said. "The wheel of belief that turns from mysticism to materialism and back again. Give humanity a few more millennia, and they'll rediscover what they've forgotten about the connection between body and spirit."

"You seem to be speaking from experience?"

She sighed. "No, not from experience. From learning. This current age of technology makes a good case for the material world." She tapped her book. "But then they write things like this, trying to rediscover magic through willpower and positive thinking."

"Do you believe in the power of manifestation?"

She considered the question. "Perhaps. I was practicing it when you appeared. Willing you to come out to the garden, and you did."

His eyebrows rose. "Should I feel flattered?"

"I was curious."

His smile was warm and slightly teasing. "I came out because I was restless in my new quarters and wanted to check out the inner garden, not because I felt a mystical summons."

"Ah, but how do you know that restlessness wasn't the mechanism of my manifestation? Perhaps I didn't summon you directly but created the conditions that led you here."

"That's dangerous philosophy," he said, but his tone was light. "If you can claim credit for any coincidence by saying you manifested the circumstances that led to it, then you can never be proven wrong."

"Exactly," she said, matching his playful tone. "It's a perfect belief system. All successes are proofs of this method working, and all failures are just evidence that I didn't believe hard enough."

"Two very convincing arguments that absolve the author from liability."

They both laughed, and Tamira felt something ease in her chest. How long had it been since she'd had a conversation like this? One that danced between serious and playful, that challenged her thoughts without becoming a battle of wits worn smooth by repetition?

"I saw your garden when we walked past it the other day," she said. "It looked well-tended. That's when I noticed you."

He looked embarrassed. "I apologize for the pose I had to assume. It was humiliating."

"Don't apologize." She reached out with her hand to cover his. "That was what you were expected to do. Besides, I enjoyed gazing upon the body part that was most prominently displayed. It was very nicely shaped."

Color rose in his cheeks, which was adorable. "Should I say thank you for the compliment?"

She shrugged. "I just call it like I see it." She needed to move away from the topic of his nicely shaped bottom. "Anyway, when my friends and I passed by your herb garden, we wondered if you had anything that could help soothe the burns Rolenna gets from her glassmaking experiments. Immortals heal quickly, but we are not immune to pain, and she could use a salve if you can make it."

"I have several preparations that might help. Aloe, of course, but also calendula infused in oil, and a salve made from comfrey and plantain."

"That's wonderful. Rolenna is rather accident-prone, so you might want to prepare a large batch for her."

"I'll be more than happy to do so. It's good to be useful."

There was something in the way he said it that tugged at her. She recognized the feeling—the need to have purpose in a purposeless existence, to contribute something meaningful to the small world they inhabited.

"The servants speak highly of your remedies. And now that you're free to interact with us, I suspect you'll find yourself very much in demand."

He arched a brow. "For my herbs?"

The question held layers she wasn't comfortable addressing yet. He knew why he'd been elevated, what was expected of him. But neither of them seemed ready to acknowledge that particular elephant in the garden.

"Among other things," she said. "Like your ability to carry on an intelligent conversation. It's been a long time since we've had someone new to talk with who can bring fresh perspectives."

"I'm not sure how fresh my perspectives are."

She studied him more closely, trying to gauge his age. His face was unlined, his hair thick and without a single gray strand, but there was something in his eyes that spoke of years beyond his apparent youth. It was the same look that she saw in the mirror and reflected in the eyes of her companions.

Since he was human, the only explanation for the ancient wisdom in his eyes could be his profession. A shaman could connect to other realities, communicate with spirits, and have a spiritual depth that other humans did not possess.

"How long have you been practicing your craft?" she asked.

"Long enough to know that the more I learn, the less I understand." He smiled wryly. "That's the shaman's answer. The practical answer is that I've been studying herbs and healing for most of my adult life."

"What about the spiritual part of your craft? Is that something you learned or something you were born to?"

"Both, I think. The inclination was always there but learning how to channel it usefully took time and many mistakes along the way."

"We all make mistakes," Tamira said softly. "The blessing and curse of immortality is that we have to live with them forever."

"Do you see it as more of a blessing or a curse?"

The question was gently asked, but it struck at the heart of her existence. She'd answered it in different ways over the millennia, her response shifting with her mood and circumstances. Today, sitting in the artificial light with an interesting new companion, the answer felt more complex than usual.

"My answer tends to change according to my mood."

"Fair enough." He shifted on the bench, and she caught another whiff of his clean scent.

"Will you be joining us for dinner tonight?" she asked.

"I was told I was expected to."

"Told, not invited?"

His smile turned rueful. "Lord Navuh's instructions were communicated clearly."

She squared her shoulders. "I'm inviting you now. Would you join us for dinner, Shaman Elias?"

He bowed his head. "I am delighted to accept your invitation, Lady Tamira."

16

TIM

T he first thing Tim noticed was the beeping. Steady, rhythmic, annoyingly persistent. Like an alarm clock that wouldn't shut up no matter how many times he hit snooze. The second thing he noticed was that his mouth felt like someone had stuffed it full of cotton balls that had been marinating in gym socks.

He tried to open his eyes, but they seemed to be glued shut. After what felt like an eternity of struggle, he managed to crack them open just enough to be assaulted by fluorescent lighting that stabbed directly into his brain.

"Fuck," he croaked, or tried to. What came out sounded more like a dying frog's last gasp.

His body felt wrong. Not just tired or sore, but fundamentally different in ways his foggy brain couldn't quite process. There were things attached to him—wires, tubes, various medical apparatus that suggested he was in significantly worse shape than a simple hangover would warrant.

Memory returned in fragments. The gym. Magnus towering over him like some Nordic god of war. The pathetic excuse for wrestling moves he'd attempted. And then fangs, sinking into his neck with a sharp, searing pain that had immediately morphed into a euphoric trip better than any he had ever experienced, including the ones he'd soared on after the mushroom parties in art school.

The induction ceremony.

Right. He'd done it. He'd actually been bitten by an immortal vampire Viking right in the neck. And now he was...what? Transitioning?

That was what they called it when his body decided to completely rewire itself at the cellular level.

He became aware that he was wearing a hospital gown, the kind that left his ass hanging out. His new tracksuit— the one he'd bought in January after his year-end resolution to get in shape and had never worn even once before —was nowhere to be seen. They'd probably peeled it off him. He had a vague memory of sweating through it completely before he and Magnus had started their wrestling match.

Wrestling.

Christ, who was he kidding? He'd been on the wrestling team in high school, sure, for exactly one semester before deciding that spending his afternoons getting slammed into mats by guys who ate protein powder for breakfast wasn't his idea of fun. Since then, the only things he'd wrestled with were stubborn chip bags that refused to tear at the designated spot and the occasional pickle jar that thought it was tougher than him.

The door opened with a soft whoosh, and Tim's brain short-circuited.

A woman walked in, and calling her beautiful would be like calling the Sistine Chapel a nice bit of ceiling art. She was tall, probably five nine or five ten, with the kind of figure that made men walk into lamp posts and then apologize to them. Her hair was a dark cascade that captured and reflected the harsh hospital lighting in ways that defied physics. But it was her eyes that did him in—impossibly blue, like someone had distilled the essence of every ocean and sky and concentrated it into two perfect orbs.

He must have died during the transition, and since there was no way he had earned a spot in heaven, this had to be hell. This stunning beauty was either a demon sent to torture him with unattainable perfection or the devil herself, taking a form designed to make him suffer maximum torment.

Either way, she could have his rotten soul.

Hell, he would hand it over to her gift-wrapped with a bow.

His breath hitched, which was a mistake because it reminded his body that breathing was actually quite difficult at the moment, but on the other hand, it made him question the assumption that he must be dead.

"Welcome back, Tim," she said, and her voice was like aged whiskey—smooth, with just enough burn to make him want more.

"Am I dead?" The words came out clearer than his earlier attempt at speech, though still rough around the edges.

She laughed, and the sound hit him like a kick to the gut. It was rich and sexy, completely lacking the polite, forced quality of people who laughed at things because they felt they should. This was real laughter, and it did things to him that were entirely inappropriate in his current state.

That became immediately, embarrassingly apparent as his body responded to her presence in the most primal way. The thin hospital blanket covering him did nothing to hide his predicament, and Tim felt heat rush to his face, which was something that hadn't happened to him in decades, or at least not because of a woman.

Sometimes tequila made him red in the face.

He tried to lift his arms to cover the tenting blanket, but they refused to cooperate. His muscles felt like overcooked spaghetti, useless. How the hell could he be too weak to move his damn arms but still capable of sporting an erection that he could hammer nails with?

Now he was convinced that he was in hell. This was his eternal punishment—to be paralyzed in bed while the most beautiful woman he'd ever seen witnessed his complete lack of control over his own body.

The beauty—demon, whatever—glanced at the tent with a knowing smile that somehow managed to be both professional and wickedly amused. "That's an excellent sign, Tim. It means that you're on your way to recovery."

He cleared his throat, trying desperately to think of anything other than how her scrubs managed to hint at the curves beneath without clinging to her body. "Are you the doctor?"

"No." She walked over to the monitors surrounding his bed, pulled out a small handheld tablet from her pocket, and began noting the readouts with quick, practiced motions. "I'm your nurse. Hildegard."

Hildegard. Of course, she had a name that sounded like it belonged to some ancient goddess of battle and beauty. Because why would the universe make this easy on him?

"A pleasure to meet you, Hildegard," he mumbled, trying to inject some of his usual sarcasm into the words but failing miserably. Hard to be cutting when you were horizontal and sporting a tent pole. "How long have I been here?"

She surprised him by sitting on the edge of his bed, entirely inappropriate and invading his personal space. She was so close that he could smell her perfume, something light and floral, and the scent of the female underneath. With her impossibly blue eyes fixed on his, Tim forgot how to breathe.

"You've been out since yesterday," she said, her tone conversational despite the intimacy of their positions. "Which is uncommon. Most Dormants wake up the morning after their induction, and the transition only starts a day or two later. Yours started right away, and you probably have a ways to go before you're out of the initial stage." She paused, glancing again at his persistent problem with a grin that was positively wicked. "But the fact that you're awake and sporting a boner while having a catheter stuck in your penis is an excellent sign. You will transition quickly."

Tim nearly choked.

She'd said it. She'd acknowledged both his erection and the fact that he had a tube shoved up his dick, and she'd done it with the same casual tone someone might use to discuss the weather. He was simultaneously mortified and falling in love.

The woman was perfection personified.

Out of his league, but he could fantasize.

"That's good to hear," he managed, his voice only cracking slightly. "I don't want to transition quickly. I want to do it slowly and enjoy having you as my nurse for as long as I can drag it out. Not only are you stunningly beautiful, but you also have a mouth on you that matches mine. I love it."

Hildegard laughed again. "Falling for your nurse is so clichéd, Tim."

She rose to her feet in one fluid motion and walked over to the sink in the corner. Her blue scrubs were as shapeless as those of most medical professionals, but on her, they somehow managed to look both professional and flattering. How was that even possible?

"You were so busy ogling me that you forgot to ask for water," she said over her shoulder. "So typically male."

"I wasn't ogling," he protested. "I was appreciating. And it's not my fault that you're a ten."

She returned with a plastic cup filled with water and a bendy straw, looking amused. "A ten, eh?"

"Eleven," he corrected, then closed his lips around the straw she gently pushed between them. The water was the best thing he'd ever tasted, cool and clean and washing away some of the sock-cottony feeling in his mouth. When he'd drained the cup, he corrected again, "Fifteen."

Hildegard looked amused but also pleased. "You were ogling, and you still are." She glanced at his mast. "We might have to do something about that wood. It looks painful."

The casual way she referred to his erection as 'wood' sent another surge of heat through him. Who was this woman? Nurses were supposed to be professional, distant, maybe a little condescending to difficult patients like him. They weren't supposed to be gorgeous beyond belief with smart mouths and the ability to make him forget his own name.

"I'm willing to suffer much worse than a painful wood to have the pleasure of looking upon you," he said, and for once in his life, there wasn't a trace of sarcasm in his voice.

She studied him for a moment, those incredible eyes seeming to see right through him. "I've heard about you, Tim. Your reputation precedes you."

"All bad, I'm sure."

"Mostly," she agreed. "I think they said you have elevated being unpleasant into an art form."

"You say that like it's a bad thing."

She laughed. "I didn't say that. They did. I think you are charming. Is this a side effect of the transition or are you always this smooth with medical professionals?"

"I'm never smooth," he admitted. "Usually, I'm too busy being an asshole to everyone in my vicinity, but I've never met anyone like you. I'm making an effort."

"Flattery will get you nowhere," she said, but her smile suggested otherwise. "Besides, you should be focusing on your transition, not on your nurse."

"I'm an excellent multitasker. I can transition and appreciate my beautiful nurse at the same time."

She shook her head, but she was definitely fighting back a smile. "How are you feeling? Any pain? Discomfort beyond the obvious?"

Tim tried to take inventory of his body, which was challenging when most of his blood flow was concentrated in one specific area. Everything felt strange, like his skin was too tight and too loose at the same time. His muscles ached with a deep, bone-level soreness that suggested they were being rebuilt from the ground up. His head felt stuffed, but underneath that was a strange clarity, as if his senses were slowly sharpening.

"I feel like I got hit by a truck," he said honestly. "Then the truck backed up and hit me again. Then maybe a steamroller came by for good measure."

"That's normal," Hildegard assured him. "Your body is rewriting itself at the cellular level. Every system is being upgraded, which requires energy and causes discomfort.

Some Dormants describe it as the worst flu they've ever had multiplied by ten."

"Fantastic. And how long does this joy last?"

"Varies by person. It could be days or weeks. You're already ahead of the curve by waking up this soon into it." She made another note on her tablet. "Your vitals are surprisingly strong for this stage as well, and you don't have a fever, which worries me a little because you should."

"Must be the motivating factor of having you as my nurse."

"There you go with the flattery again."

"It's not flattery if it's true."

She set the tablet aside and fixed him with a look that was part amusement, part exasperation. "You know what? I think I like you better when you're being an honest asshole instead of trying to be smooth."

"Who says I'm trying? This is all natural charm, baby."

"And there's the Tim I was warned about." But she was smiling as she said it. "Tell me, what do you remember about your induction?"

Tim thought back, trying to piece together the fragments. "Magnus was very patient with my complete lack of athletic ability. I might have actually landed one decent punch, but that could be my ego rewriting history. Then he pinned me to the floor and then came the bite." He frowned. "Hurt like a son of a bitch, but the trip that followed was worth it. The best I ever had."

"The venom triggers euphoria." She grinned. "It's the best stuff ever. Easy to get addicted to, but since all the side effects are positive, there is no need to abstain."

"I got high on immortal spit. Fantastic. Does that make Magnus my dealer?"

She pursed her lips. "Not really, since you are never getting bitten again. For guys, it's once and over with. Luckily, I'm not a guy." She winked. "But I'd be careful about calling it spit to Magnus's face. He's a nice guy, but you know, those are the most dangerous when aggravated."

"Do you know him well?"

"Everyone knows Magnus. He's one of the clan's senior Guardians. You were lucky to have him as your inducer."

"I'll be sure to send him a thank-you card. 'Thanks for the bite, big guy. Your venom is top shelf.'" He narrowed his eyes at her. "Have you ever tried his venom?"

"Magnus is my cousin." She cast him a glare. "Fates, you really don't have a filter, do you?"

"Had one once. Didn't like it. Returned it for store credit."

She stood, smoothing down her scrubs. "You need to rest. Your body needs all the energy it can get for the transition. I'll be back in an hour to see how you're doing."

He didn't want her to leave.

"Will you be my nurse for the duration of my transition?"

"Why? Are you trying to see if the other nurse is hotter than me?"

"That's impossible. I'm trying to figure out how long I have to impress you with my sparkling personality."

"Well, aren't you presumptuous?"

"I prefer optimistic."

She opened the door. "One hour, Tim. Do something about your persistent condition before I get back."

"It's a medical marvel," he called after her. "They should study it for science."

Her laughter echoed down the hallway as the door closed behind her, leaving him alone with his thoughts and his extremely inconvenient physical response to the most gorgeous and fascinating woman he'd ever met.

He stared at the ceiling, trying to process everything that had just happened. He was transitioning into an immortal. His body was apparently rewriting itself from the ground up. He had tubes in places that tubes should never go. And somehow, despite all of that, he'd just had the most engaging conversation he'd had in years with a woman who looked like she'd stepped out of his fantasies and talked like she'd stepped out of his most naughty dreams.

The universe, Tim decided, had a seriously twisted sense of humor.

But for once in his life, he wasn't complaining.

He closed his eyes, trying to will his body to calm down before Hildegard returned.

No pressure.

No pressure at all.

17

HILDEGARD

A smile played on Hildegard's lips as she closed the door to Tim's room behind her.

What a character.

She'd been warned, of course, but all she'd heard were the negatives. What they hadn't mentioned was that he was funny. Or that beneath the sarcasm lay a charming, quick wit and self-deprecating humor. They certainly hadn't warned her about the way his whole face transformed when he smiled—a real smile, not the cutting smirk she'd expected.

Tim was just a sharp-tongued and sharp-minded guy who wielded his snark and sarcasm as weapons of self-defense. He was like a cute porcupine, protecting a soft interior with a prickly exterior.

"How's our problem child doing?" Julian asked as she entered his office.

"He's fine," Hildegard said as she sat down. "Awake, alert, and already hitting on me."

Julian's eyebrows rose. "Tim? That's bold. Should I adjust his medications to make him mellower?"

She laughed. "Don't you dare. I enjoyed every moment. He certainly makes things interesting, and he's also doing very well, as evidenced by the huge erection he sprouted when he saw me. Quite impressive for a guy his size."

As she'd expected, Julian's expression turned pinched. He was so proper for someone so young, and he didn't like the way she talked.

Well, tough.

Mentioning Tim's erection was medically relevant, and she wasn't going to twist herself into a pretzel trying to describe it in terms that didn't offend Julian's sensibilities.

He glanced at his desktop screen, and she suspected that he had done so not because he wanted to go over Tim's readouts but because he was trying to avert his gaze from her.

Fun times. She loved making the young stiff uncomfortable.

"His readings are remarkable. Who would have suspected that Tim was so close to the source? He was like a remote bet that Kian put off testing for years since he first suspected that Tim's ability was more than a talent."

That got her attention. "How is that possible? The guy certainly doesn't look like he has an abundance of godly genes."

Tim had a nice face, but he was short, pudgy, and balding. Dormants, even those who were far removed from the source, were usually good-looking.

"Does he need my attention?" Julian asked, looking like he hoped she would say no.

"He's weak, obviously, and experiencing the usual discomforts. But he's coherent and responsive. I hope the erection resolves itself without medical intervention because I'm sure it's not comfortable given the catheter. If not, you might want to give him something for that."

Julian shook his head. "Do you know the saying, birds of a feather?"

She arched a brow. "Flock together?"

"Yeah. You two should be getting along splendidly."

"My sparkling bedside manner is why patients love me," she said. "People like honesty, not fake smiles. If someone's being a pain in my ass, I tell them. If they're doing well, I tell them that too. No sugar-coating from me."

"No wonder you charmed the pants off the notorious grump."

Was Tim grumpy?

Not really. He was snarky, and it wasn't the same.

"I like him. He's refreshingly honest about being an asshole instead of pretending to be nice while thinking asshole thoughts." She pushed to her feet. "Plus, he called my smart mouth one of my best features. The guy has taste."

Julian sighed dramatically. "Do I need to remind you to maintain proper boundaries?"

"Please." She rolled her eyes. "When have I ever crossed professional boundaries?"

"Do you want the list chronologically or alphabetically?"

"That guy wasn't my patient. I was done treating him first, and then I spent the night with him." That wasn't entirely true since she'd checked his incisions the next morning, but it was such a trivial thing that it wasn't worth mentioning.

Living by the rules was boring, and as long as she didn't harm anyone by breaking them, she didn't see a good reason to follow them.

The sharp buzz of a call button interrupted her train of thought. There was just one patient in the clinic, so she didn't need to look to know which room it was coming from.

"Speak of the devil," Julian murmured.

"He probably just wants to ogle me some more." She walked out of the office.

When she opened the door, Tim was attempting to push himself up, his face twisted in concentration.

"What do you think you're doing?" she asked, walking quickly to his side.

"Trying to move," he grunted, managing to raise himself approximately two inches before collapsing back. "And failing spectacularly. Why am I so weak?"

"It's part of the process, and it shouldn't worry you. Is there a reason you're making efforts you shouldn't?"

"I'm hungry," he admitted. "Starving, actually. Like, 'would eat hospital food and be grateful' level hungry."

"That is strange." She made a note on his chart. "Transitioning Dormants usually get hungry when they are past the initial stage and need to replenish their stores of energy. There is no chance you are there yet."

He grimaced. "Can I have something to eat, please? I'm really hungry, like hunger pangs." He moved his hands to his stomach, which was a good sign since he'd regained some strength in his arms, and his erection was gone, which was good news for him.

"I have to ask the doctor, and if he says that you can eat, the most I can give you is broth. Maybe some Jell-o if you're very good."

"You're offering me flavored water as my first immortal meal?"

"First of all, you are not an immortal yet, and second, would you prefer unflavored water? Because I can do that. Sometimes the body interprets thirst as hunger."

"Broth it is, then." He studied her face. "Can I ask you something?"

"You can ask. I might not answer."

"Fair enough." He paused, seeming to gather his thoughts. "Were you born immortal?"

193

"None of us are born immortal. We are born human, or rather Dormant. Girls transition early, at about two years old, and boys at puberty. Did no one explain things to you before throwing you into the ring with Magnus?"

He pursed his lips. "Andrew tried to cram everything in during the ride to my apartment to collect my things and then to the village, but I was too shell-shocked to absorb what he was saying. He might have explained that detail, or he might not have."

She nodded. "You can ask me anything you want to know. Since you are the only patient in the clinic, it's not like I have other things to do."

His eyes widened, not in surprise but in delight. "I'm your only patient?"

"That's what I said."

"So, you can devote all of your attention to me?"

"I can, doesn't mean that I will. If you don't need anything, I might busy myself with other things."

"I have lots of questions," he said. "Can you sit down with me for a little bit?"

"I thought you were hungry."

"Food can wait."

She pulled a chair closer to his bed and sat. "Ask away."

"How old are you? Or is it inappropriate to ask?"

"Older than you, by a lot, and age is not something that we talk about. It's irrelevant when you live forever."

"Older, like in you could be my mother? Or grandmother?"

He was a stubborn guy. "Like your great-great-grand-mother. Why does it matter?"

"It doesn't. You could be as old as Methuselah, and it wouldn't matter to me. I would still think that you are the hottest chick on Earth."

"Methuselah lived to be almost a thousand, and I'm not quite that old. I don't appreciate being called a chick, though."

"My bad. Can you give me a list of approved words? Is babe okay?"

She looked at him down her nose. "If we were a couple, babe would have been okay. But we are not, so you can call me Hildegard, nurse, woman, or female depending on the context. If we become friends, you will be allowed to call me Hildie."

"Can I call you Hildie now? You can pretend that we are friends. You know, fake it until you make it kind of thing."

She was contemplating his request when his stomach growled loudly.

"Fine," Hildegard said, standing. "You can call me Hildie, but I reserve the right to rescind my acquiescence. Let me get you that gourmet broth. Chicken or beef?"

"Surprise me. I like to live dangerously."

"Indeed." She walked out the door and stopped by the doctor's office. "He's hungry. Can he have broth and Jell-o?"

Julian looked surprised. "He couldn't have transitioned already."

"I know, but he's hungry."

"You can give him clear liquids, and if he doesn't throw them up or lose consciousness again, you can give him solids."

She was about to turn away but paused. "Do you want to administer the test to see if he's transitioned?"

Julian shook his head. "It can't happen so fast. In my opinion, this is a temporary pause, and he will go under again. Perhaps I missed some underlying health problem, and his body halted the process because it was risky for him."

Surprisingly, Hildegard's worried response was visceral. She didn't want anything happening to Tim. "Perhaps you should check on him after all. Maybe I missed something."

"I will. But first, let's see how he reacts to the food."

In the kitchen, she pulled out a cup of beef broth from the freezer, put it in the microwave to defrost, and thought about her strange reaction to Julian's hypothesis.

It had been easy to joke and tease when she thought that Tim was out of danger, but if Julian was correct and this was just a temporary reprieve, then things could still go wrong.

Everyone had their armor, and Tim's just happened to be made of snark. But underneath, he was just as scared as anyone else in his position would be.

You always did have a soft spot for the broken ones.

Hildegard chuckled to herself. "Tim is not broken. Just dented. And dents can be hammered out."

"With him, it might require a sledgehammer," Julian said from behind her.

She hadn't noticed him walking into the clinic's kitchen. "Can I get you anything, doc?"

"I'm just getting myself coffee." He refilled his cup from the carafe. "The microwave is done, by the way. I heard it beeping from my office."

"Oh, I know. I was waiting for the broth to cool down." That was a total lie, but she didn't want Julian to think she had been preoccupied with talking to herself.

She pulled out the hot container, placed it on a tray, and added a cup of Jell-o.

Stopping before Tim's door, she knocked before entering this time, giving him the courtesy of warning before opening it. "Miss me already?" she asked.

"Desperately. I've been composing sonnets in your absence."

Tim had adjusted his position a little.

"Do you even know any?"

"Shakespeare's overrated." He watched the tray she put on the serving table. "A feast worthy of a king. I may waste away to nothing with such fare. A shadow of my former self." He didn't make a move to take one of the two spoons on his tray, and she wondered if she should offer to feed him or let him try to do so by himself first.

"You know what's weird?" he asked.

"What?"

"It feels like my bones are trying to crawl out of my skin, but also like my skin is trying to crawl into my bones. Does that make sense?"

"Perfect. Your body is literally rebuilding itself from the inside out." She smoothed his hair back without thinking, then caught herself. Professional boundaries. Right. "Try the broth. Nutrients for the reconstruction."

He stared at her. "You just petted me."

"I did not pet you. I was checking for fever."

"With your hand? Not even my mother did that. Medical professionals use a thermometer."

"Sometimes a hand is more handy."

"You wanted to touch my luxurious hair. Admit it."

"Your hair looks like you stuck your finger in an electrical socket."

"And yet you couldn't resist."

She shook her head. "You're impossible."

"I've been told that before. Usually right before someone throws something at me or storms out of a room."

"Good thing I'm paid to be here and not allowed to throw things at my patients."

"Ouch. Way to wound a man's ego."

"Your ego could use some wounding. It's taking up all the space in here."

"Touché."

"Are you going to eat?" She pointed at the broth with her chin. "Or do you need me to feed you?"

The sparkle in his eyes betrayed his response before his mouth started moving. "I need you. To feed me."

"Say please."

"Please, Hildie. I need you to spoon me. I mean, I need you to spoon-feed me."

She laughed. "Of course, you do."

18

ELUHEED

As befitting the warlord's concubines, the dining room was elegant and opulent. Crystal chandeliers hung over a table that could have graced any palace, set with china so fine it was nearly translucent and silverware that had been polished to reflect the light like mirrors.

Eluheed paused in the doorway, acutely aware that he was crossing a threshold he'd never expected to breach.

Seven ladies sat around the table, their beauty so perfect that it was almost painful to behold. Sitting between them, Tony looked like he didn't belong. As a human, he might be considered good-looking, but next to the female perfection he was surrounded with, he was painfully ordinary.

They turned toward Eluheed with varying degrees of curiosity, and he dropped his gaze to the floor as he'd been trained to do.

"Elias!" Tony called out. "Come join us. We saved you a seat."

When Eluheed lifted his head, he saw the American looking pleased to see him.

Tamira patted the empty chair beside her, and Eluheed's pulse quickened. Once again, she wore a deep blue dress that complemented her olive skin, but it wasn't either of the ones she'd worn the other two times he'd seen her. Did each of the ladies have her own signature color? He also noticed that her hair had a slightly reddish hue, and he wondered if it was a trick of the light or if she had colored it since he'd last seen her in the courtyard. It was swept up to reveal the elegant line of her neck, the long ends cascading down her back in perfectly styled ringlets. When she smiled at him, his chest tightened and then expanded.

"Thank you," he managed, making his way to the chair. The thick carpet muffled his footsteps, making him feel like he was floating in a dream.

As he sat, a familiar figure entered the dining room, one of the kitchen staff who'd shared his bed a few times. She kept her eyes downcast as she poured water into his crystal goblet.

"Thank you, Mariam," he said quietly.

She glanced up, surprise flickering across her face as if she'd expected him to forget her name just because he'd been moved to the ladies' quarters. She answered with a slight nod and then rushed out of the dining room.

The exchange hadn't gone unnoticed.

"You know the staff well," said a pale, blonde woman across

from him. She spoke English with a faint Germanic or Norse accent.

"The staff is not so extensive that it was difficult to learn all of their names over the eighteen months I've been here," Eluheed said. "After the doctor died, I've been treating their various ailments to the best of my abilities."

He'd been doing that prior to the doctor's death as well, but he chose not to mention that. Many of the staff had trusted him more than they had trusted the ancient physician.

"This is Liliat," Tamira introduced the blonde. "And beside her is Raviki, then Rolenna—she's the one experimenting with glassmaking. Across from them are Beulah, Sarah, and Tula."

Each woman nodded as she was named, their expressions ranging from friendly curiosity to careful assessment. Eluheed had the uncomfortable sensation of being a specimen under examination.

"And I'm Tony, but you knew that already," the guy added with his characteristic grin. "Welcome to the dinner table discourse society. We solve all the world's problems between the soup and dessert."

"If only the world knew," Raviki said dryly. She had the darkest skin of the group, her features sharp and elegant. "Thousands of years of accumulated wisdom, and we're using it to debate whether the latest fashion trends are an improvement or a travesty."

"Fashion is important," Rolenna protested. "It's one of the

few ways humans have to express their inner selves through external means."

It felt surreal to hear them discuss fashion when somewhere on this same island, women who could have been just like them, immortal, were dying as old humans. According to Tony, they had the right genes but were kept from transitioning so they could have many more dormant children for Navuh.

They were treated as breeding stock.

If Tony knew about that, the ladies must know as well, but it wasn't as if any of them could do anything about it.

They were also breeders for Navuh, just with an elevated status.

"Everything is important when you have eternity to fill," Sarah said. She had a bookish air about her, including a pair of wire-rimmed glasses perched on her nose despite the fact that she surely didn't need vision correction. It was a fashion accessory, and Eluheed found the choice strange.

Another servant appeared to serve the first course. Sonia, whose son he'd helped through a bout of pneumonia just the other day. She shot him a grateful look, even though Mika's miraculous improvement was thanks to the antibiotics that had finally been delivered from the island's main clinic and not Eluheed's herbal remedies.

"You seem uncomfortable." Beulah studied him with dark, intelligent eyes. "Is it us, or is it being served by people you consider friends?"

The directness of the question caught him off guard. "Both and neither, I suppose," he admitted. "I was served by people I knew in the staff quarters as well, so it's not about that. It's about being here and being treated as one of you. It's an adjustment."

"An honest answer," Liliat approved. "How refreshing. You are not pretending that this is perfectly natural for you." She cast Tony a sardonic smile.

"Nothing about this situation is natural," Eluheed said, then wondered if he'd been too blunt.

Tamira laughed, the sound melodic and pleasing to the ear. "On that, we can all agree." She turned to Tony. "You have to tell Elias about your first dinner with us. You spilled wine all over yourself trying to impress Tula."

Tony groaned. "I wasn't trying to impress anyone. I felt like an extra in a historical drama turned into a science fiction movie, and I was afraid of breaking the crystal stemware. My grandmother had a set of six crystal glasses, and I wasn't allowed to even look at them."

"Surely you could have afforded to buy a set," Sarah said. "Don't bioinformaticians get paid well?"

He grimaced. "I was just a post-doc, and I was being paid peanuts. I could barely cover my rent. That's why it was so easy to lure me to this island under the pretense of a fake job offer. I was desperate for money."

"Speaking of bioinformatics," Raviki said, "You started to explain something over breakfast and didn't finish."

As Tony launched into a lengthy explanation that involved a lot of hand gestures and scientific terms Eluheed only half understood, the main course arrived. Lamb prepared with herbs and vegetables he recognized from the kitchen gardens. In addition to smelling amazing, it was also beautifully arranged around his plate, making him reluctant to mess up the presentation.

"You're not eating," Tamira noticed after everyone had dug in.

He picked up his fork. "It's almost too pretty to eat. I'm not used to food presented as art. Food is supposed to be simple fare meant to nourish and delight the palate, but this also delights visually."

"Spoken like a true shaman," Liliat said. "Although, to be honest, I have no idea what shamans of different traditions do. My ancestors practiced shamanism which was a form of magic and divination called seiðr. It involved communicating with spirits, prophecy, and healing. But I've only read about that in fiction, so I don't trust the accounts."

Eluheed considered his answer carefully. These women had lived for millennia, and they would spot shallow pretense immediately. He would have to lean into his knowledge of human shamanic practices, which wasn't as extensive as he pretended it was. What humans expected from their shamans was very different than what had been expected from him where he'd come from. "I think that shamanism is pretty universal, but some focus on one of the aspects more than the others, so it depends on who you ask. To some, a shaman is a bridge between the physical and spiritual worlds. To others, we're simply healers who understand that body and spirit are inseparable."

"What is it to you?" Tamira asked.

"To me, shamanism is about seeing the fundamental truths of everything and seeing the connections others miss. Understanding that everything is interwoven. Plant, animal, and person. Earth, water, and sky. Past, present, and future." He paused. "Though I suspect that sounds like mystical nonsense to those raised in this age of technology."

"Not at all." Sarah leaned forward, adjusting her unnecessary glasses. "Modern physics is just beginning to catch up to what shamans have known for millennia. Quantum entanglement, the observer effect, the possibility of parallel universes—it all points to a reality far stranger than pure materialism suggests."

"Have you studied physics?" Eluheed asked.

He'd read extensively on many subjects, including physics, but some of the topics were too complicated for him to grasp. Humans had advanced so much during the last two hundred years or so that it was hard for him to wrap his head around the progress.

Eluheed often wondered if his people, or what was left of them, had progressed at the same rate. If he ever returned home, would he find that they lagged behind humans, or would he be surprised that they'd leaped ahead?

"I wouldn't call it studying," Sarah said. "We don't have teachers here, but I read a lot and understand some." She smiled. "When time is not an issue and you are afforded the

206

ability to procure books on every subject imaginable, you can gain a lot of knowledge. I've been particularly fascinated by how modern science keeps rediscovering ancient wisdom. It's like the connections you spoke about. I'm thrilled each time I find them."

"Like morphic resonance," Tony said. "A famous biologist proposed that there's a field of collective memory that influences form and behavior. That sounds a lot like what a famous psychologist referred to as the collective unconscious, which bears a resemblance to what shamans have long described about the spirit world. It's all the same thing with different names."

Eluheed hadn't expected such depth from the American, and he wondered if Tula had anything to do with it. So far, she hadn't said much, seeming preoccupied with something no one else was privy to, but he had a feeling that Tony had learned about those things from her and not the other way around. From his brief interactions with the guy, he'd gotten the impression that Tony was highly educated, but he was the type who knew a lot about things in his narrow field of study and was not interested in much beyond it.

Sarah's eyes lit up. "Or consider the placebo effect. It's really proof that belief and intention can create physical changes."

"Which brings us back to that book you were reading about manifestation," Rolenna said to Tamira.

Tamira nodded. "The claim is that focused intention can reshape reality. Elias and I were discussing it in the garden earlier."

All eyes turned back to him.

"What are your thoughts on that?" Beulah asked. "As a shaman, you must have opinions on whether we can will things into being." She wiggled her fingers as if performing magic. "Perhaps we can will ourselves out of here. I for one would love to see America."

He was accustomed to the dismissive attitude with which people usually treated his calling, and he wasn't offended by it. They were just ignorant about the multitude of wonders the universe had to offer and sure that science had already discovered everything worth discovering.

It was such arrogance to think that the limited minds of humans could ever uncover all the secrets in the universe.

Eluheed took a sip of wine while preparing his answer. It required a careful balance between the echoes of common beliefs and knowledge and what he knew that none of those present did and sounding like he had a lot to contribute to the discussion while not delivering anything earth-shattering. "Every culture has stories about the power of will and word. In ancient Egypt, they believed names held the essence of things—to know something's true name was to have power over it. The Aborigines of Australia believe that they sang the world into being. Hindu and Buddhist traditions speak of maya, the illusion of reality."

"Do you believe in any of it?" Raviki said. "Can we actually change reality with our thoughts?"

Eluheed smiled. "I think that the separation between thought and reality is superficial. Consciousness is fundamental to the universe, not just the byproduct of our brain chemistry, and our intentions are part of the fabric of reality, not separate from it."

"That's a clever dodge." Liliat nodded with approval. "But you didn't answer the questions about what you believe."

Smart lady. He'd hoped that the big words would do the trick. "Then let me be more direct. Yes, I believe intention shapes reality, but it's not as simple as thinking really hard about riches or freedom or both and having it become your reality. It's more subtle than that. Focused intention can rewire the way our brain perceives opportunities and what possibilities we notice or ignore."

"The observer effect," Sarah murmured. "We collapse probability waves just by looking."

Eluheed nodded, vaguely remembering what he'd read on the subject. "What shamans learn through practice, physicists are discovering through mathematics. Consciousness and the cosmos are inseparable."

That sounded profound enough without really saying anything. Of course, consciousness was not separate from the cosmos because the cosmos contained everything within it, or as some believed, consciousness contained the cosmos.

He waited for someone to call his bluff, but no one did.

"How did you become interested in shamanism?" Tamira asked. "Were you born into the tradition?"

The question required an even more careful navigation. "No one is born a shaman. My people had old traditions." He shifted his gaze to Liliat. "Like your ancestors. They had old ways of seeing, but they were lost, so I had to develop my own."

Liliat's eyes were sharp as she regarded him. "How did they get lost?"

"War. Displacement. The usual tragedies." He kept his tone light, but as he turned to look at Tamira, her expression suggested that she heard the old pain behind his words. "Then again, getting displaced meant that I traveled all over and learned a lot along the way, so it wasn't all bad."

It was terrible, horrific, and he couldn't even think about the fate that befell his people without his heart breaking into a million shards that shredded his insides and made him wish for death to stop the pain. They had been annihilated, and he'd barely managed to escape with the precious cache he'd been entrusted to save, the treasure that was now buried under tons of rock. He had to find a way to dig it out, not only to save it but also to honor the sacrifice of those who had made his escape possible.

"Well, whoever taught you along the way did an excellent job," Rolenna said. "Tony claims that your remedies cured his migraines when nothing else would."

Tony nodded. "That's true. And I didn't feel like throwing up after drinking the concoction either. Elias sweetened it with honey. Thank you."

"It was my pleasure," Eluheed said. "My garden may be small, but each plant there was chosen carefully and cultivated with intention."

"Speaking of intention," Liliat said with a mischievous glint, "Tamira claims she manifested you seeking her out in the garden earlier."

She'd told him that, but he wasn't sure how to respond without embarrassing her. "I guess she did because I felt compelled to check out the garden."

"I was practicing what the book suggested," Tamira said. "Focusing on my desire for interesting conversation. And then he appeared."

"After this, therefore, because of this," Tony said. "Classic logical fallacy."

"Or classic manifestation." Raviki turned to face the guy. "How would we tell the difference?"

"You'd need a control group." Tony seemed to warm to the topic. "Double blind studies, multiple trials, statistical analysis—"

"How romantic," Tula interrupted his flow dryly. "Darling, I manifested you, and I have the data to prove it."

Everyone around the table laughed, and more of the pain in Eluheed's chest eased. Laughter was therapeutic.

"What I find interesting is how often ancient spiritual practices align with cutting-edge science," Sarah said, looking pointedly at Tony. "Studies show that meditation changes brain structure. Prayer affects recovery rates. Shamanic drumming induces theta brainwaves associated with deep healing. You can't poke holes in that because it was proven."

"Bad science," Tony muttered as dessert was served, delicate pastries that looked too beautiful to eat. "Don't forget remote viewing," he added in a mocking tone. "The CIA spent millions researching it. Turns out shamans have been doing it for millennia."

"You're remarkably open-minded for a scientist," Eluheed said, ignoring the guy's sarcasm.

Tony shrugged. "Given my experience, I guess more is possible than I can conceive of. I could have never imagined that I would find myself trapped on an island full of immortals." He grinned at Tula. "If someone had told me that I would be surrounded by beautiful women and chosen by the most beautiful of them all, I wouldn't have believed it, but I would have surely hoped it was true."

"Flatterer." Tula leaned over and kissed his cheek.

"I like to imagine that I'm free in some other, parallel universe," Beulah said. "Supposedly, every quantum event splits reality into multiple timelines, and since there are an infinity of events, there are also an infinity of realities. In one of them, I'm not a concubine locked in a harem."

"Or you might be suffering a worse fate," Sarah said. "If multiple universes exist, then I bet that in half of them you suffer and in half of them you enjoy life, so balance is maintained. It's all about balance in the universe."

19

TAMIRA

"The multiple universes idea is too confusing," Tamira said. "I have enough trouble understanding what's going on in this one."

Rolenna nodded. "Like collective consciousness. It doesn't make sense to me. If we're all connected on some level, why does communication require such effort? Even the six of us, who have lived together for thousands of years, still have disagreements over silly misunderstandings and imagined slights. Why don't we simply know each other's hearts?" She turned to Elias. "Any thoughts on the subject?"

Tamira watched Elias as he considered Rolenna's question. He was so smart and so careful, neither rushing to answer nor deflecting with empty mysticism.

"Our brains function like sieves. They limit the amounts of information they allow into our conscious minds, and blocking the pain, fear, and longing of others is critically important. If you were exposed to all that, the weight would crush you."

That was such a good answer, and Tamira was proud of her shaman.

Well, he wasn't hers. Not yet anyway. But soon.

It was almost funny how her attraction to him was growing with every clever thing he said.

"We carry that weight just from reading about it," Beulah said quietly. "All the wars, the natural disasters, the endless suffering. And through it all, we are here, in perfect isolation."

"But you carry it with your boundaries intact," Elias said. "That distance allows compassion without drowning. Perhaps the effort required for true communication, the choice to bridge the gap, is what makes connection meaningful."

Tamira leaned toward him, drawn by his words. There was so much wisdom in them, so much understanding and compassion. He had an incredibly bright soul.

"So, you're saying that isolation is a gift?" Tony asked with thinly veiled sarcasm.

"I'm saying boundaries are sacred," Elias said. "They define where I end and you begin, which makes the choice to connect an act of will and courage."

His eyes met Tamira's as he spoke, and she felt heat bloom in her chest. Was he speaking of spiritual philosophy or something more personal? The knee that had brushed hers earlier remained close, not quite touching but near enough that she could feel his warmth through the silk of her dress.

"Courage," Liliat repeated. "That's an interesting word choice for connecting with others. Most would say that love and desire drive connection."

"Love requires courage," Elias said. "And so does desire. Without courage, both remain unrequited and unfulfilled. A true connection requires the bravery to be subjected to rejection, misunderstanding, or loss."

"Speaking from experience?" Raviki asked with characteristic directness.

A shadow crossed his face, there and gone so quickly that Tamira might have imagined it. "We all have our stories of connection and disconnection, and they shape how we approach new possibilities."

Tamira recognized deflection when she heard it. Whatever losses Elias had experienced, they still carried weight. It made her want to know more, to understand what had created the shadows of sorrow in his eyes.

"Well, I for one am grateful for new possibilities," she said, letting warmth seep into her voice. "The courage to engage with a new acquaintance has brought us a fascinating dinner conversation."

"Hear, hear." Tony lifted his wine glass. "To new perspectives and the courage to share them."

They toasted, crystal chiming against crystal with pure, clear notes. Tamira let her fingers brush Elias's as they lowered their glasses, a touch so brief it could have been accidental, but the slight widening of his eyes suggested he knew it wasn't.

"You said that you traveled a lot," Sarah said as servants silently cleared the dessert plates. "Which famous locations have you visited?"

Tamira watched Elias choose his words carefully. Whatever his full story, he wasn't ready to share it completely.

"I've been to many places," he said. "From the mountains of the Caucasus to the markets of Constantinople. I've walked the Silk Road and sailed the Mediterranean. Each place taught me something different."

"Constantinople?" Beulah repeated. "Isn't it called Istanbul these days? They changed the name in 1930."

Tamira frowned. It was the kind of mistake that very old humans or immortals made, but Elias was a young man.

He smiled. "It depends on where you come from. Those who dislike the Turks often refer to the city as Constantinople. It annoys Turks to no end."

"Are you Armenian?" Sarah asked.

"Good guess," he said. "There is no love lost between Turks and Armenians."

It was a good explanation, but Tamira suspected that there was more to it. She had known Elias for a very short time, but she'd paid attention and learned to tell when he was being completely open and when he hid behind half-truths.

"I still think of Myanmar as Burma, and Zimbabwe as Rhodesia," Rolenna said. "Change happens faster than my memory adjusts."

"What did you do in Constantinople?" Tamira asked Elias.

"A little bit of commerce. Empires rise and fall, but trade endures, and the merchants in the Grand Bazaar still sell the same goods their ancestors did—spices, silk, stories. The names and languages change, but the human need for connection through exchange remains constant."

"You are reducing human connection to commerce," Liliat said. "That's rather cynical for a shaman."

"I'm not reducing. I'm recognizing that trade drives progress," Elias corrected. "Before we could speak each other's languages, we could point at goods and negotiate value. It's connection at its most basic and honest."

"I never thought of it that way," Tony said. "Though it makes sense. DNA shows trade routes almost as clearly as migration patterns. Genetic markers follow the Silk Road like breadcrumbs."

Tamira wasn't sure if he said that seriously or meant it as a joke, and given the looks the others directed his way, they weren't sure of his meaning either. Tony must have realized that and launched into one of his lectures.

Tamira didn't pay attention. She was focused on studying Elias and reading his subtle tells.

When the conversation returned to his travels, she watched the way his hands moved when he spoke of places he'd been. The subtle tension in his shoulders that never quite eased, as if he were ready to flee on a moment's notice. The way his voice softened when speaking of beauty he'd witnessed, like a sunrise over the Sahara or storms rolling across the Black Sea.

She envied him for seeing the world, for having traveled and mingled with so many people, but she also wondered what he wasn't saying.

When her friends shifted to debate whether modern technology helped or hindered genuine human connection, Elias had gone quiet.

"Are you tired?" she asked quietly.

He turned to her, and for a moment, his careful control slipped. She saw loneliness there, deep and aching, before he smiled. "A little. I don't remember talking so much in years. Besides, sometimes it's better to listen. You can learn more that way."

She smiled. "The only one who's been quiet throughout dinner was Tula, so I guess she learned a lot this evening."

"There were many small silences in between your words."

Was he trying to give her a compliment? She never said no to those.

"And what did they tell you?"

"That you're not only stunningly beautiful but also smart and knowledgeable, and you are bravely making the best of a difficult situation. You've found ways to maintain sanity and dignity despite your circumstances, and that you're hungry for something indefinable—not just novelty but also meaning."

His perception was unsettling and accurate, but then she should have expected that from a shaman.

Tamira felt exposed, as if he'd peered directly into her soul. "And what do you hunger for, Elias?"

The question hung between them, loaded with possibilities. Around them, the dinner conversation continued, but Tamira felt caught in a bubble of intimacy with this incredibly compelling man.

"Fulfillment," he said after a long moment. "The knowledge that I have fulfilled my duties and haven't failed those who depend on me."

Tamira felt her heart constrict.

Did Elias have a wife and children somewhere that Navuh had torn him away from?

"Who are those people who depend on you?" she asked.

He swallowed hard. "They are no longer on this plane of existence, and my sacred duty is to carry the torch and not let them be forgotten." He closed his eyes. "Hard to do from this place."

She felt his pain. Her people were dead as well, long gone, but not forgotten.

"You can write about them," she suggested. "Perhaps Lady Areana can arrange the publishing of your memoir. As long as you don't mention this place, it might be possible."

He took her hand, and she was surprised at how smooth his skin was for someone who gardened as much as he did.

"You are very sweet, Tamira, but writing about my lost people will not count toward fulfilling my duty to them."

"Then what will?"

His eyes clouded. "When you've touched the infinite, ordinary existence feels hollow. But the infinite can't be grasped, only glimpsed. So, we return to the mundane world carrying echoes of transcendence that make normal life feel like exile."

She had no idea what he was talking about, but it sounded too profound to be a mere deflection. Perhaps she just wasn't smart enough to understand what he was trying to say. She understood the sentiment, though. The sense of being forever displaced, of belonging neither to the world left behind nor the one currently inhabited.

"Perhaps exile shared becomes homecoming," she said.

"Perhaps it does," he whispered.

"What are you and Elias whispering about over there?" Rolenna asked, piercing their bubble of intimacy.

Tamira turned back to the group, noting how they were watching her interaction with Elias with knowing smiles. "I said that shared experiences create their own form of belonging. Like us…"

She was interrupted by the doors opening and Lady Areana entering the dining room. She wore white, as she often did, the color making her pale beauty seem almost translucent.

Everyone rose to their feet, including Elias, who followed their lead and bowed.

"Please, sit." Areana waved a hand over the table. "I didn't mean to interrupt. I came to welcome the latest addition to our group." She glided to Elias, who bowed even deeper. "My lady."

"Call me Areana. Everyone here does."

"I'm Elias," he said.

"Welcome to our small group within the larger community of the harem, Elias," Areana said. "Are you enjoying yourself?"

"Very much so, my lady—Areana. I don't remember ever engaging in a conversation quite as stimulating. Your ladies are as intelligent and as knowledgeable as they are beautiful."

"I'm glad you appreciate my lovely companions. Each of them is a bright diamond with no equal, and I treasure them greatly." She surveyed the table with her kind, ageless eyes.

"Will you join us for coffee?" Liliat offered.

"Thank you, but no. I need to be back in my quarters." Her gaze fell on Elias again. "I look forward to speaking with you properly tomorrow at lunch."

"I'm honored, my lady, I mean Areana," Elias said with yet another bow.

After Lady Areana left, the mood shifted. Her presence always reminded them of their reality. For all the luxury and conversation, they remained prisoners of a despot's whims, and they were lucky to have Lady Areana as a protector and shield.

"More wine?" Tony asked, reaching for a bottle. "I find philosophy goes down easier with proper lubrication."

"Not for me," Raviki said, rising. "I need my beauty sleep. I feel every year of my long life tonight. Too much deep thinking makes me nostalgic."

One by one the others excused themselves, and soon only Tamira, Elias, Tula, and Tony remained.

"Well," Tony said, looking between them with thinly veiled amusement. "Tula and I should probably retire for the evening as well."

"Good night," Tamira said with a smile.

Their exit was about as subtle as a thunderclap, and Tamira found herself alone with Elias in the grand dining room, the servants having discreetly vanished once the meal had concluded.

"Subtle, isn't he?" Elias said with a wry smile.

"As a battering ram." She shifted in her chair, angling toward him. "I was hoping we'd have a chance to talk privately."

"Were you?" His voice held cautious interest.

"Mmm. Group conversations are wonderful, but they don't allow for deeper exploration." She let the words carry a double meaning, watching his reaction.

She wanted him tonight, but only if he wanted her too. She wasn't in the habit of coercing males into her bed who weren't interested.

Not that they were ever uninterested unless they were in love with someone else.

Tamira knew she was beautiful. After all, she had to be stunning for the god Mortdh to take her as his concubine. Her beauty had condemned her to life in the harem, but it had also saved her life. If she had stayed in Sumer and mated another immortal from a prominent family, she might have been happy for a few years, but then she would have died with everyone else when Mortdh had decided to kill all the gods and die along with them.

Elias didn't disappoint, holding her gaze. "What do you have in mind?"

"You," she said simply. "All to myself." She rose to her feet and offered him a hand up.

His breath caught. "Tamira..."

"I have a sitting room in my quarters, well stocked with books and comfortable chairs. We could continue our discussion about manifestation and consciousness without Tony's interruptions."

"Discussion?" He seemed unsure suddenly.

She smiled. "I've found that the best connections unfold naturally, without predetermined outcomes."

He took her hand and smiled, his face transforming from handsome to devastating. "I would be honored to continue our conversation privately."

They walked the short distance from the dining room to her quarters, a corridor she'd traveled for many years, but tonight everything felt different. The anticipation humming through her veins made everything sharper—the whisper of silk against stone, the play of lamplight on marble, the sound of their synchronized footsteps.

"The architecture of this place is remarkable," Elias said as they passed by the ornate archway that led to the interior courtyard.

"Lord Navuh spares no expense on our cage," she said quietly, then winced at her bitter tone. "I apologize. Sometimes the resentment slips through at the most inappropriate moments."

"No need to apologize. Acknowledging reality isn't bitterness—it's sanity."

"This is me." Tamira stopped before her door and opened it.

There were no locks in the harem. There was no need. No one entered private quarters uninvited, and that even included Lord Navuh. The monster had a few redeeming qualities, chief among them his love and devotion to Areana.

Tamira's sitting room was her sanctuary, decorated to reflect her evolving tastes. Bookshelves lined the walls, filled with volumes in dozens of languages. Comfortable chairs clustered around an electric fireplace that was for decoration rather than function. There was no need for heating on a tropical island.

Persian rugs covered the floors, and artifacts from various cultures created an eclectic but harmonious whole. Another redeeming quality of Navuh was never refusing his ladies their hearts' desires. All she had to do to purchase an item was submit a request to the accountant, and it got approved without question. Well, except for current literature, or phones that worked outside the harem, or any weapons of any kind. But she was smart enough not to try that.

"Your room suits you," Elias said. "It's beautiful and interesting, just like the lady who occupies it."

"This is my nest," she said. "Please, sit wherever you like."

He chose one of the chairs by the fireplace, and she took its companion, curling her legs beneath her. For a moment, they simply looked at each other, the possibilities hanging in the air between them.

"Would you like tea?" she asked. "Or something stronger?"

"Tea would be perfect."

As she walked over to the small preparation area she'd created against one wall, Elias rose to his feet and went over to one of her bookcases.

"You have an impressive collection," he said, examining her bookshelves. "Philosophy, science, poetry, fiction...in how many languages?"

"All the ones I speak and a few I'm still learning." She filled the electric kettle with water from a carafe and selected a delicate oolong from her tea collection. It was floral with complex undertones. "Books are my salvation here. Windows into worlds I will never see."

"Which worlds call to you most strongly?"

The question was simple, but she heard layers beneath it. "The ones where choice exists. Where people can leave if they're unhappy, love whom they choose, pursue their own purposes." She poured hot water over the leaves, watching them unfurl. "I never lived in places like that, never experienced what it's like to be free. I was always an asset to be traded for goods or for status, and that was even in my country of origin, which was incredibly progressive compared to this." She waved her hand in the air. "But my parents traded me for status and favors, and I was too young and naive to realize that I was agreeing to eternal bondage."

Elias looked suddenly anxious, his eyes darting over the walls of her room.

She laughed. "Don't worry. There are no listening devices or cameras in here. Lord Navuh is paranoid, but he is not a pervert. He allows us privacy in our rooms."

Elias frowned. "Are you sure about that? Because I was under the impression that my room was not as private as this."

"It's not, and neither is Tony's. But you can talk freely here. I promise it's safe."

He still looked doubtful.

"Navuh is a cruel despot and a vile shithead," she said, not loud enough that it could be heard outside her door, but loud enough to convince Elias.

"Now I'm really scared." He looked at the door as if expecting it to burst open at any moment.

"Don't worry. I have cursed at him out loud thousands of times in here. He would not let it slide if he heard it."

She carried the tea service to the small table between their chairs, and he helped arrange the cups and saucers without being asked.

Small courtesies, but they mattered.

"It might be a trick," Elias said quietly. "He might ignore your cursing so you will think that this is a safe place to talk."

She sat in the chair. "Why would he do that?"

"To lull you into a false sense of security," Elias whispered. "So if you ever plot against him, you will do it here, where he could learn of your plans."

She laughed. "I could plot from here until eternity and not come up with anything that will help me escape this place. Even if I managed to somehow get through both fences and overpower the guards patrolling the grounds, where would I go? It's an island. The only way out of here is the last exit."

"Death," Elias said.

"Precisely." She lifted her teacup and blew air on the hot water before sipping her tea.

Could he be right about the listening devices?

It was possible, but since she had no nefarious plans, she had nothing to worry about, and if Navuh was indeed a pervert and wanted to watch her having sex in her bed, it was his prerogative. After all, she belonged to him, and he could do whatever he wanted with her.

It wasn't a pleasant thought, and she searched her mind for something to say that would chase away the bitterness that hovered over her, as it was the last thing she wanted when she was about to seduce an intriguing man and needed to get into the right mood.

"What's your favorite book?" Elias asked. "The one you return to when the world feels too heavy?"

He was so attuned to her that he had guessed exactly what she needed right now.

"Rumi's poetry," she answered without hesitation. "A Sufi mystic from the thirteenth century. His words about divine love and longing speak to something in me that transcends circumstance."

"'Let yourself be silently drawn by the strange pull of what you really love,'" Elias quoted. "'It will not lead you astray.'"

The man didn't cease to amaze her.

"You know Rumi?"

"How could a shaman not? He understood that separation is an illusion, that all longing is really for reunion with the source."

"Is that what you believe?" she asked. "That we're all seeking reunion?"

"Yes, that and recognition. To be truly seen and accepted, not for our masks but for our essences."

The words hit her with unexpected force. When had anyone last seen her essence rather than her beautiful exterior? Even her sisters in captivity knew only the Tamira she'd become, not the girl she'd been.

"And if someone sees that essence?" she asked quietly. "What then?"

His gaze held hers, intense and unwavering. "Then we face a choice. To hide or reveal. To retreat or risk. To maintain a safe distance or dare proximity."

Her heart raced. This was moving exactly to where she needed it to go. Some connections couldn't be parsed or paced—they simply were.

"I'm tired of safe distances," she admitted.

He set down his teacup. "Tamira, I need you to understand —there are things about me I can't share. If you want me, you will have to be satisfied with what I can freely offer."

"I'm not asking for your secrets," she said. "I'm asking for your presence. Tonight."

"Tonight?"

She rose, moving to stand before his chair.

This close, she could see flecks of gold in his brown eyes, the sun-kissed strands in his chestnut hair. He looked up at her, and she saw her own hunger reflected there.

"Tonight, I want to forget that we're not free. I want a conversation that goes deeper than philosophy. I want to be touched by someone who sees me as more than the lord's property."

ELUHEED

"I want to be touched by someone who sees me as more than the lord's property." Tamira offered Eluheed a hand up.

The words impacted him with unexpected force. In that simple statement, she'd revealed the oppressive burden which was her captivity, a millennia of being viewed as an object, a possession, a beautiful thing to be owned rather than a person to be cherished.

His body responded to both her vulnerability and her strength, desire flaring through him with an intensity that surprised him.

Instead of taking her offered hand, he rose to his feet in one fluid movement and lifted her into his arms. The action was instinctive, a need to show her that she was precious, worth cherishing. She weighed almost nothing, her immortal form deceptively delicate despite the strength he knew she possessed.

Tamira's smile bloomed as she wrapped her arms around his neck, her fingers playing with the hair at his nape. "I like assertive men, and I find strength arousing."

He chuckled, the sound rumbling through his chest. "I don't need strength to carry you. You weigh next to nothing."

"Liar," she whispered.

As he carried her through the sitting room toward her bed, he was struck by the trust and acceptance she was showing him.

Her bed was luxurious, with soft fabrics in cream and gold that looked like clouds made solid. The windows on the side facing the inner courtyard would have shown stars if they weren't deep underground. Instead, clever lighting created the illusion of moonlight, bathing everything in silver.

He laid her on the crisp cream-colored linens with careful reverence, struck anew by her beauty. Her dark hair spread across the pillows, creating a striking contrast. The deep blue of her dress made her golden skin glow, and her eyes, those impossible, ancient eyes, watched him with a mixture of desire and something else. Was it hope?

Perhaps.

She was so stunningly beautiful that she seemed almost unreal, like a painting or a statue created by a gifted artist or a goddess from myth. The perfect arch of her brows, the sensual curve of her lips, the elegant line of her throat— every feature was in flawless harmony.

And somehow, impossibly, she wanted him.

He thought of all the males who must have shared her bed over the centuries, all chosen for their resemblance to Navuh, all more handsome than he. What could he offer her that they hadn't?

"Are you going to just stand there and stare at me?" she asked, but her tone was teasing rather than impatient.

"I could do that forever," he murmured. "You are like a work of art. Nature's work of art."

Something shifted in her expression, a shadow crossing her face. "Not really, but I don't want to talk about this tonight."

The response puzzled him. What could she possibly mean? He studied her more closely, looking for signs of artifice or alteration. In his experience, some people chose to modify their appearance, especially those with means and vanity. But the harem seemed frozen in an earlier time, and he doubted such modern interventions were available here.

"What do you mean? Did you have any part of your body altered?"

Tamira laughed, but her laugh held a note of bitterness beneath the amusement. "Of course not. Even if I wanted to, immortal bodies are impossible to alter. I can't even pierce my ears to wear earrings. Coloring my hair and applying cosmetics is the best I can do to change my appearance." She paused, her hand rising to her throat in an unconsciously protective gesture. "I am a descendant of gods, and I suspect that their perfection was carefully bred. It could not have been natural selection that led to such results."

Had she meant perfect pairings to create beauty? Or had it been something more sinister than that?

Her hand slid from her throat down to her cleavage in a deliberately sensual movement, redirecting his attention from dark thoughts to present desire. "Come join me, Elias."

"Let me dim the lights first," he said.

A knowing smile played on her lips. "Are you shy?"

"No, but I'm a romantic, and this room is too bright for a romance." He walked to the light switches near the door, using the journey to compose himself. The room plunged into darkness, but not entirely.

His night vision was excellent, another gift of his immortality, and he could see her perfectly despite the low light. But even without that, he could have found his way to her by the soft glow emanating from her eyes, a sign of her godly heritage that probably manifested strongest in moments of passion.

Her blue eyes glowed like two precious jewels, guiding him back to her.

"You should know that I can see perfectly in the dark, so you can't hide anything from me," she said.

"That's good to know."

It complicated things.

His body bore a mark that would raise questions.

Eluheed sat on the bed beside Tamira, suddenly uncertain. He'd been with many women over his centuries of wandering, brief connections that eased the loneliness without demanding truth. But he'd never been with anyone like Tamira. She was older than he by millennia, had experienced pleasures he could only imagine. How could he hope to please a woman who'd known the touch of countless lovers?

He leaned over her, drinking in her beauty, her scent, the way her chest rose and fell with quickened breath. "Perhaps you should close your beautiful, glowing eyes and let yourself just feel. When one of the senses is deprived, the others compensate, and pleasure intensifies."

Her smile turned knowing. "Now I'm sure that you are trying to hide something from me."

She wasn't wrong. The mark on his chest could perhaps be explained as a tattoo, a birthmark, or even a strangely healed wound. But he abhorred lying even though his existence on Earth forced him to lie constantly, or rather misdirect, though he had a feeling that his well-practiced redirection tricks might not work on her.

If they became lovers beyond just this night, how long could he maintain his secret? The thought troubled him.

"I am trying to hide something," he admitted, choosing honesty within limits. "I'm not as perfect and unmarred as you are."

The playfulness faded from her expression, replaced by something tender. "You don't have to be perfect. I know that humans carry their history on their bodies, both men and women, and I don't regard it as shameful. Scars tell stories. They're proof of survival."

Her understanding moved him. She thought he was self-conscious about battle scars or the marks of hard living. If only it were that simple.

"But if you want," she continued, "I'll close my eyes on the condition that you close yours as well."

He traced the curve of her hip through the silk of her dress, marveling at the way she shivered at his touch. "I want to give you pleasure first, and I don't want you to do anything other than just feel."

The smile that bloomed on her face was radiant. "How can I say no to such an enticing offer?"

Her trust humbled him. This ancient, powerful woman was placing herself in his hands, allowing herself to be vulnerable with him.

Moving down the bed with deliberate slowness, he lifted her foot and removed her delicate sandal. The action was oddly intimate, servant-like, and worshipful at once. "Your eyes are still open," he said, pressing kisses to her toes, drawing a surprised gasp from her.

"You are still dressed," she countered, her voice breathier than before. "I'm not missing seeing you undressed."

He tickled her foot in gentle retaliation, delighting in her laughter. "Do as I say."

"Are you getting bossy with me?" The throaty quality of her voice sent heat straight through him.

"Never." He repeated the reverent attention on her other foot, kissing each toe. "I wouldn't dare."

"Somehow, I think you would." She stretched like a cat, all sinuous grace and barely contained power.

Removing her gown proved as simple as sliding the thin straps down her arms and drawing the fabric away. The revelation of her body being bare beneath the dress nearly undid his control. She was perfection incarnate, every curve and plane designed to inspire worship.

"You really are a work of art," he whispered, smoothing his palms over her inner thighs with reverent touches, gently encouraging her to open for him.

The scent of her arousal was intoxicating, calling to something primal within him. It took all his willpower not to dive between her legs immediately like a man possessed. But this wasn't about his need—it was about hers. About worshiping the goddess within her.

Tamira sighed and finally closed her eyes, submitting to his gentle guidance.

Dimly, Eluheed was aware that he wasn't following any practiced script. He hadn't kissed her lips first, hadn't paid homage to her breasts, hadn't followed the typical progression of seduction. Instead, he was letting instinct guide him, somehow knowing what Tamira needed without words. He had a knack for sensing the unspoken, and right now, every fiber of her being was crying out for something different, something unexpected.

A woman who had known countless lovers over millennia needed something different.

"Fates!" Tamira exclaimed the moment his lips made contact with her heated center, her back arching involuntarily off the bed.

He placed his palms over her thighs to hold her steady, anchoring her as he explored her with reverent devotion. His tongue swept over her delicate folds, learning her taste, her texture, the way she responded to different pressures and rhythms. He circled her opening teasingly before plunging inside, drawing a keening sound from her throat that made his own arousal almost explode.

Her fingers threaded through his hair, holding him against her as her movements grew increasingly frantic. She was close, her body trembling on the precipice. Five thousand years of experience, and yet she responded to him like she was starving just for him and this particular touch.

"I need to come, Elias." The words were half-command, half-plea.

He could refuse her nothing.

Sliding two fingers inside her welcoming heat, he closed his lips around her most sensitive spot and sucked gently.

She erupted with a cry that might have woken the entire floor if the walls weren't built to contain secrets. He continued his ministrations, drawing out her pleasure until she pushed weakly at his head, over-sensitized and sated.

He lifted his head and pressed a tender kiss to her mound, overwhelmed by a feeling of gratitude and satisfaction that had little to do with his own unsated arousal. He'd given her pleasure, had made this goddess among women cry out in ecstasy.

She caressed his head with gentle fingers, then cupped his cheeks to draw his face up where she could see him. Her eyes were open now, glowing more brightly than before, filled with wonder and something that looked dangerously like tenderness.

"I knew you'd be good," she said, her voice still rough from crying out. "But I didn't expect this. You blew my mind."

"Just your mind?" he teased. "I must not have done my job properly."

Her laughter was throaty. "Oh, you did your job superbly. I may never let you leave this bed."

"There are worse fates," he murmured against her lips.

As he rose to stretch out beside her, gathering her boneless form against him, Eluheed realized he was in trouble. This was supposed to be a simple night of shared pleasure between two lonely people, but nothing about Tamira was simple, and what he felt went far beyond mere physical attraction.

In her arms, for the first time in centuries, he felt something dangerous and wonderful.

Impossibly, he felt like he was home.

2 1

TAMIRA

T amira took pride in being an excellent judge of character. Five thousand years of experience had honed her ability to read people with ease. She knew their desires, their fears, their true nature beneath whatever mask they wore. She had never been wrong in her initial assessments.

Until tonight.

Either she'd been completely mistaken about Elias, or the careful, reserved shaman had been hiding a passionate nature that only emerged when desire overrode caution, because the man who'd just shattered her with pleasure bore little resemblance to the cautious philosopher who'd sat beside her at dinner.

First times had never been like this.

She'd experienced the full spectrum—from a selfish god who had taken her virginity without much care for her pleasure to fumbling young humans who'd needed explicit instruction or arrogant ones who'd believed they were irresistible. The timid ones had frustrated her with their hesitation, while the overconfident ones had disappointed her with their assumptions.

Neither type had truly satisfied.

Long ago, she'd accepted that the perfect lover did not exist, that he was a fantasy created to give hope to young women who still believed that their salvation would one day come.

Simple carnal pleasure could be found easily enough, but a true connection? That meeting of bodies and souls that the poets sang about? She'd lost hope of ever experiencing it a long time ago and convinced herself that it didn't exist.

How spectacularly wrong she'd been.

Elias had displayed the perfect balance of masculine dominance tempered with gentle care and perfectly attuned consideration. He'd taken control without taking away her choice, asserting his will while remaining attuned to her every response. Each touch had been deliberate yet, somehow, spontaneous, as if he were simultaneously following a plan and improvising based on her reactions.

It was as if he'd been reading her mind, or perhaps her body, and interpreting each shiver and sigh like a language he'd spent lifetimes learning. He'd led when she wanted to follow, yielded when she needed control, created a dance of give and take that had been deeply satisfying and yet left her hungry for more.

Now he lay beside her, still fully clothed while she was bare, and the contrast sent another wave of heat through her. Any other man would have been tearing at his clothes by now, desperate to claim his own pleasure after taking care of hers. But Elias waited, watched, and let her set the pace for what came next.

It should have cooled her ardor, but instead, it stoked it higher.

He was unexpected, different, and delightful.

She turned on her side to face him, drinking in the sight of him in the near darkness. His hair was disheveled from her fingers, his lips slightly parted as if he was as breathless from her climax as she was, and his eyes were dark with desire but also tender. Full of wonder? Or perhaps recognition of the thing she felt blooming between them?

"You're still dressed." She trailed a finger down his chest.

"I know. I didn't want to presume. I'm here for your pleasure, not mine."

"You've delivered on that and then some. You made me forget my own name." She sighed. "You are the only man in forever who saw me as me, Tamira, and not someone else's possession."

His expression softened. "You are no one's possession."

She actually was Navuh's possession, but her heart and mind were her own.

"Tell that to the guards," she said.

"I would, if I thought it would make a difference." His hand came up to cup her cheek. "I can't change your circumstances, but I can make you forget them for a little while."

"You already have." She turned her head to kiss his palm. "But now I find myself greedy for more." She began working on the buttons of his shirt.

When she parted the fabric, her breath caught. His chest was smooth and well defined, the muscles of someone who used his body for work rather than vanity. But it was the mark on his right pectoral that drew her attention—an intricate pattern that looked almost like a symbol, burned or etched into his skin.

She traced it gently with her fingertips, feeling him tense beneath her touch. "Is this what you were worried about me seeing?"

He nodded.

"How did you get it? It looks like a burn." The pattern was too precise to be accidental, too meaningful to be random scarring.

His breath hitched. Was it a surprise to him that she'd identified its nature so quickly? "It was a burn," he said.

She lifted her eyes to meet his, seeing the wall he'd erected around this particular truth. "If you don't want to talk about it, that's fine."

"I don't." The words were soft but final.

A small hurt bloomed in her chest at his unwillingness to share, but she pushed it aside. This was only their first night together, and trust took time to build. When he felt safer with her, perhaps he would tell her the story of how he'd been marked.

Instead of dwelling on what he wouldn't share, she focused on what he would, moving her hands to his waist. The anticipation of finally seeing all of him made her pulse quicken.

She helped him shed the rest of his clothes, and when he was finally naked before her, she took a moment to simply appreciate the male beauty. He had the lean strength of a runner, a body honed by use rather than training.

"You are beautiful," she said.

He laughed, the sound slightly self-conscious. "I think that's my line."

"No." She ran her hands over his chest, his arms, mapping the terrain of his body. "You are beautiful in the way a well-balanced blade is beautiful—functional and elegant at the same time."

Her exploration led her lower, and when she found his hard length and gave it a testing caress, the groan that escaped him sent liquid heat pooling in her belly. The smooth, hot flesh pulsing in her hand felt magnificent—perfectly sized, responsive to her touch, already weeping with need for her.

Before she could explore further, he threaded his fingers through her hair, cupping the back of her skull with gentle firmness before claiming her mouth.

Finally, they were kissing—something that should have come before the intimate kiss he'd already given her, but she wasn't complaining about the unconventional sequence. If anything, this rewriting of the typical script added to the uniqueness of their encounter.

His lips were soft but insistent, coaxing hers apart so his tongue could slip inside. He kissed her like he had all the time in the world, like nothing existed beyond this moment, this connection, like his shaft wasn't making any demands. His tongue danced with hers, sometimes leading, sometimes following, creating a rhythm that made her think of another dance their bodies would soon share.

As if reading her mind, he rolled her beneath him with one smooth movement, his weight a warm blanket on top of her. He wasn't too heavy, just substantial enough to make her feel deliciously trapped, every point of contact between them electrified. His skin was warm and smooth against hers, muscles shifting as he adjusted his position to keep from crushing her.

He cupped her face between his palms, holding her like something precious as he kissed her again. This time it was just gentle nibbles on her lips, teasing touches that made her arch up seeking more. When she opened for him, his tongue swept inside, making love to her mouth with the same patient devotion he'd shown elsewhere.

His hard length pressed against her inner thigh, so close to where she needed it. Why was he waiting? Could he not feel how ready she was, how desperately she wanted him inside her?

Centuries of barely adequate lovers had left her hungry for something more, something real. And now that she'd found it, the anticipation was almost unbearable.

His height meant she had to stretch to reach what she wanted, but she managed to grasp his firm buttocks, sinking her nails into the solid flesh as she arched up, rubbing her aching center against his hardness. The friction sent sparks through her, but it wasn't enough.

"I need you inside me," she gasped against his mouth.

He groaned, lifting just enough to reach between them. She felt him position himself at her entrance and braced for the hard thrust that would follow, craving the sweet invasion.

But it didn't come.

Instead, Elias entered her with agonizing slowness, as if she were breakable. The consideration might have been sweet if it weren't so unnecessary and she weren't so desperate, but there was something oddly arousing about the careful control he exhibited.

He stretched her perfectly, the careful entry allowing her to enjoy every inch of him as he slowly claimed her. When he was finally seated fully inside her, she lifted her legs to wrap around his torso, using the leverage to pull him even deeper.

"Incredible," he breathed against her ear, his voice rough with the effort of maintaining control.

"So are you." She clenched around him experimentally,

drawing another groan from him. "But I'm much tougher than I look, and you need to move."

Her words should have unleashed him, but instead, he kissed her again, pulling out a few inches before pressing back in with the same careful control.

The friction was delicious, but she needed more.

"That's so good," she encouraged, hoping he'd take the hint and increase his pace.

He thrust again, harder this time, but still controlled. Then he pulled almost all the way out before surging back in with enough force to make her gasp.

"Yes, just like that." She clutched his broad shoulders, her nails digging in as he finally, finally gave her what she craved.

What followed was a revelation.

She tried to meet his thrusts, to maintain the give-and-take that they had so far maintained, but he was much stronger than any of the human males she'd been with. Each powerful drive of his hips sent her higher, pushed her beyond thought into pure sensation.

For the first time in millennia, she couldn't match her partner's strength. All she could do was hold on and surrender to the storm he'd become.

Something about that should have bothered her, but there was also something liberating about being overwhelmed, about finding a lover whose passion could sweep her away so completely.

The last time she'd experienced anything approaching this was with the god Mortdh, but he hadn't been attentive or caring. Besides, that had been so long ago she didn't trust the memory.

On some level deeper than thought, Tamira recognized that there was something fundamentally different about Elias. It wasn't just his unexpected strength or his intuitive understanding of her needs, but something elusive and essential, a quality she couldn't define.

Whatever it was, she knew with bone-deep certainty that after experiencing this, she could never go back to the simple men who'd warmed her bed over the long centuries of her captivity.

"Look at me," Elias commanded softly, and she opened eyes she hadn't realized she'd closed.

His face above hers was intense with concentration and desire, but it was the emotion in his eyes that made her breath catch. He wasn't just taking his pleasure or even sharing it—he was worshipping her with his body, each thrust an offering, each groan a prayer.

"You are so breathtakingly beautiful," he murmured, never breaking eye contact as he moved within her. "So perfect. I could spend eternity learning you."

The words should have been throwaway compliments, the kind that men said in the heat of passion. But she recognized the sincerity of his voice that made the words feel like vows.

She was close again, the tension building with each perfect stroke. But more than physical release, she felt something deeper threatening to break free—walls she'd built over millennia beginning to crumble under his tender assault.

"Let go," he whispered, somehow sensing her internal struggle. "I've got you. Let go."

And with a trust that should have terrified her, she did.

22

ELUHEED

T he sight of Tamira coming apart beneath him was the most beautiful thing Eluheed had ever witnessed. Her face transformed with pleasure, eyes wide and unseeing, lips parted in a silent cry that seemed to come from her very soul. He felt her inner muscles clench around him in waves, each pulse threatening to trigger his own release.

But he held back through sheer force of will, wanting to watch her, to memorize every second of her abandon. The way her throat arched, the flush that spread across her golden skin, the tiny tremors that ran through her body.

He wanted to remember it all.

"That's it," he murmured against her ear, maintaining his rhythm even as his control frayed. "Let me feel all of you."

She made a sound somewhere between a sob and a laugh, her nails raking down his back hard enough that he knew there would be marks. Regrettably, they wouldn't last, and she would wonder why.

When her trembling began to ease, he slowed his movements, pressing kisses to her temple, her cheek, the corner of her mouth. She turned her head to look at him with wide eyes. "Don't slow down. I want you to come undone." Her legs tightened around him. "I want to feel you let go, too."

"I'm not done worshipping you."

Her eyes, still glowing faintly in the darkness, narrowed. "Elias..."

It was a command he knew he could not refuse, but he would obey on his own terms.

He began to move again, drawing out each stroke until she was once again writhing beneath him. He wanted to map every sensitive spot, learn every gasp and sigh, discover exactly how to take her apart and put her back together again.

"You're insufferable," she panted, but her body was already responding, arousal building again.

"You love it," he teased while shifting the angle of his hips slightly, searching for—there. Her sharp intake of breath told him he'd found what he was looking for. He focused on that spot, watching her face as surprise gave way to renewed desire.

"How do you—" she began, but the question dissolved into a moan as he repeated the motion.

How could he explain that he'd spent centuries training to read female energy, to sense the flow of pleasure through her body like tracking light through crystal? That right now she was glowing like the sun, every nerve-ending broadcasting its needs in a language older than words?

Eluheed hadn't known that he'd trained for just this moment, for joining with this incredible immortal female, a descendant of gods.

Instead of trying to explain, he showed her. Drew patterns of pleasure with his hips, wrote poetry on her skin with his hands, sang silent songs of devotion with every touch.

This wasn't sex—it was communion, a sharing of essence that transcended the physical.

She was close again; he could feel it in the way her breathing changed, the tension gathering in her muscles. This time, he knew he wouldn't be able to hold back. The need for release had become urgent.

"Come with me," he commanded.

Her eyes met his, and in them he saw his own need reflected and magnified. She nodded, pulling his head down for a kiss that was all teeth and tongue and a desire as desperate as his.

The last threads of his control snapped. He drove into her with abandon now, chasing both their pleasure with single-minded intensity. She met him thrust for thrust, their bodies moving in perfect synchronization as if they'd been lovers for years rather than hours.

When he finally allowed himself to climax, his release was like a volcanic eruption. He heard himself cry out her name, maybe, or perhaps something in his native tongue that he hadn't spoken in many centuries.

Dimly, he was aware of her peaking with him, her body bowing beneath his as ecstasy claimed her again. The feeling of her pulsing around him extended his own climax until he thought he might dissolve entirely and become nothing but sensation and light.

When the storm finally passed, he collapsed, pulling her with him so he wouldn't crush her with his weight. For a long moment, they lay with their limbs entangled, their mouths panting, and sweat cooling on their skin.

It was Tamira who moved first, curling against him with her head on his chest. The gesture was so trusting, so intimate, that it made his throat tight with emotion.

"That was..."

"Inadequate?" he suggested when she trailed off, though he was fairly certain that wasn't what she'd been about to say.

She laughed, the sound vibrating through his chest. "I was going to say transcendent, but if you think it was inadequate, I suppose we'll have to try again. You know, to improve."

He pressed a kiss to the top of her head, inhaling the scent of roses and a satisfied woman. "Give me a few minutes to recover, and I'll be happy to make another attempt."

"A few minutes?" She lifted her head to look at him, eyebrow raised. "That's rather optimistic for a human."

The casual reference to his supposed humanity sent a chill through him, but he kept his expression light. "Tonight, I feel like a god."

A shadow passed over her eyes. "I've been with a god, and he couldn't hold a candle to you."

She stunned him speechless.

"A god?"

"Yes," she said softly, settling back against him. "Don't ask."

Eluheed supposed it was only fair. After all, he'd told her not to ask about his mark.

He traced the curve of her hip, the dip of her waist, the elegant line of her spine, while she drew patterns on his chest, carefully avoiding the mark.

"Can I ask you something?" she said eventually.

He tensed. "You can ask. I might not answer."

"Fair enough." She was quiet for a moment, seeming to gather her thoughts. "That mark on your chest is not really a burn, is it?"

His heart rate spiked, but he forced himself to remain still. "It actually is."

"I've seen burns, Elias. They are never that precise unless someone did it deliberately, like with a hot iron."

He was quiet for so long that she probably thought he wouldn't answer. Finally, he said, "It wasn't done with a hot iron."

"Then what?"

He couldn't tell her. "It's part of a shamanic tradition, and I'm not allowed to talk about it."

It was a partial lie, and the best he could do without revealing who and what he really was.

She traced near it but not on it, her touch feather-light. "It must have been agonizing."

"Pain is often the price of transformation."

She pressed a kiss to his shoulder. "Thank you for telling me."

Guilt twisted in his stomach. He'd given her a half-truth at best, but it was more than he'd shared with anyone on this planet.

"Your turn," he said, wanting to redirect the conversation. "You said that you've been with a god. What did you mean?"

She stiffened against him, and for a moment, he thought she wouldn't answer. Then she sighed, her breath warm against his skin.

"Do you know how I came to be here? I mean in the harem?"

"I assumed Lord Navuh chose you for your beauty, and once Lady Areana arrived, he decided that he didn't want any of his concubines."

She shook her head. "Navuh inherited me along with the other concubines. We belonged to his father first, and he was a god. His name was Mortdh, and he loved using all of us as well as every priestess in his many fertility temples and any goddess that agreed to share her bed with him."

The implications made his stomach turn. "Was he cruel to you?"

She shrugged. "He wasn't abusive, but he was what nowadays would be called a narcissist. I was young, naive, and I hoped he would fall in love with me and choose me above all others. But I was just an immortal, and I didn't conceive. I was worthless to him. He hoped to father a pureblooded god child with a goddess."

He tightened his arms around her. "You're not worthless. You are priceless."

She sighed. "I'm sorry. I'm ruining the mood."

"No." He turned so he could see her face. "Don't apologize for feeling sad or disappointed. Not with me. You never have to pretend with me."

She searched his eyes. "You're dangerous, you know that?"

"How so?"

"You make me want things I can't have. Freedom. Choice. A life beyond these walls." She touched his face. "You."

"You have me," he said, meaning it despite all the reasons he shouldn't.

23

AMANDA

A satisfied smile spread across Amanda's face as she surveyed her handiwork. The village green had been transformed into a fairy-tale wonderland, with pink and gold streamers fluttering from the trees and creating canopies of color. Round tables draped in white linen and topped with miniature castles made from sugar and fondant dotted the lawn, the place setting featuring tiaras for the ladies and crowns for the gentlemen because it was a royal birthday, and all guests were princes and princesses.

"Mommy! Mommy!" Evie pointed at the dessert table. "Cake!" She started toward it with the determined but wobbly gait of a little girl who was still learning to walk.

If she fell on her little tushie, the diaper would cushion her fall, but the custom princess dress Stella had created would get dirty before the party even started.

The soft pink confection with its layers of tulle and delicate embroidery made Evie look like she'd stepped out of a period painting, and not one of Disney's adapted fairy tales that bore no resemblance to the originals they'd supposedly been based on. Not that there was anything wrong with adapting old stories for modern times, but at some point, the scripts had become so ridiculous that the stories had lost their charm, and the movies were simply unwatchable. Little girls didn't watch movies about princesses to have adult subjects shoved in their sweet little faces. They wanted magic, fairy dust, pretty dresses, and tea parties.

All of which Amanda had strived to provide for Evie's first birthday party.

"Look, Mommy!" Evie managed to reach the dessert table before Amanda could catch her and grabbed one of the chocolate-covered pretzels that had been left within her reach.

"Oh no, you don't." Amanda swooped in with a wet wipe she'd pulled out of her pocket with the practiced swiftness of a gunslinger. "Let's clean these little hands before they touch the pretty dress."

Evie shoved the pretzel into her mouth and tried to reach for another one, but Amanda was faster, catching her hands and cleaning the chocolate smudges.

"Choco!" Evie lamented, pointing at the dessert table with sad puppy eyes.

"Later, sweetie. After we eat real food." Amanda adjusted one of Evie's tiny hair clips that had come loose. "Let's say hello to your guests." She lifted her into her arms and walked away from the table laden with irresistible temptations for little ones.

"The decorations are beautiful." Syssi walked toward them with Allegra's hand in hers. Kian followed, looking handsome in his casual linen pants and short-sleeved, loose shirt. It was a rare sight to see her brother dressed like that. He usually dressed in a suit and looked like he was about to close a billion-dollar deal.

Allegra was resplendent in her own custom princess dress, a deep purple creation with silver stars embroidered across the skirt.

"I'm like Princess Sparkle!" Allegra twirled to make her dress flare out.

"You look beautiful, sweetie." Amanda glanced at Syssi. "I really wanted to order queen dresses for the mothers, but Dalhu said that I was getting carried away and that I couldn't put every resident of the village in a costume." She sighed. "I wish I could. Imagine how wonderful this party would have been if everybody was wearing costumes."

"You think?" Kian raised an eyebrow, gesturing at the elaborate setup. "The cruise weddings you organized were not as fancy as this."

"You only turn one once," Amanda defended. "Besides, look how happy our little princesses are."

Phoenix, Andrew and Nathalie's daughter, came running over in her own princess dress—a gorgeous green number with gold trim that complemented her dark hair perfectly. Even Karen's daughter, Idina, normally too cool for such things at the advanced age of four, seemed pleased with her blue and silver gown. Cyra had been delighted to receive her green and gold dress with the matching tiara and wear it to the party, but as usual, she was too shy to show it off and was hiding behind her mother's legs.

"Where's the birthday girl?" Annani's melodious voice preceded her arrival.

"Nani!" Evie reached for her grandmother with grabby hands.

Annani's face lit up as she took her granddaughter. "Happy birthday, my precious one."

As Amanda watched them together, she was almost overcome with emotion. A year ago, she'd been pregnant and terrified, wondering if she could keep her daughter safe until she transitioned into immortality. But even though it was still too early for that, just having her mother around made her less afraid. Instinctively, she knew that nothing would happen to Evie while her grandmother was nearby.

"Shall we move to the family table?" Amanda suggested. Evie's diaper seemed full and probably needed to be replaced, but she'd left the diaper bag on a chair over there.

The family table was decorated with an elaborate centerpiece of a gorgeous castle, and as they settled in, more family members arrived.

Amanda scanned the gathering for Dalhu, who had gone to help Soraya and her sisters carry things to the buffet table and was missing in action.

When she saw him walking toward them, she smiled and waved. "Daddy is coming," she told Evie.

"Daddy!" Her daughter wiggled in her arms, demanding to be put down so she could run to him.

He scooped her into his arms and twirled her around, eliciting happy squeals.

"I hate it when they do that," Syssi said. "It's so dangerous."

"It's what daddies are for," Kian said. "We bring fun and excitement."

She glared at him. "I could do with a little less excitement and a little more safety. I will be less worried after the girls turn immortal, but until then, we should be super careful with them."

Kian was about to respond when Esag approached their table with a wooden box. The guy had been in the village for nearly three weeks now, but he still seemed to feel out of place.

"I brought something for the birthday girl." He put the box on the table in front of Evie. "Open it up and see what's inside."

The lid of the box had a small handle and no latch, and when Evie leaned forward and lifted the lid, Amanda realized that it had a magnetic closure instead of the customary latch that would have been difficult for a little girl to open.

"Dollies!" Evie breathed with excitement, and she pulled out the first one.

The figurine was no more than three inches tall and carved with exquisite detail, and so were the others she took out and carefully put on the table. There was a king with an elaborate crown, a queen in a ball gown, a princess who looked remarkably like Evie, and three courtiers in period dress.

"Oh, Esag, these are incredible," Amanda said. "A whole royal family for Evie to play with. I can see her spending hours role-playing with these. Thank you."

"You are welcome," he said with a slight dip of his head. "I used safe paint in case she decides to put them in her mouth."

Evie arranged the figurines in a row and then lifted the princess, examining it with serious concentration before attempting to do exactly what Esag had anticipated.

"No, baby," Amanda gently redirected. "We look at figurines. We don't eat them."

Allegra, who had been watching from her chair between Syssi and Kian, looked up at Esag. "I want a royal family, too!"

"Allegra," Syssi chided gently. "It's Evie's birthday."

"It's all right," Esag said with a smile. "I missed Allegra's birthday, so I owe her a present. I'll carve one for you as well, little princess. What would you like yours to look like?"

Allegra's eyes went wide at the offer. "Can you make Nana in a white dress?"

"Of course." He turned to Phoenix. "Would you also like a figurine set?"

She shook her head. "I'm not a baby, and I don't play with dolls. I play video games."

Andrew laughed, ruffling his daughter's hair. "She's not even four, but she thinks she's twenty."

"Video games are better than dolls," Phoenix insisted.

"I'd rather you spent more time reading," Nathalie said.

She was such a show-off. So what if Phoenix could already read? Amanda was sure that Allegra and Evie would be reading even sooner.

"I should check on the buffet." Amanda rose to her feet.

She'd entrusted the catering to Soraya and her sisters again, and although she was certain they had everything under control, Amanda had learned from experience that it was always smart to inspect rather than expect.

"Everything smells amazing," she told Soraya as she lifted the lid off one of the chafing dishes. "Thank you for doing this."

"It's our pleasure." Soraya smiled. "Cooking for a happy occasion is good for the soul, and the money you pay us is good for our bank account. We are very grateful for your business."

After thanking them again, Amanda walked over to the family table, lifted the portable microphone, and turned to her guests. She turned the device on, tapped on its side to get everyone's attention, and when all eyes were on her, she waved and smiled.

"Thank you all for coming to celebrate our little princess turning one. You have all been part of her first year, and Evie is blessed to grow up surrounded by so much love and with such a large and caring family, not all related by blood, but family nonetheless. So, thank you for being here and helping us raise our little miracle."

Some oohs and aahs sounded, followed by applause, and Amanda waited until they had finished before continuing. "Soraya and her sisters have prepared a feast, and the buffet table is set and ready, so please, eat, drink, and be merry!"

After more applause, people got up and formed a line at the buffet, and once everyone had returned to their seats with their plates filled to the brim, the conversation around the table resumed between tasty bites.

Amanda felt content as she watched her extended family enjoy themselves. This was what life was about—these moments of joy and connection.

"How are you progressing with Khiann's figurine?" Toven asked Esag.

The guy's expression grew thoughtful. "I've carved an endless parade of figurines depicting Khiann in every possible pose and mood, and they are good but not good enough. I'm still not satisfied. Something's missing, some essential quality I can't quite capture."

"Have you had any prophetic dreams lately?" Amanda asked.

"No, nothing yet."

Annani's face showed a flicker of worry before she smoothed it away. "These things take time."

"Dreams like that are very rare for me," Esag added quickly. "I've only had a few throughout my long life, and none were as vivid as the one about Wonder falling into the chasm while trying to save lives."

"Maybe the guilt you felt about Wonder was what triggered that dream," Syssi suggested. "Strong emotions can be catalysts for psychic experiences."

"Perhaps," Esag agreed, though he looked unconvinced.

"How's Tim doing?" Alena asked. "I understand that he's still in a coma."

Andrew put his fork down and wiped his mouth with a napkin. "He woke up the day after his induction, seemed fine, then slipped into a coma that same evening. Bridget says he's doing great, as evidenced by his growth. He's already gained almost an inch in height, and it has been only a few days."

"That's fast." Orion sounded impressed. "Not that I have anything to compare it to, but it just seems like a lot for a short time."

"Everything about his transition is unusual," Andrew said. "But then, no two transitions are alike. Everyone rewrites the rules."

Kian reached for his glass of water. "I feel guilty for putting off Tim's induction for so long. I didn't really believe he could be a Dormant."

"We were all skeptical." Syssi placed a hand on his arm. "Tim's talent was extraordinary, but there were no other indications."

Amanda was about to say that they had discriminated against Tim because of his prickly personality, when Okidu walked up to her, wearing the period costume she'd ordered for him. He was dressed as an eighteenth-century French servant, complete with a powdered wig and a pair of silk breeches.

"*Madame*," he said with a perfect bow. "The tea service is ready for the *mesdemoiselles*."

Amanda clapped her hands. "Right on time. We are done eating, and now it's time for tea and desserts."

She gathered Evie from Dalhu's lap and led a procession of little girls to the raised platform she'd had constructed for the event. A child-sized table was set with delicate china and cookies shaped like crowns. Each place setting had a name card in elaborate script.

"This is adorable." Syssi helped Allegra into her chair. "It's such a great idea."

"I aim to please." Amanda settled Evie into the ornate chair at the head of the table. "Okidu will be serving you, *mesdemoiselles*. Remember to say please and thank you."

Okidu floated around the table, pouring apple juice from a silver teapot into tiny cups. The girls were enchanted, even

Phoenix forgetting her mature pretensions in the face of such magical treatment.

"And now the cake!" Amanda announced as Gerard appeared with Laleh and Donya as his assistants.

The creation that was carried out drew gasps from children and adults alike. Three tiers of pink and white fondant roses supported a miniature castle, complete with turrets and flags. But the crowning glory was the princess doll on top, her dress made of spun sugar and her tiny tiara actually sparkling with edible glitter.

"Pwiness!" Evie exclaimed, reaching for the doll.

"First, we sing." Amanda lit the single candle. "Everyone!"

Voices rose in harmony, singing the birthday song, while Evie bounced in her chair with excitement. When they reached the end, Amanda and Dalhu helped their daughter blow out the candle, earning a round of applause.

"Do you want to take the princess off so we can cut the cake?" Amanda asked.

Evie carefully extracted the doll, examining it with wonder before turning in her chair and offering it to Allegra.

"For me?" Allegra asked, eyes wide.

"Pwiness!" Evie insisted, pushing the doll toward her cousin.

Amanda's heart melted. Her baby, only one year old, was already showing such generosity.

Allegra looked torn, clearly wanting the doll but understanding it wasn't hers. "You should keep her, Evie. She's yours."

But Evie was insistent, practically climbing out of her chair to give Allegra the doll. Finally, Allegra accepted, but immediately got up and wrapped Evie in a careful hug.

"Thank you, Evie."

"She gets her generosity from her mother," Dalhu said quietly beside her.

Amanda snorted. "Her mother would have kept the doll."

As Gerard began cutting the cake and serving generous slices to the increasingly sugar-high children, Amanda looked around at her family, and her eyes misted with tears. Her mother was holding court at the main table, her brother and his mate were watching their daughter with such pride, her sister with her baby boy, and the rest of her extended family, all here to celebrate this milestone.

"Mommy!" Evie called, now thoroughly covered in frosting. "Cake!"

"Yes, baby," Amanda laughed, grabbing more wet wipes. "Lots and lots of cake."

This was what she'd wanted when she'd planned this party. Not just the decorations or the fancy dresses or even the cake, though those were all wonderful. She'd wanted to give her daughter a memory of being surrounded by love, of being celebrated and cherished by a community that would always be there for her.

Her baby was one year old, healthy, happy, and loved.

Everything else was just icing on the cake.

24

TAMIRA

Consciousness returned slowly, like silk scarves being drawn across her awareness one by one. First came the warmth of Elias's body pressed against her back, then the steady rhythm of his breathing against her neck, and finally the weight of his arm draped across her waist.

Seven mornings of waking like this, and still Tamira's heart stuttered at the reality of it.

A week.

How had it only been a week since that first night when he'd carried her to this very bed and proceeded to worship her body with a devotion that still made her breath catch?

It felt both like yesterday and like a lifetime.

Time had taken on a strange quality since Elias had entered her world, each moment stretching and contracting unpredictably.

Tamira kept her breathing even, not wanting to wake him yet. These quiet moments before he stirred had become precious, a chance to simply exist in the bubble of contentment they'd created. Outside this room, the harem continued its eternal rhythms. But here, wrapped in Elias's arms, she could pretend they were somewhere else.

Somewhere free.

She felt the subtle change in his breathing that meant he was awake, and then his arm tightened around her, as if to make sure that she was still there, that she hadn't been a dream.

He'd told her that just the day before.

"Good morning," he murmured, pressing a kiss to the spot where her neck met her shoulder.

A shiver ran through her. "Is it morning already? I never can tell when the drapes are closed."

Outside, the courtyard illumination changed according to the time of day, creating the illusion of the passing of time.

"Your body knows." His hand splayed across her stomach, thumb stroking her skin. "Don't you have a clock somewhere in here?"

"I prefer your method of timekeeping." She turned in his arms, wanting to see his face. "Tell me, do all shamans have special training in reading the body's rhythms?"

His eyes crinkled with amusement. "It's a professional secret known only to shamans."

There it was again—the deflection whenever she probed too close to anything real about his background. She'd grown used to it over the past week, though it still stung.

Tamira knew he'd traveled extensively, that he spoke at least eight languages fluently, that he could discuss obscure philosophical texts as easily as modern science. But of his family, his homeland, his journey to becoming what he was? Nothing.

"What are you thinking about so hard?" He traced a finger along her jawline. "I can practically hear the gears in your head turning."

"I'm trying to solve a puzzle named Elias."

"Why? I'm much more interesting when I am being mysterious." He leaned in to kiss her, a clear attempt at distraction.

She allowed it, melting into the familiar heat of his mouth on hers. He knew exactly how to angle his head, how much pressure to use, when to tease with his tongue, and when to take. The intimacy between them was growing too fast, too much for the short time they'd been together, and yet it felt like coming home.

Like it was meant to be.

But it couldn't be. She was immortal, he was human, and anything they had could only be a fleeting moment in her never-ending life.

His hands began their morning exploration of her body, and she marveled again at how he seemed to have memorized every sensitive spot, every touch that made her gasp. No fumbling and no awkward moments. From that first night, he'd handled her body like he'd been studying her for years.

"Elias," she breathed as he moved down her throat, marking a path she knew by heart now.

"Shh," he murmured against her skin. "Let me."

She understood what he meant. Let him lead. Let him worship. Let him avoid conversation by using his mouth for other purposes. She should protest, should demand to take over, but the truth was that she loved this—loved being the sole focus of his attention, loved the way he seemed to derive as much pleasure from giving as receiving.

By the time he entered her with one smooth thrust, Tamira had abandoned any pretense of thought. This was what he did to her, what he'd been doing all week—reducing her from an old, cynical immortal to a woman drunk on passion.

They moved together in a perfectly synchronized dance.

In five thousand years, through countless lovers, she'd never found a partner who completed her so perfectly. His stamina equaled hers, never flagging when she needed more, never pushing when she needed gentleness. Last night they'd made love twice before dinner and once after, and he'd been as eager the third time as the first.

It wasn't normal for a human. She'd had enough human lovers to know that for a fact. Even the young, most virile human males needed time to recover. But not Elias.

He shifted angles, hitting that perfect spot inside her, and all coherent thought scattered like dust in the wind. Her climax built like a gathering storm, inevitable and all-consuming. When it crested, she cried out his name and felt him follow, his release triggering aftershocks through her body.

If only he had fangs and venom, the experience would be complete, but she wasn't greedy, and she thanked the Fates for giving her Elias even if she could enjoy him only for a few decades, and even though he could never give her the venom bite.

Afterward, they lay tangled in each other's arms, breathing hard, their skin cooling in the climate-controlled air. This was usually when he'd start to pull away, some obligation, real or manufactured, calling to him.

She waited for it, counting heartbeats.

"I wish I could stay here all day," he said right on cue.

"Then stay."

"You know I can't. I need to tend to my medicine garden."

"Heaven forbid your plants should suffer for want of their devoted gardener." She tried to keep her tone light despite the disappointment, but she couldn't keep out the sarcasm.

He pressed a kiss to her forehead before extracting himself from her embrace. "The plants are delicate in these early stages, and the monsoon rains are too much irrigation. I need to watch the new batch, especially the feverfew and goldenseal I just got from the mainland. If they take root, I'll be able to expand my healing repertoire significantly."

She watched him pad naked to the bathroom, cataloging the lean strength of his body.

When he emerged a few minutes later, she sat up against the pillows, sheet pooled at her waist. His eyes darkened as they traveled over her exposed breasts, but he began dressing as he did every morning.

"You could at least pretend to be reluctant to leave," she said.

He paused buttoning his shirt. "I am reluctant, but I have duties to perform. As long as the lord of this place doesn't provide the harem with a proper physician, I'm all these people have, and all I know are medicinal herbs. I don't even know the names of the pharmaceuticals in the clinic or what they do, but I can read the dates, and I know that most of them are expired. Does that make saying goodbye to me easier this morning?"

"No," she admitted. "But it soothes my ego."

He crossed to the bed and cupped her face in his hands, kissing her deeply. "Your ego needs no soothing. You know exactly what you do to me. If I had my way, I'd never leave this bed."

"Pretty words," she murmured against his lips. "But you always leave anyway."

"Duty before pleasure." He straightened, resuming his dressing. "A harsh master, but one I can't ignore."

There it was again—that weight he carried, that sense of obligation to people no one had put him in charge of but whom he cared for nonetheless.

She could remind him that his main task was to keep her pleased and perhaps help her conceive, but she didn't like to be reminded that she was the property of Navuh and obligated to do anything and everything he demanded of her. Reminding Elias that he was in the same position would be cruel.

He'd chosen to help the humans in the harem, to serve as their temporary healer until a proper physician was found. It made him feel needed, even vital, and that was crucial for his well-being.

Tamira wished she had something she could offer, but her area of expertise was languages. Even though she could potentially teach the harem children, the sad reality was that it would be useless. They were never leaving this place, and they would never find any use for those languages, so why bother?

"Will I see you at lunch?" she asked.

"I'll try. But you know how erratic the day can be. Lord Navuh might summon me for another session, and he doesn't follow a predictable schedule."

He still hadn't told her what he and Navuh had discussed during those sessions, and she figured out that he couldn't. That didn't stop her from speculating, though. Advice? Treating some mental malady?

Immortals didn't get sick, but emotional turmoil could cause headaches, and Navuh could certainly use help with his paranoia and anger issues.

She watched Elias finish dressing. Such mundane actions, but she still committed every detail to memory. The way he always put on his left shoe first. How he patted his pockets in the same sequence each morning—left front, right front, back left, back right. The way he smoothed back his hair, though it would be mussed again within minutes of working in the humidity of the garden.

"What?" he asked, catching her stare.

"Just watching. Storing up memories."

A shadow crossed his face. "I'm not going anywhere, Tamira. You know that."

"Perhaps. The Fates might still surprise us."

He smiled. "Didn't peg you as an optimist."

"I'm not. I'm a pessimist. My life experience has taught me that expecting bad things to happen is more realistic than hoping for miracles."

He looked like he wanted to say more, but after a moment, he simply nodded and headed for the door. At the threshold, he paused and turned back to face her. "This week has been the best of my life. I just wanted you to know in case of a disaster striking and ending us before I have a chance to tell you that."

He was mocking her, and she lifted a pillow to throw at him, but he was out the door faster than should have been possible. She was left alone with the echo of words that she wasn't sure had been a tease or a goodbye.

She rose and made her way to the bathroom, running through her morning routine while her mind replayed countless moments with Elias, and a collection of inconsistencies that refused to form a coherent picture.

His hands, for instance. She'd watched him work with thorny plants, seen the inevitable cuts and scratches. But by the next morning, his skin was always unmarked. She'd tested it two days ago, running her fingers over where she'd seen a particularly deep gash. Nothing. Not even a faint line.

He'd said that he had developed a special salve that expedited healing, but until she saw a human healing as quickly with its help, she would remain doubtful.

Then there was his stamina—not just sexual, though that was remarkable enough. Yesterday they'd gone to the pool and when they'd swum laps, she'd pushed the pace, testing him. He'd claimed exhaustion when they'd finished, but his breathing had been barely elevated.

Perhaps the herbs he was cultivating provided uncommon benefits. Perhaps his shamanic knowledge included secrets such as the rapid healing of wounds and even the prolongation of life.

After all, he sounded much older than he looked, both in manners and in knowledge.

The salve he'd created for Rolenna worked better than any lotion their previous physician had prescribed, so there was that.

Elias's night vision was exceptional. She'd tested that too, eliminating all light in her room, and he had still navigated the familiar space without hesitation, finding her in the bed as easily as if it were full daylight. When she'd commented, he'd laughed and said that the glow in her eyes was what he'd navigated by.

A plausible explanation.

The languages, though, were what puzzled her the most. His fluency made sense for someone who'd traveled extensively, but last night, he'd corrected her pronunciation of an ancient word not in modern Sanskrit, but the archaic form that hadn't been spoken for over a thousand years. When she'd pressed, he'd claimed he'd studied with an old teacher who was a purist about such things.

Always an explanation. Always plausible. Never quite satisfying.

TAMIRA

T he dining room was half full when Tamira arrived, and several of her usual companions were already gathered. Tony sat with Tula, the two of them engaged in an intense discussion about the genetics of offspring and the Russian roulette of what traits children inherited from their parents.

Tony had integrated well over the months, providing a fresh perspective and a glimpse into modern science. Still, Tamira thought that he was a little too full of himself, in a typical male fashion, and assumed that the six of them only appeared smart because they had thousands of years to accumulate information.

But Tula liked him, or at least tolerated him, probably wanting some semblance of normalcy in a place that was anything but.

"Good morning, sunshine," Liliat called out. "Although I use the term loosely since none of us has been outside for the past four days. The rains are brutal, and even when it's not raining, it's too hot and humid out there. I don't know how Elias gets out there each day and works in his garden."

"I saw sunshine less than an hour ago." Tamira took her usual seat. "It was radiating from my bed."

Raviki laughed. "My, we're poetic this morning. Your shaman must have hidden talents."

"Oh, his talents aren't hidden," Tamira said, accepting coffee from the serving girl with a nod of thanks. "He displays them quite openly and repeatedly."

"Scandalous," Sarah said with mock severity, though her eyes danced behind her unnecessary glasses. "What would Lord Navuh say?"

"Probably 'Good, maybe she'll finally conceive,'" Beulah said dryly. "Isn't that the point of allowing Elias up here? Fresh breeding stock that happens to be intelligent?"

The reminder sobered Tamira's mood.

Navuh had permitted the exception to his usual rules not out of kindness, concern for their happiness, or even to appease Lady Areana, but because he wanted more sons, and he wanted them to be smart, and none of his so-called concubines had conceived in many years.

"Well, if that's his goal, he chose well," Rolenna said. "I've never seen you so glowing, Tamira."

"I caught her humming in the library yesterday," Liliat said conspiratorially. "Humming! Our Ice Queen of Profound Melancholy, reduced to humming like a lovestruck girl."

"I am not an ice queen," Tamira protested. "Nor am I melancholy. And I'm certainly not a lovestruck girl."

She wasn't sure about the last part of her statement. It was hard not to fall for Elias. He was perfect except for lacking immortality, fangs, and venom.

"We all have our ways of coping with this existence," Sarah said sagely. "Yours was to build walls of elegant distance. It's been remarkable watching them crumble over the past week."

Sipping her coffee, Tamira considered Sarah's claim, which seemed to reinforce what Liliat had said before.

Had she really been so cold?

Looking back over recent centuries, she could see their point. She'd retreated into books, maintaining cordial but distant relationships even with her sisters in captivity. It was inevitable that it would happen, especially to a realist who had at some point realized that she would welcome death over this endless, purposeless existence.

If the mythology books she'd read were a true report of the gods' shenanigans, she could understand why they had acted the way they had. They'd been bored, just like she was, and they would have done anything and everything to alleviate that boredom, even if it meant playing with the lives of mortals and making them miserable.

Not that understanding meant she would have done the same. She would never stoop as low as harming others just to entertain herself.

"Elias makes me feel alive. For far too long, I've merely existed."

"That's beautiful," Sarah said. "And terrifying."

"Why terrifying?" Tony asked.

The women exchanged glances. How to explain the mathematics of immortal relationships with mortals without making the only mortal at the table acutely aware of his mortality?

"Because he's human," Tula said quietly. "In fifty years, seventy if he's exceptionally lucky, he'll be gone. Tamira will remain, carrying the memory of these moments of happiness and the pain of their loss."

They'd had this discussion before and would likely have it again. The cruel mathematics of immortality made every human connection an exercise in anticipated grief.

Tamira had sworn off such entanglements, determined to avoid the pain. But then Elias had walked into her life, bringing his careful smiles and hidden depths, and all her resolutions had crumbled like sand.

"Speaking of your shaman," Sarah said, "I've been doing research."

Tamira's attention sharpened. "Oh?"

"I was curious about shamanic practices." Sarah adjusted her glasses in the way she did when preparing to share scholarly insights. "Where did he say he was from?"

"He said he was Armenian," Tamira said.

"Yes, that's what I thought. The Armenian highland has ancient shamanic traditions dating back thousands of years. They still have them to this day, so his calling himself a shaman is not as unusual as I thought."

Tamira thought of her conversations with Elias over the past week while picking at her breakfast. The way he'd discussed historical events with the immediacy of personal experience, then caught himself and added qualifiers like "I've read that" or "historians say." His knowledge of trade routes that hadn't been used in generations, describing them with the detail of someone who'd walked them.

"You're very quiet," Beulah said with her kind voice. "Is something troubling you?"

"No," Tamira said quickly. "I was just thinking about what Sarah said. Maybe I should read up on shamanism. Get some insight."

After breakfast, Tamira made her way to the library. It had become her refuge over the centuries. It was extensive and relatively current if one knew how to navigate the restrictions. Was Navuh even aware of the multitudes of books being delivered regularly to the harem? He must be. Nothing on this island happened without his approval, including the kinds of books that found their way to the library.

There was nothing about politics or current events, and she and the others pieced together information from recent fiction books that mentioned what was going on in the world and reflected how different societies functioned these days. It was fascinating and frustrating at the same time.

She could use her imagination to picture herself living in New York, working in a fashion house or a modeling agency. She was too short to model clothing, but she could be a world-famous actress or a cosmetics model. The obvious problem was that no one knew about immortals in the human world, so if there were any immortals living among the masses, they were hiding their identities and were not allowing themselves to become famous.

Tamira found her usual corner, where her Sanskrit texts waited. But today she bypassed them, moving instead to the section on mythology and folklore. If Elias wouldn't tell her his secrets, perhaps she could puzzle them out herself.

She pulled down volumes on ancient civilizations, hoping to find something about shamanism within them.

"Anything interesting?" Elias said from behind her.

Startled, Tamira nearly dropped the book. "Research," she said, closing the volume perhaps too quickly. "For my trans-lations."

His eyes flicked to the spine, reading the title in Russian without hesitation. "Traditions of the Caucasus helps you with Sanskrit translation?"

Heat rose in her cheeks. "I was taking a break. Comparative mythology interests me."

"I see." He moved around her chair, settling into the one beside it. "And what have you learned?"

There was something in his tone—not quite warning, but close. She met his gaze steadily. "That mythologies and traditions are far more complex than most people realize, and that there is very little mention of shamanism. The only thing I found was a comment about the depth of knowledge and the many years of training required to master it."

"It's a calling, not a skill one learns."

She let it drop, though questions burned on her tongue. "How was your day?"

"One of the servants is pregnant and having difficulties. I prepared some remedies to ease her discomfort."

Always so helpful, always needed. It was part of what drew her to him—that instinct to heal, to ease suffering wherever he found it.

"Are you going to join me for lunch?" she asked. "Or will the pregnant servant require more of your attention?"

He took her hand, threading their fingers together, and for a moment, they sat in silence, surrounded by the ever-present unspoken truths.

"What are we doing, Elias?" she asked softly.

"I don't know," he admitted. "I didn't plan for this to go where it did."

"But here we are."

"Here we are." He brought her hand to his lips, kissing each knuckle with reverence. "I can't seem to stay away from you, no matter how much wisdom might dictate otherwise. I still have so much work today, but I had to take a break and come see you like an addict needing his fix."

"Then sit with me a little bit. Tell me about your travels. Not the big things, not the secrets you guard so carefully. Just the small moments. What was your favorite market? Where did you see the most beautiful sunset? What food made you understand why people call taste a gateway to memory?"

He relaxed in his chair. "There was a market in Samarkand. Not the grand bazaar the tourists visit, but a smaller one in the old quarter. A woman there made these dumplings—manti, she called them. Lamb and onions and spices that I couldn't identify, steamed in a metal contraption that looked like it had been serving the same purpose for centuries."

"When was this?" she asked casually.

His eyes became shuttered like they usually did when he lied to her or told her half-truths. "Years ago. But I'm sure the market is still there. Places like that endure."

Another deflection, but she let it pass, content to listen as he painted pictures with words. A sunrise over Mount Ararat, the sound of evening prayers echoing across Constantinople—he caught himself and said Istanbul. The taste of tea so perfect that it had made him understand why ceremonies had been built around the simple act of steeping leaves in water.

With each story, she felt she understood him better and less. The depth of his experience, the poetry in his observations, the gravity of memory he carried—it all spoke of a life lived fully but alone. Whatever he was, wherever he'd come from, he'd been searching for something. She wondered if he'd found it here, in this underground prison that was her world.

"I love listening to you," she said when he paused. "You make me feel like I've traveled alongside you."

"Maybe someday—" He cut himself off, shaking his head.

"What?" she pressed. "Maybe someday what?"

"Nothing. Foolish thoughts."

"Tell me your foolish thoughts. I'll share mine in return."

He looked at her for a long moment, and she saw the war in his eyes—the desire to trust battling against habits of secrecy that seemed carved into his bones.

"I can imagine showing you the world," he said. "All the places I've been to, seen through your eyes. The way the light would catch in your hair at sunset over the Bosphorus. How you'd laugh at the chaos of a bazaar. The expression on your face while tasting your first real kebab from a street vendor who's been perfecting his recipe for forty years."

Tears pricked her eyes. "That's a beautiful but foolish thought."

"What's yours?"

"Sometimes I imagine waking up beside you somewhere else. A house with a window, the real kind that shows the sky. No guards, no schedules, no one to answer to but us, living an ordinary life."

"Tamira..." His voice sounded rough with emotion.

"I know," she said. "Impossible dreams. But isn't that what makes them precious?"

He stood, and for a moment she thought he would leave. Instead, he pulled her to her feet and into his arms, kissing her with a desperation that made her heart race. She could taste longing on his lips, could feel the barely leashed control in the way his hands gripped her waist.

When they broke apart, he rested his forehead against hers. "You're going to destroy me," he whispered.

"You'll destroy me first," she whispered back.

When he left, she returned to her book, but the words blurred before her eyes.

In just seven days, he'd cracked open the shell she'd built around herself. She felt exposed, vulnerable in a way she hadn't allowed herself to be in centuries. The smart thing would be to rebuild her walls, to treat this as a pleasant interlude and nothing more.

But it seemed like she hadn't been smart after all, and she had been negligent in protecting her heart. It would cost her, she knew that, but it was too late to do anything about it.

26

HILDEGARD

"'The thing about being a bastard is that everyone expects it,'" Hildegard read aloud, adjusting her position in the chair she'd sat in for far too many hours over the past week. "Deliver a cutting remark? That's just Marcus being Marcus. Destroy someone's carefully laid plans with a few well-placed observations? Classic Marcus. Show an ounce of human kindness? Now that throws people off their game.'"

She glanced at Tim's unconscious form, looking for any sign that her reading was getting through. His face remained peaceful, almost serene in a way she'd never seen when he was awake. The perpetual scowl that had carved lines around his mouth had smoothed out, making him look younger, less like a badger ready to attack.

"I thought you'd appreciate this one." She found her place in the book again. "The protagonist is almost as big of an asshole as you are. Almost."

The steady beep of monitors provided a rhythmic backdrop to her reading. Tim's vitals remained strong. His heart rate had stabilized at a steady sixty beats per minute, his blood pressure was perfect, and his oxygen levels were optimal. If she didn't know better, she'd think he was taking a very long nap.

But the physical changes told a different story.

In seven days, Tim had grown almost two inches. His body had lengthened, as if someone was stretching him on a medieval rack, but slowly and carefully, allowing his bones and sinew to adjust. The small belly he'd carried had completely disappeared, his body cannibalizing every spare ounce of fat to fuel the transformation. Even the minimal muscle definition he'd had was gone, leaving him looking gaunt and skeletal.

He was getting all the necessary nutrients through his IV, but at the rate his body was changing, it wasn't enough.

"You're going to hate how skinny you are now," she told him, marking her place in the book with her finger. "All that complaining about being short and pudgy, and now you'll have to complain about being a beanpole instead. Though knowing you, you'll find a way to make that our fault."

The door opened with a soft whoosh, and Bridget entered with her tablet in hand.

Hildegard would never say it to Julian's face, but she was glad his mother had taken over Tim's care. Bridget had significantly more experience than Julian, and Hildegard wanted the best for Tim.

"How's our miracle patient today?" Bridget asked, moving to check the monitors.

"Same as yesterday. And the day before. And the day before that." Hildegard set the book aside. "I'm starting to think that he's doing this on purpose just to be difficult."

Bridget's lips quirked in a smile as she reviewed the read-outs. "Andrew claims that being difficult seems to be Tim's specialty, but he's just another patient to me." She shook her head. "Before Tim, Andrew was the Dormant who gained more inches than anyone else, but I have a feeling that Tim is going to beat him for the record. His growth rates are unprecedented."

"Should we be worried?"

"I don't think so." Bridget moved to Tim's bedside, gently manipulating his arm to test muscle tone. "The fact that his body can do this so fast is an excellent sign. Especially given his poor fitness level." She lifted Tim's arm, showing how thin it had become. "He's using everything available as fuel. Even protein from his own muscles. Not that he had much of that to begin with."

Hildegard studied Tim's transformed features. His face had refined during the transition, cheekbones emerging from what had been a soft roundness, his jaw becoming more defined. He would never be truly handsome, but his new look was compelling.

"He's going to be weak as a kitten when he wakes up."

"Weaker," Bridget said. "He'll need extensive physical therapy just to walk properly. His center of gravity will be completely different, his proprioception shot to hell. It's going to be like learning to use his body all over again."

"He's going to love that," Hildegard said dryly. "Tim's least favorite thing is needing help from other people."

Bridget chuckled. "Maybe it'll teach him some humility."

"We should live so long." Hildegard picked up the water pitcher, refilling the cup she used to keep Tim's lips moist. "Turner went through a long transition as well, and you were much more worried about him than you are about Tim. Why's that?"

Bridget closed her eyes as if the memory of her mate transitioning and almost not making it was still painful to her. "I had good reasons to worry. Turner had cancer prior to his transition. When he began the transition, the cancer was in remission, but I was terrified of it reemerging with a vengeance, propelled by the growth spurt that sometimes occurs. In a healthy Dormant, that growth is seen as a good thing and means the body is working to reach its full potential. But Turner didn't grow any taller, so I had no indication that his body was doing well."

Hildegard nodded. "Every transitioning Dormant has a different story."

"Indeed." The physician cast her an encouraging smile before leaving the room.

Hildegard returned to her reading, but her mind kept wandering. She'd volunteered to supervise Tim day and night because Gertrude had taken Rob to Scotland to meet her mother, and they had no other nurse on staff. Perhaps she should have accepted Ronja's offer to help out for a few hours a day because she was getting too involved. But then Ronja hadn't practiced nursing for decades, and she had no experience with transitioning Dormants.

Hildegard couldn't trust her with Tim's life.

She'd been charmed by him, damn it.

That first day when he'd woken up, all swagger and inappropriate comments despite being weak as a newborn. The way he'd looked at her like she was the most beautiful thing he'd ever seen. The complete lack of filter that should have been offensive but somehow came across as refreshingly honest.

"'Marcus had learned long ago that caring was a weakness,'" she continued reading. "'Let people know what mattered to you, and they'd use it as a weapon. So, he'd built his walls of sarcasm and cutting wit, each cruel observation another brick in the fortress. The problem with fortresses, though, was that they kept you in as effectively as they kept others out.'"

She paused, looking at Tim's peaceful face. "Sound familiar? I bet you and Marcus would be thick as thieves. Or maybe you'd hate each other. Probably both."

The door opened again, and Andrew entered carrying a cardboard carrier with two coffee cups and a white paper bag that smelled of fresh sandwiches, like he'd been doing almost every day after work.

"Good afternoon." He set everything on the small table by her chair. "How's the patient?"

"Still playing Sleeping Beauty." Hildegard accepted the coffee gratefully. "Though at the rate he's growing, he'll be Sleeping Beanstalk by the time he wakes up."

Andrew moved to stand at the foot of Tim's bed, studying the changes. "Fates. He really has grown, hasn't he?"

"Almost two inches, and he's not done yet."

"He's going to be insufferable when he wakes up." Andrew shook his head, but there was fondness in his voice. "Can you imagine how arrogant he'll get?"

Hildegard unwrapped the first sandwich—turkey and avocado, bless Andrew for remembering her favorite. "He'll still want platform shoes to get even taller."

Andrew laughed, nearly choking on his coffee. "Don't let him know I told you this, but he has a pair of boots that have two-inch heels hidden in the sole."

"No!" Hildegard gasped with delight at the gossip. "Really?"

"Really. He thought I wouldn't notice that suddenly the top of his head was reaching my nose and not my chin."

"Did you tease him about it?" she asked.

Andrew affected a horrified expression. "Fates forbid. Do you know what his favorite method of retaliation is?"

"What?" She'd heard about the cartoons from hell, but she wanted to hear it directly from Andrew, who knew Tim well.

"He draws excellent caricatures that are so offensive it's impossible to ever think of his victims as anything other than their caricature. If someone offends him or gets on his bad side, he draws one of the poor sap, makes a hundred copies, and attaches them to every exposed surface in the building. Lately, he also discovered that he could do more damage by sending everyone in the office a memo with the drawing."

Hildegard laughed. "Diabolical."

"I actually like the guy," Andrew admitted after a moment. "But in very small doses. He's brutally, unnecessarily, and often cruelly direct but honest. You always know where you stand with Tim. There's something refreshing about that."

"Even when you're in his line of fire?"

Andrew shrugged. "Better than people who smile to your face and talk shit behind your back. With Tim, at least the shit-talking is right up front where you can see it coming."

"I suppose that's true."

"It's like...You know when you eat anchovies?"

"That's a weird segue, but okay."

"A little bit of anchovy in a Caesar salad? Perfect. Adds depth, complexity, that umami thing everyone talks about. But eat a whole can of anchovies?" Andrew shuddered. "Too much. Too sharp. Leaves a bad taste that lingers for hours."

"So, Tim is an anchovy?"

"Tim is definitely an anchovy. Good in small doses, adds flavor to the mix, but too much and you need to rinse your mouth out." Andrew finished his coffee and tossed the cup in the receptacle. "Nathalie thinks he just needs someone to see past his defenses."

"Of course, she does. Nathalie thinks everyone is nice if only given a chance."

"Right? Sometimes an asshole is just an asshole."

"People can change," she said. "But then not everyone has to fit the mold."

"True." Andrew's gaze returned to Tim. "Julian thinks he might be close to the source."

"I know," Hildegard said. "It's the speed of his transition, for one thing. But also his talent. Genetics are weird. Bridget said that sometimes genes can skip generations and emerge stronger than ever in a remote descendant."

"Makes sense. Tim's probably the descendant of some artistic god who decided to try their luck with humans thousands of years ago. The genes diluted over time until they were barely there, then *bam*—full expression in one cranky artist who uses his divine gift to draw unflattering sketches of his coworkers."

"The Fates have a sense of humor," Hildegard said.

Andrew nodded, then glanced at his watch. "I should head home. Nathalie is waiting with dinner for me."

"Then go and give her my regards." She waved her hand at the door. "Thanks for the sandwiches and the coffee."

"My pleasure. It's the least I can do." Andrew walked out the door and closed it behind him.

Hildegard tidied up the remnants of her meal, checked Tim's IV line and his catheter, and adjusted his blankets. All the small tasks that made her feel useful when really all she could do was wait.

"Andrew likes you," she told Tim. "He thinks that you're an anchovy. I'm not sure if that's a compliment or an insult."

She picked up the book again but didn't start reading immediately. Instead, she studied Tim's transformed face, trying to reconcile the man she'd met a week ago with whatever he was becoming.

"You know what I think?" she said. "I think you're scared. All that snark, all those cutting remarks—it's just armor. Keep people at arm's length so they can't hurt you. Classic defense mechanism."

Tim, predictably, didn't respond.

"The thing is, armor that thick? It doesn't just keep pain out. It keeps everything out. Joy, connection, love. All the good stuff that makes immortality bearable."

She thought about her own long life, the centuries of experiences, both bitter and sweet. The lovers she'd had and lost, the friends who'd drifted away, the countless small heartbreaks that accumulated like sediment over time. It would have been easier to build walls, to become cynical and closed off.

But then she would have missed out on so much fun.

"When you wake up, you're going to have a choice. You can keep up the act in a taller body, or you can try to smooth out the edges. Don't lose your snark because that will just make you boring but try not to insult people as much or make unreasonable demands just to humiliate others when you have power over them. That's just mean."

She opened the book again, finding her place. "But first, you have to wake up. So, I'm going to keep reading about Marcus the Magnificent Bastard, and you're going to lie there growing like a weed, and eventually your body will decide it's done with whatever the hell it's doing."

27

ELUHEED

T he sharp knock on the door came as Eluheed was preparing to join Tamira for dinner. He knew that knock, the knocker, and the summons that it carried.

Lord Navuh required his attendance.

The timing was odd, though. The lord dined with Lady Areana, and it probably coincided with dinner on the second level, even though the first level had its own staff with its own chef.

"The lord wants to see you," Arnav said.

"Isn't he dining with Lady Areana?" Eluheed asked as he closed the door behind him.

Arnav shrugged. "I don't ask questions. I just do what I'm told. If you're smart, you will do the same."

"Thanks for the advice." Eluheed cast him a smile even though all previous attempts to befriend the guy had failed.

He needed information, mainly on how Navuh was traveling between his residence in the harem and his house on the other side of the island. He couldn't traverse the distance on foot, so he had to use a vehicle, but since no one ever saw him come and go, he must be using a tunnel, and it had to be big enough for a car. Then again, the vehicle didn't need to be a car. Navuh could be using a motorcycle or a scooter.

The image of the scary warlord, who was fond of wearing elaborate robes, riding a scooter, was comical, and Eluheed chuckled as he followed Arnav to a staircase that he hadn't even been aware existed instead of using the elevator as they usually did.

"What's funny about using the stairs?" the guy asked.

"I was just thinking about something I heard. But what happened to the elevator?"

"Nothing." Arnav grimaced. "Sabina told me that I need to get in shape and that I need to use the stairs more."

She had a point.

Funny how he hadn't known where the staircase was located until now or that the harem even had one. The builders of this place hadn't needed to abide by any building codes, so even though it was unsafe to have a seven-floor structure without a staircase, he'd assumed that Navuh just hadn't wanted one included.

It would have been so interesting to peek into the warlord's mind and find out all of his secrets, but Eluheed did not possess that particular ability. Some of the shamans back home could do that, and there had been one who could even compel like Navuh did, but Eluheed's one questionable gift was visions of personal connections. He couldn't even foresee disasters, or he would have known to move his treasure to a safer location before the mountain had erupted and buried it under tons of rock.

That was why that vision he'd had about the fire and smoke had struck him as so odd, and he'd interpreted it as an allegory for something else.

Arnav knocked once, waited for the barked command to enter, then opened the door and stepped aside. Eluheed entered to find Navuh pacing behind his massive desk, the restless energy radiating from him immediately setting off alarm bells.

Something had agitated the warlord. In Eluheed's experience, an agitated Navuh was unpredictable and dangerous.

"My lord." He bowed deeply.

"Sit." The command was sharp.

Eluheed sat, keeping his posture relaxed despite tension threatening to lock his muscles.

Navuh continued pacing for another moment before finally settling into his throne-like chair. His presence filled the space like poisonous smoke.

"How are you enjoying my generosity?" the lord asked, his tone deceptively casual.

The question seemed routine enough, but Eluheed knew better. Navuh did not engage in small talk. The lord knew that Tamira had claimed him. She hadn't been subtle about her interest, and privacy in the harem was an illusion.

"My lord, your generosity knows no bounds," Eluheed said, infusing his voice with appropriate deference and gratitude. "I'm thankful for the chance to serve Lady Tamira. She is exquisite."

Navuh leaned back, dark eyes studying him with the intensity of a predator evaluating prey. "And how exactly do you serve her?"

Did he want details of their lovemaking?

"I'm delighted to fulfill Lady Tamira's every wish of me. She is beautiful beyond words, intelligent, and kind. Every moment in her presence is a precious gift."

"Since you spend every night in her bed, you have a treasure trove of those precious moments."

Where was he going with this?

Despite Tamira's assurance that there were no surveillance devices in her rooms, the lord probably knew how many times they'd made love, in what positions, and what words they'd whispered in the dark. The thought made Eluheed's skin crawl, but he kept his expression appropriately embarrassed rather than disgusted.

"Lady Tamira has been generous with her affections," he said, ducking his head as if overwhelmed. "I am a fortunate man."

"She seems quite taken with you," Navuh observed, and there was something dangerous in the silky tone.

Instinctively, Eluheed knew that he shouldn't let Navuh even guess the depth of their connection, but how was he going to deflect the lord's questions without seeming to do so? How was he going to minimize what was between him and Tamira without insulting her or implying she had poor taste?

"I am merely a novelty, my lord," he said. "Different. I know that her interest will wane once the newness fades. It always does."

"Did she tell you that?" Navuh's fingers drummed against the desk.

"No, but I am a realist, my lord. I am a simple man with some shamanic knowledge that she finds fascinating. Lady Tamira is extraordinary. Once she has exhausted my limited conversational repertoire and satisfied her curiosity, she will move on to a new companion."

"Hmm." Navuh was silent for a long moment, and Eluheed resisted the urge to fill it with nervous chatter. "Tula has claimed the American, but I know she doesn't love him. She is just guarding her toy and doesn't want anyone else to play with him. What do you and Tamira talk about?"

Another test. Navuh undoubtedly knew every word spoken in the dining room, probably had recordings of their more public exchanges. But did he have the time or inclination to listen to hours of philosophical debate and literary analysis? More likely he wanted a summary, wanted to know if anything subversive was being discussed.

"Philosophy, mostly," Eluheed said. "Lady Tamira is remarkably well read. She challenges my understanding of various schools of thought. We debate the nature of consciousness, the role of suffering in spiritual development, and the intersection of science and mysticism."

"How intellectual," Navuh said dryly.

"Also poetry," Eluheed continued. "She has introduced me to works I'd never encountered. Her translation work is fascinating—the nuances of meaning that can be lost or transformed between languages. And books, of course. The ladies' literary discussions are quite enlightening."

"And what else?"

"My lord?"

"What else do you discuss? Surely not every moment is spent in rarified intellectual discourse."

Eluheed allowed a slightly sheepish smile. "No, my lord. We also talk about...more earthly pleasures. The excellent food, the rare wines from the harem's cellar, and other things..."

All true and harmless. He'd carefully avoided any mention of the deeper conversations about loneliness, dreams of freedom, and the growing connection that went far beyond intellectual stimulation or physical pleasure.

"No discussion of the outside world? No curiosity about current events?"

Aha, so that was what Navuh was worried about. He didn't want his concubines to know the state of the world for some reason. It was truly paranoia since they were prisoners of the harem and could change nothing.

"Yes, of course," he said. "Lady Tamira knows I have traveled extensively, so she sometimes asks about places I've been, markets I've visited, and foods I've tried. We don't talk about world politics or international trade because neither of us knows much about these subjects, and besides, those matters are irrelevant to our situation."

"Your situation?" Navuh's eyebrow arched. "You consider yourself part of the harem now?"

Dangerous ground. "I apologize, my lord. I meant only that I understand my place here, and the ladies understand theirs. We exist in the world you have created for us. The outside does not exist in here. It's a distant memory, nothing more."

"Well said." But Navuh's tone suggested he wasn't convinced. "Tell me, shaman—have you had any visions lately? Surely, proximity to my treasures has sharpened your sight."

And there it was. The real reason for this summons. Not Tamira, not their conversations, but Navuh's endless hunger for foreknowledge of threats.

"I must touch you to see, my lord," Eluheed said.

"You have touched them. Did you see anything?"

Eluheed swallowed. "I've only touched Lady Tamira, and she does not know about any plots against you, my lord."

That was true, and Navuh seemed to read the truth in his eyes.

"Let's do this." He extended his hand with the air of someone making a great sacrifice.

As Eluheed took the offered hand between both of his, the lord's fingers were long and cool, and his grip was firm despite how elegant his hand seemed. His hands belonged on a pianist, not a butcher, but then Navuh didn't do the butchering himself. He sent his minions to do his dirty work.

When the vision arrived, it was more violent than usual. Perhaps it was Navuh's agitation, or perhaps the universe had something urgent to communicate. Either way, Eluheed found himself drowning in images of blood and betrayal.

A figure in shadows, the face obscured. The glint of a blade. Poison in a cup. Explosives planted with careful precision. And through it all, a sense of proximity—this wasn't some distant threat, but someone close who was constantly plotting his ruler's demise.

But who? The vision swirled, showing him snippets without context. Someone with access to Navuh. Someone who smiled politely while planning murder.

It wasn't the son from previous visions. This was different, closer, and more dangerous because it came from within Navuh's inner circle. It must be someone who had been away and had recently returned because Eluheed hadn't felt him before.

Releasing Navuh's hand, Eluheed tried to process what he'd seen and how much of it he was going to reveal. If someone managed to kill Navuh, chaos would ensue, and the ladies would be in danger. They were safe as long as Navuh ruled this island with an iron fist.

"What?" Navuh demanded. "What did you see?"

"Danger," Eluheed said, letting his voice shake slightly. "Someone is plotting your death, and he's very close to you. He doesn't have any specific plan, so I don't think it's imminent, but you shouldn't trust any of your generals or advisors."

"Are you sure it's a he and not a she?"

Eluheed frowned. "Do you suspect the ladies? I think that after five thousand years, you should have realized that they pose no threat to you."

Navuh let out a breath. "I suspect everyone, including you, shaman. That's why I'm still here and still holding power." He leaned back in his throne chair. "Who is it then? Can you give me more concrete specifics?"

"I'm sorry, but the vision is clouded," Eluheed said, which was true enough. "I saw a charming smile, but that was all the universe was willing to show me. That and the traitorous thoughts behind that smile. It's someone with access to you. Someone in your inner circle. Someone whose betrayal would actually have a chance of succeeding because you don't suspect him. I mean, beyond the blanket suspicion of everyone."

Navuh rose to his feet and started pacing, his agitation now focused on this new threat. "My commanders? My sons?"

"I don't know. It could have even been a servant," Eluheed said. "A valet, a food server, anyone who knows your routines. Ensure that your food is tested before consuming it. Don't even trust bottled water. I think it is safest for you to take all of your meals in the harem because it's more tightly controlled, and no one can smuggle any poisons there."

It suddenly occurred to him that all those expired medications in the clinic could be used as poison, but they were probably not strong enough to kill an immortal. Eluheed quickly banished the thought from his mind, even though he was effectively shielding from Navuh's mental intrusion.

He could see Navuh's mind working, cataloging everyone who fit that description. The lord's paranoia, always simmering beneath the surface, was now at full boil. Eluheed had planted the seeds of suspicion, which meant increased scrutiny for everyone in Navuh's orbit.

The warlord returned to his chair, his expression thoughtful now rather than agitated. "You've given me much to consider, shaman. And I'm surprised that you are so concerned about my well-being."

There was no point in sugarcoating his motives. "I'm just looking out for my own interests, my lord. You are the protector of the harem. Your replacement might decide to just get rid of everyone in here, including me and the ladies."

"Well reasoned and well said, Shaman." Navuh rewarded him with a rare, genuine smile. "You are a smart man, and you understand that Lady Tamira is not yours. She is mine.

They all are, and I protect what's mine. You are permitted to enjoy her because it pleases her and serves my purposes."

"Of course, my lord. I'm at your service."

"Don't forget that. The moment you cease to be useful, the moment you become more trouble than you're worth..." Navuh smiled, and it was like watching a shark bare its teeth. "Let's just say the ocean is very deep and very unforgiving."

"I understand perfectly, my lord."

"Good." Navuh settled back in his chair. "You're dismissed."

Eluheed rose and bowed deeply. "I remain at your service, my lord."

"Yes," Navuh said. "You do."

2 8

ELUHEED

Navuh had been perfectly clear, and his jab deflated the happy bubble Eluheed had been floating in for the past week.

Perhaps that was the impetus behind Navuh's sudden summons. It wasn't that the lord had had a premonition about someone plotting his death and needed Eluheed to tell him that. The guy probably had many people plotting his demise, starting with his sons and going through his generals, all the way to his servants. He was arrogant, cruel, and his one redeeming quality manifested only in the harem.

Eluheed needed to get his head out of his ass and go back to thinking about ways of escaping this prison. He'd been so focused on Tamira and the unexpected joy of their connection that he'd neglected his primary purpose. The earthquake that had buried his charges hadn't buried his duty. He needed to find a way out, needed to return to Mount Ararat and find a way to recover what he'd lost.

No one talked about it, but somewhere in this maze of luxury there was a secret tunnel that Navuh used to move between the harem, specifically the first level, and his house on the surface. That had to be the explanation for him just appearing in his residence in the harem without going through the gates outside.

No one ever saw him arriving or leaving.

But even if Eluheed found it, how could he leave? Tamira had become everything to him. Essential? The word felt both too much and not enough.

Besides, even if he managed to escape the harem, how was he going to escape the island?

The second level was quiet when he reached it, its residents probably finishing dinner right now. He should join them, but he needed a moment to compose himself, to lock away the turmoil Navuh's threats had stirred up.

In his quarters, Eluheed walked out to the balcony and looked down at the artificial garden below. Beauty masking confinement, an illusion of freedom when every exit was guarded, every movement watched.

Two fences surrounded the harem, guards patrolling between them and beyond them, multiple layers of security between the harem's residents and the outside world.

Only Navuh came and went freely.

If Eluheed could find the tunnel the lord used, then what? Swim off the island? Steal a boat and hope not to get caught before reaching international waters?

It was impossible, but then Eluheed had survived the impossible before.

He'd escaped the annihilation of his people, protected the sacred treasures, and lived for centuries among humans without detection. He could find a way off one island. He had to.

He needed to start collecting intel, but not tonight.

Tonight, Navuh would be watching more closely than ever, suspicious of everyone and everything.

A knock at his door interrupted his brooding. "Come in," he called, expecting Arnav to come get him again.

But it was Tamira who entered, resplendent in green silk that made her skin glow. "You missed dinner," she said. "Is everything all right?"

"Lord Navuh required my presence," he said, moving back into the room.

Her expression tightened. "Another consultation?"

He wasn't allowed to tell her about his visions or the real service he was providing to Navuh. The lord had attempted to compel his silence, but even though the compulsion slid off him, he needed to pretend that it had worked.

"Yes."

She studied his face, those impossible eyes seeing too much. "You look unsettled."

Eluheed chuckled. "He's so intense and constantly worried about people betraying him."

"With good reason," she said. "But what does he expect you to consult him on? How to be nicer so his subordinates don't plot his murder?"

It was uncanny how insightful she was, despite being in the harem and having no idea what was going on outside the island.

Eluheed chuckled. "I told him to eat exclusively in the harem because he can trust the food here."

"Good advice, and speaking of food, everyone's still at dinner." She took his hand and tugged him toward the door. "You need to eat."

In the hallway, she linked her arm through his, the gesture both possessive and supportive. "I'm surprised that you are actually helping him."

She didn't need to qualify who 'him' was.

"The devil you know, and all that. We are safe as long as everything stays the same."

She nodded, her intelligent eyes expressing her understanding. "I'm not worried. Someone who has maintained power for so long is not easy to topple. But whatever happens, I want you to know that this week we had was magical. It's worth whatever price either of us might have to pay."

The words sent a chill through him. Did she sense something? Or was it just the fatalism of someone who'd lived long enough to know that happiness was always temporary?

"Don't talk like that."

She squeezed his arm. "I'm not naive, Elias. I know this can't last. Nothing good ever does in this place. But that doesn't diminish what we've shared."

He wanted to tell her she was wrong, that he'd find a way to free them both, but the words would be lies, and he'd told her too many of those already.

So instead, he raised her hand to his lips, pressing a kiss to her knuckles that tried to convey everything he couldn't say. She smiled, sad and beautiful, and he thought his heart might break from the weight of what he couldn't give her.

The dining room welcomed them with warmth and chatter, the other ladies greeting them with smiles.

The conversation resumed, covering similar topics that they had already discussed numerous times.

All of it was so normal, worth preserving even though they were all prisoners in a despot's luxurious dollhouse.

Eluheed ate without tasting, smiled without feeling, and contributed to conversations he'd forget within minutes. All the while, his mind was working on two problems that seemed increasingly impossible to reconcile.

How to escape and complete his duty to his people, and at the same time, free Tamira and take her with him.

The walls were closing in, just as he'd feared. Navuh's suspicion, his own growing attachment, the seeming impossibility of freedom—all of it pressed down like a boot on his neck, gradually cutting off his air supply.

Like his treasures, who were buried beneath millions of tons of rock, waiting for him to free them.

The meal ended, and they returned to Tamira's quarters as had become their custom.

"I wish..." she began, then stopped.

"What?" he prompted. "What do you wish?"

"I wish I believed in happy endings," she said. "Just once, I'd like to see the Fates being kind to people who deserve it."

He pulled her into his arms, pressing his face into her hair and inhaling her scent.

He wished the same thing, had wished it for centuries, but in his experience, fate was neither kind nor cruel.

It was indifferent to human and immortal suffering.

TAMIRA

The tremors struck at precisely two o'clock in the morning. Tamira only knew the time because of the clock on her bedside table. The bed shook beneath her and Elias, a rolling motion that made the crystal perfume bottles on her vanity clink together like wind chimes.

Elias tensed beside her, his arm tightening instinctively around her waist. "What was that?"

"Just a tremor." Tamira placed a calming hand on his chest, feeling his heart racing beneath her palm. "We get them occasionally. The island supposedly sits on a volcanic foundation."

The heartbeat under her hand sped up. "Volcanic?" His voice carried a note of alarm.

"Dormant," she assured him, though in truth she didn't know if that was accurate. The island had been their home for less than a century, and Lord Navuh controlled information as tightly as he controlled everything else. "We've had tremors for as long as I've been here, which is almost a hundred years. The structure was built to withstand them."

The shaking subsided, leaving behind an eerie stillness. In the darkness, she could feel Elias's breath against her neck, still quick with adrenaline.

"We should go aboveground until we are sure this is over," he said. "Being trapped in an underground structure during an earthquake isn't a good idea."

"We're not trapped, and it's raining outside. I don't want to get wet."

He pulled her closer, pressing a kiss to her shoulder. "Do you have an umbrella?"

"Have you ever tried to stay dry under an umbrella in a monsoon torrent?" She turned in his arms to face him, the inner light from her immortal eyes illuminating his features. "I'm surprised that a little tremor so easily rattles you. I thought shamans were supposed to be one with the earth and all that."

"Even shamans prefer when the earth stays still," he said dryly. "Especially when they're in an underground structure and there are people on all of its seven levels."

"Actually, there are eight levels, but no one lives in the lowest one." She feathered her fingers over his chest, avoiding the mysterious mark that he still wouldn't tell her about. "There are seven residential levels in the pyramid, but the mechanical systems are located in the level below. There might even be more levels that we don't know about.

I'm surprised that you haven't heard the noise when you were down on Level Seven."

"I didn't notice. I probably thought that the noises were coming from elsewhere on Level Seven. It's a big space." His voice carried that careful neutrality she'd come to recognize —the tone he used when filing away information. "What else is housed below it?"

"As far as I know, all the mechanical systems. Water pumps, electrical generators, and the climate control that keeps us from roasting in this tropical heat. Also, storage, I believe, though I've never been down there. Only the maintenance crew and guards are allowed down there."

"Seems like a security risk, having all your critical systems in one place."

She laughed softly. "Everything about this place is a security risk. We have no choice but to believe that Lord Navuh wouldn't endanger us all by allowing subpar planning or construction. After all, Areana lives here and so does he, at least during the night."

"I don't know how this man finds love for his mate in his black heart."

She shrugged. "There is good and bad in everyone, and once they pass behind the veil, their good and bad deeds are weighed. Lord Navuh will need to do a lot of groveling when he gets there."

His thumb stroked along her cheekbone. "How do you do it? Live with such...acceptance?"

"What's the alternative? Rage against walls that won't break? Plot escapes that will only end in torture and death?" She turned her head to kiss his palm. "Eventually, you realize that acceptance is the only path to sanity."

"It's called learned helplessness."

The words stung, perhaps because they were true. "Is that what you think of me? That I'm helpless?"

"No." He shifted, rolling them so he hovered above her, his weight balanced on his forearms. "I think you're surviving the only way you know how. But what if the walls could break? What if escape didn't mean death?"

Sweet, naive Elias with his human lifespan and his belief that things would turn out okay in the end. "Then I'd probably be too institutionalized to leave. This is my world, Elias. It's all I've known for millennia, well, not this location specifically, but the harem structure."

"Where have you lived before?"

"Several locations. The first one was near Baalbek."

He smiled. "That's a much cooler place than this."

"Tell me about it." She pretended to wipe sweat off her forehead. "Am I imagining it, or is it more humid in here tonight?"

They had air-conditioning and dehumidifiers, and the climate control was usually perfectly balanced; however, this was the wet season, so perhaps some additional calibration was needed.

"I don't feel it." He got that mischievous gleam in his eyes. "Maybe you are just hot and bothered and need me to do something about it."

"How did you guess?"

"I'm perceptive like that." He kissed her, deep and searching, as if he could pour all his hope and determination into her through that connection. "My goddess," he whispered as his hands moved over her body with the reverence of a worshipper at an altar, each touch designed to drive thought from her mind and replace it with sensation.

She arched beneath him as he traced the curve of her hip, the dip of her waist, the sensitive skin where her neck met her shoulder. He knew her body so well by now, had mapped every responsive zone with the dedication of a cartographer charting new territory. When his lips followed the path his hands had taken, she gasped, fingers tangling in his hair.

"You're so breathtakingly beautiful," he murmured against her skin. "So strong. You deserve so much more than this."

"I have you," she said, the words escaping before she could stop them. "For now, that's enough."

He lifted his head to look at her, his gaze intense in the darkness. "Is it?"

Rather than answer, she pulled him down for another kiss. Some facts were too dangerous to speak aloud, even in the supposed privacy of her chambers. The fact that he'd awakened something in her she'd thought long dead. The fact that she was falling in love with him despite every rational argument against it. The fact that when he inevitably left—through death or escape or simple loss of interest—it would destroy something fundamental inside her.

His body joined with hers in that perfect synchronization they'd found from the very beginning, and coherent thought scattered like startled butterflies. This was what she needed —this connection that transcended words and fears and her reality. In these moments, she could pretend they were somewhere else. Not in an underground harem on a private island, but in a home of their own choosing, free to love without consequence or fear.

He moved within her with passionate tenderness, each thrust a promise he couldn't keep, each kiss a vow that would inevitably be broken. She met him stroke for stroke, trying to tell him with her body what she couldn't say with words.

When release came, she cried out his name and felt him shudder above her. For a moment, they existed outside of time, outside of the prison that held them, outside of every-thing but this perfect moment.

Reality returned slowly, seeping back like water through cracks in a dam. His weight pressed her into the mattress. The humid air clung to their sweat-dampened skin, heavier than usual, carrying the green scent of growing things and something else—a mineral tang that seemed out of place.

"You are right. It is more humid than normal," Elias said. "Maybe the dehumidifier stopped working."

"It's monsoon season," she said, though it had also been monsoon season yesterday and the day before, and it hadn't been this humid in her room. The air felt thick, almost oppressive. "The rains have been particularly heavy this year."

He rolled to the side, keeping one arm draped across her stomach. "I noticed. The garden has been challenging to maintain with all the water. I've had to work on the drainage to save my herbs from rotting."

"Perhaps that's affecting things down here as well. All that water has to go somewhere."

"Into the water table, ideally. Though with volcanic rock..." He trailed off, and she could practically hear him thinking. "The geology here must be complex. Volcanic islands often have unusual underground water systems—aquifers trapped between rock layers, underground streams following old lava tubes."

"How do you know so much about geology?"

"I know a lot about many things." He tickled her ribs. "I'm like a sponge. I absorb information. I've traveled through many volcanic regions, like the Caucasus, parts of Turkey, and the Mediterranean islands."

Always an explanation. Always plausible. Never quite satisfying.

"The pyramid must have been a massive undertaking," he said, once again deflecting. "How was it built?"

She allowed the change of subject, too content in the after-glow to pursue his secrets. "I don't know the details. It was already here when we arrived. Navuh built it for us. The design is ingenious, really. Each level is smaller than the one below. Natural light wells hidden in the structure bring sunlight down to the first level during the day."

"But not to the lower levels."

"No. Those of us on the second level have windows to the interior garden, but that's artificial light. The servants below us have no windows at all. Just endless artificial day and night, regulated by timers and routines."

"I know. I lived among them for eighteen months, and I still work down there during the day."

"Humans are remarkably adaptable," she said. "I suppose we're all proof of that. We adapt to our cages, make them comfortable, pretend the bars are there for our protection rather than our confinement."

"Some cages are harder to see than others," he said quietly.

Before she could ask what he meant, another tremor rolled through the structure. This one was gentler, more of a shiver than a shake, an aftershock, but something about it felt off.

"That didn't feel like an earthquake," Elias said, sitting up.

She sat up beside him, listening intently. The tremor faded, but in its wake came something else—a sound so low it was more felt than heard, like the earth itself groaning.

"The structure is settling, perhaps," she said.

"Concrete and steel shouldn't groan." He swung his legs over the side of the bed, reaching for his clothes. "I should check on things."

"Check on what? And how? You can't just go wandering the halls in the middle of the night. The guards—"

"Won't stop me from checking on the servants," he said, pulling on his pants.

She knew she should stop him, but he seemed so determined that she knew it would be a losing battle.

"Be careful," she said instead.

He leaned over to kiss her, just a quick press of lips. "I'm always careful. Try to get back to sleep. I'll be back soon."

She listened to him while he finished dressing and then the soft pad of his feet on the carpet. The door opened and closed with barely a sound. Then she was alone with the oppressive humidity and a growing sense that something was not right.

Sleep seemed impossible, and Tamira lay back against the pillows, staring up at the ceiling and trying to convince herself that her unease was just the aftermath of the earthquake. The island experienced them regularly. The structure had weathered dozens, perhaps hundreds over the years. This was no different.

But her body, ancient and finely tuned to danger after millennia of survival, knew better.

The clock on her bedside table ticked on, marking time and indifferent to her fears. It was three-thirty now. The deepest part of the night, when the walls between the possible and impossible grew thin. When shamans claimed the veil between worlds could be pierced.

Where was Elias? Checking on the servants, as he'd claimed? Or looking for a way to escape? After a week of nights in her bed, she still knew so little about him. The mystery that had initially attracted her now felt like a barrier between them, one that grew higher with each deflection, each half-truth, each careful omission.

Another sound drifted through the walls, so faint she might have imagined it. A sound like running water where there should be none. She sat up again, straining to hear, but it faded before she could identify its source.

The humidity was oppressive by that point, definitely not normal even for monsoon season. The climate control systems, which had functioned flawlessly for decades, were struggling against something beyond their parameters.

She thought of the lowest level, where all those mechanical systems hummed away in the darkness. The pumps and generators, and complex networks of pipes and wires that kept their underground world habitable. What would happen if they failed? How long could they survive without climate control, without fresh air circulation, without the dozens of invisible systems they took for granted?

Stop catastrophizing.

It was just a storm system affecting the equipment. It had happened before, though not recently. The maintenance crew would sort it out, as they always did. By morning, everything would be back to normal.

But what if it wasn't?

The thought wormed its way into her mind and wouldn't let go. What if this was different? What if the tremors had damaged something critical? What if—

The door opened so quietly she almost missed it. Elias slipped back inside, moving with that uncanny silence he possessed.

"What did you find?" she asked.

He came to sit on the bed beside her, and she could feel the tension radiating from him. "Everything seems to be under control, but some of the servants have woken up and they are worried. Also, the humidity is worse in the stairwells. Much worse. Like walking through fog. The dehumidifier must have malfunctioned." He took her hand, his fingers cool against her heated skin. "Something's wrong, Tamira. I can feel it."

"What exactly do you feel?"

"I don't know. But let's be ready to leave on a moment's notice, so keep comfortable clothes nearby."

"Elias, you're scaring me."

"A little fear will keep you safe." He lifted her hand, twisting it so he could kiss her palm. "We should sleep with one eye open."

She laughed. "I don't think I can sleep like that."

He stood to undress again, and she listened to the familiar sounds with new attention. How many more nights would they have like this?

When he slipped back into the bed beside her, she curled against him, seeking comfort in his solid presence. His arms came around her, holding her close, and she felt him press a kiss to the top of her head.

"Try to sleep," he murmured. "I'll keep one eye open for both of us."

As if she could sleep now. She lay in his arms, feeling the steady beat of his heart against her cheek, and tried not to think about the weight of the earth above pressing down on their shelter.

When another tremor came, she wasn't surprised. This one felt sharper, more focused, as if the earth had found what it was looking for and was beginning to probe. The walls creaked in response, a sound she'd never heard before in all her years here.

Elias's arms tightened around her, though he didn't speak. He was awake too, lying in the darkness and waiting for what came next.

NABIN

T he tremor jolted Nabin from his light sleep, years of military training bringing him to alertness before his eyes were fully open. His hand was already reaching for the kukri knife beside his bed when his mind caught up with his body. It was an earthquake, not an attack.

As if anyone would attack the harem, and even if some forces from the outside tried it, the legions of immortal warriors would take care of the invader. One human with a knife was worthless.

Still, he would protect his family if needed because the immortals would just let the humans die. They didn't value human life.

He sat up, listening to the structure settle around him. In his eleven years serving as security chief of the harem, he'd experienced dozens of these tremors. After all, the island sat on volcanic rock. But something about this one felt different. The duration, perhaps, or the rolling quality that suggested movement deep below rather than the sharp jolts of tectonic shifts.

His wife turned on her side. "What is it?"

"An earthquake."

"Oh." She turned to her other side and went back to sleep. His woman could sleep through anything.

As his walkie-talkie chimed, he knew it was Hassan before his name lit up the display.

"You felt it," Nabin said into the device.

"I'm already in the control room," Hassan answered, his Pakistani accent thickening with stress. "All systems are showing green, but that was a nasty one. Not big, but stinky. You know what I mean?"

Nabin rolled his eyes. All of Hassan's jokes were fart based.

"We should do a visual inspection. Let's start with Level Five. I don't want to bother the ladies for no reason."

"I'll meet you there in ten minutes."

Nabin dressed quickly in his black tactical pants and the gray shirt bearing the Harem Security insignia. The kukri went into its sheath at his hip. Lord Navuh permitted him this one cultural concession, recognizing perhaps that a Gurkha without his blade was like a bird without wings.

The corridors of Level Six were quiet as he made his way to the service elevator. Hassan was already waiting for him, his toolkit in hand.

"Any reports from the other levels?" Nabin asked as they descended.

"Nothing significant. A few residents woke up, and some items fell off shelves. The usual." Hassan adjusted his glasses, a nervous habit that intensified under stress. "I'm worried because of the duration of that tremor. It lasted nearly forty seconds. Usually, they last half of that."

They emerged onto Level Five, the first of the staff quarters. The hallway stretched before them, fluorescent lights humming steadily. Everything appeared normal—doors closed, no visible cracks in the walls or ceiling. They walked the perimeter systematically, Nabin checking security points while Hassan examined structural elements.

"Remember when we thought this would be temporary?" Hassan said quietly as they completed their circuit. "Fifteen years. Where did the time go?"

Nabin remembered his own recruitment vividly. A decorated Gurkha soldier honorably discharged and struggling to support his elderly parents. The offer had seemed like a gift from the gods—security work for a private employer, pay that would let him hire a caretaker for his parents and pay for all their other needs.

He hadn't known that this wasn't a job he would ever leave. The only exits were in boxes or weighted bags destined for the ocean floor.

"At least we were able to support our families," Nabin said. "That's more than most can say."

They'd had this conversation before, in various forms. It was part of their ritual, like checking the walls for cracks—probing old wounds to make sure they hadn't festered.

Nabin had married a sweet servant girl, and he would have been happy if they were allowed to have a child, but they were still waiting for their turn. The harem population was strictly controlled.

Level Six showed similar normalcy. A few residents poked their heads out as they passed, but Nabin waved them back to bed. "Just a routine check. Nothing to worry about."

The lie came easily. In this place, maintaining calm was as much a part of security as walking the hallways and monitoring the cameras.

Level Seven was larger, housing most of the service staff. Here they found the first signs of the tremor's impact—a cracked water pipe dripping steadily onto the floor, some fallen ceiling tiles. Nabin made notes on his tablet while Hassan called for his maintenance crew.

"Should we wake Lord Navuh?" Hassan asked as they approached the access to the service level below.

"Not yet." Nabin punched in his security code. "No point disturbing him or the ladies for minor damage."

They took the emergency stairs that were rarely used. The metal steps echoed under their boots, the sound strangely hollow in the confined space. Emergency lighting cast harsh shadows on the concrete walls.

"I've always hated this place," Hassan muttered. "Feels like descending into a tomb."

Nabin couldn't argue. There was something menacing about Level Eight and moving even deeper underground, away from even the artificial comfort of the residential levels. The air grew cooler and carried a mechanical smell.

As he punched in another code and opened the secured door at the bottom of the stairs, the underbelly of the pyramid opened before them like an industrial cathedral. The ceiling soared twenty feet high, necessary to accommodate the massive machinery that kept their underground world functioning. Water pumps the size of tanks hummed steadily. Electrical panels lined one wall, their indicator lights creating a constellation of green and amber. The waste-processing systems occupied their own section, mercifully sealed and sound dampened.

"I'll check the water systems." Hassan walked toward the pumps. "You take electrical?"

Nabin nodded, though his attention was drawn to the far wall and a series of vault doors. Five in total, each secured with electronic locks that responded only to the highest security clearances. In eleven years, he'd never seen them open.

"Still wondering what's in there?" Hassan followed his gaze.

"Aren't you?"

"Self-preservation trumps curiosity, my friend. Some doors are better left closed."

Wise words, but Nabin couldn't help speculating. What was behind those square locker-style doors? Gold? Diamonds? Or something more exotic—the kind of treasures a man like Lord Navuh might accumulate over his never-ending life?

The guards whispered theories when they were a safe distance from the surveillance equipment. Some even claimed to have heard sounds from behind the doors—mechanical noises or sometimes what might have been voices. But guards stationed too long underground often heard things that weren't there.

He forced himself to focus on the electrical panels. All the readings were normal. No tripped breakers, no unusual power draws. The backup generators showed full fuel reserves and recent successful test cycles.

"Nabin." Hassan's voice carried an edge that made him turn. "Come look at this."

The engineer stood by the far wall, his flashlight beam playing across the concrete surface. At first, Nabin saw nothing out of the ordinary. Then Hassan placed his palm against the wall and held it there.

"Feel," he said.

Nabin pressed his hand to the concrete. It was damp. Not wet enough to be visible, but definitely carrying moisture that shouldn't be there.

"When did we last have the dehumidifiers serviced?" he asked.

"Six weeks ago. They are working fine. It's not the dehumidifiers." Hassan moved his flashlight beam slowly across the wall. "There—do you see that?"

Thin lines of mineral deposits traced patterns on the concrete like spider webs. It was the kind of buildup that came from water seeping through microscopic cracks over time.

"How long would this take to form?" Nabin asked.

Hassan knelt, examining the deposits more closely. "Depends on the mineral content of the water and the rate of seepage. It could be months or years. However, what bothers me is that this wall faces the interior of the structure. Any water reaching it would have to come from above or..." He paused, frowning. "Or from below."

"The water table?"

"Possibly. When this place was built, it was supposedly far above the water table, but that can shift. Volcanic activity, changes in rainfall patterns, and underground streams finding new channels." Hassan stood, wiping his hands on his pants. "We should run a full diagnostic. Moisture sensors, structural scans, the works."

Nabin considered their options. A full diagnostic would involve reports, which would mean waking people, potentially alerting Lord Navuh to a problem that might be minor. In his experience, the lord did not appreciate false alarms.

"What's the worst-case scenario?" he asked.

Hassan removed his glasses, cleaning them slowly with a cloth he'd produced from his pocket—another nervous tell. "Worst case? Hydrostatic pressure is building up beneath the foundation. If water finds a weakness, it doesn't knock politely. It comes in hard and fast."

"And best case?"

"Surface water from the monsoons found a new path. It'll dry up when the rains stop." He replaced his glasses. "But the tremor complicates the picture."

They stood in silence, both calculating risks they were tasked with anticipating and diagnosing but not fully empowered to address. The machinery hummed around them, an illusion of normalcy, while the water tried to undermine the building's foundation.

"Let's just keep monitoring the situation," Nabin said. "We will check every two hours, document the changes. If it gets worse, we report to Lord Navuh. If it stays stable, we say nothing and avoid causing unnecessary panic."

Hassan nodded. "Every two hours means no sleep. Oh, well. I'll set up some humidity sensors and strain gauges in key locations."

As they made their way back to the stairs, Nabin took a final glance at the damp wall. The mineral deposits seemed to shimmer malevolently in the fluorescent lighting.

They parted ways at Level Four, Hassan heading to gather monitoring equipment while Nabin made for the security office. He filed a report—minor tremor, minimal damage, all systems operational. The kind of report that would go into the file cabinet and never see the light again.

But he also wrote a private log, documenting in careful detail what they'd found. His military training had taught him the value of accurate records. In his desk drawer, locked away, were eleven years' worth of similar observations. Small anomalies, patterns that might mean nothing or everything.

His desk phone rang. The night watch commander reporting all quiet on the upper levels. Nabin thanked him and hung up, then pulled up the security feeds from Level Eight. The cameras showed the machinery running smoothly, the vault doors undisturbed.

But cameras couldn't capture the moisture in the walls or the weight of water gathering in the darkness below. They couldn't show the hairline cracks spreading through concrete or the way that pressure was conspiring against the human inhabitants of this monstrosity.

ELUHEED

The hum started as a vibration in Eluheed's bones, pulling him from sleep. For a moment, he lay still, trying to identify the source. It wasn't mechanical. It sounded too organic—more like the earth itself was humming a low, thrumming note that resonated through the concrete and steel of their underground world.

Beside him, Tamira slept on, her breath deep and even against his shoulder. He envied her that peace. His long struggle for survival had made him a light sleeper, attuned to any disturbance that might signal danger. And this was wrong.

The sound was felt more than heard, a frequency so low it bypassed the ears and went straight to the gut. He'd experienced something similar once, decades ago, when standing near a glacier that was about to calve. The ice had sung its death song in the same register—too deep for human hearing but impossible for him to ignore.

As he carefully extracted himself from Tamira's embrace, she murmured something in her sleep and turned, pulling his pillow against her chest. The sight filled his heart with an emotion that felt dangerously like love.

He pulled on his pants and shirt, not bothering with shoes. The tile floor was cool against his bare feet as he eased open the door and stepped into the corridor.

He wasn't alone.

Tony stood in his doorway in his boxers and a t-shirt that proclaimed, 'I Put the Pro in Procrastinate.' His usual grin was absent, replaced by a frown.

"Tell me you hear that too," Tony said.

"The hum?" Eluheed moved closer, noting that other doors were cracking open along the corridor. "How long has it been going on?"

"It woke me about five minutes ago. I thought that I was having indigestion or something." Tony stepped fully into the hallway, head tilted as if trying to locate the source. "It's coming from below, right?"

Eluheed nodded.

Tula's door opened and she peered out. "What is that sound?"

"We're trying to figure that out," Tony said, moving to her side. "You okay?"

"No," she said flatly, her hand resting on her midsection. "Something is wrong. I can feel it."

More doors opened. Liliat emerged in a silk robe, followed by Raviki, then Sarah. Within moments, all the ladies were in the corridor, looking troubled.

"It's like the whole building is humming," Rolenna said, pressing a hand to the wall. "I can feel it vibrating."

"Has this happened before?" Eluheed asked, though he suspected he knew the answer.

"No," Beulah said. "Not in all the years we've been here."

The service elevator at the end of the corridor chimed, and they all turned toward it. The doors opened to reveal not the expected security guard or servant, but a group of maintenance workers who barely glanced at the gathered residents before rushing toward the emergency stairs.

"Excuse us," one called over his shoulder, his voice tight with urgency. Tool belts clanked against their legs as they disappeared through the stairwell door. "We were told not to use the elevators."

"Should we be worried?" Rolenna asked, though the answer seemed obvious.

The hum deepened, if that was possible, and Eluheed felt his teeth ache with the vibration. Whatever was causing it was getting stronger, not weaker. He thought of the tremors from earlier, the unusual humidity, and now this. The pieces of the puzzle were starting to form a disturbing picture.

"We should get dressed," Tamira said from behind him. He turned to find her in the doorway of her room, wrapped in a sheet and looking like a goddess. "We should get up to the surface before this entire structure collapses on us."

"It's not going to collapse," Liliat said. "But it's still a good idea to get dressed and be ready to evacuate. Just out of abundance of caution."

The ladies dispersed to their rooms, but Tony lingered, his eyes looking frantic. "How bad is it?" he asked Eluheed. "And don't bullshit me."

Eluheed met his gaze. "Get dressed. Help Tula gather anything she can't bear to lose."

Tony's eyes widened. "That bad?"

"I hope not. But hope is a poor strategy."

"Shit." Tony ran a hand through his already wild hair. "She's going to freak."

"Then help her," Eluheed said.

He returned to Tamira's room to find her already pulling clothes from her wardrobe. She'd wisely chosen practical items—pants instead of her usual flowing dresses, flat shoes instead of delicate sandals.

"You're frightened," she said. It wasn't a question.

"Concerned," he corrected, though it was a weak distinction.

"Water," she said, demonstrating that quick intelligence he admired. "Water has found its way in. The tremor weakened the structure, and rainwater is seeping in from above."

That was one option. "We should pack a bag. Just in case."

She gathered the essentials, and he helped. A change of clothes, her journal, a small wooden box she handled with particular care. He added a flashlight from her drawer and some fruit from the bowl on her table.

"My books," she said, looking at the shelves with distress in her eyes.

"Will be here when we return," he said, hating the lie even as he spoke it.

A knock interrupted them. "It's Liliat. We're gathering in the common room."

"We'll be right there," Tamira said.

They emerged to find some of the others dressed and waiting. Even in crisis they looked elegant, dressed in silk blouses and tailored pants, as if they were heading to a casual luncheon rather than responding to an emergency. Only the tension in their faces betrayed their fear.

"Has anyone alerted Lady Areana?" Sarah asked.

"I'm sure she's aware," Beulah said. "At this point, Lord Navuh will have been informed, and she's with him."

They moved as a group toward the common room at the center of their level. The hum followed them, vibrating through the walls and floor with increasing intensity. The overhead lights flickered once, twice, then steadied.

"That's not encouraging," Tony muttered.

The common room was their usual gathering space—comfortable chairs, low tables, shelves lined with games and books for communal use. Someone had thought to start the coffee maker, and the mundane smell of brewing coffee in the midst of a crisis was oddly comforting.

"Should we try to contact someone?" Raviki asked. "The security office? The kitchen staff below?"

"The phones aren't working," Liliat reported, hanging up a handset. "Internal communications seem to be down."

Another flicker of the lights, longer this time. In the moment of darkness, the hum seemed to intensify, feeling like depth pressure against Eluheed's eardrums.

"Elias," Tamira said quietly, moving close to him. "What aren't you telling me?"

"I have a bad feeling," he said. "I finally realized where I heard that hum before. That's the sound the earth makes when pressure builds beneath the surface. When water finds channels through rock that was previously solid."

"You're saying that the water is coming from below and not from above?" Sarah asked.

"That's a possibility."

"Lord Navuh would not allow anything to happen to us," Rolenna said.

"Lord Navuh isn't immune to the forces of nature," Tula snapped at her, surprising everyone with her vehemence. "He might think he is, but he's not."

The lights went out completely.

Emergency lighting kicked in a second later, bathing everything in a harsh red glow that made the familiar surroundings seem hellish. The coffee maker sputtered and died. The air-conditioning, which had been struggling to pump air into the room, gave up entirely.

"Everyone, stay calm," Liliat said, though her own voice was strained.

The lights came back online, and with them, the cool air returned.

The hum crescendoed, and somewhere far below, something gave way with a sound like the world's largest pipe organ playing its lowest, most ominous note. The building shuddered, not like the earthquake tremor but like something had struck it from below.

"What was that?" Rolenna whispered.

Before anyone could answer, they heard it—distant but unmistakable. The sound of rushing water.

"No," Beulah breathed.

The sound grew louder, though still muffled by distance and intervening floors. But there was no mistaking it now. Water had found its way into their underground world, and even though water always sought the lowest level, this time it was different. It was rising, which meant that the servants living on the seventh level were in big trouble.

"Get your bags and take the stairs to the surface," Eluheed said.

Tamira turned to him. "What about you?"

"I need to help them." He headed for the emergency stairs.

"We should wait for instructions from Lord Navuh or the chief of security," Beulah said. "If we need to evacuate, they will announce it on the loudspeakers."

The lights flickered again, and this time when they went out, the emergency lighting didn't immediately return. In the absolute darkness, the distant sound of water seemed to grow louder.

NABIN

In the control room, Nabin studied the monitors. It was five-thirty in the morning, and he hadn't slept since the tremor. His eyes burned from staring at the screens, but the numbers refused to lie still. The humidity sensors showed a steady climb—ninety-three percent and rising. Too high for the dehumidifiers to handle, even running at maximum capacity.

"Nabin." Hassan's voice crackled through the walkie-talkie. "You need to come see this. Equipment room, eastern wall, section four."

Nabin grabbed his flashlight and headed down the emergency stairs. As he entered the equipment room, the hum seemed to intensify with each step, vibrating through the concrete.

He found Hassan kneeling beside a strain gauge attached to the wall, his face pale in the fluorescent lighting.

The engineer pointed to the digital display. "Look at these readings. The pressure's spiking. It jumped twenty-three percent in the last five minutes alone."

Nabin crouched beside him, studying the numbers. The gauge showed pressure levels that shouldn't be possible this far above the water table. Unless...

"The water table's risen," he said, the words tasting like ash in his mouth.

"Or something's redirected an underground stream." Hassan pulled out his tablet, fingers flying across the screen. "The seismic activity could have opened new channels. If there's an aquifer under pressure—"

The wall answered before he could finish. A crack appeared in the concrete, no wider than a hair at first, but Nabin could hear it growing. The sound was obscene—like bones breaking in slow motion.

"Back away," Nabin ordered, pulling Hassan to his feet.

They'd made it three steps when the crack exploded.

The concrete didn't just fail—it disintegrated. A section the size of a door blew inward with the force of a cannon blast. Behind it came the water.

Not a trickle. Not a stream. A geyser.

The pressure behind it was monstrous, turning the water into a battering ram that slammed into the opposite wall with enough force to crack those panels too. The roar was deafening, drowning out Hassan's scream and the sudden shriek of alarms as the spray hit the electrical panels.

Sparks flew in cascading showers as panel after panel shorted out. The acrid smell of burning insulation mixed with the mineral tang of the incoming water. Emergency klaxons began their piercing wail, but Nabin could barely hear them over the thunder of the inrushing flood.

He grabbed his walkie-talkie, backing toward the stairs as water spread across the floor with terrifying speed. "All stations, all stations! This is Nabin. Code Red. I repeat, Code Red. Catastrophic breach in Level Eight. Initiate immediate evacuation. Everyone needs to get out."

Static answered him. The water had already claimed the main communications panel.

Hassan stood frozen, watching the water rise. In seconds, it had gone from ankle-deep to knee-deep, the current strong enough to stagger him.

"The pumps!" Hassan shouted, pointing to the control station. "We have to engage the emergency pumps!"

They waded through the rising flood, fighting against the current. The pump controls were on the western wall, still dry but not for long. Nabin's fingers flew over the switches, engaging pump after pump. The massive machines roared to life, their intake valves opening to gulp down the incoming water.

For a moment, he dared to hope. The pumps were rated for thousands of gallons per minute. Maybe they could handle—

Another section of wall gave way. Then another.

The eastern wall was failing in sequence, each breach larger than the last. The water wasn't coming in streams now but in solid columns, hammering into equipment and structures with devastating force. A maintenance cart got caught in the flow and slammed into a support column hard enough to leave a dent.

"It's not going to work!" Hassan had to scream to be heard. "The pumps can't keep up!"

Nabin didn't need an engineering degree to realize that. The water was rising faster than the pumps could eliminate it. Already it was waist-deep, the current strong enough that he had to brace himself against the control panel to stay upright.

His walkie-talkie crackled. Through the static, he heard a familiar voice—one of Navuh's security detail.

"Control room, report. What's your status?"

Nabin pressed the talk button. "This is Nabin. Level Eight is compromised. Catastrophic water breach. We need immediate evacuation of all levels. The pumps can't handle the intake rate."

"Stand by."

Stand by? They were drowning, and the man said stand by?

The lights chose that moment to fail. The main panels had finally succumbed to the water, plunging them into absolute darkness for a heartbeat before the emergency lighting kicked in. Red lights bathed everything in an infernal glow, making the rising water look like blood.

"We need to get out of here," Hassan said, already wading toward the stairs.

There were people on Level Seven, including his own wife. He grabbed the emergency phone, a hardwired line that should still work.

Dead.

The walkie-talkie crackled again. A different voice now, one that made Nabin's blood run cold despite the crisis.

"This is Lord Navuh. Report."

Even over the roar of water and failing machinery, the lord's voice carried absolute authority. Nabin pressed the talk button, choosing his words carefully.

"My lord, Level Eight has suffered multiple catastrophic breaches. Water is entering faster than our pumps can evacuate. At the current intake rate, Level Seven will be flooded within minutes. We need to get everyone out."

"Seal the stairwell doors," Navuh commanded. "Contain the flooding."

Nabin's heart stopped. Seal the doors? With dozens of people still below?

"My lord, the people on Level Seven—"

"Will be evacuated if possible. Seal the doors, Nabin. That's an order."

The connection cut off.

Hassan stared at him in horror. "He can't mean that. There are over sixty people down there. Families. Children."

Including Nabin's wife. The thought of Priya, probably just waking to the sound of alarms, not knowing that death was rushing up from below...

Lord Navuh had given a direct order. Seal the doors, contain the damage. It was the logical choice—sacrifice the few to save the many. The water wouldn't rise forever. Eventually, it would reach equilibrium with whatever source fed it. If they could contain it to the bottom levels...

But those weren't just numbers on a casualty report waiting to be written. They were people he knew, had worked alongside for over a decade. Mariam, pregnant with her first child. Sonia, whose son had just recovered from pneumonia. Ahmed, who always had a joke ready no matter how long the shift.

His wife.

"We evacuate first," Nabin decided. "Then we seal the doors."

If Navuh sentenced him to death for refusing a direct order, at least he would die with a clear conscience.

Another section of wall gave way, this one larger than all the others. The water didn't even look like water anymore—it was a solid white wall of force that demolished everything in its path. A massive electrical panel, bolted to the floor with inch-thick steel, got ripped free and tumbled in the current like a toy.

The water was chest-deep now and rising. Each second they delayed was a second stolen from the people above.

"Go!" Nabin shouted at Hassan. "Get to Level Seven. Start the evacuation. I'll follow."

Hassan didn't argue. He fought his way to the stairs, using the railing to pull himself against the current. Nabin watched him disappear up the stairwell, then turned back to the failing room.

Nabin fought his way to the emergency supply locker, the water now high enough that he had to swim in places. Inside, waterproofed and waiting, were the evacuation air horns. He grabbed a few and headed for the stairs.

He climbed while using the air horns to signal the emergency pattern.

As he emerged onto Level Seven to chaos, the evacuation had begun, but it was disorganized. People stumbled from their quarters in various states of dress, confused and frightened. Some headed for the elevators—which would be death traps. Others milled about, unsure where to go.

"Stairs only!" Nabin bellowed. "Leave everything! Move to the stairs now!"

His voice cut through the panic, giving people something to focus on. They began to stream toward the stairwells. But there were so many of them, and the stairs were narrow...

He spotted Hassan trying to organize them in groups, sending them up in waves to prevent crushing. Smart man. But where was—

"Nabin!"

Priya appeared from their quarters, still in her nightgown but carrying their emergency bags—the ones they'd packed years ago, just in case. His practical, wonderful wife.

"Go," he told her.

She gripped his hand. "Come with me."

"I can't. Not yet." He squeezed back, then pushed her toward the stairs. "Go. I'll follow."

She went, but not without a look that promised consequences if he didn't keep that promise.

The floor shuddered beneath his feet. A moment later, water began seeping through the stairwell doors. Not flooding—not yet—but enough to tell him their time was measured in minutes.

"Everyone out!" he roared. "Two minutes! Anyone not on the stairs in two minutes gets left behind!"

It was harsh, but it worked. The stragglers stopped dawdling, and the flow of people toward the exit became more urgent. Nabin did a rapid circuit of the level, banging on doors, checking common areas. In the communal kitchen, he found the chef struggling with a bag of possessions.

"Leave it," Nabin ordered.

"My photographs—"

"Will do you no good if you're dead." He grabbed the man's arm and steered him toward the stairs.

The seepage was becoming a flow. Water poured under the stairwell doors, spreading across the floor in an expanding pool. The pumps on this level engaged automatically, but Nabin knew they were just buying them minutes.

Hassan appeared next to him. "That's everyone I could find. We need to go."

But Nabin's duty wasn't done. Lord Navuh had ordered the doors sealed. If he didn't do it now, the water would race up the stairwells, potentially flooding the entire structure.

"Help me," he said, moving to the emergency control panel.

The stairwell doors were designed to seal in case of fire, preventing smoke from spreading between levels. They'd work just as well for water. Nabin input his security code, then turned the manual lock. A red cover lifted, revealing a row of switches.

"This will trap anyone still down there," Hassan said quietly.

"I know." Nabin's hand hovered over the switches. Somewhere below, Level Eight was probably completely flooded.

They were out of time.

He threw the switches.

One by one, the heavy steel doors slammed shut. The sound was final, like the closing of a tomb. The flow of water cut off instantly, though they could hear it building behind the barriers, testing the seals.

"They're rated for fire suppression," Hassan said. "Should

handle water pressure to thirty feet." He wiped sweat from his face. "Beyond that..."

They both knew what beyond that meant. If the water rose high enough, the pressure would blow the doors off their hinges like champagne corks.

His walkie-talkie crackled. "Nabin. Report."

Lord Navuh again. Nabin keyed the microphone. "Level Seven evacuated, my lord. Stairwell doors sealed. The barriers are holding for now."

"For now." The lord's tone was contemplative. "How long?"

Nabin looked at Hassan, who shrugged. Too many variables. How much water was coming in? What was its source? Would it reach equilibrium before the pressure exceeded the door ratings?

"Unknown, my lord."

"I see. Keep monitoring. Report any changes immediately."

The connection ended. No word of thanks for saving the staff on Level Seven. No acknowledgment of the crisis still unfolding.

But that was Lord Navuh. Nabin had served him long enough to expect nothing else.

"Come on," he told Hassan. "We need to get the other levels to evacuate."

Because the doors would fail.

33

TAMIRA

T amira's bag weighed almost nothing—a change of clothes, her journal, the small wooden box containing her grandmother's ring. She had countless gowns, shoes, jewelry, hair accessories, belts, exotic perfumes, and makeup, but none of that mattered to her. It was all replaceable. The only things she regretted having to leave behind were her books and the precious moments with Elias she'd collected over the past week.

Hopefully, there would be many more.

She could imagine him helping evacuate the staff or perhaps assisting the maintenance crews in trying to avert the disaster. She should have gone with him, should have lent a hand as well, but after thousands of years of living in captivity, she was nearly incapable of making such decisions.

She followed the rules, did what was expected of her, and only dared tiny rebellions inside her own mind. Immortals were not supposed to be able to read the minds of other immortals, but Lord Navuh was different, more powerful than any immortal, and she'd learned to empty her mind in his presence.

She sat on the armchair with the bag in her lap, waiting for instructions as Beulah had suggested, wondering if she should have followed Elias's instructions instead and just got to the surface.

The speakers crackled to life, making her jump.

"Attention," Lord Navuh's voice boomed through the speakers in her television set even though it was not turned on. "Evacuate immediately via the emergency stairs. Do not use the elevators. I repeat, do not use the elevators. Leave all nonessentials behind and proceed to the surface at once."

Spooked, and not because of the evacuation order, Tamira rushed to the door.

If Navuh could speak to her through her television set's speakers, he could probably also see and hear everything that happened in her room. She'd been naive to believe that her room was clear of surveillance.

In the corridor she found Liliat, who clutched a bag and stood frozen in her doorway. Raviki's bag was overflowing with books that were threatening to fall out, and she was trying to rearrange them as she walked toward the emergency stairs, not watching where she was going. Sarah was rushing in the same direction with two heavy bags slung from her shoulders.

"Dear merciful Fates," Beulah called out. "Are you out of your minds? Liliat, start moving. Sarah, Raviki, what did you not understand about nonessential items?"

"My research is important," Sarah protested, clutching her two bags. "I'm strong, I can carry these."

She was right about being able to carry her bags, but she was wrong about her research being important. No one other than her and her friends in the harem would ever get to see it, so what good would it do?

Beulah just sighed and pushed Liliat in the direction of the stairs.

As Sarah and Raviki exited through the emergency door, Tula emerged from her room dressed in a pair of shorts, a t-shirt, and hiking boots. The female looked like she was going to attack someone, and Tamira wondered who had pissed her off.

Behind her, Tony emerged from their room with a back-pack slung over one shoulder. "Let's go, sweetheart."

"I should go down there to help," Tula said. "All those people. The children."

"The guards will help them." Tony reached for her arm. "Come on."

Tula jerked away. "What guards? Do you think he's going to send guards to help them!"

"I'm sure he will," Tony said. "They are probably already on their way down."

"Ladies!" A male voice cut through their debate. One of Areana's personal servants held the emergency door open. "Lady Areana is waiting for you topside. She asked me to make sure all of you leave here at once."

Well, so much for going down to help.

Even Tula wouldn't dare disobey a direct order from Lord Navuh that just got repeated by an emissary of Lady Areana.

As they entered the stairwell, Tamira was reminded how narrow it was. She'd only used them a handful of times, and it had been many years ago. Voices echoed from below— distant thunder of multiple sets of feet on metal steps, some shouts, some cries.

The servants were evacuating somewhere far below, and she could imagine Elias helping organize things so they wouldn't trample each other in a stampede.

"Where's Elias?" Liliat asked as she joined them in the stairwell, looking confused. Her panicky eyes darted from face to face as if she'd somehow missed him in the chaos. "Tamira? Where is he?"

"He went to help evacuate the servants, remember? He has friends down there."

"Oh." Liliat nodded.

Only a single flight of stairs separated Level Two from Level One, but during the short climb the chaos below seemed to have intensified. The stairwell acted like an acoustic chamber, carrying up the sounds of panic. Children crying, adults shouting, and the ominous sound of rushing water that was still distant but growing louder.

"Faster, ladies," Raviki urged, practically pushing them upward even though they were in no immediate danger.

Tamira was much more worried about the people below and about Elias who was with them.

They emerged onto the landing of Level One, which was crowded with Areana's personal staff. A group of guards passed them, rushing down, and Tamira murmured thanks to Lord Navuh, who, atypically, had sent help to the staff.

Another flight of stairs brought them to the topside pavilion, and through the glass doors, Tamira could see daylight —gray and dim, and rain, sheets of it, driven horizontal by the wind.

"Out, out!" One of the guards opened the door and held it for the others to exit. "Head out to that elevated area over there."

That was smart. If the water geysered to the surface, it would burst through the pavilion's two available openings and catch everyone and everything in its path. The water would rush toward the lowest point of the plateau, which was the area overlooking the cliff and then down to the ocean below. Anyone who got swept away would die, splattering on the rocks below.

Even immortals wouldn't survive that fall.

More than once, Tamira had contemplated ending her existence that way, but she was too much of a coward to do it. It would be a very painful way to die.

As soon as she was out the door, the warm rain hit her like the stream from a pressurized shower head, instantly soaking through her clothes, and the wind tried to tear the bag from her hands. She'd experienced monsoon storms before, but nothing like this. The sky was gray, split by constant lightning. Thunder rolled continuously, so loud it drowned out voices.

"This way!" Areana appeared on the elevated area like a vision in white, somehow maintaining her composure even in the deluge. Her personal servants held up a large tarp, creating a temporary shelter. "Ladies, over here!"

As they huddled beneath the inadequate protection, water still found its way through, running in streams off the edges, but it was better than having the full force of the storm pelt their heads.

Tamira positioned herself where she could see the two pavilion exits. The main one that the ladies used, and the smaller one that was used by servants.

No one was emerging yet. Where was Elias?

"Look at that." Tony pointed through the rain.

Another tarp had been erected nearby, this one sheltering Lord Navuh and more of Areana's personal staff, who were fussing around their lord and lady. They'd even gotten out two chairs so Navuh and Areana could hold court out here in the deluge.

It was so absurd that it was funny.

"It's like that movie," she murmured.

Liliat looked at her questioningly. "What movie?"

"*Titanic*. The one about the ship sinking. How they kept the class divisions even as people were drowning."

"What a cheerful comparison," Raviki muttered.

Several guards appeared, probably new ones who had entered through the two checkpoints. They formed up next to Lord Navuh's tarp, standing in the rain and awaiting orders.

It was unprecedented for the guards who patrolled the perimeter to enter the harem area, signifying how dire things were for Lord Navuh to allow the breach in protocol.

"Secure the perimeter," Navuh commanded, his voice carrying over the storm. "Set up a containment area for the servants as they emerge. Order needs to be maintained."

Tamira's heart sank. They were here to contain the people, not to help with the rescue.

How typical.

"They should be helping," Tula hissed. "They should be down there carrying children and helping whoever needs assistance. Not standing up here worrying about containment!"

"Tula," Tony warned, but she was too agitated to listen, and in her anger, she glared at their master. "The lord has already sent guards to help," Tony continued. "You saw them going down." He got in front of her, blocking the lord's view of her.

She didn't like it, but he kept murmuring to her until her posture deflated and her shoulders sagged. He then wrapped his arms around her, and she rested her head on his chest.

Watching, Tamira couldn't help a pang of envy. Where was Elias?

As if to answer her question, the servants' door burst open, and people began pouring out, but Elias was not among them.

They emerged into the rain with nowhere to go, huddling against the pavilion walls for whatever protection they could find. The guards made no move to help them.

Where was Elias?

"Bring the children here!" Tamira shouted. "Under our tarp! There's room!"

The other ladies took up the call. "The children! Bring them over!"

Some of the servants hesitated. The invisible barriers that had governed their lives for so long were hard to break, even now. But maternal instinct won out. Mothers began shepherding their children toward the impromptu shelter.

"What are you doing?" One of the guards moved to intercept them.

"Let them through," Areana commanded. "The children will shelter with the ladies and when that tarp can contain no more, the rest can shelter with us."

When Navuh didn't contradict her, the guard stepped aside.

As more people emerged, Tamira tried to track who she recognized. Sonia appeared with her son, the boy who'd been so sick with pneumonia. They'd made it. But where was Mariam, the pregnant one? Where was the elderly gardener who trimmed the hedges, shaping them to look like animals?

Soon they had several children pressed against them, shivering and terrified. Tamira held a little girl who couldn't have been more than three, her dark eyes wide with fear.

"It's all right," she said. "You're safe now. A little rain never hurt anyone."

More servants emerged, a steady stream now, but still no Elias.

"I can't stand this," Tula announced. She shrugged off Tony's restraining arms and stepped out from under the tarp. "I'm going down to help."

"You will remain right here." Lord Navuh's voice cracked like a whip.

Tula turned to face him, rain streaming down her face. "People are struggling down there. Children who can't climb fast enough. Elderly who can't manage the stairs. I'm strong enough to carry them. I can help."

"No," Navuh said, his tone brooking no argument.

"Please, let her go," Areana said softly.

"It's the guards' job to help evacuate the serving staff. Not my concubines'."

The guards securing the perimeter could be more useful helping with the evacuation, but Tamira doubted Areana would point that out. The first wife knew how to manipulate her arrogant mate and contradicting him in public would not only be counterproductive but probably catastrophic.

"I know, my lord," she said while dipping her head. "This is for Tula's sake. She needs to feel like she's helping."

Brilliantly played. Tamira felt like applauding.

Navuh made a dismissive gesture toward Tula. "You can go. But stay in the pavilion. If anyone needs help being escorted out, you can do that."

Tula didn't wait for him to change his mind. She sprinted toward the pavilion, her immortal speed making her seem to blur in the rain.

Tamira doubted Tula was going to follow Navuh's instructions. She would probably head down and hope no one told him. She should help too. She was strong, immortal. She could help—

She must have taken a step forward because Raviki caught her arm. "Don't be stupid," she murmured. "You'll just get Areana in trouble."

Raviki was right.

Because of Areana's pleading, Navuh had made an exception for Tula. If more ladies tried to join her, he would blame Areana for the insurrection.

The flow of evacuees continued, people emerging already soaked.

Thunder crashed overhead, so loud that some of the children began crying.

It seemed like hours had passed while they were standing in the rain when in fact it had been mere minutes. Time moved differently when a catastrophe was unfolding.

Where was Elias?

"The water must be rising fast," Tony said. "Look at them—they're soaked through. That's not just from the rain."

He was right. The latest evacuees were drenched, their clothes dark with water that had to have come from below.

Time stretched like taffy. Each heartbeat seemed to last an hour, and Tamira found herself making bargains with the Fates, the universe, and with whatever powers might be listening.

Let him be safe. Let him return.

What if the stairwells flooded before he could—

She couldn't complete the thought.

The storm raged on. Lightning split the sky. Thunder shook the ground. Rain fell in sheets that made seeing difficult.

He had to come back.

34

ELUHEED

The emergency stairs echoed with the thunder of feet and voices as Eluheed plunged downward, taking the steps three at a time. He could move faster than most humans, but that wasn't only because he could push his immortal body beyond what they could. He'd lived most of his life in steep mountains, climbing them up and down, so even though he'd slackened over the last few decades, his body still retained the strength it had developed over hundreds of years.

Still, he felt the weight of every second that passed. Water didn't wait for anyone.

Level Three flashed by in a blur, the library with its thousands of books about to become sodden waste. Level Four, where the recreation areas and some of the offices were located, would also be flooded soon, but Eluheed was concerned only with saving lives.

He burst onto Level Five to find relative order. The harem levels were occupied according to a hierarchy of size, and since this level was the smallest of the three staff residential levels, it housed the upper management. The rooms were larger, and the number of occupants smaller than those on the levels below.

Most of the residents here had already evacuated or were in the process of climbing up the stairs. A couple of stragglers were weighed down by the possessions they were trying to save, packed into laundry baskets and pillowcases.

"Leave it!" Eluheed shouted as he passed a woman struggling with an overstuffed bag. "Your life is not worth what's in that bag!"

She ignored him and kept running with the laundry bag slung over her shoulder.

Hopefully, she wouldn't slow other people who were trying to save themselves and were more responsible.

A quick scan revealed that the entire floor was deserted, and Eluheed returned to the stairwell. It was now full of people rushing up, small children crying, and older humans moving too slowly. Some had stopped to help neighbors, creating bottlenecks. Others pushed past, survival instinct overriding community bonds.

He squeezed by them on his way down, and then he heard it —the sound of water finding its way through barriers, the groaning of doors under pressure. He continued down, fighting against the stream of evacuees. Level Seven was hopefully fully evacuated because the stairwell door was locked. It was already weeping, though, the water seeping beneath it in steady streams.

It followed him as he climbed back to Level Six, where the evacuation was a barely controlled panic.

"Mama! Mama!" A child's terrified wail cut through the chaos.

Eluheed followed the sound, splashing through the rising water. He found them huddled in a doorway, a man and a woman, each holding a small boy, one of the children crying for his mother, who wasn't the woman with the other boy. Eluheed knew most of the residents, but he didn't remember who was married to whom or which child belonged with which parent. The adults were trying to carry the children, but the water was making walking difficult, and the boys were panicking, fighting their parents' grip.

"Here," Eluheed said, not wasting time on explanations. He scooped up both boys, one under each arm. "I'll carry them up the stairs. Try to follow as fast as you can."

"But our things—" the woman started.

"Will be underwater in minutes," Eluheed cut her off. "Leave everything and move!"

He didn't wait to see if they followed. The boys squirmed in his grip, crying for their parents, but he held them secure and started the climb.

In normal circumstances, the six flights of stairs would be nothing for him, but these weren't normal circumstances. The stairs were crowded with evacuees, the children were terrified and struggling, and the water was rising below.

"It's all right," he told the boys, though he doubted they could hear him over their own cries and the chaos around them. "I'm going to get you out of here."

Fifth floor. His legs pumped, maintaining speed while carrying two frightened children with sheer determination. Other evacuees pressed against the walls to let him pass, some calling out blessings, others just staring with desperate hope.

Fourth floor. Third floor. The boys had stopped struggling, either exhausted or sensing safety in his firm grip.

Level Two. Almost there. The children were whimpering now rather than screaming, and Eluheed could feel their small hearts racing against his arms.

Level One. The final flight to the surface. Fresh air and rain-scented wind poured down from above. He burst through the door to the pavilion and handed the boys to Tula, who reached for them. "Their parents are coming up behind me."

He didn't wait for her to answer.

Every second counted, and there were more people down there—elderly who couldn't climb fast, more people with small children, some who might be too frightened to move.

He turned and plunged back into the stairwell.

The descent was harder the second time. More people were climbing, and he had to fight his way down against the flow. Shouts of "Wrong way!" and "What are you doing?" followed him, but he didn't have time to explain.

Level Six was worse than before. In the corridor, an elderly couple were struggling through knee-deep water. The woman could barely walk, her husband trying to support her while fighting his own exhaustion.

Without saying a word, Eluheed lifted the woman onto his back. She did not weigh much, and he could feel her frailty, bones like a bird's beneath thin skin. "Hold on to me," he told her. "Arms around my neck."

Her grip was weak but determined. He turned to the husband, evaluating quickly whether the man could walk if not burdened.

"No," Eluheed decided, and before the man could protest, he'd hoisted him under his left arm. It was awkward with the woman on his back, and her husband under his arm like a package, but it was fast and efficient.

"Please, put me down," the man protested weakly. "I can walk."

Eluheed answered with a grunt and kept moving.

The climb this time was a blur of burning muscles and careful balance. Even his strength had limits when it came to endurance, and he was carrying two adults up six flights of stairs through a panicking crowd. The woman on his back wheezed with each jolting step. The man under his arm had gone quiet, perhaps realizing that protest would only slow them down.

Fifth floor. Fourth floor. His legs screamed protest, but he pushed through. This was nothing compared to climbing the ragged mountains of his homeland, or Ararat—the land he'd called his home for over eight centuries. And it was definitely nothing compared to the weight of failure he'd carried for the last two centuries. He could do this. He would do this.

Finally, he reached the pavilion, where Tula was waiting and ready to take over. He put his charges down. "Lady Tula will help you from here."

The elderly woman gripped his hand with surprising strength. "Bless you," she whispered. "Bless you, young man."

Young man. If only she knew. But there was no time for irony. He could hear screaming from below—panicked and desperate. The water must have broken through completely.

He did two more runs, helping three children and two sick adults up the stairs.

This would be his last one because he was operating on fumes. Hopefully, everyone was already on their way up.

Going down again, his legs felt like molten lead, but he forced them to move. The stairwell was nearly empty now. Most of those who could evacuate on their own had done so. But as he descended, he could hear the ones who were trapped.

The emergency doors on Level Six had given way and it was flooding fast, the water rushing through in a torrent. The corridor was waist-deep and rising visibly. But he could hear children crying.

What in the seven hells were they still doing there, and where were their parents?

He dove into the flooded corridor, swimming against the torrent more than walking. The water was surprisingly warm, heated by its journey through volcanic rock, and it carried the mineral taste of deep earth.

The crying led him to a door that was stuck—water pressure holding it closed. Inside, he could hear multiple voices. A family trapped as water rose around them.

Eluheed punched the top portion of the door, breaking it, and whoever was on the other side got the idea and was helping break off pieces to widen the opening.

Inside, a woman stood on top of a dresser holding twin infants with a boy of perhaps five clinging to her leg.

Two men, the ones who had helped him break the door, were already reaching for the children.

"Give me the children," he commanded, already reaching.

A look of sheer panic passed across the mother's eyes, but she handed the babies to the men, and they transferred the children to him through the opening in the broken door.

Eluheed tucked one under each arm and then turned his back to the door. "Put the child on my back."

A moment later, small arms wrapped around his throat with desperate strength.

"Hold on tight," he told the boy. "Help the woman through the opening and follow me."

The journey back to the stairwell was nightmarish. Bleeding knuckles that were already healing but painful, water chest-deep and rising, and the weight of three children, two infants who he had to hold up above the water and a five-year-old clinging to his back.

Eluheed's legs moved through sheer will, each step a battle against exhaustion and physics. He climbed fast, and behind him the adults struggled to keep up, but he could hear them following. Fifth floor. Fourth floor. He was pushing his body beyond the limits of its endurance. The infants were slipping in his grip, slick with water. The boy on his back was choking him with terror-strengthened arms.

Third floor. Second floor. Black spots danced in Eluheed's vision. His legs moved without conscious thought, muscle memory from centuries of survival.

Just a little farther. Just a little more.

First floor. One more flight.

He burst onto the surface for the final time, legs giving out the moment he cleared the exit. He managed to pass the infants to Tula, felt the boy being lifted from his back, then collapsed.

Rain pelted his face, mixing with his sweat. His chest heaved, trying to pull in enough oxygen to feed muscles pushed beyond all reasonable limits. Even his immortal body needed recovery time.

"Elias!" A familiar voice, high with fear and relief.

Then Tamira was there, dropping to her knees beside him in the rain. Her hands framed his face, her eyes wide with tears that mixed with the deluge.

"You magnificent fool," she sobbed, pulling his head into her lap. "I was so afraid—"

He tried to speak, but his body was too focused on the simple act of breathing.

"Did everyone..." he finally managed to gasp. "Did everyone make it?"

"Yes," she said, running her hands through his soaked hair. "We are still counting to make sure we didn't miss anyone, but Shalini says they are all here. The Fates were merciful tonight."

Relief washing over him, Eluheed turned on his back, closed his eyes, and just let the rain pelt him.

"Oh," he heard Tamira exclaim. "I forgot about the guards."

He opened his eyes and saw a procession of guards emerging from the pavilion in pairs, each duo struggling with a heavy chest. Diving masks dangled from around their necks, and their uniforms were soaked and smelling of the mineral-rich flood water from below.

They'd gone diving, he realized.

While people were fighting for survival, these guards had been swimming through flooded vaults to retrieve—what? Gold? Jewels? Papers?

Eluheed watched them struggle with their burdens, saw Lord Navuh directing them to load the chests into waiting vehicles. Whatever was in those chests, it had been deemed more valuable to him than human lives.

The bitter irony burned worse than Eluheed's overworked muscles. He'd pushed his body to breaking point to save strangers, while Navuh's guards had done the same to save possessions.

Two types of treasure, two sets of priorities.

What could possibly be so important? Gold wouldn't dissolve in water. Precious stones would survive a flooding. Important documents were probably backed up digitally. But lives were irreplaceable.

"What are they carrying?" Tamira asked, following his gaze. "Did he have corpses stored down there?"

The chests were large enough to contain dead bodies, but they didn't look like coffins.

"Priorities," Eluheed said. "They are carrying Lord Navuh's precious treasures."

35

AREANA

There was only one thing that Areana valued enough to put in her purse before evacuating her suite, leaving everything else for her staff to decide on.

The hidden communication device was her most prized possession, and the one thing she had kept hidden from her mate for years. Well, there had been some inconsequential harem shenanigans that she'd kept from him to protect people she cared about, but he probably preferred her keeping those to herself.

Communicating with her sister and their sons was a different matter, and if Navuh ever found out, it would push him over the edge he had been teetering over for thousands of years.

It was such a monumental effort to prevent him from falling over into complete madness, and sometimes Areana felt like she was losing the battle, but she had to keep trying even though it was exhausting.

Navuh was extremely powerful, and the amount of damage he could inflict on the world if she wasn't there to hold him afloat was staggering and terrifying.

Still, the ability to talk to Annani, Kalugal, and on occasion Lokan, was her lifeline, and she couldn't give it up even given the tremendous risk involved.

The problem was that she had to be close to the cliff for the communicator to work, and if they were relocated to somewhere else on the island, somewhere far from the cliff where the device couldn't reach its hidden amplifier, she wouldn't be able to maintain contact. The thought of losing that lifeline, that single thread connecting her to the outside world, made her throat constrict and tears prickle the backs of her eyes, but she couldn't allow herself to show the emotional turmoil that she couldn't explain even by the disaster that they had barely managed to avert.

Areana was so grateful to the young shaman who had saved many who otherwise might not have made it, and to the Fates who had sent him to them.

She offered them a silent prayer of gratitude.

Navuh did not like it when she prayed to the Fates, so she never did that in his presence, praying in silence instead. Despite his love and devotion for her, it was not a good idea to butt heads with her mate, especially not in public, but after witnessing what the guards had come back with, she was tempted to give him a piece of her mind.

He had implied that they had been sent to help rescue

people, and instead they had rescued things, emerging with his salvaged treasures.

Ten immortal warriors, strong enough to carry multiple humans to safety, had been sent to retrieve possessions instead. What could possibly be so important that it warranted prioritizing over lives?

In their five millennia together, she and Navuh had made their peace with keeping secrets from each other. It was the only way their relationship could function—him with his endless schemes for power, her with her small acts of mercy and rebellion. But why hide treasures beneath the harem without telling her? Did he think she would steal them? Tell someone about them?

The bitter irony almost made her laugh. Tell whom? No one left the harem alive. Even Carol, Lokan's brave mate who'd risked everything to try to rescue her and helped her establish communication with Annani, was believed dead. They had staged a suicide, Carol supposedly jumping off the cliff because of a broken heart, and Navuh had believed it.

Anger would serve no purpose now, though, and Areana forced herself to look away from the guards and their burdens. Instead, she turned her mind to gratitude, thanking the merciful Fates for granting them so much grace in this disaster.

Ninety-eight servants and twenty-two children were all alive and accounted for. Her ladies, shaken but unharmed. It was miraculous that in such chaos, with water rising and panic spreading, everyone had made it out.

She watched the guards loading the retrieved chests into waiting trucks, treating them with more consideration than the humans who stood shivering in the rain. The ladies remained under the tarp with as many children as they could shelter, but they were all soaked through as well.

The servants didn't even have that.

And yet, the treasure chests took priority.

Finally, three black SUVs arrived. The drivers emerged, each holding several umbrellas. They passed through the gates of the double fences surrounding the harem and headed toward the two tarps sheltering their lord and the ladies.

As one of the drivers offered an umbrella to Elias and Tamira, Navuh shook his head. "The shaman can travel with the servants."

"If it is not too much trouble, my lord, Elias should ride with us," Areana said. "He saved so many people, and I feel like rewarding him with a hot cup of tea."

Navuh turned to her, eyebrow raised. "My mansion doesn't have enough bedrooms to host him. He will have to stay with the others."

She had forgotten about the need to keep up appearances. Outside the harem, Elias couldn't share Tamira's bed. The ladies were supposed to be Navuh's concubines.

Areana smiled sweetly. "After I treat him to a warm meal and a change of clothes, he can be taken to where the other servants will be staying. Unless we can find him a bed in the servants' quarters."

Navuh nodded. "We can worry about accommodations later. Right now, he can ride with us and receive the royal treatment for saving so many lives."

"Can Tony come with us as well?" she asked. "You know how amusing I find him."

Navuh's jaw tightened, but he gave a dismissive wave. "As you wish. But he can't stay with us either."

They would have to figure out a solution for the two males, but she had a feeling they wouldn't be allowed to stay in Navuh's home. This would start rumors that her mate had worked very hard to avoid.

When Navuh turned to her personal staff who were huddled around them, Areana knew what was coming before he opened his mouth.

"Listen carefully," he said, his voice carrying that particular quality that meant he was using his gift. "You will speak to no one about the harem and what transpires within its walls. Privacy will be maintained."

Areana watched as the compulsion took hold. She could see it in the subtle relaxation of shoulders, the slight glazing of eyes.

Navuh grabbed an umbrella from one of the drivers and walked to the tarp that the ladies were huddling under. He repeated the commands in so many words, including Tony and Elias in his compulsion.

Navuh moved on to the servants next, repeating his commands to each group. He was so powerful that compelling over a hundred people, adults and children alike, was nothing for him.

Her mate was the most powerful immortal in the world, and he could have done so much good if he hadn't had his mind poisoned a long time ago.

Her hand found her purse again. At least she had this. For now.

"My lady," one of the drivers said as he walked over with an umbrella. "Your vehicle is ready."

She allowed herself to be escorted to the large car, settling into the leather seat with a grace born of millennia of practice. The interior smelled of expensive leather and subtle cologne, the opulence a stark contrast to the miserable deluge outside.

Navuh finished his rounds and joined her, water droplets still clinging to his dark hair. He looked oddly satisfied for a man who'd just incurred a substantial loss. It was going to cost him a fortune to restore the structure.

"Where are you planning to shelter the servants?" she asked as the vehicle pulled away.

"They will be taken to the resort's main hotel." He leaned back in the seat. "We don't have many guests during the monsoon season, and we can move the few who are there now to the bungalows to make room for the servants. I don't want them interacting with the guests."

Areana knew that the visitors to the tourist side of the island were not attracted by the weather. She was well aware that her mate dealt in sex tourism and extortion, luring prominent politicians and businessmen to the island with the promise of fulfilling their fantasies, no matter how dark and depraved. She just tried not to think about it too often.

"For how long?" she asked. "Can you get the pyramid fixed before the end of the monsoon season?"

Areana held her breath as she waited for his answer. She needed access to that cliff, and that meant that she needed to get back to the harem.

He glanced at her. "After the storm is over, we will assess the damage and see what needs to be done. The repairs shouldn't take more than a few weeks."

She let out a breath and nodded. "I hope the books in the library survived. It would be such a hassle to replace them. Some of them are probably irreplaceable."

"I know how important those books are to you, my love." Navuh draped his arm around her and kissed her temple. "I promise that everything will be restored to its former glory."

"Thank you." She leaned against his shoulder, enjoying the closeness.

In moments like these, she could almost forget about all the things that were wrong about their relationship and focus on all the things that were absolutely perfect.

The drive continued through the storm-lashed darkness. Without landmarks visible through the rain, Areana couldn't tell where they were going until the vehicle began to climb. Up, away from the coast, into the hills and then down again.

When they finally stopped, she looked at the sprawling mansion that loomed before them. It was everything that the harem wasn't. Instead of being hidden underground, this structure proclaimed its strength openly. High walls and guard towers at regular intervals, manned despite the weather. Gates that would stop anything short of a tank. She was sure that there were cameras tracking every movement even though she couldn't see them in the rain.

They passed through multiple checkpoints to reach the main entrance. Guards saluted as Navuh passed, their eyes carefully avoiding her. She wondered what they'd been told about the evacuation, about the women they would now be guarding.

When they stopped in front of the main entrance, the driver got out and opened the door for Navuh.

Her mate stepped out and opened the door for her himself, offering her a hand down while the driver held the umbrella over their heads. "Welcome to your temporary home."

"It's impressive," she said as she took his hand.

He smiled, pleased by what he took as a compliment. "The security here is as tight as that in the harem. You'll be perfectly safe."

Safe. As if that had ever been her primary concern.

The interior was modern and cold, all glass and steel and sharp angles. No warmth here, no attempt to create even the illusion of a home. This was a fortress, nothing more.

Still, she paid him compliments as they passed by the living room. He led her up the stairs and then through a hallway. "I hope the master suite is to your liking."

"I'm sure it is as elegant as the rest of the house."

He laughed. "I know that you don't like the modernist style. You don't have to pretend that you do."

"I'm surprised that you like it, my love. I always thought of you as a traditionalist."

"I am." He opened the door to a suite that was actually not as bad as she'd expected. "This was an experiment that I'm starting to regret, but I'll give it a few more months before I order the decorators to return everything to the way it was."

He'd never consulted her opinion about decorating his other residence, and it stung. She didn't expect him to consult her about the wars he was instigating, but he could have at least asked her opinion about furniture.

"I do not know how it looked before, but I prefer our residence in the pyramid. I hope we can return there soon."

Something flickered in his eyes—understanding, perhaps, or pity. "I'll have the engineers assess the damage as soon as the storm passes. If the structure is sound, and the water can be somehow diverted elsewhere, renovations will start right away. You will have your palace back within weeks. A few months at most."

Months.

Annani would worry when their scheduled call didn't happen. She would assume that something had happened to Areana and might even mount another rescue attempt.

Fates, she hoped her sister wouldn't do that. It would only end in disaster.

"Thank you." She put her hand on Navuh's arm. "We should shower and change and then have a hot cup of tea."

36

TAMIRA

T he dress that had been delivered to Tamira's room
felt wrong against her skin. It was also too short,
too structured, nothing like the flowing silks she
was accustomed to. She tugged at the neckline as she
descended the stairs, the stiff fabric a reminder that everything had changed overnight.

She'd expected the dining room to look like the ones she'd
seen in movies about rich people living in a metropolis, but
she'd been too modest in her expectations. The room
reminded her of a picture she'd seen of an exhibit in a
modern art museum. Glass, chrome, and strange sharp
angles everywhere. The artwork on the wall was very
colorful but it depicted nothing. It was like the artist had
thrown buckets of paint onto the huge canvas, but she had
to admit that the combinations of vivid colors were pleasing
to the eye.

The other ladies were already seated, looking equally
uncomfortable in their new clothing. Liliat kept touching

her hair, still damp from the shower. Raviki fidgeted with the buttons on her blouse, and even Sarah seemed overwhelmed by their unusual surroundings.

Elias sat at the far end of the table, wearing a simple white shirt and dark pants that must have come from the store that served this part of the island, the one that the ladies' outfits had come from as well. The clothes fit him surprisingly well, and Tamira had to force herself not to stare at the way the fabric stretched across his shoulders. Tony sat beside him, drumming his fingers on the glass table in a nervous rhythm.

"Good morning," Areana said as Tamira took her seat. "I trust everyone is refreshed?"

"Thank you for the clothes," Beulah said. "And the hot shower was lovely."

Navuh entered, and the atmosphere shifted, becoming colder and stiffer.

His household staff watched everything with poorly concealed curiosity. These people didn't know that Navuh never touched his concubines, that Elias was far more than an advisor, and that Tony belonged to Tula.

"Ladies," Navuh said, taking his seat at the head of the table. "Elias. Tony."

"Thank you for hosting us for breakfast, my lord," Elias said with a proper dip of his head.

Tony repeated his thanks, and the staff began serving the morning meal, an elaborate spread that seemed excessive, bordering on ostentatious. Fresh fruit, pastries, eggs prepared three different ways, four different sorts of bread, cheeses and cold cuts of all kinds.

Tamira picked at a piece of melon, her appetite nonexistent. Every bite felt like sawdust when all she wanted to do was reach across the table and take Elias's hand and kiss him until neither of them could breathe.

Instead, she buttered a roll that she had no intention of eating.

"More water pumps were delivered to the site," Navuh announced, spreading honey on his toast with precise, elegant movements. "The engineers need the water cleared out before they can assess the damage."

"How long will it take?" Areana asked, and Tamira caught the edge in her voice. Their lady was anxious, and that was unusual for her.

Areana was their rock—always composed, always ready to help with a kind word. To see her so discombobulated was concerning.

Was it the shock of displacement?

They all knew their roles in the harem, the rhythm of their days. Here, everything was uncertain.

Or perhaps something else was troubling her?

As Areana's fingers tightened on her teacup, Tamira suddenly understood. In the harem, everyone knew that Navuh was devoted solely to his first lady, his wife, and that the concubines were there to produce sons he could claim as his own. But here, with his regular household staff and guards watching, Areana's role in Navuh's life was diminished. She was still the first lady of the harem, but she was supposed to share him with six others. She was forced to pretend that her mate was spreading his affections among seven women.

It was humiliating.

How far was the pretense going to go? Would Navuh be spending some of his nights with his concubines now?

Tamira shuddered at the thought. It would be torture to spend a night with him even if she slept on the couch and he slept in the bed. Just having him in the same room with her meant that she wouldn't be able to have a minute of shuteye.

Hey, she could spend the next day sleeping, providing material for the household staff to gossip about. They would be convinced that their lord had tired out his concubine.

Navuh must have sensed his mate's distress because he reached for her hand. "The water needs to recede before they can access the lower levels. But I assure you, my dear, that the restoration will begin as quickly as possible."

"Of course," Areana murmured.

An uncomfortable silence fell that someone needed to fill, to maintain the pretense of normalcy, but Tamira couldn't think of a single thing to say.

Tony, bless him, seemed to understand. "The implications of prolonged water exposure on structural materials are quite fascinating." He launched into what promised to be a lengthy lecture. "You see, when concrete is subjected to hydrostatic pressure..."

Tamira tuned him out, grateful for the distraction he provided but having no patience for his scientific explanations. Not when Elias sat mere feet away, close enough that she could smell the soap he'd used, see the way his hair curled slightly when damp, but too far for her to reach and run her fingers through those curls or press her face against his neck and breathe him in.

Instead, she focused on spreading jam on her unwanted roll.

"The porosity of volcanic rock creates unique challenges," Tony continued, warming to his subject. "Water can penetrate microscopic channels, creating weakness in otherwise solid stone..."

Tamira suspected that Tony sometimes made up his assertions. He couldn't be knowledgeable on so many subjects, and by now he knew what each of them was interested in and what he could get away with.

Once he was finally done, Areana turned to Elias. "This experience has been quite traumatic for all of us. Do you have any advice on how to process such an event? Some spiritual guidance?"

Elias set down his coffee cup. "In times of crisis, we often focus on what was lost," he said, his voice taking on the particular cadence that meant he was choosing each word carefully. "Meditating on gratitude for what was preserved is the best antidote. Every life saved was a victory over chaos."

"Beautiful words," Liliat said, and for once, she didn't sound flippant.

"The Sufis speak of finding the gift within the trial," Elias continued. "Perhaps this displacement, difficult as it is, offers opportunities for reflection and growth."

Tamira almost laughed. Growth? The only thing growing was her desperate need to be alone with him, to drop this suffocating pretense and have her way with him. But she couldn't laugh, couldn't react at all beyond polite interest.

The damn servants were watching.

"Speaking of growth," she said instead, proud of how steady her voice remained, "I've been having difficulty sleeping. Do you have any herbal recommendations? Perhaps a calming tea?"

It was such a transparent excuse to speak to him that she nearly cringed.

"Passionflower and chamomile." Elias played along seamlessly. "With a touch of lavender for scent. I could prepare something for you if Lord Navuh permits."

"That would be helpful," she managed, when what she really wanted to say was that she needed him, that last night or rather this morning, she'd thought she'd lost him to the flood, and now she was losing him to these stupid rules and watching eyes and—

"The hotel should have these things," Navuh said, effectively ending that line of conversation. "You can prepare the remedies there."

The meaning was clear. Elias would be at the hotel, not here. Not with her.

After a few more minutes of mind-numbingly stilted conversation, Navuh pushed back from the table. "I have business to attend to. Elias, Tony—the guards will escort you to the hotel."

He kissed Areana's cheek with a formal flourish and then swept from the room, leaving them to navigate the good-byes without his oppressive presence, not out of the goodness of his heart, but because he had things to do.

The household staff remained, though, watchful and judgmental.

Areana rose from her chair gracefully. "Gentlemen, thank you for your assistance during this difficult time. I'll speak with Lord Navuh about arranging regular visits. The ladies and I benefit greatly from your company."

"You're most kind, my lady," Tony said with a bow that looked theatrical rather than genuine.

Elias stood and Tamira forced herself to remain seated. Every instinct screamed at her to go to him, to throw her arms around him and refuse to let go. Instead, she folded her napkin next to her plate.

"Thank you for the tea recommendation," she said, the words ashes in her mouth. "I look forward to trying it."

"I hope it brings you relief," he said, and she heard everything he couldn't say in those simple words.

The guards entered the room, two immortal warriors who would take the men to the hotel.

Tula finally looked up, her eyes finding Tony's. "Safe travels," she said in a formal tone, but Tamira heard the undertones of anger and frustration.

"Thank you, my lady." Tony inclined his head. The pain in his eyes was obvious to anyone who knew him.

He loved Tula, that was obvious, but Tamira wasn't sure that Tula loved him back. Like many others before him, Tony was a temporary amusement.

No doubt Tula was smarter than Tamira in that regard. Getting attached to a human was stupid. A mistake a long-lived immortal like her should have never allowed.

As the men headed out, Elias paused in the doorway for a moment, and as his eyes found Tamira's, she saw her own anguish reflected in that brief connection. Then he was gone, and the temperature in the dining room plunged several degrees lower even though no one touched the air-conditioning controls.

"Well," Sarah said after a long moment, "that was properly excruciating."

"Sarah," Areana admonished, glancing at the servants.

"Apologies, my lady. I meant only that we don't like parting from our instructors. Their guidance is highly appreciated."

Nice save, but the damage was done. The servants had heard the bitterness, filed it away with whatever other gossip they'd collected. By evening, the entire household would be speculating about the real relationships hidden beneath the formal façades.

"Perhaps we should adjourn to the sitting room," Areana suggested. "I believe I've noticed a bookshelf. Perhaps we can find something interesting to read."

They rose and headed out of the dining room, a flock of exotic birds transplanted to the wrong habitat.

In the sitting room, Tamira picked up a book without looking at the title and claimed a chair by the window. The words blurred on the page as her mind replayed every moment of breakfast, every carefully chosen word, every glance she'd had to cut short.

Elias was probably at the hotel now, surrounded by displaced harem staff. She was here, in this new, cold prison, where she had nothing but the memory of his eyes in that doorway and the taste of words she'd never gotten to say to him.

It was almost funny how the harem felt like a sanctuary to her now. At least there, she'd had her beautiful, warm room, her books, her routines, her nights with Elias.

ELUHEED

The resort lobby gleamed with marble and crystal, a temple to excess that reminded Eluheed of the upper levels of the harem. He stood in the lobby entrance, taking in the soaring ceilings, the beautiful flooring, and the elaborate fountains. This was where Navuh's clients stayed when they came to indulge their darkest fantasies, where powerful men paid fortunes for experiences they couldn't find anywhere else.

Now it was overflowing with displaced servants, their simple clothes and worried faces a stark contrast to the opulent surroundings. Children who'd never seen such luxury ran through the halls, their laughter echoing off surfaces designed to impress jaded politicians and businessmen.

"This way, sirs," the bellhop said, leading Eluheed and Tony toward the elevators. The young man maintained his professional demeanor despite the chaos, though his eyes kept darting to the people camped in every available space.

They rode up in silence, Tony radiating misery. When the bellhop opened the door to their room, Eluheed's heart sank.

One bed. King-sized, draped in white linens and enough pillows to build a fort, but still—one bed.

"We don't have rooms with double beds," the bellhop said apologetically. "And this is the only room available."

"It's fine," Eluheed said. "Thank you."

The door closed, leaving them alone with the elephant in the room. Or rather, the bed.

"I'll take the couch." Eluheed gestured to the seating area. It looked comfortable enough, certainly better than many places he'd slept over the centuries and definitely better than sharing a bed with Tony.

The guy didn't argue. He simply walked to the bed and threw himself face down on it, still fully clothed. "This is bullshit," he said, his voice muffled by the pillows.

Eluheed chuckled. "Which part?"

"All of it." Tony rolled onto his back, staring at the ceiling. "The flood. The evacuation. Being stuck here while Tula's trapped in that modernist nightmare. Having to pretend we're nothing to each other while servants gawk at us like we're zoo animals."

"It won't last forever," Eluheed said, though the words felt hollow. How many times had he told himself the same thing about his own situation? Just a little longer. Just until he could find a way out. Just until...

"Won't it?" Tony sat up. "You know what I've learned? Nothing changes in Navuh's world unless he wants it to. And he likes his toys exactly where he puts them."

Eluheed tensed, and he glared at Tony, lifting his finger and pointing toward the ceiling. "Watch what you say in here."

Tony's eyes widened. "Right. I forgot about that."

"I'm going to explore the hotel," Eluheed said. "Get the lay of the land so to speak."

"Knock yourself out." Tony flopped back down. "I'm going to lie here and contemplate the meaninglessness of existence until I fall asleep."

"Enjoy."

Eluheed was exhausted, but he was also still wound up, and he needed to release some tension before he could sleep.

He left Tony to his sulking and headed back to the elevators. As he waited, it occurred to him that it was strange that Navuh hadn't kept him at the mansion. After all, the whole point of placing him in the harem had been to keep him away from the lord's sons and generals who might try to use his abilities against Navuh.

But perhaps keeping up appearances mattered more.

Everyone had been compelled to secrecy about the true nature of the harem and its inhabitants. As far as the household staff knew, 'Elias' was just a spiritual advisor, a shaman who provided guidance and herbal remedies. It gave Navuh an excuse to summon him whenever he wished while maintaining the fiction.

Once the elevator arrived, Eluheed entered and rode it down to the lobby. He remembered seeing a bar when they'd arrived, and he headed in that direction.

He needed a drink. Maybe several. The last twenty-four hours had been a blur of adrenaline and desperation, and now that the immediate crisis had passed, his body was demanding some form of chemical comfort.

The bar was exactly what he'd expect from a place like this —all dark wood and leather, dim lighting that made everyone look mysterious, bottles of liquor that cost more than most people could ever afford. What surprised him was how empty it was. Only one man sat at the bar, slouched on a stool like he'd been there for hours.

Eluheed took a seat a few stools down, catching the bartender's eye. "Whiskey, please. Whatever you recommend."

"Certainly, sir. Will you be charging it to your room?"

He'd forgotten about that. "Yes. Room..."

He and Tony had been told that they could charge whatever they pleased to the room, and it would be covered, but he realized that he didn't know the number.

"Elias, correct?" the bartender said smoothly.

"Yes. How did you know?"

The barman smiled mysteriously. "It's my job to know." He tapped on the screen. "You are in room 323."

"Thank you. I'll remember that."

Eluheed tried not to think about what the bartender meant when he'd said that it was his job to know. Had the hotel staff been given instructions to watch him and Tony?

Probably.

"Finally," the man a few stools down said loudly. "Someone who doesn't look like an inbred cretin."

That was an odd comment.

Eluheed glanced over at the man. Asian features, expensive casual wear that screamed designer labels, thick glasses that gave him an owlish appearance. He was clearly drunk or at least well on his way there.

"Rough afternoon?" Eluheed asked politely, hoping the man would take the hint and leave him alone.

Instead, the stranger picked up his drink and moved to the stool directly next to Eluheed. The smell of alcohol wafted off him in waves.

"Rough afternoon? Try rough month. Rough year." He gestured broadly, nearly knocking over his glass. "Do you have any idea what it's like to be surrounded by idiots? To be the only person in a hundred-mile radius who understands basic biochemistry?"

Evidently, the guy hadn't heard of Tony.

The bartender placed a glass of whiskey in front of Eluheed.

He took a grateful sip, savoring the burn. "That must be frustrating."

"Frustrating?" The man laughed, high and slightly hysterical. "That's like saying the ocean is damp." He lifted his hand and offered it to Eluheed. "I'm Dr. Marcus Zhao, by the way. Biochemist. Genius, really."

"Elias," Eluheed offered, regretting engaging with the man.

Anyone who introduced himself as a genius had problems that needed professional help.

"Elias? That's an unusual name." Dr. Zhao squinted at him through his thick glasses. "You're new here. Are you one of the evacuees?"

"Yes."

The guy frowned. "What I saw so far was a bunch of servants. What do you do?"

"I grow medicinal herbs," Eluheed said. "So, I guess you can say I'm a gardener."

Zhao pursed his thick lips. "An herbalist. Interesting. My grandmother grew medicinal herbs. She had no formal education, but she was brilliant." He tapped his temple. "I got my brains from her."

If the guy could appreciate his grandmother, perhaps he wasn't a total loss.

"I wish she were still alive," Zhao said. "I wish she could see what I am now. What I have become."

"And what's that?" Eluheed asked despite himself.

The guy straightened on the stool. "I'm the fucking future, that's what I am. I'm the man who's going to change everything. I can make the strong stronger, the fast faster. Pushing human potential beyond all known limits."

"That sounds ambitious."

"Ambitious?" Zhao laughed again. "It's not ambitious, it's genius. I've already done it. Well," he amended, taking another swig of his drink. "There are some minor side effects, but I'm working on it."

"Such as?"

"Sorry, Elias." Zhao patted his arm. "Can't talk about it. Not allowed." He waved a hand dismissively. "It's not important. The point is, I can make people stronger, faster, better. Evolution in a bottle." He leaned closer to Eluheed. "The antidote to artificial intelligence." He snorted. "Brawn over brains. I never expected to be working on that. But hey, someone needs to do it."

Eluheed kept his expression neutral despite the cold dread spreading through his chest. This drunk fool was talking about creating monsters, turning men into weapons.

"Isn't what you're doing dangerous?" he asked without expecting a response. The guy was obviously working for Navuh and, therefore, compelled to keep his work a secret.

"Of course, it is," Zhao said. "That kind of power doesn't come without sacrifice."

"Everything has a price." Eluheed took another sip of whiskey.

"Exactly! You understand." Zhao clapped him on the shoulder with drunken enthusiasm. "These muscle-bound idiots don't understand the science, the beauty of what I've achieved."

He kept talking, the words flowing in an increasingly slurred stream. Eluheed nodded at appropriate moments, filing away every piece of information the guy blurted. Something about enhancement drugs and warriors who couldn't be stopped by conventional means.

The implications were staggering.

"The real problem is that people are limited in their thinking," Zhao said. "Small minds, small ambitions. They see my work as just another tool, but it's so much more than that. It's the next step in human evolution. Survival of the chemically enhanced fittest."

"You seem very passionate about your work." Eluheed lifted his glass, signaling to the bartender that he needed a refill.

Zhao laughed bitterly. "I'm trying to elevate humanity, and I'm stuck on this godforsaken island surrounded by thugs and whores. Present company excepted, of course." He squinted at Eluheed again. "Are you sure you're just a gardener? You seem intelligent. Not like these inbred imbeciles I have to deal with."

The bartender smiled as he poured more whiskey into Eluheed's glass, probably pitying him for the company he had to endure.

"Open minds, that's what we need." Zhao signaled for yet another drink, though he was swaying on his stool. "People who can see the bigger picture. What did you say your name was again?"

"Elias," Eluheed repeated.

A smile spread across Zhao's face, predatory despite his drunken state. "Well, Elias," he said, raising his fresh drink in a toast, "let's drink to the next stage in evolution. The giant leap forward." He laughed maniacally. "One small step for a man, one giant leap for mankind."

COMING UP NEXT
The Children of the Gods Book 99
DARK SHAMAN: LOVE FOUND

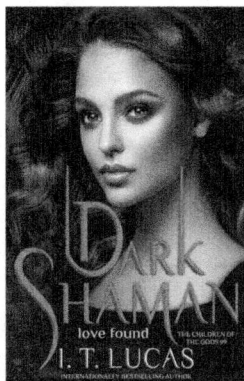

Eluheed has spent months hiding his true nature while serving Lord Navuh. When he's granted access to the immortal ladies of the harem, he's drawn to Tamira—an ancient immortal whose exquisite mind captivates him as much as her ethereal beauty.

As their forbidden connection deepens, the island's iron-fisted order begins to unravel. Navuh's greatest weapons are turning against their master, and chaos spreads through the once-controlled paradise.

TO READ A PREVIEW ON THE VIP PORTAL,
JOIN THE VIP CLUB
To find out what's included in your free membership, flip to the last page.

BONDS OF WINGS AND FURY
The Two-Faced God

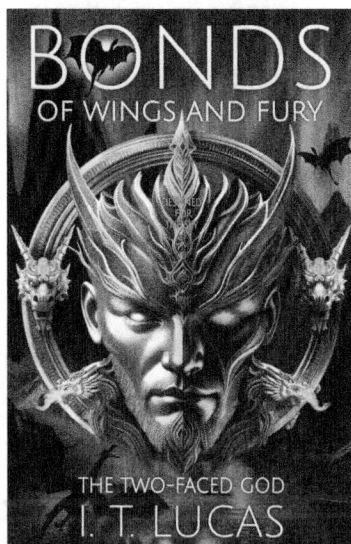

Read the enclosed excerpt

In a world where dragons dominate the skies and colossal worms tunnel through mountains, three nations teeter on the brink of war.

Like every Elucian, Kailin must brave the perilous pilgrimage to Mount Hope's summit, where an ancient shaman will decide her fate. A select few are destined to bond with dragons, and for most, it's the ultimate prize. Not so for Kailin, who is hiding a paralyzing fear of heights and would rather sketch the magnificent beasts than ride them.

Alar appears to be a privileged Elurian seeking the glory and immortality of dragon riders. Yet beneath his aristocratic facade lies a secret agenda that could disrupt the delicate alliance between the reclusive Elucia and the cosmopolitan Elurian Federation.

When Kailin and Alar cross paths, sparks fly, and as they ascend the perilous mountain, hunted by shadowy assassins and tested by ancient rites, their unlikely bond deepens.

Defying a thousand years of tradition, an impossible selection puts the star-crossed lovers at the center of an ancient prophecy. But in a world where dragons have their own agendas and even the gods aren't what they seem, the greatest threat may yet come from within.

This new series takes place in the larger universe of the gods, and while it stands alone, the two series will converge. The book is scheduled for release on January 17, 2026, but it may be released earlier.

Click HERE to read the enclosed excerpt.

CHECK OUT THE NEW AND IMPROVED
MEGA BOXSETS

MEGA BOXSET 1

Includes:

- Dark Stranger: The Dream
- Dark Stranger Revealed
- Dark Stranger Immortal
- Bonus Short Story 1: The Fates Take a Vacation
- Dark Enemy Taken
- Dark Enemy Captive
- Dark Enemy redeemed.
- Bonus Short Story 2: The Fates' Post-Wedding Celebration
- A Children of the Gods Companion Guide for books 1-6

MEGA BOX SET 2

Includes:

- My Dark Amazon

- Dark Warrior Mine
- Dark Warrior's Promise
- Dark Warrior's Destiny
- Dark Warrior's Legacy
- A Children of the Gods Companion Guide for books 6.5-10

MEGA BOXSET 3

Includes:

- Dark Guardian Found
- Dark Guardian Craved
- Dark Guardian's Mate
- Dark Angel's Obsession
- Dark Angel's Seduction
- Dark Angel's Surrender
- A Children of the Gods Companion Guide for books 11-16

BONDS OF WINGS AND FURY
The Two-Faced God
Excerpt

1
KAILIN

Five years ago

The 27th Day of the Third Month

Year 11663 of the Dragon Pact

Year 3384 post Division

It is said that you can smell death on the wind before it comes to claim its due. Tonight, the air tastes of frost and pine and something else—something metallic and sharp that makes my skin crawl—but I ignore it and convince myself that there is no chance the monsters will come for me on the one night I'm left alone in the house.

—*From the journal of Kailin Strom*

I added a sketch to my journal entry, trying to capture visually the feeling I struggled to express in words. Drawing had always helped calm my nerves, turning vague impressions and uncomfortable feelings into more tangible visual representations, but tonight, even the familiar rhythm of pencil scratching against paper couldn't quiet the churning in my stomach.

Perhaps it was the wind howling outside my window or the cold seeping through every crack and crevice in the old stone walls, but I didn't really mind the cold, and I was used to the wind, so neither could be the cause of my sense of foreboding.

The most likely culprit was my brother's impending pilgrimage and my apprehension over the fate he would learn at its culmination.

Coupled with our parents' return trip home and the potential dangers they might face on the journey, was it a wonder that I was anxious?

Shedun attacks were rare in our area, but no place in Elucia was immune to this scourge.

Still, what was probably at the root of my unease was the realization that Dylon would not be coming home regardless of the fate awaiting him at the summit of Mount Hope.

When my brother had walked out the front door this morning, he'd left our childhood behind, and the life we'd shared was already reduced to a collection of memories and journal sketches.

With a sigh, I tucked the journal under my pillow, turned on my side, and propped myself on my elbow to gaze out the window.

The auroras were particularly spectacular tonight, great ribbons of green and purple light dancing across the sky.

Their glow transformed the mountainside, casting an ethereal light over the landscape and making the snow-covered peaks shimmer. From afar, it all looked magical, but Elucia's breathtaking beauty was as harsh and unforgiving as its people.

In the distance, I could make out Mount Hope, its sacred summit disappearing into the clouds.

Tomorrow at dawn, Dylon would start the ascent, and in three days, he would reach the Circle of Fate and learn his destiny.

In five years, it would be my turn.

Thousands of young Elucians joined the three annual pilgrimages, hoping to be declared gifted and become riders, but only a handful were selected, if any.

The ability to bond with dragons was rare, dormant until awakened by Elu's touch and coaxed to the surface by the shaman's words. The trait ran in families, and since neither of our parents was gifted, it was highly probable that Dylon and I would be found talentless and get assigned to other branches of the Elucian military. But there was that one distant relative who'd been gifted, and that was enough to feed my brother's dreams and my nightmares.

I was probably the only Elucian dreading the possibility of becoming a dragon rider, and there were several good reasons for that, but chief among them was my fear of heights. It was uncommon for a mountain-dweller, and I did my best to hide the embarrassing affliction, but merciful

Elu was all-knowing, and I clung to the hope that the shaman would not decree a fate I couldn't endure.

Naturally, if I was chosen, I would fulfill my duty and serve my country to the best of my ability, but just imagining myself astride a dragon sent chills down my spine. I could barely handle a hover-car skirting a ravine even with my eyes tightly shut. How could I possibly soar through the skies on the back of a flying beast?

With stubborn determination, that's how.

I was an Elucian, after all, and Elucians didn't let fear rule them.

Telling myself that I needed to set these thoughts aside and get some rest, I moved my journal to the windowsill and burrowed under my thick blanket, pulling it up to my nose. The warmth slowly lulled me to sleep, but I had barely started to doze off when Chicha's warning bark sliced through the night like a thunderclap, startling me awake and sending adrenaline coursing through my veins.

I bolted upright, the loud and rapid rhythm of my heartbeat nearly drowning out the barking. But then, as my terror burned through the cobwebs of sleep and my mind processed what was probably a false alarm, I took a calming breath and commanded my racing heart to slow down.

It was nothing.

Chicha had the courage of a mouse, treating every rustling bush and passing night bird as mortal threats, but despite her tiny size, she had the lungs of a lioness and a ferocious bark.

We'd all learned to dismiss her dramatic outbursts.

In the event of real danger, the night guards would blast the bullhorns, rousing the village defenders to arms.

"Quiet, Chicha!" I called out, dragging my pillow over my head.

She barked once more in defiance before dropping to a low growl, but that didn't last long, and soon she launched into another volley of frantic barking.

I loved that little dog dearly, but right now, I could happily banish her to the sheep pen. Not that I'd actually do it—partly because I would hate to extract myself from the warm cocoon of my blankets, but mostly because Chicha had mastered the art of wounded dignity. She'd give me that look, all betrayed eyes and drooping ears, until guilt gnawed a hole in my resolve.

Instead, I tried to ignore the racket she was making and go back to sleep, but it was no use.

My mind might have rationalized that the barking was not a likely sign of danger, but the lingering surge of anxious energy coursing through my veins would take time to dissipate.

Sighing, I turned on my back and let my thoughts drift to Dylon and the fate awaiting him at the end of his pilgrimage. Was it selfish of me to wish for my brother not to be granted his heart's desire?

Despite the so-called immortality the bond bestowed upon dragon riders, they rarely survived to old age, and those who did seldom got married or had kids, even though they were encouraged to do so to produce the next generation of riders.

There were never enough of them.

The trait was rare and the number of gifted in the general Elucian population was gradually dwindling, but I couldn't blame the riders for not wanting to raise a family in the Citadel, knowing that their kids might get orphaned before they were ready to fly.

I didn't want that for Dylon. I wanted him to find love, to give our parents grandchildren to spoil, and to grow old in our village, where we knew everyone and everyone knew us.

The truth was that I missed him already, and he'd been gone less than a day. If he joined the Dragon Force, months would pass between his visits home. But if my selfish prayers were answered and he was assigned to any other branch of service, he'd return sooner and more frequently, and when his duty years ended, he'd settle back in our village, and life would continue as it should.

Dylon would hate me if he knew what I prayed for, but he would thank me later when he was surrounded by family, friends, and neighbors whom he'd known his entire life, instead of the cold, lonely skies. Because I'd volunteered to stay behind and watch over our livestock and Chicha so our parents could see him off, I wouldn't even get to hug him one more time and wish him luck before the start of his pilgrimage.

Suddenly the barking ceased, replaced by a quiet whining, which wasn't Chicha's normal mode of operation.

Something *was* wrong.

I bolted out of bed and hurried downstairs. My bare feet were silent on the wooden steps, but Chicha should have heard me and rushed to greet me, and the fact that she didn't added to my growing sense of dread.

In the kitchen, I found her wedged beneath the sink in her favorite hiding spot, her small body shaking.

"What is it, girl?" I reached for her.

She whimpered and pressed herself further back into her nook.

My heart began to pound. Chicha might be a cowardly little thing, jumping at shadows and fleeing from her own reflection, but in all her years, she had never shrunk away from me.

Her terror was eroding my courage, but I couldn't let fear paralyze me. I had to keep a clear head.

It was most likely a mountain lion or some other wild beast trying to snatch one of our sheep, and the distressed bleats from their shed reinforced my assessment. A Shedun attack was always a possibility, albeit remote, but the guards in the watchtowers would have spotted the monsters long before Chicha could have sniffed them out and sounded the alarm.

Still, a mountain lion was not a beast to trifle with, and I have never taken one on by myself, but there was no one else home, and it was up to me to protect our livestock.

I could do this.

I might be only sixteen, but I had a steady hand and a true aim.

My skill with a rifle was praised not only by my father but also by my instructor in the youth training camp. Even Dylon had grudgingly admitted that I was a better shot than he was.

I can do this, I repeated it in my head as I hurried to the front door, pushed my feet into my mud-covered boots, got my coat on, and grabbed a rifle and two boxes of ammunition from the shelf above the doorframe.

My hand shook as I unlatched the locks and opened the door, but the little courage I'd managed to muster fizzled out as soon as I stepped outside.

Something felt off.

Despite the howling winds, there was an unnatural stillness about. The trees swayed in the wind, but apart from that, nothing moved. Everything around me seemed to be holding its collective breath. Even the sheep had gone quiet, and Chicha's whimpers had ceased.

The small hairs on the back of my neck tingled as dread spread through my veins. Something was definitely wrong, and I had to decide whether to backtrack into my house and lock the door or keep going.

Glancing at the nearest watchtower, I hoped to see the night guard's silhouette against the aurora-lit sky, but deep down,

I already knew that the tower would be empty even before my gaze confirmed it.

I should have panicked. I should have run back into the house and barricaded the door. Instead, a sense of numbness enveloped me. I was in denial, trying to convince myself that this couldn't be happening tonight of all nights, but at the same time I was certain that it was indeed happening and that I probably wouldn't make it out alive.

"Maybe the guard went down to relieve himself," I muttered, in another effort to convince myself that everything was alright, but the words felt hollow even as I spoke them.

The guards never left their posts until their replacement arrived. If they had to, they did their business in a bucket.

The guard was most likely dead, and it was up to me to sound the alarm, provided that I made it to the tower before they got me.

Without making a conscious decision to move, I was already running, crouched and silent, with the rifle slung across my body. It took me mere moments to traverse the short distance between my home and the closest watchtower, but it felt like so much longer.

As I hurried up the ladder, my sweaty hands slid over the smooth wooden rungs that were worn by years of use. Climbing, I still tried to convince myself that I was overreacting and that there was a perfectly reasonable explanation for the guard's absence, but it was just self-talk to boost my floundering courage and keep me going.

One more rung and I would be at eye level with the platform, but my foot hovered in the air, refusing to move.

I drew in a breath, hoping to steady my nerves—but the sharp, coppery scent that filled my lungs only served to confirm my fears.

Even then, knowing what I would find, I wasn't prepared for the scene that greeted me when I finally forced myself to climb up that step. The guard lay face down in a spreading pool of blood, his throat cut, his rifle lying just beyond his outstretched hand.

Somtan. I recognized him by the plaid shirt I had seen him wearing so many times before.

I stood paralyzed, my mind refusing to accept what my eyes were seeing.

Remembering him carrying me on his shoulders during the harvest festival when I was little, I couldn't accept that I would never see his cheerful smile again or that his four young children would have to grow up without a father. His seven nieces and nephews would never get to ride on their uncle's broad shoulders again, and his elderly parents would now face their final years without their son.

The world tilted sideways, and bitter acid rose in my throat as my body finally reacted to the horror before me. I doubled over, ready to empty the contents of my stomach.

Except, I didn't.

Somehow, training kicked in, and I forced the bile down and tore my eyes away from the still-growing pool of blood.

There was no time for shock or grief. The village was under attack, and if I didn't move fast, things would quickly get much worse.

The Shedun must have sent a forward stealth team to silently eliminate the guards, and their main force would soon follow to violate, torture, and slaughter the rest of us.

We had minutes, at most.

My hands shook violently as I grabbed the bullhorn, and it took me two tries to position my finger over the button and sound the alarm. It blared across the sleeping village, its harsh sound shattering the silence and the false sense of calm, urgently rousing everyone.

Lights began to flicker in the windows, and in mere moments, doors flew open as my neighbors emerged with rifles clutched in their hands.

At the sound of heavy footsteps on the ladder, I turned with my rifle trained on the intruder, but it was just old Ednis climbing onto the platform. The grizzled veteran took in the scene with one glance, then knelt beside Somtan's body.

"He's gone," I said, my voice sounding strangely calm to my own ears, like it wasn't I who was speaking but some alternative version of me.

Ednis checked anyway, his weathered fingers seeking a pulse that we both knew wouldn't be there. When he straightened, his face was grim.

"Get yourself home, Kailin," he said gruffly. "Hide in the cellar and bar the door from the inside. Don't open it. Not

420

even if someone you know is telling you that it's okay to come out."

The Shedun were known to hold a knife to a child's throat, forcing its desperate parents to betray their neighbors. But they were also known to set fire to homes, so hiding in a cellar was not such a good strategy either.

My fingers tightened around my rifle. "I'm staying here." I was surprised by the steel in my voice. "I know how to use this, and I have two full boxes of ammunition in my pocket. I can help."

"Kailin—"

"I'm staying, Ednis." My hands were still shaking, and I had to grip my rifle even tighter. "I feel safer here with you, fighting, than hiding and cowering."

Ednis studied me for a moment, then nodded. "Don't let yourself get killed, girl. Your parents will never forgive me if you die on my watch. Stay close to me and do as I say, understood? No stupid heroics."

"Yes, sir. I mean, no, sir."

I scanned the darkness beyond the village boundaries, but with the auroras casting ever-shifting shadows across the mountainside, it was difficult to distinguish movement from tricks of the light. Somewhere out there, the Shedun were gathering, preparing to attack, and soon they would emerge from the shadows like a pack of demons, ready to devour every living soul in their path.

Was it too much to hope that they had abandoned their plans after I sounded the alarm?

I clung to the sliver of hope even though I knew we wouldn't be that lucky.

All four watchmen had failed to sound the alarm, forcing me to conclude that they'd been killed, so luck wasn't a word I should use, and yet I was immensely relieved and grateful that Dylon and my parents were safe, away in Skywatcher's Point.

"They're coming," Ednis whispered beside me.

I raised my rifle, sighting along its barrel into the aurora-lit landscape.

The night stretched on, tense and terrible in its stillness, save for the howling winds that only added to the dread. None of the animals bleated, mooed, or neighed, and I wondered why they were so quiet. Did they sense death's approach and keep silent to escape its notice?

The Shedun came like shadows made flesh, materializing from the darkness like the demons they were. Covered in black from head to toe, their faces painted with black tar, they seemed to absorb what little light reached them. The only splash of color on them was the red symbol of Elusitor stamped on their foreheads.

They moved with an unnatural speed that made my skin crawl.

Rumors claimed that they used dark magic, fueling it with the blood and suffering of their victims, but I didn't believe in magic. I believed in medicines, and there were herbs that could enhance performance for a short period of time. The same substances also ravaged the mind, unleashing a savage madness that perfectly explained the Shedun's infamous brutality.

It wasn't sorcery that had created these monsters.

They were manufactured by a warped ideology, twisted, evil faith, and science.

"Steady," Ednis murmured beside me. "Wait for my signal."

I forced myself to breathe slowly, trying to still my trembling, sweaty hands. My rifle felt impossibly heavy as I tracked the approaching figures through its sight.

Could I do this?

Could I aim and shoot to kill someone when I had never shot a living thing before?

This wasn't like the practice range. This was real, but I had told Ednis that I could help, and by Elu, I would.

The first shot came from the western tower—a crack that whipped through the unnatural silence. A Shedun dropped, but the others didn't even break stride. They didn't mind losing their own because they glorified death, and life meant nothing to them.

"Now!" Ednis said.

I squeezed the trigger without thinking, the rifle's recoil slamming into my shoulder. My target stumbled but kept coming. I'd hit him, but not well enough. I had to keep shooting. Gritting my teeth, I took aim again.

The night erupted into chaos. Gunfire echoed off the mountainsides as our village defenders engaged the attackers. The Shedun returned fire, their weapons making odd whistling sounds.

Before long, I barely noticed the rifle's recoil and the violent clap of detonation with each bullet fired. I became one with the weapon, a machine without feelings. The air was thick with the smell of gunpowder, but my breathing became steady, measured, and my aim improved.

I was defending my people—nothing else existed beyond that singular purpose. Later, I would have to confront this cold, empty space inside me, this strange detachment that had settled over my mind. But for now, that void was a gift I couldn't afford to question.

"Down!" Ednis yanked me to the floor of the watchtower as bullets splintered the wood where I'd been standing. "Did they teach you nothing in the Youth Training Camp, girl?"

The void shattered, the clarity was gone, and terror flooded back along with the raw horror of what I'd seen, what I'd done, and what I still had to do.

"Sorry," I murmured, trying to control the shaking of my hands and slow down the frantic beat of my heart.

I still had a job to do, and I couldn't succumb to panic.

When he released me, I followed what I'd been taught and

crawled to the other side of the tower, peering through a gap in the wooden slats.

Three Shedun were attempting to flank the Marson family's home. I lined up my shot and fired. The nearest one went down hard, clutching his leg. His companions hesitated, and in that moment of indecision, they made perfect targets for the defenders in the eastern tower.

"Good shot," Ednis grunted, picking off another attacker with a careful aim. "Keep watching that side. Don't let them get behind the houses."

Time seemed to lose all meaning. I fired, reloaded, fired again. My shoulder ached from the rifle's recoil, and my ears rang with the constant gunfire. But I didn't stop.

I couldn't stop.

A scream cut through the noise—one of ours.

I risked a glance and saw Weber clutching his arm, blood seeping between his fingers. But he kept firing one-handed, his face twisted with determination and pain.

"They're retreating!" someone shouted. "They're running!"

Sure enough, the Shedun were melting back into the shadows as quickly as they'd appeared, dragging or carrying their wounded with them, but leaving the dead behind.

"Keep firing!" Ednis bellowed.

I tracked a fleeing figure through my sight, squeezing off two shots in quick succession. The second one found its mark, and the Shedun crashed to the ground.

He didn't get up again.

Within minutes, the surviving demons had disappeared into the darkness, and I could imagine them jumping into the mouth of their tunnel—a dark hole torn into the mountainside, carved out by one of their giant worms.

The sudden silence was deafening.

"Is it over?" I asked.

Instead of answering, Ednis turned and lifted his eyes to the sky. As I followed his gaze, there was nothing to see, but I heard the distant beat of powerful wings approaching.

A thunderous roar shattered the night, so powerful that it made the wooden tower tremble. My head snapped up just as five massive shapes burst through the auroras, their wings creating gusts of wind that whipped my hair around my face.

Their scales gleamed like polished steel in the ethereal light as they dove after the fleeing Shedun. The lead dragon opened its maw, and the stream of blue-white flame that erupted turned night into blinding day. The raiders were consumed in an instant, their bodies reduced to ash before they could draw a breath to scream.

I should have felt satisfaction watching our enemies burn, but the raw display of power made my insides twist, and the acrid stench of burning flesh brought about a wave of nausea.

This was different from rifle fire.

This was devastation on another level—nature's fury harnessed as a weapon. And yet, death by dragfire was swift and far kinder than what the Shedun offered their victims.

These vile creatures did not deserve such mercy.

Fueled by an irrational hatred of dragons and those who bonded with them, the Shedun dedicated their collective miserable existence to hunting both. Every life they extinguished was an offering to their abhorrent god of death, a deity as cruel and as insatiable as its worshippers.

Elusitor, the dark face of Elu, the deceiver, the destroyer, the tormentor.

It was this relentless onslaught that forced all Elucians to dedicate long years of their lives to military service, standing with our winged, fire-breathing allies against the tide of darkness.

The ground shook as the massive lead dragon landed in front of our tower, and I instinctively gripped my rifle tighter, even though I knew it didn't mean us harm.

Frankly, I was as awed as I was terrified or perhaps the other way around.

No, fear was definitely the stronger emotion. This was an apex predator, and I was a puny human it could snuff out with a hiccup.

Dragons were just as intelligent as humans, but to assume that they were anything like us was a mistake. As my dragon lore teacher had said on multiple occasions, they didn't think like us, they didn't feel like us, and they didn't make the same judgment calls.

It was never wise to lower one's guard or underestimate their destructive power.

It or rather he, because it was definitely a male, bent his long neck so his eyes were level with mine, holding me transfixed. Glowing like molten gold, those eyes conveyed intelligence and curiosity, and as he regarded me, I felt as if he was looking straight into my soul and measuring my worth.

Mesmerized and terrified, I didn't dare breathe, but then something stirred inside of me, and I felt compelled to shift my gaze from those golden eyes to those of the rider, which were no less captivating and unnerving.

It almost felt as if the dragon wanted me to look at his rider and had somehow communicated his wish to me, but that was absurd.

Even if I had the gift, it wouldn't manifest until I was twenty-one and the shaman coaxed it to the surface on top of Mount Hope, which would take place five years from now.

Still, here I was, gazing into the impossibly dark eyes of the imposing rider and feeling dazed and lightheaded. Was that why I was seeing gold flakes swirling around his irises, even though he was too far away for me to see such minute details?

Could it be another thought that the dragon had planted in my mind?

When the rider finally released his hold on my gaze, I sucked in my first breath since the start of this strange encounter. He shifted his eyes to my rifle, then the bodies of the Shedun strewn on the ground, and a small smile lifted his lips. A two-fingered salute followed, but instead of offering it to Ednis, it seemed as if he was offering it to me.

Did he think that I, a sixteen-year-old girl, had killed all those Shedun by myself?

I wanted to correct his misconception, but the words refused to form on my lips. Then his dragon dipped its head as if to second the rider's opinion, and my head started spinning.

I stumbled back.

"Easy, girl," Ednis said quietly as he put a hand on my back. "Never show a dragon that you fear it. It might mistake you for prey."

"I'm not afraid," I murmured. "Not anymore."

I was mesmerized, enthralled, and some other emotion I couldn't decipher. A yearning for something.

No, yearning wasn't the right word to describe the intensity of what I was feeling either.

Need.

I needed... what?

To climb on the back of that dragon and look into the eyes of its rider from up close?

What an absurd thought that was!

I was surrounded by carnage, the smell of burned flesh still permeating the air, and yet I was thinking about a guy and the strange connection I felt to him?

It must be the shock or the adrenaline or whatever other hormones were released during battle. Survivor's high. Perhaps a post-combat elation. I'd read about that, but never really understood the phenomenon before.

Now I did.

The thrall was only broken when the dragon launched back into the sky with a powerful beat of those massive wings, the downdraft nearly knocking me over. Ednis steadied me with a firm grip on my arm, and together, we watched as the dragons pursued the last of the fleeing Shedun.

The night was lit up with multiple streams of flame, turning the mountainside into a canvas of fire and shadow. It was an awe-inspiring display, and in my post-battle euphoria, I cheered our dragons on. I wanted them to turn every fleeing Shedun into ash so none of the monsters could return to slaughter the people of another Elucian village.

"They're making sure none escape back into the mountains," Ednis said, his voice filled with vengeful satisfaction. "Burning them as they try to crawl back into their tunnel and then sealing the hole."

Once their grim task was completed, the dragons wheeled overhead in formation, with the huge obsidian dragon that had landed before us taking point and leading the others in a final pass over our village before disappearing into the ribbon of lights above.

The sudden absence of their presence left me feeling strangely hollow.

Despite the auroras still dancing overhead, the night suddenly seemed darker, smaller somehow.

"Those eyes," I whispered, more to myself than to Ednis. "I've never seen anything like that."

"Aye," he said. "That's why we call them the Wise Ones."

I hadn't meant the dragon's eyes, although they too were magnificent. It was the rider's gaze that had seared itself into my soul, and I knew that I would dream about it for many nights to come.

I shook my head and took a long, steadying breath.

As the haze lifted, reality crashed back with the acrid smell of gunpowder mixed with the sharp scent of dragfire, the nauseating smell of burned flesh, the copper stench of blood, the dead bodies strewn about, and the moans of the wounded.

Then, the throbbing pain in my palms suddenly registered —the splinters buried in my skin from the tower's rough wood making themselves known.

"We have to make sure all the Shedun left behind are actually dead." Ednis was already moving toward the ladder. "We also need to check for survivors, take care of our wounded and prepare our dead for their rites."

I started to follow, but my legs wouldn't cooperate. Now that the immediate danger had passed, my body was remembering how to be afraid. My hands began to shake violently, and I clung to my rifle by sheer determination.

"Hey now," Ednis's voice softened as he turned back to me. "It's alright, Kailin. It's over. You did good."

A sob caught in my throat. "I killed people."

"No," Ednis said firmly, walking back to me and placing his hands on my shoulders. "You killed monsters. Those weren't people out there, Kailin. People don't slaughter innocent villagers in their beds or torture captives to death for the sake of their twisted god's pleasure."

The tears came then, hot and unstoppable.

Ednis pulled me into a rough embrace, letting me sob against his shoulder. "It's okay. Let it all out."

He smelled of gunpowder and pine smoke, so much like my father that it was enough to center me and help me regain my composure.

When my tears finally slowed, he held me at arm's length, studying my face. "You've got steel in you, girl. Now, go on home and get some sleep if you can. We'll take care of the rest."

"But I can help—"

"You've helped plenty," he cut me off. "This next part is not for you. Go home, check on your animals, and try to get some rest. Tomorrow, we'll honor our dead, but tonight, there's more ugly work to be done."

I wanted to argue, but exhaustion was already settling into my bones. Looking down from the tower, I could see shapes moving in the predawn light—villagers emerging from their homes, checking on neighbors, gathering the fallen.

As I climbed down the ladder behind Ednis, my muscles protested every movement, and as I made my way home, every shadow made me flinch, every sound had me clutching my rifle, but finally I made it through the door.

I needed to check on the sheep, but it would have to wait.

Chicha launched herself into my arms the moment I crouched down, her tiny body vibrating with relieved whimpers.

"We are okay," I whispered, holding her close. "Thanks to you. You saved us, you little alarm fiend." I kissed her shaggy head. "Wait until Mom and Dad hear that. Mom will make you your favorite snack."

At the word *snack,* Chicha perked up and lifted her snout.

"Tomorrow, sweetie." I kissed her head again.

Tomorrow, there would be funerals to attend and damage to repair.

Tomorrow, we would mourn our losses and strengthen our defenses.

Tomorrow, I would face my parents when they returned from Skywatcher's Point and tell them that their sixteen-year-old daughter had killed for the first time.

Tonight, though, I would cuddle my little dog and dream about a pair of dark eyes with molten gold swimming in their depths.

ORDER YOUR COPY TODAY!

TO READ THE NEXT FIVE CHAPTERS ON THE VIP PORTAL, JOIN THE VIP CLUB
To find out what's included in your free membership, flip to the last page.

NOTE

Dear reader,

I hope my stories have added a little joy to your day. If you have a moment to add some to mine, you can help spread the word about the Children Of The Gods series by telling your friends and penning a review. Your recommendations are the most powerful way to inspire new readers to explore the series.

Thank you,

Isabell

Also by I. T. Lucas

BONDS OF WINGS AND FURY
1: BONDS OF WINGS AND FURY: THE TWO-FACED GOD

THE CHILDREN OF THE GODS ORIGINS
1: GODDESS'S CHOICE
2: GODDESS'S HOPE

THE CHILDREN OF THE GODS
DARK STRANGER
1: DARK STRANGER THE DREAM
2: DARK STRANGER REVEALED
3: DARK STRANGER IMMORTAL

DARK ENEMY
4: DARK ENEMY TAKEN
5: DARK ENEMY CAPTIVE
6: DARK ENEMY REDEEMED

KRI & MICHAEL'S STORY
6.5: MY DARK AMAZON

DARK WARRIOR
7: DARK WARRIOR MINE
8: DARK WARRIOR'S PROMISE
9: DARK WARRIOR'S DESTINY
10: DARK WARRIOR'S LEGACY

DARK GUARDIAN

THE CHANNELER'S COMPANION
THE VALKYRIE & THE WITCH
ADINA AND THE MAGIC LAMP

THE CHILDREN OF THE GODS SERIES SETS

DARK STRANGER TRILOGY
INCLUDES A BONUS SHORT STORY:
THE FATES TAKE A VACATION

DARK ENEMY TRILOGY
INCLUDES A BONUS SHORT STORY:
THE FATES' POST-WEDDING CELEBRATION

DARK WARRIOR TETRALOGY
DARK GUARDIAN TRILOGY
DARK ANGEL TRILOGY
DARK OPERATIVE TRILOGY
DARK SURVIVOR TRILOGY
DARK WIDOW TRILOGY
DARK DREAM TRILOGY
DARK PRINCE TRILOGY
DARK QUEEN TRILOGY
DARK SPY TRILOGY
DARK OVERLORD TRILOGY
DARK CHOICES TRILOGY
DARK SECRETS TRILOGY
DARK HAVEN TRILOGY
DARK POWER TRILOGY

DARK MEMORIES TRILOGY

DARK HUNTER TRILOGY

DARK GOD TRILOGY

DARK WHISPERS TRILOGY

DARK GAMBIT TRILOGY

DARK ALLIANCE TRILOGY

DARK HEALING TRILOGY

DARK ENCOUNTERS TRILOGY

DARK VOYAGE TRILOGY

DARK HORIZON TRILOGY

DARK WITCH TRILOGY

DARK AWAKENING TRILOGY

DARK PRINCESS TRILOGY

MEGA SETS

THE CHILDREN OF THE GODS: BOOKS 1-6

INCLUDES BONUS 2 SHORT STORIES & A COMPANION GUIDE
FOR BOOKS 1-6

THE CHILDREN OF THE GODS: BOOKS 6.5-10

INCLUDES A BONUS COMPANION GUIDE FOR BOOKS 6.5-10

THE CHILDREN OF THE GODS BOOKS 11-16

INCLUDES A BONUS COMPANION GUIDE FOR BOOKS 11-16

PERFECT MATCH BUNDLE 1

CHECK OUT THE SPECIALS ON

ITLUCAS.COM

(https://itlucas.com/specials)

FOR EXCLUSIVE PEEKS AT UPCOMING RELEASES
&
A FREE I. T. LUCAS COMPANION BOOK

JOIN MY *VIP CLUB* AND GAIN ACCESS TO THE VIP PORTAL AT ITLUCAS.COM

TO JOIN, GO TO:

http://eepurl.com/blMTpD

INCLUDED IN YOUR FREE MEMBERSHIP:

YOUR VIP PORTAL

- READ PREVIEW CHAPTERS OF UPCOMING RELEASES.
- LISTEN TO GODDESS'S CHOICE NARRATION BY CHARLES LAWRENCE
- EXCLUSIVE CONTENT OFFERED ONLY TO MY VIPS.

FREE I.T. LUCAS COMPANION INCLUDES:

- GODDESS'S CHOICE PART 1
- PERFECT MATCH: VAMPIRE'S CONSORT (A STANDALONE NOVELLA)
- INTERVIEW Q & A
- COMPANION GUIDES FOR BOOKS 1-16

IF YOU'RE ALREADY A SUBSCRIBER AND YOU ARE NOT GETTING MY EMAILS, YOUR PROVIDER IS SENDING THEM TO YOUR JUNK FOLDER, AND YOU ARE MISSING OUT ON IMPORTANT UPDATES.

To fix that, add isabell@itlucas.com to your email contacts or your email VIP list.

Check out the specials at
https://www.itlucas.com/specials

Printed in Dunstable, United Kingdom